THE BOOTLACE MAGICIAN

CASSIE BEASLEY

THE BOOTLACE MAGICIAN

DIAL BOOKS FOR YOUNG READERS

DIAL BOOKS FOR YOUNG READERS

An imprint of Penguin Random House LLC, New York

Text © 2019 by Cassie Beasley

Visit us online at penguinrandomhouse.com

Library of Congress Cataloging-in-Publication Data is available.
Printed in the United States of America
ISBN 9780525552635
1 3 5 7 9 10 8 6 4 2

Design by Jason Henry • Text set in Stempel Garamond
Page iii illustration © 2019 Andrew Bannecker
Interior illustrations © 2019 Erin Kono

for everyone who believes

PROLOGUE

The Idea was born in darkness.

It flashed to life deep, deep in the sea, in a place so far below the waves that the warmth of the sun was only a rumor. There, beneath the cold weight of the ocean, the Idea shone dazzling and new. The drifters and skitterers that lived in that black abyss fled from its light. And it was alone.

It had been born, as Ideas often are, much too soon. But it had been born, too, with a certainty, right at the center of itself, that it would not be alone forever.

One day, Someone would understand the Idea. They would meet at the perfect Moment, and together, they would do great things. But their meeting would not come soon, and it could not be here, in this dark place.

The Idea would have to go up, into the world, to wait.

It set out—a brilliant spark spiraling up and up toward the surface, toward its Someone, toward their destiny.

And also toward a hungry fish, which gulped it down in a single bite.

Fortunately, Ideas are not digestible.

The tuna endured a few queasy hours, then it spat the spark of light back up and swam off to find a less troublesome lunch.

The Idea was delighted by this experience. In the whole of its short life, nothing so interesting had ever happened to it. A fish, it decided, was a wonderful creature to be.

So, it grew fins. It figured out scales and gills. It gave itself a lovely silver tail, and with a few experimental twitches, it was off—a tiny, gleaming dart of a fish heading for the waves above.

The Idea-that-was-now-a-fish breached the surface with barely a ripple. It looked around.

How bright it is up here! it thought, though the day was gloomy.

It spied the rocky line of the nearby shore. *Aha!* it said to itself. *I am supposed to go in that direction.*

And so it did.

Standing on the pebbly beach, quite unaware of the fish heading toward him, was a boy. His name was Ephraim Tuttle, and he had come to the beach, as he often did, to write letters to his father, who was a soldier in the war overseas.

Ephraim was used to the beach's chilly breeze and its

dark water and the steady clack of pebbles as the waves lapped onto shore. But he was not at all used to the strange thing that was happening around him now.

Only moments ago, a great wind had swept up out of nowhere, blowing so fiercely that Ephraim had to lean into it to keep himself standing upright. But instead of whipping the waves into a froth, as it should have, the wind was pressing the whole ocean flat.

Flat enough, Ephraim thought, *to walk on.* Flat enough, he hoped, that a determined son might be able to cross all the way to Europe to fetch his father back home.

He headed toward the water.

Now, the fish didn't understand any of this. It couldn't feel the wind underwater, and it couldn't yet tell the difference between a boy and a barnacle. What it *did* know was that the creature it had seen on the beach would take it where it needed to go.

It felt the truth of this like a tug deep inside its fishy belly. *That way to safety. That way to the future.*

And so it swam toward shore, and it was pleased when Ephraim waded confidently into the ocean, wearing all his clothes and a pair of boots with leather laces tied into neat bows.

Hello, the fish said when it reached the boots. *Here I am! Pick me up.*

The boots didn't answer.

I am on a mission. The fish nudged one of the bootlaces with its nose. *You are supposed to help me.*

But Ephraim's feet didn't speak the language of Ideas, and the boy himself had no way of knowing what was going on beneath the water's surface. He felt wet and silly and disappointed, and—what was that sound?

Ephraim tilted his head, listening.

A song drifted on the wind, one filled with pipes and drums. To Ephraim, the music sounded like an invitation; he decided to accept it.

He turned his body, and his boots, back toward dry land.

Unwilling to be left behind, the fish took matters into its own fins. It flicked its tail and wriggled itself inside Ephraim Tuttle's left boot, which was just loose enough around the ankle for a very small sea creature's comfort.

The tug in the fish's belly was satisfied.

The two of them were headed out of the ocean and in the right direction, and beyond that, the fish did not worry. As it sloshed along in the boot, it went back to imagining its Someone.

They would meet at exactly the right Moment, in exactly the right way, and together, they would change everything. The fish believed in this the way people believe in the sunrise.

Of course, of course, of course, it thought. *There is no other way for the world to be.*

SEVENTY-FIVE YEARS LATER

A RARE SPECIMEN

Circus Mirandus did not sleep, but in the wee hours before sunrise, its music faded to a hush. The sound of the pipes became a breath. The drums thrummed low as a heartbeat. The crowds thinned, and many of the performers sought their beds.

Yet every night, a few determined children remained, and they found wonders aplenty.

Some explored the foggy twists and turns of the mist maze, while others sat by glowing pools in the circus's nocturnal garden, sipping mugs of hot cocoa. And on the darkest nights, when the moon was hidden, almost everyone could be found lying in the grass on the midway, watching the magician Firesleight send her power aloft.

Just such a moonless night arrived one August, while the circus was in the middle of its South American tour.

They had settled in Brazil a few days before, the dense vegetation of the Amazon rain forest parting to make room for the grassy meadow that surrounded the circus no matter where in the world it traveled. Now the noises of the jungle—whistle, shriek, and hoot—echoed across the grounds, mingling with applause as Firesleight lifted her arms skyward and flames blossomed in the air.

At the magician's command, deep orange fire skated along the peaked roofs, casting strange shadows against the brightly colored tent fabric. It swirled around and around before condensing into white-hot motes that twirled and danced with the fluttering pennants.

And that was only the beginning. The fire show was a spectacle no child would dream of missing. Except . . .

One boy at Circus Mirandus wasn't paying any attention to the performance at all.

Inside Mr. Head's Menagerie, Micah Tuttle sat with his legs crossed on top of a tall wooden barrel, his back resting against the glass wall of an aquarium that encircled the tent's huge center pole. His hands were busy, fingers tugging and tweaking an elaborate knot he had tied into a strip of aged leather. When he bent his head low over the project, his brown bangs fell into his eyes so that he had to shake them out of the way to see properly.

"Almost done," he said, though no human being was nearby to hear him.

Around Micah, the air was warm with the smell of

scales and fur, sawdust and hay. The menagerie's nocturnal animals bustled, carrying on as usual despite the fact that their admirers had all abandoned them in favor of Firesleight's performance.

The pangolins rolled themselves into balls for their nightly bowling tournament. The funny fox laughed at its own jokes. And a trio of bioluminescent bush babies were trying to steal one of the treat buckets that Mirandus Head, the circus's manager, kept secured on pegs around the walls of the tent.

But as flames raced through the air a few feet above the menagerie's open skylights, the animals paused. Eyes all over the tent blinked shut at the sudden brightness. Heads tilted up, and large ears swiveled to catch the distant sound of cheering from the midway.

Micah didn't look away from his work.

As the first round of applause faded, he put the finishing touches on the leather strip. He ran his hands over every turn and twist in the knot, then he made a small adjustment, picking at a particular loop with his fingernails until it was arranged to his liking.

Finally, he smiled and maneuvered himself around to face the aquarium. Light filtered through the water, greenish and wavering, and when the enormous silver fish in the tank swam past, it cast a shadow over Micah's face.

"I'm trying something new," he said, pressing the knot to the glass. "I hope you like it. It's my first time tying memories for an animal."

The fish didn't answer him.

An engraved bronze plaque was embedded into the aquarium, just above Micah's barrel. Like all the circus's signs, the engraving changed to match the local language. But even though Micah couldn't read Portuguese, he knew the words by heart.

FISH: A RARE SPECIMEN COURTESY OF EPHRAIM TUTTLE

He slid his fingers over the plaque, tracing the letters of his grandfather's name.

Micah had grown up hearing stories about Circus Mirandus, but he'd never dreamed they were true. The mysterious Lightbender, the beautiful Bird Woman, the little fish that had traveled to the circus in a boot—they had seemed like characters in a wonderful fairy tale.

Then Grandpa Ephraim had found out he was dying. And Micah had found out that the fairy tale was real.

"Neither of us would be here without him," he said to Fish, gesturing with the knotted leather strip. "I've explained it all in this knot. When you touch it, you'll understand. You'll see why we should be friends."

In the three months he'd been living at Circus Mirandus, Micah had had a lot of conversations with Fish. Whenever nightmares about Grandpa Ephraim's death drove him out of bed, he headed for the menagerie. It had seemed like the perfect solution. Micah didn't want to bother his new guardian every time he had a bad dream, and he'd assumed that Fish, who wasn't very popular with the crowds, could use the company.

Micah had thought that the two of them might have a special connection because of Grandpa Ephraim, but unfortunately, the relationship was beginning to seem a little one-sided.

Fish swam past again.

"You remember my grandpa's boot, don't you?" Micah said. "You remember how he followed the music to the circus, and he gave you to the ticket taker? To Geoffrey?"

Fish didn't pay attention to him. Or the knot. And he didn't show any hint of recognition for Geoffrey the ticket taker, even though they'd been living at the same circus for seventy-five years.

Micah was disappointed but not surprised. No matter how long he talked or what stories he shared, Fish never responded with more than an occasional flick of his tail.

For a while, Micah had assumed that Fish, being a fish, just wasn't great at expressing himself. But as time passed, he was forced to admit that Fish seemed to enjoy his company about as much as the company of the barrel he was sitting on.

He hoped the knot he'd tied would change that.

He had picked the strip of leather because it matched Grandpa Ephraim's old bootlace, which he wore as a bracelet around his own wrist. He'd spent hours and hours trying to put everything about himself and his grandfather into the knot in a way that a fishy brain might understand.

He could feel the buzz of magic in the leather right now. If he focused, he could even hear Grandpa Ephraim's voice saying, *I gave them a fish for a ticket! Can you believe it? Oh, Micah, I hope one day you get to see the circus. I hope one day you'll find a magic of your own.*

He shifted his grip on the knot, and another memory sparked against his fingers.

The Bird Woman. Victoria. She—

Micah shook his head and told the knot to be quiet. It had seemed important to include the whole story for Fish, but that didn't mean he wanted to think about his evil, long-lost grandmother right now.

A sudden rush of heat caught his attention, and he looked up to see flames washing over the menagerie's skylights again.

Micah had decided to give Fish the knot during Firesleight's show for a couple of reasons. For one thing, he didn't want to tell anyone why he had made something so personal for a fish, and for another, if the magic just didn't *work*, he would rather not have an audience. He was doing his best to prove that he could fit in here at the circus, but that was tough when he had only just turned eleven and most of the other magicians had been mastering their power for centuries.

The menagerie was usually empty during the fire show, and right now, nobody was around except for the creatures. Even the manager was gone. Micah glanced across the tent toward the secret seam in the scarlet fabric that served as the door to Mr. Head's office.

It was closed. There would never be a more private moment.

Micah climbed off the barrel, gripping the leather strip tightly in his fist. Then, he took a deep breath, drew his arm back, and tossed the knot up and over the rim of the aquarium.

It plopped into the tank and sank slowly through the clear, greenish water.

Micah had timed the throw well. Fish was about to pass by on another circumnavigation, and the knot would brush across one of his fins.

That will be enough. It has to be.

Suddenly, Fish stopped swimming.

"Fish!" Micah protested, pressing his face to the glass. "What are you doing?"

Fish eyed the knot.

"Touch it!" Micah said encouragingly. "Just with your fin. Don't let it sink to the bottom."

He flapped one of his arms like a fin, hoping that would give Fish the right idea, but Fish didn't budge.

"Come *on*," Micah begged as the knot drifted down. "Please, *please* touch it."

As if he'd heard, Fish swished his tail until the knot was right in front of his nose. But he didn't brush his fin against it. Instead, he did something Micah had never seen him do before. He opened his mouth wide as a shark's.

"Wait a second," said Micah.

Fish did not wait a second. He swallowed the knot before Micah could even blink.

Micah stared into one of his big silvery eyes. "Why would you do that?" he said slowly.

Fish didn't eat; it was the weirdest thing about him. But now, he was floating in place, apparently considering the flavor of Micah's offering.

"You shouldn't have eaten it," Micah said. "It wasn't food."

He had no clue what a magic-imbued piece of leather might do to Fish. He had tied dozens of knots and bracelets, filled with hundreds of memories, but he'd never once wondered what might happen if somebody *swallowed* them.

Some of Micah's knots were permanent. He didn't want the important ones to snap without his permission, so they didn't. He'd figured out the trick of making them thoroughly indestructible.

So the knot Fish had just eaten wouldn't dissolve in his stomach.

He's so big, Micah thought, worry growing in him. *And it's only a little knot. Why is he so still?*

"Don't you want to swim in circles some more?" he asked hopefully.

Fish was frozen in place, his eyes wide and staring.

Micah tapped gently on the glass. "Fish?" he murmured. "Are you okay?"

For an agonizing minute, nothing happened.

Then, Fish's tail twitched. Once. Twice.

And he shot out of the water like he'd been fired from a cannon.

Micah yelled and stumbled back, tripping over his own feet. The impact when he hit the ground knocked the breath from his lungs.

Fish soared toward the roof of the tent, his scales flashing like silver coins. He hung in the air for an impossibly long time, as if he didn't feel the need to obey the laws of gravity. But then he plunged . . .

down,

down,

down.

Micah struggled upright. What if Fish hit the side of the tank? What if he landed in the sawdust? What if—

SPLASH.

Fish belly flopped back into the aquarium, and a wave of cold, salty water knocked Micah down again.

He crawled toward the tank on his hands and knees, sputtering and shaking his wet hair out of his face. Fish was rocketing around, crashing into the walls so hard that Micah was sure he was about to break the glass.

"Stop! Stop!" he cried, clambering to his feet. "Fish, don't!"

But Fish didn't stop. He bashed into the side of the tank again and again, thrashing his tail wildly.

The other menagerie animals, curious about the commotion, were climbing out of their habitats. They were scurrying, slithering, and waddling toward the aquarium en masse, and Micah didn't know if he should order them to stay away for their own safety or ask them for help.

His heart battered against his ribs, every bit as determined to burst out of its confinement as Fish was. He shooed off a mousebird that was twittering around his head and raised a hand toward Fish, willing him to calm down.

"It's okay," Micah said. "It'll be okay, Fish. I'm going to get help!"

2

IDEAS

"Mr. Head!" Micah shouted, bursting through the hidden seam into the manager's office. "It's Fish! I'm so sorry, I . . ."

No one was there. Micah spun around, taking in the whole room, half expecting the manager to materialize.

It was a peculiar office—circular, with no filing cabinets or calendars, no desk filled with tape dispensers and paper clips. Instead, Mr. Head had a hodgepodge of pillowy sofas and stout armchairs. A cavernous fireplace was set into one curved wooden wall, and the floor was made of wood as well, inlaid with a compass rose design. A peculiar white plant vined over the mantelpiece, and a tapestry map of the world hung beside the door, embroidered with dots to represent major cities but with none of the usual lines to demarcate the borders of countries.

The only other thing in the room was a mattress (bigger than the one Micah slept on and made of the finest red and gold velvet) that belonged to the circus's guard tiger, Bibi.

"Bibi!" Micah shouted. "Are you here?"

He heard a chuffing sound, and he turned to see Bibi appearing out of thin air. She was sprawled across an aggrieved-looking sofa, the cushions squashed nearly flat under her weight. The tip of her white, striped tail brushed the floor.

Micah hurried toward her. "Where's Mr. Head?"

Bibi yawned.

"Bibi! Fish could break out of his tank any second! We need to get help!"

Curiosity lit the tiger's piercing blue eyes. The sofa groaned pitifully as she stood.

Micah shifted from foot to foot, his wet clothes dripping, while Bibi stretched. It only took a second, but it felt like ages before she plonked onto the floor, her huge paws hitting the polished wood with all the delicacy of sledgehammers.

She slinked past Micah and out the door.

"Is Mr. Head in one of the private paddocks?" Micah asked anxiously. He was following so close behind Bibi that her tail kept swishing against his legs. He winced as Fish leaped again and landed with another loud *SPLASH*.

He looked around at the walls of the menagerie. He didn't know where all the hidden seams were, but surely if Mr. Head were close by, then he could hear the commotion.

Bibi headed directly for Fish's tank.

The menagerie creatures still surrounded the aquarium, bleating and barking with enthusiasm. Several of the animals were drenched, but most had backed far enough away to stay out of the splash zone. They all parted respectfully as Bibi approached.

Maybe Bibi doesn't need to find Mr. Head, Micah thought. *Maybe she can fix this by herself.*

He latched on to this notion. Of course Bibi could do something! She was Mr. Head's companion and the boss of pretty much every other animal in the menagerie.

If Bibi stopped Fish quickly, then maybe Micah could clean up the flooded sawdust before the manager returned. He would still have to explain what had happened, but it wouldn't sound so reckless and irresponsible if he had a chance to put the menagerie back to rights first.

Bibi stopped walking. She settled onto her haunches and stared at the aquarium. She chuffed once, and Fish quit smashing the glass to look at her. Relief filled Micah for all of a second. Then, Bibi roared at the aquarium in a way that could only be described as *encouraging*.

To Micah's horror, Fish shot out of the water again.

"Bibi!" he cried. "This is serious!"

The tiger ignored him. She watched Fish soar toward the ceiling, a delighted gleam in her eyes.

Betrayed and outraged, Micah pushed his way past her and through the throng of gathered creatures. He ran out of the menagerie into the night, his sodden sneakers squelching on the grass. But as soon as he opened his mouth to shout for help, a magician appeared out of the darkness.

Even before Micah could make out the messy hair and the large nose, he knew who it was. He would recognize that long leather coat anywhere.

"Hello, Micah," his guardian said, stepping into the warm light that poured from the menagerie's open entrance.

"Oh," said Micah. "I . . ."

He had wanted help. And here help was. But he hadn't thought it would be the Lightbender. What on earth was the illusionist doing here at this hour?

"I didn't mean to—"

SPLASH.

Micah winced. The sound of Fish's watery landing was every bit as loud outside the tent.

The Lightbender leaned forward, peering over Micah's head into the menagerie. Micah didn't have to turn around to know what he was seeing.

"I fed Fish a knot," he confessed in a rush. "I mean, I wasn't trying to *feed* it to him, only he decided to eat it, and now he's going to break out of his tank, and I don't know how to help him, and—"

"Micah—"

"I'm *so* sorry. I understand if you want to give me back to Aunt Gertrudis—"

"I have no intention—"

"Only please save Fish first. I don't want anything bad to happen to him."

By the time he finished talking, Micah couldn't meet the Lightbender's eyes. He stared down at his feet and waited for the magician to yell at him.

But when the Lightbender spoke, he sounded as composed as always. "Micah," he said, "no one will send you back to your great-aunt."

Micah looked up. "But Fish—"

"The Fish has certainly had more alarming things than knots throw into its tank by curious children."

"You don't understand," said Micah urgently. "It wasn't just a knot. It was magic. I was trying to explain to him that we could be friends, but what if I've *poisoned* him?"

What if he dies?

Micah's hand went automatically to his bootlace bracelet. He gripped it so tightly that he could feel the two knots he always kept tied in it leaving dents in his skin.

Even if he wasn't poisoned, Fish could shatter the walls of the tank. All the water would flood out, and he wouldn't be able to breathe. Just like Grandpa Ephraim hadn't been able to breathe at the end.

But the Lightbender only blinked and tipped his head to the side, as if Micah's behavior were baffling. "Ah," he said. His brows lifted in surprise. "You don't know."

In the menagerie, Bibi was roaring again, apparently egging Fish on.

"What don't I know?" Micah said.

"Fish is not a fish." The Lightbender smiled. "It is something far more special than that."

✧ ✧ ✧

"I have ideas all the time," Micah said a short while later. "They don't start out as fish."

He and the Lightbender were sitting together on top of a pair of wooden barrels beside the funny fox's habitat. It was far enough out of the way that they wouldn't get wet, but still close enough to keep an eye on the situation.

Fish's last big *SPLASH* had been several minutes ago, and Micah hoped he was almost tired out.

"Ideas are the very stuff of creation," the Lightbender replied. "The purest sort of magic. The world is full of them, and human beings generate more than the universe will ever make use of. But some ideas are so powerful they must come into the world in a different way. Such Ideas are born. And when they are born before the world is ready for them, they must wait."

"But are they all born as *fish*?" Micah asked. He was wringing the hem of his T-shirt between his hands, trying to squeeze out some of the water.

"No," said the Lightbender. "This one seems to have developed some unusual ideas of its own."

Fish leaped again, and a clamor went up from the watching animals.

This time, the sight of him soaring through the air didn't fill Micah with panic. Instead, he found himself looking at Fish with fresh respect, his brain awhirl with everything the Lightbender had told him.

Fish was pure magic. The very stuff of creation. Micah could almost imagine there was a glow to those silver scales he'd never noticed before, as if some potent source of light was hidden within.

"He's here for a reason, then," he said as Fish landed and a wave crashed over the side of the aquarium. "He's important."

"We are all here for a reason, and we are all important," the Lightbender said. "But yes. It's impossible for us to tell exactly what kind of Idea Fish is, but we know it is something the world needs badly. And we believe its Moment will come soon."

Soon. Micah felt a pinch of sadness in his chest. "When exactly . . ."

He struggled to find the right words. Apparently, Fish had to find a particular Someone when the time was right. But was he just going to vanish from his tank one day and appear in some random person's head?

Micah hoped not. It would be terrible to come to the menagerie and find him suddenly gone.

"I do not know for certain." The Lightbender squinted toward the aquarium as if he were trying to judge Fish's precise size and weight. "Nor does the manager."

"So, it might *not* be soon. It could be months and months from now. Or years."

The Lightbender gave him a funny look.

"What?"

"I forget," said the illusionist, "how time moves for the young. It may indeed be another year before the Moment arrives. Or two. Or three. Which is *soon* by my own reckoning, but perhaps not by yours."

"Well, that's good," said Micah. Three more years with Fish around would be great. And maybe it would be five years. Or ten. To someone like the Lightbender, a decade must feel like a blink.

People who lived at the circus didn't age normally, thanks to the manager. Mirandus Head wasn't quite a magician. According to the Lightbender, he wasn't even quite human. And he gave off a power that caused all living things under his care to flourish.

A few days after he'd moved in to the Lightbender's tent, the thought that he might be a child forever had struck Micah. He'd run straight to Rosebud's wagon to ask the circus's healer if she had a potion that would turn him into an adult on schedule. But she'd explained that there was no need.

"The manager's power always works for our good, duckling. It wouldn't be good for anyone to be an eternal child."

So Micah would grow up. *And maybe,* he thought suddenly, *Fish will wait until then.*

By the time he was a full-grown magician, he would have learned enough to help the Idea do whatever it was meant to do. It would only be right. Fish had been the start of Grandpa Ephraim's story, and Micah's, too. They should stick together for as long as possible.

And what if . . .

"Could Fish choose a magician as his Someone?" Micah asked.

The Lightbender stopped brushing tiny specks of sawdust off the sleeves of his coat and looked over at him. "It's not likely, considering how few magicians there are compared to everyone else."

"But it's not against the rules or anything?"

"Not that I know of," said the Lightbender. Then he added, "But I would remind you that there are billions of people in the world, and the chances that Fish is meant for anyone at Circus Mirandus are small."

Micah sighed. Of course that was true. And Fish didn't seem interested in *listening* to Micah, never mind choosing him to enact some world-changing vision.

The Lightbender cleared his throat. "It will still be exciting for us when the Moment arrives," he offered. "The circus plans to help the Idea reach its Someone. If it needs us to. Porter is already hoping that Fish will demand we go to Bora-Bora."

Micah snorted a laugh.

Porter was the magician who made it possible for the circus to travel the world. He could open magical Doors to just about anywhere, and Micah had heard him mention more than once that it was a shame their tour schedule didn't include more tropical islands.

"What happens if Fish can't find his Someone? What if they refuse to help him? Or they just aren't in the right place at the right time?"

"It has happened before," said the Lightbender. "But even if an Idea fails in its mission, it can still bring much good into the world. It will still release its power. If the person who is meant to have the Idea isn't prepared when the time is right, it will transform itself into a burst of pure inspiration and magic for anyone nearby to use. Some of the greatest scientific discoveries, some of the most profound works of art, have arisen from such missed Moments."

"That doesn't sound so bad," Micah admitted. "But it's not going to happen to Fish. He's going to do exactly what he came into the world to do. He's going to be *great* at it."

If Grandpa Ephraim's fish was going to disappear no matter what, then Micah wanted it to be for the best reason possible.

"I agree," said the Lightbender, gesturing toward the aquarium, where Fish had calmed down at last.

He'd gone back to circling his tank at a speed that was only a little faster than usual, and as he passed around the side facing Micah and the Lightbender, he gave the glass a cheerful whack with his tail.

Micah decided to think of it as the fishy version of a wave hello.

The menagerie animals, satisfied that the night's entertainment was over, began to make their way back to their habitats. The Lightbender helped Micah down from his barrel.

"Come," he said. "I think it best that we close up the menagerie. The animals have had enough excitement, and we should let the Strongmen deal with the flooding before we allow the crowds back in."

"I was going to help clean up!" Micah said quickly. "I don't want Mr. Head to be mad."

"I doubt he will be," said the Lightbender. "I believe you said you were trying to befriend Fish? That's hardly a crime."

It might not have been a crime, but Micah could tell the Lightbender thought it was odd. He felt his face heat. "I was just—I wanted to try something new with my magic. I've been here for months, and I'm still only tying memories into things. I thought trying to do it for an animal would be different."

"I see," said the Lightbender.

"And I picked Fish because I thought he was lonely." Micah didn't see any reason to mention that the knot he'd given Fish was full of his memories of Grandpa Ephraim. Or that he'd wanted to have someone to talk to who knew his grandfather as well as he had. "Only I guess Ideas probably don't get lonely, do they?"

"I cannot say for certain." The Lightbender hesitated, then added, "I believe I promised you that I would speak to the manager about allowing Jenny Mendoza to visit. I apologize for not doing so yet, but I—"

"It's fine." Micah could feel the knot that represented his friendship with Jenny tied into his bootlace bracelet right now. He would love to see her, but he didn't want his guardian to feel like he *had* to offer. "We've been sending each other so many letters."

"Still," said the Lightbender, "I will speak to him about it."

When they got outside, the illusionist showed Micah how to close the flaps over the menagerie's entryway. He ran two of his fingers in a neat circle over a certain spot, and the scarlet fabric on either side of the entrance drew itself together like a set of curtains, shutting the two of them out. Not even a crack of light showed from inside the tent.

For a moment, it was so dark that Micah could barely make out the shape of the Lightbender standing beside him. Then, an enormous fireball exploded overhead, painting the night sky in orange light.

Micah yelped and jumped, his heart racing. Wild cheers came from the midway. For a few seconds, he didn't know what was going on, but as the fire roiled overhead, he realized it was only the grand finale of Firesleight's show.

Micah gazed up. It seemed like ages had passed since the fire show started.

As he watched, the flames morphed, shaping themselves into a mythical creature with a spike-crested head, a long tail, and bat-like wings. The dragon roared silently.

The Lightbender *hmm*ed. Micah looked over at him and saw the corners of his mouth lifting mischievously. All at once, the fiery dragon turned a deep blue-green.

"That's my favorite color," said Micah.

"Is it?" The Lightbender gave him a knowing look.

Micah wondered if everyone could see the teal flames, or if his guardian had spun the illusion for him alone.

The Lightbender turned to go.

"Are you sure I shouldn't stay?" Micah asked. "I could shovel sawdust with the Strongmen. Or fetch water buckets to help refill Fish's tank."

He figured if an Idea wanted to look like a fish, then it probably wanted plenty of water to swim around in, too.

"A generous thought. But the Strongmen can shovel more wet sawdust in a moment than the two of us could manage if we worked until dawn. And we will let the Inventor deal with the aquarium. It is one of her magical creations, and she no doubt has a clever way of refilling it."

These were good points, but they left Micah feeling deflated.

He kept running into the same problem. Whenever he tried to lend a hand around Circus Mirandus, there was always someone who could do the job quicker and better than he could. Of course, it was smarter to let the magicians who knew what they were doing take care of things, but never being able to help in any real way reminded Micah that he was still an outsider.

And it was even worse when the mess that needed cleaning up was one he'd made himself.

The Lightbender was watching him closely. He cleared his throat. "I realize the Idea did not respond in the way you expected," he said, "but it was clearly enthused by your offer of friendship."

Micah considered the way Fish had whacked the wall of the aquarium with his tail. That could have been a friendly gesture, couldn't it? And perhaps he should think of Fish's decision to eat the knot as a *compliment*.

"That's true," he said, smiling. "Maybe he did appreciate it."

Buoyed up by this happy thought, Micah followed the Lightbender back to his tent.

Over their heads, the teal flames flickered and died. When Micah looked up one last time, nothing was left of the magnificent dragon but a drifting skeleton of smoke.

3

TERPSICHORE

Micah slept until noon the next day, and even then, it was only the sound of loud splashing that woke him.

Fish! his sleep-addled brain thought. *Not again!*

He fought to get out from under his covers, struggling against the weight of the oversize patchwork quilt the Strongmen had given him as a welcome-to-the-circus present. He fell out of his bed and flopped around on the floor for a few seconds before he realized that the splashing sound couldn't possibly be coming all the way from the menagerie.

In fact, it was coming from his own bathroom.

"*Chintzy,*" he groaned, his face smooshed into the soft blue rug. "You'd better not be in my sink."

He was answered by the familiar *whom-whom-whom*

sound of the messenger parrot beating her wings to dry
them off. His bathroom would be completely splattered.

"Don't use my toothbrush on your toenails!" he
shouted.

"Mind your business!" Chintzy squawked back.

So, she was definitely using his toothbrush.

"Yuck," Micah muttered, finally extricating himself
from the quilt. He stood and saw that his bedroom must
have been trying to wake him for a while. The lamps were
shining at full brightness, illuminating a cozy space that
was starting to look familiar, if not quite like home.

Micah hadn't had many possessions when he moved in
with the Lightbender, just a couple boxes full of clothes
and knickknacks. He'd been touched when he arrived to
find that everyone at the circus had pitched in to decorate
his new room.

The magicians had given him odds and ends from their
own tents. A small bookcase doubled as Micah's bedside
table, and two green glass floor lamps turned themselves
on whenever they thought he needed light. The chest of
drawers in one corner folded anything you put in it, which
was so convenient he didn't even mind the odd creases it
left down the fronts of his shirts. And, of course, there was
the patchwork quilt, so large that even after Micah had
spread it back out over the bed it trailed off the edges and
onto the rug.

He dressed and threw open the flap that led into the
bathroom, where he found his toothbrush lying suspi-

ciously in a puddle. Chintzy, who didn't look even a little bit guilty, was standing on the edge of the sink, carefully rearranging her bright red tail feathers with her beak.

"Is this going to be an everyday thing?" Micah asked her. "Why can't you use the birdbath in the menagerie?"

"Ha!" Chintzy squawked around a mouthful of feathers. "Me! Use public facilities! Why don't you go use one of the other humanbaths if you don't like sharing?"

"But . . ." Micah didn't know which he should address first—the fact that *humanbaths* wasn't a word or the fact that he would like sharing fine if the person he was sharing with didn't leave wet feathers and bird poop on the floor.

"Anyway," said Chintzy, shaking her tail at him, "I should be allowed to take a bath because I brought you mail."

Micah's annoyance evaporated. Mail meant a letter from Jenny Mendoza. When he had left her behind in Peal, she had promised to write him weekly, and of course she had proven better than her word. She'd written him a long letter every other day, and she had even come up with a way of keeping Chintzy happy about making so many deliveries.

"What was it this time?" Micah asked.

"Guava jam!" Chintzy said. "A whole spoonful of it! And she used my special plate and . . ."

Micah nodded politely while Chintzy described, for the dozenth time, the ceramic plate Jenny had bought for her at a thrift store. Jenny had painted the parrot's name on it, and when Chintzy was scheduled to arrive she filled it with treats and left it on her nightstand beside her latest letter.

The treats were always different, and Jenny refused to tell Chintzy what they were going to be in advance. This made the parrot intensely curious. Just last week she'd sneaked into Porter's tent in the middle of the night and woken the magician to demand that he open the mailbox Door he always used to send her to Peal.

Micah brushed his teeth as best he could with his fingers while Chintzy waxed poetic about her plate and her jam and her favorite human, Jenny, who she was sure wouldn't mind sharing a bathroom with a highly important parrot.

"And when I got back here, I flew straight to the kitchen to tell them about guava jam, and do you know what I found out?"

Micah spat into the sink. "What?"

"They *have* guava jam," she said. "Right here! At our circus!"

She peered at Micah through one bright yellow eye, clearly expecting him to be flabbergasted.

"Wow!" he said, trying to look impressed. "That's great news, Chintzy!"

The kitchen magicians at Circus Mirandus could whip up pretty much every food you had ever heard of. But Chintzy was excited, and Micah didn't want to burst her bubble. "I'd better ask if they'll let me try some of that jam before they run out."

"Yes," she said, bobbing her head. "And you should hurry because they've only got three and a half jars. I counted. You should bring me one of them. With a spoon. And a plate with my name on it. And the spoon could have my name on it, too."

"Right," Micah said.

"But not now, because the Head was in the kitchen when I flew in. He said he wanted to see you in the menagerie, and I told him you would come right over."

"You—when was this?" said Micah, hastily drying his hands on his shorts. "Was he upset?"

"No. It was before my bath. Hey, don't run away! I brought mail!"

When Micah arrived at the menagerie, he found it as bright and busy as ever. The daytime animals were all out and enjoying the company of dozens of jubilant children. A little boy was riding the two-headed camel. A trio of girls were running their fingers over a llama's glittery golden wool. And Big Jean the elephant was at her chalkboard, writing trivia questions for a competitive group of teenagers.

The sawdust was dry, and Fish swam peacefully around his aquarium, which was filled to the rim. It looked like last night had never happened.

Micah spent a couple of minutes trying to spot the manager in the crowd, but then he heard a happy chuffing sound beside him. He squinted, and sure enough, he spied pawprints the size of Frisbees in the sawdust.

"Hi, Bibi," he said. "Long time no see."

Micah thought this was a funny joke, but it was hard to tell if the invisible tiger agreed.

He stuffed his hands into his pockets and leaned toward Bibi's footprints. "Chintzy said Mr. Head wanted to talk to me. He's not mad, right?"

The Lightbender had said the manager wouldn't be, and Micah knew his guardian wouldn't lie to him. But he couldn't help feeling a little nervous when Bibi snorted and the sawdust shifted. New pawprints appeared, heading across the menagerie.

Micah followed the trail, waving at Fish as he passed the aquarium. Fish whacked the glass with his tail.

Definitely a friendly gesture, Micah decided, feeling pleased.

He was surprised when Bibi's footprints led him to the seam that hid Terpsichore's private paddock. Terpsichore was the only unicorn at Circus Mirandus—a sweet, aqua-colored foal. Micah knew everyone, especially Mr. Head, was worried about her. She had been found wandering the circus's meadow a couple weeks before Micah arrived, and she was too young to be away from her mother. Sometimes, the foal refused to eat, and she wasn't growing as she should.

"Am I supposed to go in there?" Micah asked Bibi uncertainly. He'd never been invited before.

A second later the seam opened, and Mirandus Head himself stepped out. He snapped the fabric shut behind him.

"Ah," he said, nodding to Micah. "I see Chintzy is more reliable than I thought. Hello, Micah Tuttle."

Micah swallowed. "Hello, Mr. Head."

The manager of Circus Mirandus looked a little like a military version of Santa Claus. His white hair was cropped short, and when his sleeves were rolled up for work, as they were now, you could see the compass rose tattooed on one of his muscular biceps.

Mr. Head was always kind to Micah when their paths crossed, but it was hard to forget that he hadn't been eager to let Micah live at his circus.

"I'm sorry about Fish." Micah tried to keep his spine straight in case good posture mattered to the manager. "I shouldn't have given him the knot without asking you if it was all right."

Mr. Head reached down and stroked Bibi's head. It looked like he was petting a particularly firm patch of air. "That would have been best," he said. "But it *was* all right, and no harm was done."

"I thought I'd poisoned him," Micah admitted.

He expected Mr. Head to say that such a thing was impossible. Instead, the most peculiar expression crossed his face. It was like he was looking right at Micah, only deeper. As if he could see beyond skin and blood and bone to something else. The look lasted for less than a moment, but Micah could *feel* it, like a layer of frost against his skin, the cold sinking in further than it should have.

Then the feeling passed.

"No, Micah Tuttle," the manager said. "You're not the kind of person who can poison an Idea."

Micah wasn't sure what to say to that.

The manager acted as if nothing unusual had happened. "Your guardian and I had a talk about you this morning."

Micah tried not to look alarmed.

"You've been traveling with us for long enough now to settle in, and we both think you're ready for some new responsibilities."

"Of course!" Micah said at once. "I've been practicing my knots every day."

"I'm glad you're eager," said the manager, "but the chore the Lightbender has volunteered you for doesn't involve knots."

"I'll do anything," Micah said earnestly.

"I like enthusiasm in a young magician." Mr. Head smiled. "Follow me."

Terpsichore's paddock was one of the most beautiful places Micah had ever seen. It was pleasantly warm, with springy emerald-green grass underfoot and piles of sweet-smelling hay in every corner. The tent ceiling was transparent, so that the midday sun shone down into the room, the light mingling with a soft glow coming from the walls themselves.

Music played, but it wasn't the song Micah usually associated with Circus Mirandus. This was classical music instead of pipes and drums—all fluting and tinkling and merry little trills.

The music dissolved Micah's worries in an instant. For a few blissful seconds, he forgot that he was trying to prove himself to Mr. Head. He could just lie down in this soft grass and sleep—

A furious trumpeting sound blasted through the music, and Micah looked across the paddock to see an angry baby unicorn charging toward him. Terpsichore might have been small, but in that moment, she didn't look anything like a sickly, motherless infant. Her head was lowered and her stubby horn gleamed in the sunlight.

He froze.

A second before the unicorn speared him, a strong hand grabbed Micah by the elbow and yanked him out of the way.

"Mr. Head!" said Micah. "What's going on?"

The manager ignored him and called out in a cheerful voice to someone across the paddock. "You seem to have lost control of her!"

Terpsichore ran right into a wall of tent fabric. It stretched, then bounced back like a trampoline, sending the aqua-colored foal reeling. She was unharmed but obviously enraged, and she plunged forward again, jabbing at the fabric with her horn.

"She disapproved of my attempts to alter her mind," said the Lightbender.

Micah had been so focused on the unicorn that he hadn't realized his guardian was here, too. The Lightbender stood with his back pressed against the opposite wall of the paddock. His leather coat didn't seem to have any new scuffs or scratches, but his hair looked even more like a scrambled bird's nest than normal.

"I've barely managed to conceal myself from her." The illusionist had an unusual note of frustration in his voice.

"That's because she's a clever young lady." Mr. Head smiled proudly at the unicorn.

Micah inched himself behind the manager. The clever young lady was making sharp whistling noises and attacking the tent fabric as if it were her most hated enemy.

"I fear she is more ill-tempered than clever," the Lightbender replied, "but Micah can handle her."

"*Me?*" said Micah, wondering what he had done to give his guardian the impression that he was some kind of expert unicorn wrangler.

The manager pulled him forward and clapped him on the shoulder. "It was good of you to agree to help."

"Noble even," the Lightbender murmured. He hadn't moved away from the wall, and he had a distant look in his eyes that made Micah think he was still trying to use his magic on the foal. "Micah, just walk over to Terpsichore and offer to pet her."

"What? No!"

"Unicorns like children," the Lightbender said.

"They do," Mr. Head agreed. "And they are herd animals. Perhaps what Terpsichore needs is a friend."

Suddenly, Micah understood how he had ended up in this position. He'd been trying to make friends with a fish last night. No doubt the Lightbender thought he could do with another animal pal.

"Are you serious?"

"Of course," said Mr. Head.

"At the moment," said the Lightbender.

"She needs to eat. See if you can persuade her to take a few bites of this." Mr. Head steered Micah toward a wooden bucket that lay on its side a few feet away. The bucket's contents had spilled, and a mass of something that looked like half-melted yellow marshmallows covered the grass.

Mr. Head scooped a double handful of the food into the bucket and passed it to Micah. Then he pursed his lips and whistled an elaborate tune.

Terpsichore stopped jousting with the wall. She tilted her head.

Mr. Head whistled again, and before Micah could say, "Are you sure about this?" the foal rounded on him.

Unicorns did not like children. They liked *chasing* children.

This was a very important distinction, and Micah wasn't sure he should forgive the Lightbender or the manager for not mentioning it.

Micah dashed around the paddock, the bucket swinging awkwardly from one arm, while Terpsichore capered in circles around him. Every time he thought about stopping, the unicorn would lunge, her horn pointed at the center of Micah's tender stomach.

The Lightbender was still hiding against the wall, calmly giving advice that just *had* to be wrong. He was saying things like "Hold still." And "Just stroke her mane." And "Micah, I promise, you are completely safe."

Meanwhile, the manager seemed to think it was helpful to explain the unicorn's feelings—"Oh! She'll enjoy her lunch much more after some exercise." Or, "She's so proud her horn has come in. Let her jab you a little. It's not sharp yet."

It might have gone on until nightfall, but on his next circuit of the paddock, Micah tripped and sprawled across the grass. He clenched his eyes shut and waited for the inevitable pain of being trampled and speared.

Instead, he heard a whuffling noise, and a moment later, the side of his face was being licked by a slobbery tongue.

"Gross!"

He rolled over. Terpsichore's blue-green nose was an inch from his own. The foal stamped her hooves and made a chiming sound that Micah had to admit seemed more happy than murderous.

Cautiously, his lungs still burning from the chase, Micah climbed to his feet. He brushed his hands off on the front of his T-shirt and eyed the unicorn.

A few seconds passed, and then Terpsichore lunged at him again.

Micah forced himself to stand still. The foal bumped him with the end of her horn. Several times, but gently. As if hoping she might prod him into continuing their game.

"They're not violent animals." The manager approached the two of them slowly. "The opposite, in fact. Unicorns protect creatures weaker or smaller than they are, including human children. Terpsichore will, too, when she's grown."

He picked up the bucket Micah had dropped and held it out to him.

Micah took it and offered it to Terpsichore, who ignored it in favor of licking his face again.

Mr. Head reached into the bucket for a handful of the food. The lumpy stuff glistened wetly in his palm, and the smell was cloying. The Lightbender, who had finally left his safe post by the wall, wrinkled his nose.

Micah wondered if unicorns in the wild ate this kind of thing, or if the magicians had somehow gotten the recipe wrong. Now that he wasn't running away from her, he noticed that Terpsichore looked thin. He had seen the foal on his very first trip to Circus Mirandus, before he'd known he would one day live here. She hadn't grown at all since then as far as he could tell.

"Isn't there any way to find her family?" he asked.

Mr. Head was holding the food right under Terpsichore's snout. "Not if they're unwilling to be found." He sighed. "This is the first time I have heard of a young unicorn being abandoned by her herd. Terpsichore is almost certainly the only foal in the world right now. Her mother should have been fiercely protective of her."

Abandoned. Micah hadn't realized. He'd assumed the

foal had wandered too far from her herd and been unable to find her way back.

Being abandoned was a lot like being an orphan, and Micah knew how hard that was. But at least Grandpa Ephraim would never have left Micah behind on purpose. Even when he'd been so sick he couldn't get out of bed, he'd been sending letters to the Lightbender, trying to make sure Micah found a new home.

Micah reached out to stroke the unicorn's velvety nose. "Poor Terp," he said. "You must be so confused about all of this."

The Lightbender had been easing closer to them, and now he stopped a few yards short of the foal's hindquarters. "Don't be afraid for her. Unicorns are strong. Even young ones."

"That's an understatement," said Mr. Head. "If we can get her to eat, Terpsichore will do wonderfully. She'll even be able to knock the Strongmen around in a few months."

As if she understood what they were saying, Terpsichore pranced in place and made a proud tootling sound.

Then she snorted condescendingly at the food in the manager's hand and jammed her head into the bucket Micah was holding.

Micah barely managed to keep his balance.

"Well!" said Mr. Head in a delighted voice. "This plan might work."

Micah held tight to the bucket and tried not to make any sudden movements while the unicorn ate her fill. "I can come every day," he offered. "I'll be her friend and make sure she eats."

He could even use his magic to help. If he tied a knot full of all his best food memories—orange soda and extra-cheesy macaroni and his grandfather's double chocolate brownies—maybe it would whet Terp's appetite. He'd have to get Mr. Head's approval, but it might work.

The Lightbender cleared his throat. "Speaking of friendships," he said. "Mirandus has something to tell you."

Mr. Head shot the illusionist an exasperated look before turning to Micah. "You may invite Ms. Mendoza to come for a visit," he said. "Of course."

Micah gaped at him over Terpsichore's ears.

"I am not some tyrant who prohibits the magicians who live here from having *guests*," the manager said, a hint of affront in his voice.

"I didn't think you were, sir," Micah said quickly, though he had, in fact, thought something a lot like that. "Thank you so much!"

Mr. Head nodded.

While Terp finished eating, Micah was already composing his next letter to Jenny in his head.

"Dear Jenny," it would start. "Guess what!"

4

BAD LUCK

Just before lunchtime a week later, Micah climbed the three wooden steps that led up to the door of Rosebud's wagon and knocked.

"Come in, duckling!" a booming voice called. "Terpsichore's potion is almost ready."

Micah stepped inside, and the familiar smells of strong herbs and smoke and a hundred different kinds of tea stung his nose.

Circus Mirandus's healer and potions expert stood over her worktable. Rosebud was seven feet tall, and her bald head almost brushed the ceiling of the wagon. She was uncorking a tiny glass bottle. Whatever was inside the bottle looked like condensed cobwebs and stank like old cheese, and Rosebud deftly scraped every bit of it out into the mixing bowl in front of her.

Dried leaves filled the bowl already, along with colorful powders and pale flower petals.

"Rosebud," Micah said, "do you think maybe I'm missing something about my knots? Because I can't figure out how to make them do anything new or impressive, and—"

"Shoo that mousebird off, dear," Rosebud interrupted. "They know they're not allowed in here."

Micah blinked and looked down to see that a small gray mouse had followed him through the door. It was sniffing at the laces of his sneakers.

"Not again," said Micah, nudging the mouse with the toe of his shoe. "Go away."

The mouse caught his shoelace between its teeth.

Sighing, Micah bent and grabbed it. He dropped the mouse onto the wagon's steps, and it chittered angrily at him. Halfway through its rant, it turned into a bird, and Micah shut the door on it before it could flutter back inside.

"They're always going after my shoelaces and the bracelets I tie and even my *hair*," said Micah, stepping carefully around a towering stack of books and newspapers to get to Rosebud's oversized armchair. He couldn't read any of the titles, and that wasn't unusual. Rosebud spoke more languages than anyone else at the circus.

"The mousebirds like to line their nests with magical

bits and pieces," said the healer, reaching for a cookie tin on one of the wagon's many shelves. "They can be a bother, but I do admire them. They stayed behind when the other birds fled from . . ."

Micah held his breath, but Rosebud was too considerate to finish her sentence.

Circus Mirandus had been home to many species of bird until Micah's grandmother, Victoria Starling, had gone on a rampage during her horrible final performance. She'd driven her flock of magical birds mad so that they fought one another and plummeted into the ground.

Grandpa Ephraim had fallen in love with the Bird Woman and married her without realizing that she'd done such terrible things. And Micah had never even met her. But that didn't stop him from feeling guilty about the birds. The survivors had all flown away after the disaster, and Chintzy and the mousebirds were the only ones left.

"Anyway, duckling," Rosebud said, after a moment's pause, "I'm afraid your knot bracelets will always be too much of a temptation for the mousebirds."

Micah was gripping the edge of the chair's cushioned seat so tightly his fingers hurt. He made himself relax.

"As for them stealing your hair," Rosebud said, "you could quit using your magic to untangle it, but I'm afraid you'll have to borrow a comb from someone other than me."

She smiled and pointed at her own bald head. She had painted irises on her scalp today, and the bright purple flowers stood out against her dark skin.

"I don't untangle my hair on purpose, though," said Micah. "It just happens."

Rosebud opened the cookie tin. It was full of something pale green and crumbly, and when she spooned it over the contents of her mixing bowl, everything began to liquefy.

She pulled a digital wristwatch from the pocket of her long skirt and set the timer. The *beep-beep* the buttons made as she pressed them sounded weirdly out of place in a wagon full of potions ingredients.

"Now," she said, setting the watch on the table, "you were asking me about your knots when you came in. What makes you think you're missing something?"

"It's just that I've been practicing a *lot*," said Micah. "I can tie regular knots really fast, and I don't have much trouble with the memory ones. But what if that's all I can ever do?"

"What if it is?" said Rosebud, her tone patient but no-nonsense. "Filling knots with your memories is more than most people can do."

Micah knew that. But he also knew that compared to everyone else at the circus, his magic was small. And compared to a gift like Rosebud's, or the Lightbender's, his talent might as well have been crumbs.

He said as much, and the healer stared into her mixing bowl thoughtfully.

"It seems to me," she said at last, "that worrying over what you *don't* have might take a lot of useful energy away from making the most of what you *do*. It's good that you're practicing. Try not to lose patience. Gaining new skills, magical or otherwise, takes time."

Micah sighed. "I know."

Rosebud grinned at him. "And if you hope to catch up with *me*, you'll have centuries of work ahead of you."

The digital watch beeped shrilly, and she gave the potion a stir. It was a blinding shade of yellow now, and she poured it into the same china pitcher she had used yesterday.

Micah stood, and she passed it to him.

"Do you think we might get by with less sugar in it today?" she said. "I know it tastes good, but it will work better if you can persuade the foal to eat it without the additional sweetener."

Micah was flattered that Rosebud trusted his opinion enough to ask. "I can get her to eat it," he promised. "I'll tell the kitchen magicians to change the recipe."

She opened the door for him, and he made his way toward the dining tent.

Micah went carefully, watching where he stepped and keeping his grip on the pitcher tight. Preparing lunch for a picky unicorn was a lengthy process for all the magicians involved, and he didn't want everyone to have to start over because he'd spilled Rosebud's potion.

He took a winding route to avoid the busier parts of the circus, but he still ran into a few curious kids who wanted to know what he had in his arms. He managed to convey with smiles and gestures that the pitcher wasn't full of something delicious or interesting he could share.

Nobody took the news badly. The visitors Micah encountered were almost always in a great mood. They *were* at a magical circus after all. And the potion's bizarre smell probably helped to convince everyone he was telling the truth.

The day before, a couple of boys his own age had even decided to walk along with him to make sure no one bumped into him. Micah found them later that afternoon and showed them around the midway to say thank you. He made sure they got to try a few of his favorite games and all the best snacks.

It had been a lot of fun, and it had made Micah miss Jenny fiercely. She was going to come for a day trip right before school started back, and he was already planning everything they might do together.

Eventually, Micah and the pitcher reached the Staff Only section of the circus.

The dining tent and kitchen, Porter's warehouse full of doors, the greenhouses, the Strongmen's bunkhouse, various workshops—they were all hidden back here by the Lightbender's magic so that visiting children never knew they existed. Most of these tents were dull shades of brown and green, and the dining tent blended right in with the moss-colored storage tents on either side of it. But inside, it was a warm and inviting place.

The tent had a wooden floor, and a wall with a cutout window separated the kitchen from the dining room, which looked like a tea shop that had grown out of control.

About three-quarters of the round tables had chairs for seating, and the remaining ones were covered in platters, casserole dishes, samovars, and tureens. Circus Mirandus didn't have set mealtimes, but the food that was set out in the morning tended to be breakfasty. Heavier dishes began to appear around noon, and if you came by at midnight there were always hot drinks and desserts.

Micah had been enchanted the first time he'd stepped through the door. He'd seen all the magicians eating supper together—people from different parts of the world and different centuries speaking a dozen or more languages— and he'd realized all over again how special the circus was. He still felt that way as he entered the tent now.

The lunch rush was just beginning, and when Micah headed back to the kitchen, he found it bustling with magicians who were putting the finishing touches on what looked like ten different dishes at once.

"Hi, Yuri," he said to a man who was jabbing sprigs of rosemary into some kind of roast. "Where's Terpsichore's food bucket?"

"Dulcie has it?" Yuri said, pushing his glasses up on his nose. He had a strong Russian accent, and he only ever spoke in questions. "The unicorn baby is growing better now they say?"

"She is!" Micah said proudly. "I've talked her into eating her food every day this week."

Yuri grinned at him.

Micah liked Yuri. He was the youngest magician at

Circus Mirandus, other than Micah himself, so you could talk to him about things like televisions and computers without worrying that he'd never actually seen one. And he wore his dark hair tied back in a ponytail that Micah thought looked cool.

"Where *is* Dulcie, though?" Micah asked, craning his neck to see everyone in the kitchen. The circus's candy maker wasn't there.

Then he spotted her. She was emerging from the pantry with Terpsichore's food bucket in one hand and a ten-pound bag of sugar tucked under her arm. She was humming cheerily, and the only healthy food in sight was a pineapple she had somehow managed to cram into the bib pocket of her green overalls.

"Rosebud said less sugar," Micah told the magician as she approached the counter. Dulcie set the bucket right beside Yuri's roast.

"Nonsense!" she said. The sugar bag hit the counter with a *thunk*. "Sugar is my specialty!"

It was true, and Dulcie's confectionery magic could probably make gym shorts taste like cotton candy. But still.

"Rosebud said the nutrient potion would work better if there was less sugar in the food. Maybe you could just use a spoonful or two." Micah elbowed the sugar farther away from the unicorn's bucket and set Rosebud's pitcher down.

"A *spoonful*." Dulcie was looking into the bucket, aghast. "But what else will I put in here?"

"Things that are not sugar?" Yuri offered helpfully.

"Sugar is *my* thing, though," said Dulcie. "I'm an *artist*, and it's my *canvas*."

"What about that pineapple?" said Micah. "And some vegetables."

"I tried to make a salad once," Dulcie said. "And it gave people hives."

Micah didn't think she was kidding. "What about you?" he asked Yuri. "Can you make unicorn food?"

Yuri shook his head. "I only make regular food? Without magic?"

"Oh. I thought . . . I guess that won't work."

In the wild, unicorns foraged for magical vegetation, so the food in Terpsichore's bucket had to be made with magic as well.

"It's fine, it's fine," Dulcie grumbled. "I know what to do. Let me go get more pineapple."

She left, and Micah looked at Yuri. "I thought you had kitchen magic."

He had never seen Yuri outside the kitchen, so it had been a natural assumption.

"I am a chef?" said Yuri, grabbing a potato from a pile on the counter. "Who is also a magician?"

"That's pretty neat," said Micah. It had never occurred to him that someone at Circus Mirandus might have a job unrelated to their power. "What kind of magic do you do?"

Yuri's face fell. "It's best that you do not know this?" he said. "I do not want you to be hurt?"

At Micah's alarmed look, he backtracked hastily. "Not hurt? I mean affected? Influenced?" He set the potato back down with a frustrated grimace. "It's best that I do not say certain things out loud?"

Micah hadn't realized that the way Yuri talked had something to do with his magic. He'd always assumed the chef was just shy.

"Sometimes telling it makes it stronger?"

Micah didn't understand, but the pained look in Yuri's eyes told him that the matter was serious. "That's totally fine," he said. "You don't have to explain. I'll . . . um . . ." He looked around for something to break the tension, and his eyes landed on the pile of potatoes in front of the chef. "Wow, those look delicious! I'll go get you some more of them."

"But I do not need—"

Micah was already hurrying toward the pantry.

He found Dulcie inside the cool, dimly lit room. She was already back in her usual good spirits, humming as she stuffed various tropical fruits into her overalls, which must have had magical pockets, Micah decided.

"Potatoes are over there," she said, using a banana to point toward a bin near the door. "If you're really going to make poor Yuri peel more of them."

"Well, I have to now," Micah said, embarrassed. "I'll help him peel them while you finish Terp's lunch." He hunched over the bin.

"You're doing great, you know," said Dulcie.

Micah clutched an armful of red and yellow potatoes to his chest. "Thanks. It's hard to hold this many."

"Not the *potatoes*, Micah." Dulcie stuffed a mango into her overall bib. "I meant you're doing well with the abandoned foal. I'm glad someone's finally got her eating."

Abandoned. That word again. People used it all the time when they were talking about Terpsichore, and it always rubbed Micah the wrong way.

He couldn't say why, since it was only the truth. Maybe it was just that he hated to think of Terp like that—as if she were unwanted, a castoff.

"She's really great," he said to Dulcie. "She's smart. She likes playing games. She's funny and sweet and there's nothing wrong with her at all."

"Of course not," Dulcie agreed in a kind voice.

"Everyone says unicorns take good care of their foals," said Micah. "That they're these wonderful protectors. But I don't see how they can be so wonderful if a whole herd full of them decided to leave Terp behind."

"Aw, sweetie," said Dulcie, reaching for a melon that had rolled under the shelves. "There's not always reason. Sometimes it's just bad luck."

Micah knew that as well as anyone, but it didn't make him feel any better.

Micah spent at least an hour with Terpsichore each day and sometimes more, depending on the mood she was in. An adult magician was always in the paddock in case he needed help. Usually it was one of the Strongmen or Mr. Head, so when he arrived with the food bucket, he was surprised to see the Lightbender standing outside the hidden seam.

"I just came from a meeting with the manager," the illusionist explained. "Since I was here anyway, I thought I'd stand watch."

"Aren't you coming inside?" Micah asked, running his fingers in a zigzag down the seam. The fabric split, and an eager blue-green nose shoved itself out.

"I will if you want," said the Lightbender. "But the manager feels you have a firm handle on the job. He suggested that you might try it alone today. I'll be right here if you have any trouble."

"I can do it," Micah said at once. "I've had plenty of practice."

When he entered the paddock, he was immediately greeted with a happy tootling sound and a friendly jab to the stomach.

"Oof!" he said. "Hello, Terp. You're going to be too big to do that soon. And I've brought you lunch."

He waved the bucket enticingly.

When the foal sniffed at the bucket and snorted unhappily, he set it down and pulled a strand of knots filled with special food memories out of his pocket. He'd tried many different versions of this project without much success, but he kept at it, just in case it was helping in some way he couldn't see. Today, he'd tied a line of small knots into a length of silver ribbon and stuffed them with images of frosty soda bottles on hot summer days and long night-time drives in Grandpa Ephraim's car, on the way to their favorite pizza restaurant.

He showed the knots to Terpsichore, and as usual, she ignored them completely. Micah wrapped the ribbon around the handle of the food bucket, figuring it couldn't hurt. Then, he resorted to less dignified techniques.

He danced around with the bucket, sniffing the contents and making loud yum-yum sounds. Eventually, Terp decided that it wasn't fair he was having so much fun without her, and she trotted over to stick her head in the bucket. Dulcie had worked her magic so that the new food didn't look too different from the melted yellow goop the unicorn was used to, and she dug in with gusto after she'd tasted a bite.

When she'd finished, they played tag. And after that, sweaty, grass-stained, and with an empty bucket in hand, Micah left the foal to her own devices.

"Success?" asked the Lightbender, when Micah emerged from the seam.

"She ate every bite."

The illusionist was heading back to his tent for a two o'clock show, and Micah followed him, planning to change into fresher clothes.

Outside, the drone of rain-forest insects was so loud that Micah could hear it even over the music and the excited chatter of the visiting children. It was a warm, humid day, and earlier it had been sunny. But now dark clouds were gathering in the sky overhead.

The Lightbender looked up. "Perhaps we will take a shortcut," he said, beelining toward the busy midway.

If Micah had been with any of the circus's other performers, they would soon have been surrounded by eager kids hoping to see some magic. But the Lightbender must have been using his power to hide them from the crowd. The magicians who ran the midway stalls waved at Micah, but none of the children even glanced in their direction.

Micah sped up to keep pace with the Lightbender. "I wanted to say thank you."

"Whatever for?" The Lightbender sounded bemused.

"For telling Mr. Head I would help with Terpsichore," said Micah. "I'm doing my best. The knots full of happy food thoughts don't work, but she's still eating."

The Lightbender nodded. "You are doing well," he said. "And you should not be disheartened about the knots. At least they have not been so disastrous as my own, similar attempt."

Micah remembered the scene he'd walked in on that first day, when the Lightbender had been hiding against the wall of the paddock. "You said she didn't approve of you trying to alter her mind."

The Lightbender's illusions didn't have anything to do with bending light; it just sounded nicer than the truth.

He'd told Micah that playing tricks with the light was something people had always understood, even long ago when he first discovered his power. A torch held at the wrong angle in the darkness could turn an oddly shaped rock into a beast. A stray shadow could make a man vanish.

But what the Lightbender did was much more than that. He tweaked something in your brain, so that for you, the rock *was* a beast. And if the beast growled you would feel it in your bones, and if it chased you, you would hear its footfalls on the earth, and if it bit, you would feel sharp fangs sinking into your skin.

Which was unbelievably scary if you thought about it, so Micah mostly didn't.

"I was trying to encourage Terpsichore to have 'happy food thoughts' myself," the Lightbender said. "Most animals barely respond to my illusions, so I didn't realize she would react badly. It appears unicorns take such things personally."

"I didn't know that." Micah had assumed the Lightbender's illusions worked on pretty much anything.

"There are exceptions. Creatures with human, or near-human, intelligence are susceptible. Chintzy is particularly easy to persuade."

Micah could guess how much that annoyed the parrot.

"I am glad I never had occasion to try my magic on an adult unicorn," said the Lightbender.

"Are they really as strong as everyone says?"

The Lightbender nodded. "I saw a stallion charge into the face of a cliff once." He sounded amused. "I think he must have done it for the sheer pleasure of it. A boulder the size of our tent broke free, and he crushed it beneath his hooves until it was sand."

Micah couldn't imagine Terp doing something like that.

Moments later, they reached the Lightbender's tent, and Micah blinked at the sight of all the kids waiting to get in. It was always strange to be reminded that he lived somewhere people were willing to line up to visit.

The Lightbender's tent was small compared to many of the others at Circus Mirandus, but in Micah's opinion, it was the most attractive.

Golden sunbursts glittered against the black fabric. And the tingle that filled the air around the tent was particularly interesting right now, with a storm building and the wind picking up speed. Even on sunny days, the feeling was electric and strange, like the ghost of a lightning bolt that had struck moments before.

Micah shivered even though he knew it was a special effect. The Lightbender had offered once to exempt him from the sensation. It was only decoration, he'd explained, and there was no reason for Micah to experience it since he was a resident at the circus instead of a guest.

But Micah had asked him not to.

He thought it was special to live with someone who used illusions the way most people used wallpaper. And the tingle made the Lightbender's tent feel separate from the rest of the circus, the way your home felt separate from every other house you'd ever stepped inside.

Micah also liked that the tent was the only one at Circus Mirandus with a guard stationed beside it.

"Hi, Bowler," he said as he passed by the Strongman on his way inside.

Bowler's heavily muscled arms were crossed over a chest twice as wide as Micah's whole body. He didn't have on a shirt, but he wore black suspenders that matched his bowler hat. The hat was tipped low over his eyes when they arrived, but he lifted it to wink at Micah.

"*Bowler.*" The Lightbender sighed. "It's about to rain. And I will not die during this afternoon's performance. I promise. You do not have to stand out here in a downpour."

"Hi, Micah," said Bowler, ignoring the Lightbender completely. He had an English accent and a cheerful face. "Did you have fun with our little Terpsichore?"

Micah grinned. "We're getting along great."

"No one has ever sneaked into my tent to assassinate me," the Lightbender said. He gestured at himself, as if to prove how alive he was. "And if they did, I could deal with the situation myself. I am *more* than capable."

The Strongman glanced at the illusionist and then tipped his hat back down over his eyes.

Micah tried not to laugh.

It was true that the Lightbender didn't need a body-guard, but he had saved Bowler's life almost a hundred years before, and the Strongman insisted that he had to return the favor. Whenever he wasn't busy doing other work around the circus, he took up his post and refused to budge.

Micah followed his grumbling guardian into the main section of the tent. The circular black stage at the center of the room was spotless, and so was the floor beneath the bleachers. Micah suspected Chintzy had been grubbing around for all the dropped candy and popcorn even though the parrot knew it wasn't good for her.

"Maybe you should do something dangerous," Micah suggested. "You could let Bowler save you, and then he would feel like the debt was paid."

"Tempting," the Lightbender said. "But I have learned that life holds enough danger on its own. I prefer to let it come when it must and avoid it otherwise. Are you staying for the show?"

Micah shook his head.

He opened the seam to his bedroom with a special combination of finger wiggles and stepped inside.

While he was changing clothes, the show started in the main section of the tent. If Micah listened, he could hear the muffled sounds of the audience taking their seats in the stands. But not long after, they fell completely silent.

Illusions weren't a noisy magic.

He flopped down on top of his patchwork quilt, clutched his pillow to his chest and wondered, as he often did lately, about Terpsichore. He kept turning the foal's story over in his mind, trying to come up with a version that felt right.

Unicorns were protectors. And foals were rare. So why hadn't they protected Terpsichore?

Why had they abandoned her?

Dulcie had called it bad luck, but Terp's luck couldn't be all bad or she wouldn't have ended up here, at Circus Mirandus, with Micah and other people who were trying to take care of her.

She must have been so scared, he thought. If she hadn't wandered into the circus's meadow, anything might have happened to her.

She's like me. She's lost her family, but it could be worse.

He sat up.

She's like me.

Suddenly, Micah knew what was bothering him.

5
RESPONSIBILITY

Micah waited for the Lightbender's show to end. He was sure it had never taken so long before.

To distract himself, he reached for a pile of black cord and gold ribbon he'd left on top of his bookcase the previous night.

Micah had decided a few days ago that he was going to tie a knot bracelet to represent every single magician, tent, and show at Circus Mirandus. It would be good practice, and he liked how it felt when he finished a new one and got it just right. It was like capturing a little piece of the circus in string or thread, and he'd begun to keep his favorite ones tied around his left wrist. (He wore the bootlace bracelet on his right.)

But no matter how many times he tried, Micah could

never seem to tie a bracelet that properly represented the Lightbender.

For this latest attempt, he had chosen two strands of black cord and a bright gold ribbon, and he had wound them over and around each other in a series of tiny, complicated knots. These knots were supposed to hold an impression of the illusionist—memories of his performances and his oddly formal way of speaking and his old leather coat—but for some reason, none of it was ever quite right.

Micah sat on the foot of his bed and tied knot after knot. He felt like his hands were doing battle with the cords and the ribbon. His fingers clenched, his knuckles popped, and sometimes he made such sudden, painful twists with his wrists that it was a wonder he didn't sprain them.

Almost there, he thought. *I'll get it this time.*

He tied, faster and faster, until his fingers nearly blurred. Then, all of a sudden, the gold ribbon burst. It didn't break neatly in two. It exploded.

Like a dandelion puff caught in a sudden gale, the tiny fibers that made up the ribbon blew apart, flurrying around Micah's hands.

He clutched at the destroyed bracelet. His fingers moved of their own accord, as if they thought some particular combination of twitches or tweaks might bring the gold ribbon back. Micah forced them to stop.

"Seriously?"

He'd never made a ribbon fall to pieces before. And now his fingers stung in a way that meant it would probably be a bad idea to try again. Sighing, he dropped the snarled black cords and the palmful of golden fluff on top of the bookcase.

Outside, it had started pouring. Micah could hear the rumble of thunder and the whoosh of heavy rain against the roof, though both sounds were muffled by the magical protections woven into the tent fabric.

The Lightbender's show had just ended, but Micah waited for an interminable half hour before he left his room. The performers almost always stuck around to talk to fans after their shows; it was an important part of the experience. All the kids in the audience right now would be leaving the circus soon (no one's ticket was ever good for more than a week), and they would never be back. For some of them, this would be their one and only chance to speak to the Lightbender.

Micah wouldn't ruin that for anyone. So, he paced a trail across the rug, and when the time was finally up, he let out a sigh of relief and hurried out the seam into the main section of the tent.

The stands were empty, but the Lightbender hadn't left yet. He sat on the stage in the homely, comfortable armchair his audiences never knew existed. A plate with a half-eaten fish sandwich balanced atop the armrest. The illusionist was staring thoughtfully up at a patch in the tent's dark ceiling.

The patch was Micah's fault. It had seemed like a good idea, as his grandfather lay dying, to break into Circus Mirandus and demand that the Lightbender come visit him. When Geoffrey and Bibi had refused to let Micah past the ticket stand, he'd stolen a giant gorilla balloon to mount an aerial assault. He'd fallen through the roof during the middle of the Lightbender's show.

It had been dangerous and horribly painful.

Micah didn't regret it.

"Hello," said the Lightbender as Micah stepped onto the stage.

"Everyone's wrong about Terpsichore," said Micah.

The Lightbender's brow furrowed. "In what way?"

"She's not here by accident. I think her mom must have brought her to the circus for an important reason."

"Micah, I do not think it likely—"

"*Listen,*" said Micah.

The Lightbender fell quiet.

"Something's been bothering me," said Micah, walking back and forth along the stage in front of the Lightbender's chair. "Terpsichore's story doesn't make any sense. Unicorns are good, and their foals are really rare. Even Mr. Head says so."

Micah didn't believe the manager would get the basic facts about any magical animal wrong.

"But everyone keeps calling Terp *abandoned*. And that's even worse, in a way, than what happened to me. Because Grandpa Ephraim couldn't help dying. He would have stayed with me if he could."

Micah didn't usually talk about his grandfather so openly

with people who weren't Fish, and it made him feel awkward and raw. But he had to make sure the Lightbender understood.

"He tried so hard to make sure I would be okay after he was gone. You offered him a miracle when he was ten, and he saved it for his whole life. But then he spent it on me, just to give me a chance to live here at the circus."

Micah touched his bootlace. "Even though he's gone, I'm . . . I guess I'm whatever the *opposite* of abandoned is."

The Lightbender didn't say anything. He sat very still in his chair.

"I know that Terpsichore wasn't abandoned either," said Micah. "Because this isn't the kind of place where someone *gets* abandoned. Circus Mirandus is really hard to find. Terp couldn't have made it here all on her own; she's too little. Her mother must have brought her here. And that would have been dangerous—leaving her herd and tracking you down and traveling who knows how far just to reach you. She wouldn't have gone to so much trouble if she didn't care about her foal.

"So if she left Terpsichore, after all that, it was because she *had* to. Maybe she was scared of something. Or sick. She must have thought she couldn't protect Terp anymore. Just like my grandpa couldn't protect me anymore. And she knew, just like he did, that the circus could."

Micah finally stopped pacing. He felt like he'd been running a race. It all made perfect sense to him, but the Lightbender didn't look surprised or excited at the revelation that Terp's story might not be as tragic as everyone had thought. And he didn't leap up and announce that they had to solve the mystery of what had happened to the unicorn mother and make things right.

"You believe me, don't you?" said Micah.

The Lightbender stood up from his chair. He spoke in a careful voice. "I think you are mistaken about a few things."

"I'm not, though," Micah said quickly. "I'm not here by accident, and Terp isn't either. We're the same."

"*You* are certainly not here by accident," the Lightbender said gently. "But, Micah, unicorns do not become ill. So, the foal's mother could not have been sick as your grandfather was. And while I have told you that unicorns are strong, I do not think I have managed to convey the magnitude of that strength. They are very nearly indestructible. No other living thing preys upon them or wars with them, not since the dragons of old faded from existence. I cannot imagine what would frighten them."

"But everyone says unicorns are good," Micah protested. Good people, and good magical creatures, didn't dump their kids for no reason at all.

The Lightbender sighed. "They are benevolent," he said. "But that doesn't make them flawless. Sometimes difficult, painful things happen, and there is no satisfying explanation for us."

Micah felt like the floor was crumbling away. It seemed

very important that he be right about the foal. Because if he was right, then the circus could do something to fix the problem. They could find the mother unicorn, and Rosebud could heal her. Or they could learn what had frightened her and stop it.

"I'm sorry," said the Lightbender. "I know you have come to care for Terpsichore, and you have been doing a wonderful job seeing to her needs."

She's my responsibility, thought Micah. The first real responsibility he'd ever been given at Circus Mirandus.

He wouldn't argue with his guardian. But he couldn't just give up. Whatever had made Terp's mother leave her behind—Micah would have to figure it out himself.

"Where are you going?" the Lightbender said.

"I need to ask Rosebud a question about unicorns."

"Wait a moment."

Micah turned. He thought the Lightbender was going to discourage him. Or maybe even be annoyed that Micah disagreed with his advice. But the illusionist walked over to the stands and picked up a yellow baseball cap someone had left under their seat.

Micah recognized it as one of the umbrella hats that Geoffrey, the ticket taker, passed out on rainy days. The magical umbrella would sprout right out of the top as soon as it got wet.

"It's raining outside," the illusionist reminded him.

"Thank you," Micah said, feeling a little awkward. "It's

not that I don't believe you. It's just that I'm taking care of Terp now. So, I have to do everything I possibly can to help her."

"I understand," the Lightbender said. He placed the umbrella cap on Micah's head, and it tightened on its own until it fit just right.

6

FIRESLEIGHT

Over the next few days, Micah met with frustration at every turn. He talked with all the magicians he could think of who might know anything about unicorns, and none of them had much to offer beyond what the Lightbender had already told him.

Rosebud confirmed that full-grown unicorns didn't get sick. Mr. Head agreed that they were nearly indestructible. Nobody knew of anything they might truly fear.

Even Jenny had suggested in her last letter that Micah might be chasing after a mystery that didn't exist. She pointed out that her father, who was in school to become a veterinarian, dealt with baby animals that had been left behind by their mothers all the time.

"Sometimes," she wrote, "it just happens."

Finally, with no good theories left, Micah decided to look into a ridiculous one.

The afternoon was pleasantly warm as he set out across the circus, heading for a tall, copper-colored tent. The weather had been dismal for most of the week, with so much rain that the ground was all mud in the more well-traveled parts of the circus. But today, the sun was out, and the copper tent gleamed like a new penny.

The tent was closed when he reached it, its flap drawn and a sign posted beside it. Micah studied it for a minute, but the Portuguese didn't suddenly become readable. He decided it was safest to assume it said something like KEEP OUT. He didn't know Firesleight well enough to just barge in, so he stood at the flap and shouted in his loudest voice, "Firesleight! It's Micah! Are you in there?"

A minute later, a magician with long, dark hair and a bright smile poked her head out of the flap. "Hi!" She sounded surprised. "Did you come for the rehearsal?"

Micah blinked. "I came to ask you a question."

"Perfect timing then!" Firesleight said. "I'll answer it, and you'll watch me rehearse my new show. I could use an opinion from someone your age."

She motioned for him to come inside, and Micah stepped through the entrance, looking around curiously.

Firesleight's tent had always been a little unusual. Instead of a stage, she had a small amphitheater. And stone terraces with benches for seating led down to the sandy area where she performed her magic.

Today, the terraces, the walls, and the ceiling had all been turned pitch-black. And some kind of magical barrier had been set up to separate Firesleight from her audience. It was translucent and barely visible in the dim lamps hanging from the tent ceiling, but Micah could just make it out—a distortion in the air like a soap bubble that stopped right at the edge of the sand.

"What do you think?" Firesleight asked, her voice eager. "Dramatic, isn't it?"

"It is," said Micah.

Firesleight looked pretty dramatic herself.

Normally, the fire magician dressed in modern clothes. She'd been born in Jakarta barely a century ago, which made her practically youthful by Circus Mirandus standards. She kept up with the outside world better than most of the circus's older magicians did, and she had a variety of fireproof hoodies and jeans, all in shades of red and orange, that she liked to wear when she performed.

But now she was in a long black dress that blended in with the dark amphitheater.

"Is that a new costume?" Micah asked.

"Yes," said Firesleight, spinning in place so that the dress flared out around her ankles. "It's part of the routine. The Inventor and I have been working on all of this"—she gestured around the tent—"for months."

"It's still not ready," said a magician in a green sari who had just stepped into the tent. "Hello, Micah."

The Inventor must have joined the circus later in life

than most. Her hair, clipped up on top of her head, was entirely gray, and she had lines on her face. She struck Micah as an elegant, serious-minded person, and seeing her here made him feel like he ought to be on his best behavior.

"You have three new bracelets," the Inventor said, glancing at his left wrist.

"Yes," said Micah, shocked that anyone had noticed. "I mean, yes, ma'am. Do you want to see them?"

He held out his arm, feeling a little silly, because *of course* she wouldn't.

But the Inventor unclipped a metal device that resembled a jeweler's loupe from the tool belt she always wore around her waist and held it to her eye while she inspected Micah's work.

For his part, Micah took the opportunity to admire the tool belt. He thought it looked impressive and magiciany. The belt held several small, bulging pouches and a number of mysterious, gleaming gizmos—tools the Inventor could use to fix magical devices or create them on the spot.

"These are finely crafted," the Inventor said, straightening up and attaching the loupe to her belt.

"Thank you," said Micah, pleased. He reached into his pocket and pulled out his latest half-finished attempt at a bracelet for the Lightbender. "I'm having trouble with this one, but I don't know why. I blew up a ribbon the other day trying to make it."

The Inventor looked thoughtfully at the bracelet. "Perhaps you don't yet have a firm grasp of the subject you've chosen," she said, before turning back to Firesleight. "If you truly wish to test your flames against the shield today, I'll need a few minutes to make adjustments to it."

"Sure, sure," said Firesleight. She plopped down on the nearest bench. "Come sit, Micah. What did you want to ask me?"

"It's kind of weird," Micah warned her as he took a seat.

"Well, who doesn't love a weird question?" Firesleight said.

"You know how I've been taking care of Terp?"

She nodded.

Micah took a deep breath. "I think maybe something bad happened and it scared Terpsichore's mom, or hurt her, and so she brought Terp here to keep her safe. But the Lightbender says the only thing that ever preyed on unicorns was dragons, and they're all gone. I know it's a long shot, but I was wondering if you might tell me—"

"About dragons?" Firesleight interrupted. "Absolutely! Dragons are one of my specialties."

Micah had hoped that was the case. The grand finale of Firesleight's nighttime show did involve a big fiery dragon in the sky, after all.

"Are they *really* extinct?" said Micah, embarrassed. It felt like asking if woolly mammoths might be hiding out somewhere without anyone having noticed.

"That's not a weird question at all," Firesleight said. "Dragons *loved* to hunt unicorns, so you had to ask to be sure."

"Right." Micah was glad she understood.

"Well, don't worry. The big, flying, fire-breathing kind of dragon hasn't been seen in centuries," said Firesleight. "I know, because when I was just a bit older than you are now, I traveled the world hoping to find one. The species hasn't *quite* gone extinct, though. I guess you would say they devolved, or diminished, instead."

Micah listened while she explained that dragons were predators who only ate other magical creatures and the occasional human being. They began life as draklings—small, ground-dwelling, flameless. But the magic they consumed made them grow larger and larger, until finally they were powerful enough to sprout wings and breathe fire.

"Dragonflame," said Firesleight wistfully. "I've never seen it before, but the stories I've heard . . . For a fire magician it would be the ultimate challenge. That's why I've always been interested. But the ancient dragons were horrific and greedy, and they slaughtered so many of the other highly magical species that they starved themselves out of existence. The ones who survived slowly transformed back into draklings. Most of them are no bigger than iguanas these days."

"So, they couldn't hurt a unicorn?" Micah asked.

"Definitely not," said Firesleight. "They've all been asleep for many years. They hibernate in underground burrows in isolated parts of the world. They're excellent tunnelers; they can sense magic over great distances, and they even have a sort of language. But if you dug one out of its lair, you'd see that they're closer to bloated earthworms than fearsome monsters."

Micah suspected he ought to be glad that dragons weren't flying around, eating people and animals willy-nilly, but he felt more disappointed that he'd hit another dead end. Unconscious earthworms wouldn't even scare Terpsichore, never mind a full-grown unicorn.

Then something else Firesleight had said registered. "The draklings have a language? You mean they can *talk*?"

"They can write," said Firesleight. "They have a few glyphs they scratch into mud or wood or rock. They claw their names into the dirt over the entrances to their burrows before they go to sleep. But to be honest, most of the names I've read are just different versions of the same thing."

"Like what?"

"I like to burn stuff," said Firesleight.

"Well, you are really good at it."

"No," said Firesleight with a laugh. "That was an example of dragon names! I Burn Stuff. Fire Is Great. I Burn More Stuff than I Burn Stuff. Some of the oldest draklings—the ones who were real terrors in their day—are smarter than the others. They're more dignified about naming themselves, but even they pretty much stick to the theme. I used to have a book full of all the known names, but I loaned it to . . . uh . . . to somebody. They didn't return it."

She seemed suddenly flustered.

"What's the matter?"

"Nothing," she said quickly. "Don't worry about drag-ons, Micah. Even if the draklings woke, they'd be too weak to hunt for the kind of food that would build their strength again."

"Firesleight—"

"Oh, look!" she said, leaping to her feet. "The Inventor's ready for us."

Micah looked down to the sand floor of the amphitheater. The Inventor stood there, rolling up a silver measuring tape. "The shielding isn't perfect, Firesleight," she warned. "It won't stop the hottest of your flames. If you wish to run through the entire routine—"

"Yes!" said Firesleight. "I'm ready."

She turned to Micah, grinning. "Micah, you're going to be so impressed! I hope. But you have to be honest if you're not, okay? Because I can still make changes."

"I'll be honest," Micah promised.

"Okay, great," said Firesleight. She flapped her hands a little, as if she were shaking off nerves. "Go sit in the front. These back seats are going to be for the younger kids."

Before Micah could ask why the seats needed to be arranged by age, Firesleight was gone. She dashed up the stairs and out of the tent entirely.

"Where's she going?" he called to the Inventor.

"The new routine involves a grand entrance," the Inventor said. "Come sit down here with me."

Micah went to join her on a front-row bench.

The Inventor reached into one of her tool belt pouches and removed a mechanical cylinder. It was the most complicated device Micah had ever seen—all tiny metal dials and golden knobs. It had little bubbles of glass on either end filled with something that glowed like liquid moonlight.

"What is that?" he asked.

"Something we will no doubt need before the end of the show."

The tent went dark.

The brightest light in the amphitheater was the peculiar cylinder, which the Inventor held in her lap. In its glow, Micah could make out the shadowy shape of the nearest benches and the pale color of the sandy floor, but not much else.

Then came the sound of drums.

It wasn't the music Micah usually associated with the circus. It was deeper, more foreboding. And as the drums beat louder and louder, his body picked up the rhythm until he felt like they were beating inside him.

Flames appeared. They were no more than wisps, slithering along the sand, but they multiplied quickly, spreading until they reached the amphitheater's stone stairs. They licked at the first step and began to climb, tiny drops of fire leapfrogging over each other, up step after step to the top, where Firesleight stood, looking like a shadow in her black dress.

As the first of the little flames reached her, she bent and caught it on the tip of her finger.

She smiled at the flame and blew gently on it. It drifted off her finger like a dandelion seed to settle on top of her head. It split into two flames, then four, then eight, on and on until Firesleight wore a crown of blazing orange.

The drums stopped.

The magician swept down the burning stairs, and as she went, the hem of her black dress trailed through the fire, collecting the little flames one by one. By the time she reached the sand floor, she looked like a bonfire come to life.

Micah was so impressed he half expected her to say, "Thank you for coming. The show's over." But she was just getting started.

Over the next few minutes, fire filled the center of the amphitheater, forming patterns in the air, swirling up so high that it splashed against the tent's coppery roof and fell back down like rain.

Micah understood now why the magical barrier was necessary. The fire was wilder than he had ever seen it. The tongues of flame came closer to the audience. Sometimes, they burned white-hot, and if not for the shielding, it would have been much too risky.

And then, just when he thought there were no more surprises, a whip of flame licked the air right in front of his nose.

"Whoa!" he shouted, leaning back. But the flame inched

closer until Micah was at risk of falling off the bench to get away from it.

"It's all right," the Inventor said. "This isn't the part of the show that's dangerous."

She had pulled out a pocket notebook at some point and started jotting down observations.

Micah cautiously sat back up, and the flame retreated. "What do you mean this isn't the part that's dangerous?"

"Sit closer to me," the Inventor said.

Micah scooted toward her until his shoulder bumped her arm.

The finale of the show was unlike anything Micah had ever seen. The fire filled the theater floor until Firesleight was only a dark shape, spinning at the heart of it. Golden flames crashed against the barrier, wave after wave, like a burning ocean trapped in a bottle.

Every wave hit the barrier harder, stretching it farther, until Micah found himself sitting directly under a sheet of fire that was close enough to touch. He knew the barrier was working because the air in the tent should have been scorchingly hot by now, but it was only a little warmer than it had been at the start of the performance.

"It won't last much longer," the Inventor said suddenly, peering up into the flames. "Would you like Firesleight to stop? Or should we let her finish?"

Micah didn't quite understand what she meant. "I'm okay."

He regretted saying it a minute later when the barrier shattered.

Micah had dropped a lightbulb on the kitchen floor once, and the sound was exactly the same. A loud *pop* that made your stomach flip over inside you. But this was no lightbulb.

The *pop* was followed by a roar as the whole world turned to fire.

Brilliant blue light sprang to life around Micah, and the tent was instantly ten degrees cooler than it had been. The Inventor had a tight grip on his arm, and when he looked at her, he saw her calmly adjusting one of the knobs on her metal cylinder with her free hand. The device was shining with the exact same blue light that surrounded the two of them.

"A much stronger shield," she said, by way of explanation. "You'll stay close?"

Micah would have liked to superglue himself to the Inventor. "I'm not going *anywhere*."

She let go of his arm.

The fire died a minute later, and the blue shield pulsed a few times before winking out.

"Well?" said Firesleight, running toward them eagerly. A few flames still glimmered in her hair. "What do you think?"

Firesleight kept Micah for over an hour after the show. She was convinced that the new routine could use "a little more pizzazz" even though he had assured her it was wonderful except for the near-death experience at the end.

Finally, she seemed to believe him.

"Well, all right then!" she said happily. "We'll work out the shielding issue, and we'll be ready for the public in no time!"

The Inventor had explained already that there would have to be multiple magical barriers in place to protect the audience before the show went live. She was going around the tent now, collecting the shielding devices that were hidden under the amphitheater's benches so that she could take them back to her workshop for repair.

"People will like it a lot," Micah said as Firesleight walked him up the stairs toward the exit. "But I think you should probably warn them about how close the flames will look."

"We will. We always post warnings for my shows. Some people are pyrophobic. You'd be surprised how many— oh!"

Firesleight stooped to pick up something on the step in front of them. When she stood, she was frowning down at the knotted length of black and gold cord in her hand.

"That's the bracelet I was showing to the Inventor," Micah said, checking his pockets automatically. "I must have dropped it."

He held out his hand for the Lightbender's bracelet, but Firesleight didn't notice. She was examining it, her brows drawn together in confusion. "It's not burned."

"I told the knots I wanted them to stay together," Micah said.

The bracelet *was* a little burned, though he didn't want to upset Firesleight by pointing that out. The strings had been much longer than they were now. It was only the knotted portions that had survived the performance.

Firesleight looked at him. "And that fireproofs them?"

"I guess so. I've never tried to burn one before, but it does make them unbreakable."

She passed him the unfinished bracelet. Micah checked it over. As he'd thought, the strings had burned off just below the last knot he'd tied. No big loss, since this version hadn't been much better than his last attempt anyway.

"I didn't realize your magic worked like that," Firesleight said. "I thought you only used the knots for holding memories."

"Well, they couldn't hold the memories if they came apart," Micah explained. "Then they would just be plain old string."

He attached the individual elements of each memory to a different loop or twist of the knot. If even part of it came undone, it wouldn't have worked properly.

"When I'm tying an important knot, I tell one section of string it has to stay connected to another section. And I do it over and over, and when I'm done, it should all be permanent."

"That's . . . interesting," said Firesleight. "Does the Lightbender know your knots work like that?"

"Of course!" said Micah.

But then he reconsidered. He'd never actually described the process of making a memory knot to his guardian, now that he thought about it. It had always seemed obvious to him. And he couldn't recall if he'd ever mentioned the permanence of the knots to the Lightbender or not.

"Well, maybe he knows," he corrected himself, looking down at the bracelet. "Why does it matter?"

"It's unexpected," said Firesleight, shrugging. "I was thinking of you as a magician who had a unique way of sharing his memories with other people. It's hard to figure out what that has to do with turning regular string fireproof."

"It's not the string," Micah said patiently. "It's the *knots*. If I untied them, you could burn these cords just like anything else."

"I see," said Firesleight. But she looked doubtful. "Just remember to pay attention to your magic. You're getting to know your own power, and the little details of how it works can turn out to be much more important than you think. Sometimes, your magic surprises you. Sometimes, those surprises get you into trouble."

7

READY

After supper that evening, Micah decided to visit the menagerie.

He had to let Terp know that, for now at least, her case was closed. He'd run out of leads, and Firesleight's warning about his magic had reminded him that he'd been neglecting his practice over the past few days.

It's not like Terp was worried about it in the first place, he thought as he grabbed a pear tart off a tray on his way out of the dining tent. He was trying to ease his sense of failure, but it was still true. All Terp really worried about was whether or not she would get to play games when she'd finished cleaning her food bucket.

Outside, the temperature was just right, and the sky sparkled overhead like someone had tipped over a pail full of diamonds. The circus was fifty miles south of the nearest city, Manaus, so there wasn't much light to compete with the stars.

Micah wasn't surprised to see that the crowd was bigger than usual on such a beautiful, clear night, nor to see that the menagerie was especially busy when he arrived. But he *was* startled to see Terpsichore out of her paddock and prancing around the tent like she owned the whole circus.

Normally during outings, she stood with one of the Strongmen holding her lead rope while kids pet her and asked questions about her. Apparently, she'd decided to spice things up tonight by starting a game of follow-the-leader. She capered around the tent while a Strongman jogged alongside her. Slower animals scattered out of their way, and a line of more than a dozen children trailed behind them, mimicking the honks and whistles Terp made as she ran.

Micah lifted his hand, intending to call out to the foal, but then he thought better of it. She was having fun, and he might distract her. Instead, he watched for a moment, feeling proud of how healthy Terp looked. Her aqua tail flicked happily, and she wasn't tiring out, even though the kids chasing her were starting to sound a little out of breath when they honked.

Micah stood quietly while Terp and her followers passed by, then he headed toward the aquarium. His barrel was in its usual position, and he climbed on top of it. "Hello, Fish."

Fish *thwapped* the glass with his tail. He did it every time Micah greeted him now, which made Micah certain he'd understood at least part of the story contained within the knot he'd eaten.

Micah had been thinking that he ought to ask Mr. Head if he could tie something else for Fish. Maybe a small knot every now and then that held a few memories about the day.

Most of the other animals took trips out of the menagerie. Some had scheduled appearances around the circus, and others went for an explore whenever the mood struck them. But Fish was always in his tank. It only seemed right that he should get to know what was going on around the circus, too.

"Would you like to eat another one of my knots?" Micah asked.

Fish bumped his nose into the glass.

"Well, all right, then," said Micah. "I'll ask the manager."

He talked for a few minutes while Fish swam in circles. He told him about Jenny, whose visit was only a couple of days away, and about his trouble coming up with ideas for how to improve his magic.

"I need to get better if I'm ever going to keep up with the others. Did you know Rosebud's got a potion that will eat through solid rock? I almost knocked it off a shelf yesterday, and she told me about it. And me . . . well, I've been trying to figure out how to do something new, but the memory knots are the only things that really work."

He'd tried to tie a knot that would turn invisible last week, and all he'd ended up with was hand cramps.

"I guess you can't help with that, right?" Micah said. "I mean . . . you're your own kind of Idea, and your Someone is out there somewhere. You probably don't have any answers for *me*?"

Fish's shadow passed over him as he swam by. Micah didn't have any sudden flashes of inspiration. He sighed. "That's okay."

He turned his back to the aquarium and sat, digging around in his pockets until he found a piece of yellow string. He didn't feel up to starting a brand-new bracelet. Instead, he thought about what Firesleight had said. It was important to pay attention to the little things about your magic.

So, Micah tied a regular knot. Easy as blinking. Then, he told it not to come undone.

He felt a prickle of magic at the tips of his fingers. He knew the knot would be permanent now. He could sense it, just like he could sense the permanence of the knots in his bootlace bracelet.

He ran his fingers over the bootlace's rough leather, checking. One knot to represent Jenny. One for Grandpa Ephraim. Both chock-full of magic and memories and tied tighter than tight.

He tied another knot in the yellow string. Then another. He made them both permanent, trying to pay close attention to how the magic worked.

It was almost like magnetizing the string, he decided. Or gluing it. He told the fibers on one part of the string that they needed to stick tight to the fibers on another part. Once his magic had connected them, they wouldn't let go.

"I don't know, Fish," he said. "I don't see how this is going to help me figure anything out."

Micah looked around the menagerie and realized he'd missed Terpsichore heading back to her paddock. The kids who'd been chasing her were all red-faced and panting. He was about to get up to go tell her good night, when he noticed something strange.

Fish's shadow was behind him again, blocking the light, and it wasn't moving.

Micah glanced over his shoulder. Fish had stopped swimming.

"Are you watching me?" Micah asked.

Fish didn't do anything to show he'd heard the question. But a minute later, he shivered all over, like an electric jolt had run through his body, and he suddenly grew bigger.

Micah stood up on the barrel and stared into the tank. He looked from Fish's blunt silver nose to the sharp triangle of his tail. He was longer than he had been by at least a couple of feet. Micah was sure of it.

"What the heck?" Micah whispered. "Fish, what are you *doing*?"

"It's gettin' ready," said a voice behind him.

Startled, Micah wobbled sideways on the barrel, and a hand reached out for his elbow to steady him.

Micah looked down to see Circus Mirandus's ticket taker. Geoffrey was wearing his tailcoat, as usual, and he was carrying a stack of umbrella hats under one arm. He let go of Micah's elbow and peered at Fish through his golden monocle.

"It was a tiny little thing for decades," said Geoffrey. "It's done most of this growin' in the past couple of years."

"To get ready for the Moment?" Micah said. "Is that how we know it's going to be soon?"

Geoffrey switched his monocle to the other eye. "It's what you do, isn't it?" he said gruffly. "You realize somethin' big needs doin', so you try to make sure you're up to the task."

"That makes sense," said Micah. "But how do you know that's what Fish is doing?"

"I always make sense," said Geoffrey. "And I know because the fish and I speak the same language."

Micah squinted at the ticket taker. Geoffrey did *not* always make sense, and sometimes he had a weird sense of humor.

"Fish doesn't talk," he said suspiciously.

"Oho!" said Geoffrey. "An expert on big Ideas, are we?"

Micah climbed down from the barrel, shaking his head. "What does Fish say, then?"

"Who knows?"

"*Geoffrey.*"

The ticket taker slapped one of the baseball caps sideways on top of Micah's head. "Storm's comin'," he said.

"Again?"

While Geoffrey stomped around the menagerie, passing out hats, Micah looked up at Fish and thought about what the ticket taker had said.

When something big needed doing, you had to try to get ready for it. Micah didn't know how to help Terp right now, and he didn't know exactly when Fish's Moment would arrive, but that didn't mean he couldn't prepare himself.

I'll practice my magic more than ever, he thought. *I'll do what Firesleight said and pay attention to the details even if it seems boring. I'll be ready.*

Not long after that, he said good-bye to Fish and left the menagerie. As soon as he stepped outside, he saw that Geoffrey had been right about the storm. The stars he had admired earlier were gone, swallowed by black clouds, and wind howled around the tents.

The twinkling lights that hovered over the circus at night were flickering, and not far away, he saw Rosebud leading the plump yellow ponies that normally pulled her wagon toward the safety and comfort of the menagerie.

Micah gripped the bill of his ball cap tightly and bent his head against the wind.

"I don't like the look of this weather!" Rosebud called to him, her booming voice carrying over the howl. "Best get yourself home for the night!"

Halfway back to the Lightbender's tent, Micah met Bowler, who was clutching his own hat to his head. The

Strongman walked beside him, serving as a windbreak. As they reached the safety of the black-and-gold tent, the first raindrops began to fall.

"Just in time!" said Bowler.

"Is it normal for storms to pop up this fast?" Micah asked, taking his hat off. "It was clear a little while ago."

"It was," Bowler agreed. He had a thoughtful look on his face. "We've made this stop before a couple of times, and we've never had quite this much rain. It's supposed to be the driest month of the year."

Then he laughed. "Of course, it *is* called the rain forest for a reason."

Even as he said it, rain started to blow sideways through the open tent flap.

8

TUTTLE KNOTS

The Door opened into sunlight.

Micah hovered on the threshold, in awe of Porter's magic. A neatly trimmed suburban yard lay before him, with daylilies blooming and a garden hose snaking across the grass. A bird chortled in the hedges, and though the street was out of sight, Micah could hear what sounded like a garbage truck growling past.

Peal was thousands of miles, and only a single step, away.

At Micah's back, Porter's warehouse was dim and quiet. The massive tent held doors stacked in piles that went almost to the ceiling. Porter had mailbox doors and barn doors, cemetery gates and attic hatches. And one narrow shed door with a scuff on the bottom that led to Micah's old neighborhood.

Micah had arrived at the warehouse half an hour before he was supposed to, wearing an umbrella hat on his head and his new magician's kit on his back. Inspired by the Inventor's tool belt, he had taken his old school backpack and decorated the straps and zipper pulls with teal yarn. Then he'd stuffed it full of his knot projects and tying supplies. It was part of his plan to make sure he was ready for anything.

"Looks good," Porter said, eyeing the backpack. The magician was already at work matching the shed door to one of the empty frames that stood in the center of the warehouse. The frames were arranged in a circle that reminded Micah of Stonehenge.

"And that looks even better," Porter added, nodding toward the tray Micah had brought from the kitchen. It held a mug of black coffee and a plate of the steamed buns that Yuri said were Porter's favorite breakfast. "Didn't expect the food, but thank you."

"I know it's a lot of trouble to open a Door just for me."

"It's not," said Porter. "It's a long way to send you, but I won't have to hold it open for long. And we're not even using a full-size Door."

Porter's magic was easiest when the Doors he opened were small or the distances were short. It was no big deal for him to send Chintzy out on deliveries all over the planet, since the parrot could squeeze herself through mailboxes and cat flaps. And the Doors that brought children to the circus were almost always local, covering distances of no more than a hundred or so miles; the magician could hold those open for ages. But opening the big gates the circus used on moving days always took a lot out of him.

Porter chewed on a bun while he tapped the shed door's hinges into place with a hammer. In between bites of food, he explained how important it was that the physical door he made here match the one on the other side as perfectly as possible. "Can't get a good connection between the two if they don't, and the magical Door won't form. I have to force it, and that's an exhausting business."

Porter was a few inches shorter than Micah, who wasn't tall for his age, but he never had trouble positioning the enormous gates and double doors the circus used on moving days. And he fitted the hinges of the small shed door so quickly that the coffee was still steaming when he'd finished.

Micah passed it to him.

Porter took a sip and pressed his free hand to the door, just below the knob. He narrowed his eyes and made a shoving motion. His elbow tensed, and he huffed sharply once. The shed door looked exactly the same, but when he flicked the knob open, Peal was there.

Porter eyeballed the sunny yard over his coffee mug. "Not bad," he said. "A little prosaic, but we all have to come from somewhere."

"Where did you grow up?" Micah asked.

"Istanbul," said Porter. "You remember the rule?"

"Jenny and I will be standing in front of this Door at eleven o'clock a.m., Eastern Daylight Time, and not a minute later," Micah recited.

"Excellent," Porter said. "And the Man Who Bends Light told you what will happen if you're not?"

"*Ummmm.*" It hadn't come up. Micah had expected a lot of warnings when he found out he'd be traveling to an entirely different country on his own. Things like *Be careful crossing the street,* and *Don't talk to strangers.*

But the Lightbender had grown up somewhen very different—possibly a time when boys Micah's age were expected to fight wolves with nothing but sharp rocks.

And, come to think of it, the illusionist probably didn't know much about crossing the street himself. He almost never left, since it was his magic that kept Circus Mirandus hidden.

But Porter was waiting for an answer.

"You'll leave me there?" Micah guessed.

"Oh, it'll be much more embarrassing than that." Porter grinned slyly at him. "If you're not here on time, we'll come get you."

Before Micah could process the idea of a bunch of magicians on a search-and-rescue mission in Peal, Porter gave him a push, and he stumbled through the Door.

The backyard belonged to the Greeber family, who lived not far from Micah's old house. The door on their gardening shed was a perfect match to the one in Porter's warehouse, right down to the scuffed bottom.

Micah couldn't stick around. He'd ridden the school bus with Florence Greeber for years, and she would wonder why he'd popped up beside her shed when he was supposedly living in Arizona with his great-aunt.

He tried to act natural as he skirted the hedge and set off down the sidewalk. He stuck his hands in the pockets of his shorts and stared down at his sneakers. Maybe if he didn't look up, he could make it all the way to Jenny's house without anyone recognizing him.

The plan was for him to spend the morning with Jenny's family. She would have explained all about the circus by now, but of course her parents would still have a lot of questions about magic. Micah would show them some of his bracelets, and he would tell them anything they wanted to know.

And Jenny would finally get to come back to Circus Mirandus. She'd helped Micah reach the circus in the first place, even though she hadn't believed it was real. They hadn't had much time to explore that night, and Micah had been thinking hard about how to make this trip perfect for her. She would love the maze of mists, which nobody had ever solved. Plus, they would need to spend plenty of time in the Inventor's souvenir tent, so that she could pick out a keepsake to take back home with her. And they would need to see—

Micah jerked to a stop. His face was still pointed down

at the sidewalk, and the toes of his shoes were an inch away from a familiar crack in the pavement, one that spider-webbed almost to the curb.

He hesitated. Part of him wanted to turn around and take another route to Jenny's house, but instead, he let his eyes trace the crack all the way to the grass. It had grown tall in the past four months.

He took a quick, deep breath and spun to face the house. It was small and yellow. The curtains were drawn, and weeds had started to spring up on the front walk. A red glass hummingbird feeder hung from the eaves, empty.

A plastic sign staked out front drew Micah's gaze:

FOR SALE BY OWNER
SERIOUS BUYERS ONLY
CALL GERTRUDIS TUTTLE:
520-555-0165

Micah knew he should get off the sidewalk so none of the neighbors would see him, but his body had gone as stiff as a butterfly pinned to a board. He read the sign again and again.

But I don't want anyone else to live here. Aunt Gertrudis can't sell it. She can't.

Only she could. It even made sense. There had been a lot of bills, hadn't there? After Grandpa Ephraim had gotten sick. Micah remembered them talking about it.

What did Aunt Gertrudis care about the house? There

was no record of *her* height and age written in marker on the bathroom door. *She* hadn't spent last summer building a tree house in the backyard with Grandpa Ephraim. And she had never cared enough about Micah to want to save those things for him.

Sometimes, Micah felt sorry for his great-aunt, who had loved the idea of magic when she was younger only to have Victoria ruin it for her. Aunt Gertrudis had been a kid when her older brother, Grandpa Ephraim, married Victoria. The Bird Woman had been like a mother to little Gertrudis until one day she'd tricked her into jumping off a roof. Gertrudis had expected Victoria to fly up and catch her, but she hadn't. And Aunt Gertrudis had refused to have anything to do with magic ever since.

When Micah had gone to live at Circus Mirandus, his great-aunt hadn't been too upset. In fact, Micah was pretty sure she'd been relieved.

You've got the circus now, Micah told himself. *That should be enough for anyone.*

But knowing his old house wasn't that important was a lot easier than feeling like it wasn't. Before he realized he intended to do something, he was standing in the backyard, looking up into the spreading limbs of a huge oak.

The tree house had never been finished. It had three walls and no roof, and the boards were unpainted. A rope ladder hung over the side, the ends just brushing the overgrown grass. The tree house was the last thing Grandpa

Ephraim and Micah had made together before he got sick.

Aunt Gertrudis could sell the house. And she could sell the tree house, too, since Micah couldn't do anything to stop her. But the rope ladder was a different matter.

He grasped one of the ladder's rungs and let his hands drift to the edges. Thick knots held each wooden rung in place.

They weren't the kind of knots you usually saw on a rope ladder. These were complicated—the rope weaving in and out and around, twisting in so many unexpected ways that your eye couldn't follow the pattern of it. Micah smiled, running his fingers over the knots, remembering the day he and Grandpa Ephraim had tied them together.

The Tuttle knot, they called this one. And only the two of them knew how to unravel it.

Micah looked up.

The ropes were secured around one of the beams that supported the tree house's floor. He grabbed a rung, intending to climb up, but then a thought occurred to him.

What if he didn't have to climb at all?

He was already touching the ropes. Did he actually have to touch those knots that connected the ladder to the tree house?

Micah had never tried to untie a knot without touching it directly. If he could, it would be a step forward with his magic. And the rope ladder was special—a last gift, almost, from his grandfather. Maybe it would bring him luck.

Micah rubbed his fingertips together for a few seconds, working out the problem in his head, and then he reached for the soft fibers of the ropes again.

Just the top knots. Only the top.

He closed his eyes and concentrated, picturing what he would do if his hands were on the knots. You could touch a certain loop of rope, *just so*, and the whole knot would loosen up and fall apart.

He thought, *Come loose.*

His fingers prickled. It was a sparkling sensation, almost warm. Micah imagined he saw a thread of light, connecting his fingertips to the knots at the top of the ladder.

Then he felt it happen. Inside his head. A tiny, tiny *snap*. And with a sound like a whisper, the knots at the top of the ladder came undone.

Micah looked up just in time to see the ladder slither out of the tree. The wooden rungs clacked against one another as they fell in a heap at his feet. He grinned down. Only the two knots at the top of the ladder had unwound. The others looked just like they had on the day Micah and his grandfather had tied them.

Tuttle knots—still tighter than tight.

9

PERMANENT
TANGLES

Micah had a spring in his step as he made his way
down Jenny's street. The rolled-up tree house ladder wouldn't fit in his magician's backpack, so he hugged it
to his chest, unbothered by the strange looks he got from
passersby.

Finally, after all these months, he'd had a real breakthrough.

If Micah could untie a knot just by touching the rope
it was made of, then maybe one day he wouldn't have to
touch ropes or strings at all. Maybe he would be able to tie
and untie knots with the power of his mind alone.

Micah didn't know what it would be useful for, but it
was going to look extremely cool.

He found himself searching all around him for opportunities to use his newfound skill. He spotted a woman untangling a knotted garden hose so that she could add water to a plastic kiddie pool, and he had to resist the urge to run over and say something absurd, like, "Allow me, ma'am. I am Micah the Hose Wrangler, magician extraordinaire!"

This isn't the time for that, he chided himself.

Jenny's neighborhood seemed like a cheerful, normal place. The houses mostly belonged to young families. Little kids in their swimsuits ran through sprinklers, and several girls Micah's age rode shiny new bicycles in circles at the end of the cul-de-sac, right in front of Jenny's house. They ignored Micah as he passed.

He practically skipped up the sun-bleached walk to knock on Jenny's front door.

Nobody answered.

Frowning, Micah knocked again and glanced at the curtains over the front window. It looked dark inside. He was early, but it had never occurred to him that nobody would be home.

He dropped the rope ladder and his backpack on the stoop and sat down to watch the girls ride their bikes. They were drinking energy drinks and giggling. One of them had a cell phone attached to her handlebars with an impressive amount of tape, and it played a bright pop song on repeat.

Micah had almost memorized the lyrics when Jenny appeared at the far end of the sidewalk. She had obviously been to the library, and she was balancing a tall stack of books in her arms.

He leaped up and jogged toward her. It didn't matter that Chintzy had been delivering their letters back and forth since the day he'd left Peal; he suddenly had a million new things to say.

The girls on the bikes flew past him, pedaling hard.

Micah stopped, surprised. A couple of the girls were riding right on the street, dodging around a parked mail truck. One of them shouted something to her friends. The pop music blared.

Before he could figure out why they were in such a hurry, the girl in the front of the pack threw her half-empty bottle of energy drink. It spun end over end through the air and landed in a bush just behind Jenny.

For a split second, Micah thought it was an accident. But then the other girls threw their bottles, too.

One bounced off the back of a car. Another landed in the grass. An empty bottle smacked into the tower of books in Jenny's arms, but there wasn't enough force behind the throw to knock the books over.

"Hey!" shouted Micah, furious.

Then, the last bottle hit the sidewalk an inch from Jenny's feet. It was almost completely full, and when it hit, the electric blue drink fountained up, splashing Jenny's legs, drenching her white knee socks. The bottle *pock-pock-pock*ed down the sidewalk and rolled toward a storm drain.

The girls sped away on their bikes, shrieking with laughter.

Micah rushed to Jenny.

He expected her to set the books down so that she could wipe off her legs. Energy drink was riveting down her knees. But she just stood there, completely still. Her eyes were clenched shut, and her jaw was set. Her arms were clamped on the books, which had been belted together with a strap so that they were easier to carry. They were all fantasy novels.

"Those jerks!" Micah said, when he reached her. "Are you okay?"

"I'm fine," Jenny said in a tight voice. "Thank you very m—MICAH!"

Her eyes snapped open, and the books hit the pavement with a thud. She flung her arms around him. "YOU'RE HERE!" she squealed. "I didn't know they would let you come early!"

Micah returned the hug, his anger fading. It felt so good to see her face-to-face. "I was kind of in a hurry to see my best friend."

"You know," Jenny said a few minutes later, slapping her wet blue socks on top of the washing machine, "where I used to live, the other kids *liked* that I was smart. And they *loved* my outfits. Everyone knew Mom designed some of my clothes, and they thought it was *great*."

They were in the laundry room, and Jenny was reaching for a bottle of stain remover. "And now my socks smell like fake blueberries," she said angrily.

Micah thought Jenny's outfit—a polka-dotted skirt and a shirt with a bow on the collar—looked almost like something a popular kid might wear on a television show. And he was sure that her mom, who owned a sewing shop and made custom formal wear, knew more about fashion than those girls on their bikes. But he also knew that some people would pick on anything that made you stand out, even if it was good. And Jenny had had trouble with bullies ever since she'd moved to Peal last year.

"I think your clothes are awesome. And your mom's the nicest person ever." Silvia had let him stay at their house the afternoon Grandpa Ephraim died so that he wouldn't have to face Aunt Gertrudis right away.

"Thanks, Micah." Jenny was squirting the stain remover on her socks with a lot more violence than the job required.

Micah tried to think of what his grandfather would have said in a situation like this. "Sometimes people see that you're doing something special, and that you're happy, and it reminds them that they're not. So—"

"So, they try to squash you down and make you feel as tiny as *they* are," Jenny said, shoving the stain remover back onto its shelf. "I know."

She tossed the socks into the machine and bent to collect dirty towels from a basket on the floor. "I wasn't even supposed to be here right now," she said. "I was accepted at a science camp. But they only had a couple of scholarships, and I didn't get one."

She flung a towel at the washer wildly, and Micah dodged out of the way before it could hit him in the face. Unfortunately, he tripped over the stack of books Jenny had left on the floor. He yelped and crashed into the side of the dryer.

"Oh, holy smokes!" said Jenny, reaching to help him up. "I'm so sorry!"

"That's okay," said Micah, picking a clump of lint out of his hair and rubbing a sore elbow. "Do you want me to go after those girls? And the science camp people? I could tangle their hair or something."

Jenny blinked, and a smile stole across her face. "Permanent tangles?"

"Absolutely," said Micah. "Just point me at your enemies. They won't know what hit them."

Jenny laughed. "I've really missed you. I'm sorry I'm in such a funk. I was just so excited about our day at the circus, and then those girls . . ." She shook her head. "Anyway, who cares about them? Tell me about your breakthrough! You said you had one this morning?"

"I did." Micah told her about untying the rope ladder's knots without even touching them. "I mean, I was still touching the ropes, but not the knots themselves. I know that's not a *huge* breakthrough, but I think—"

"It's great!" Jenny exclaimed. "We've got to add it to my chart."

"What chart?"

"Oh, I can't wait until you see it! I've been trying to think of ways to help you study your magic. That's why I checked out all these fantasy books for you, by the way. And I'm hoping we can categorize different magical skills. We'll ask everyone at the circus to add information about their powers to the chart, and by the end of the day, maybe we'll be able to match your magic with a category."

She beamed at him over an armload of towels. "If you have some idea about what *type* of magician you are, it might help you figure out what else your knots can do!"

Micah didn't know what to say. On the one hand, he needed all the help he could get. But on the other, it didn't seem fair to let Jenny spend her whole day at the circus trying to solve his problems.

"I have a lot of fun stuff planned, though," he said. "Don't you want to see all the shows?"

"I want to see absolutely everything," said Jenny. "But we can interview magicians in between performances. I promise it won't take long."

Micah was already rearranging the day in his head, trying to fit in all the best shows *and* interviews with the magicians. He wondered if Jenny would be willing to wear running shoes.

"We should head over to the Greebers' house as soon as we can," he decided. "Maybe Porter will open the Door early. When are your parents getting here?"

"About that . . ." Jenny dumped the towels in the wash

and stood on her tiptoes to reach the knob. "It'll be way easier not to bother them with all this. They're both busy today, anyway, and I told them I'm going to hang out with Florence Greeber."

"You lied to them?"

"Sort of," said Jenny. "But we'll be in Florence's backyard if you think about it from a certain standpoint."

Micah didn't believe Jenny's parents would be thinking from *that* standpoint.

She saw the look on his face. Her own smile drooped. "I know. I was going to tell them. I swear. I almost said something over breakfast. But, Micah, I just *couldn't*."

"Why not?"

"Because!" she said. "They wouldn't let me go!"

"Of course they would," Micah said. "They like me."

Jenny rolled her eyes. "Yes, they like you. But if you think about it from a parental perspective, which I've been trying to do, it sounds kind of *extreme* to step through a secret portal to visit a bunch of magical strangers in Brazil."

She hesitated. "And if they did say no, I couldn't stand it. I want to see the circus again. So much. And I need a break from . . . stuff."

From jerks on bicycles and blueberry energy drinks, Micah thought.

"Okay."

"Really?" she said, relieved. "You don't mind?"

Micah shook his head. "I figure pretty much nobody tells their parents they're going to the circus, right?"

"Right." Jenny smiled at him. "And I'll tell them sometime soon. I promise. I hate keeping secrets. But for now, we've got a Door to catch!"

10

AFTERIMAGE

Jenny bounded through the Door into Porter's ware-house so quickly she nearly bowled the magician over. "Sorry!" she said. "You must be Porter. I'm Jenny. It's good to finally meet—WOW!"

She'd brought a tote bag full of colorful markers and a roll of Christmas wrapping paper with her, and she dropped both onto the stone floor as she spun in circles. Her eyes widened as they took in the towers of stacked doors and the walls full of mailboxes. The skylights, high overhead, showed dark clouds.

"This place is wonderful!" Jenny beamed at Porter. "And your magic is amazing!"

"Thank you," Porter said, looking startled. "I'm fond of it."

As Micah stepped through the Door, clutching his rope ladder, Jenny was already hastening to unroll the wrapping paper. She held it up so Porter could see the chart she had drawn on the back. She had come up with magical categories ranging from Artificers (which included magicians who made magical objects) to Zoo Mages (which was for people whose talents involved animals).

Porter shut the shed Door behind them and listened with amusement as Jenny explained her plan to classify magical powers by type. "It will be interesting, don't you think?" she said. "And it will help Micah figure out what he can do with his knots besides memories."

Porter scratched the back of his neck. "It *will* be interesting," he said. "But I wouldn't let your hopes get away with you. Magic is more complicated than that."

"This is just a starting place," said Jenny. "I've already put you under Travel Magic, but if you want to change that or add any details about yourself, you can."

He took the marker she offered him, and she spread the chart on top of a short stack of closet doors. Porter made a number of notes under his name, including *doors must match* and *difficulty increases with distance*.

"Is that the kind of thing you had in mind?" he asked, passing the marker back.

"It's perfect!" Jenny said. "Thank you so much. Are there other magicians who can do what you do?"

"Not exactly. There's a man in Texas who can teleport. He can't carry other people with him, though."

Jenny made an excited noise and bent over the chart. Micah leaned over her shoulder to see what she was doing. *Teleporting Texan!* she had written. *No passengers.*

She capped the marker with a *pop.* "Let's go, Micah!" she announced. "We've got a lot of circus to see."

Micah left the rope ladder behind in the warehouse, and they set out, Jenny craning her neck as she walked, trying to see over rooftops and around corners. She was fascinated to be in the Staff Only section of the circus. "Are *all* of these storage tents?"

"A lot of them are," said Micah. He pointed to a cream-colored tent. "But that one over there belongs to Symphony. She does something that makes the circus's music. And that big gray tent is for the animals who don't want to be in the menagerie. It's got all kinds of habitats, and they can just hang out with no people to bother them."

"The menagerie!" said Jenny. "I want to be sure we leave time for that. You've written so much about Terpsichore that I feel like we're old friends. And I've made a card for Mr. Head."

"A *card*? Like a greeting card?" Micah couldn't imagine giving the manager a card himself. What would you even write on it?

"It's a thank-you note," said Jenny, as if that should be obvious. "I was afraid he wouldn't want me to come back because of how I behaved last time I was here. It was so hard for them to convince me all of this was really magic. I want him to know I appreciate the opportunity."

Micah had planned to start the day at the circus's maze, which was run by a woman named Mistsinger who could summon and shape fog. He was sure it would be one of Jenny's favorite tents, since she loved puzzles, but looking up at the glowering clouds overhead, he changed his mind.

"We need to get you an umbrella hat."

Jenny looked worriedly at her roll of wrapping paper. "I don't want my chart to get wet."

"It can have an umbrella hat, too. Come on. Geoffrey's always got a big stack behind the ticket stand."

They headed for the circus's entrance, Jenny walking so quickly that Micah could barely keep up.

"I can't believe I forgot Geoffrey," she said as they strode past the arboretum. "I don't have him anywhere on the chart. I hope he's not offended. What's his magic, anyway? Ticket-taking isn't a power, right?"

"I don't know."

"Micah, you've been living with him for months!" she exclaimed. "Didn't you ask?"

"He says he can talk to Fish," Micah offered. "But I'm pretty sure he was just kidding. I think his power must have something to do with his monocle. He's always swapping it from eye to eye."

The ticket taker's back was turned when they approached his stand. He was in his tailcoat and a pair of galoshes, bowing politely to a newcomer. The girl was a couple years older than Micah and

Jenny, and she had brought a ripe papaya as her ticket.

She passed it to Geoffrey as he finished his bow, then hurried past him, no doubt eager to explore.

"This is what I like to see!" Geoffrey said, when Micah and Jenny walked up. He hadn't yet turned around. "Comin' to visit the ticket taker first thing even though you sneaked in the back way."

"How did you know we were here?" Micah asked.

Geoffrey pointed up at the sign over his head.

CIRCUS
MIRANDUS
MAGNIFICENT SINCE 500 B.C.

"I've been here since the beginnin'," he said. "I know things."

He turned to face them, squinting through his golden monocle.

"Hi, Geoffrey," said Jenny. "It's good to see you again. I was wondering if I could ask you a question about your magic."

"It's good to see you, too, Jenny Mendoza. And nope."

"Thank—oh," said Jenny, looking flummoxed. "I *can't* ask you a question?"

"You can ask me all sorts of questions," Geoffrey said

in a cheerful voice. He tucked the papaya into a hidden compartment in the ticket stand and pulled out a purple ball cap for Jenny. "But I'm not goin' to answer any about my magic."

"I didn't mean to be nosy," said Jenny as she took the hat from him.

"It's not that you're nosy." The ticket taker raised his bushy eyebrows when Jenny put the umbrella hat on top of the chart instead of her own head. "I just don't need you two to run screamin' into the jungle when you find out I'm the scariest magician there is."

Jenny looked concerned, but Micah had been around Geoffrey often enough to know he was only being serious half the time.

"*Really?*" he asked. "Are you scarier than Firesleight?"

"Yep," said Geoffrey, reaching for a yellow cap. "And you can tell her I said so, too."

"Are you scarier than the Lightbender?" asked Jenny.

"Ha!" said Geoffrey. He set the yellow hat on Jenny's head, as if he didn't trust her to do it herself. "That old trickster? Absolutely."

Micah was almost positive now that Geoffrey's power was something harmless. "Are you scarier than Yuri?"

"Oho!" said Geoffrey. "Fishin' for information on our mysterious young chef, are we?"

Micah hadn't meant to, but he *was* curious about Yuri's power. And he didn't want to ask the Russian magician about it since it had upset him before.

"Scarier than Yuri," Geoffrey said. "That *is* a good question. And it's one I'm not gonna answer for now. I'll tell you when you're older."

"How old?" Micah asked.

"At least a hundred." Geoffrey switched his monocle to the left eye. "You might be mature enough by then."

Micah was a little offended to be called immature, but he was more grateful that the ticket taker thought he might still be at the circus a century from now.

"Enough about me." Geoffrey held out his hand toward Jenny. "Ticket?"

"Pardon?" said Jenny.

"She's my guest, Geoffrey. You know that."

"What's that got to do with anything?" Geoffrey waved his hand under Jenny's nose. "Ticket?"

Jenny was gripping her chart extra tight, as if she thought Geoffrey might be planning to grab it. "I didn't bring anything."

Geoffrey didn't put his hand down, and after a moment's thought, Jenny held out the tote bag full of markers. "Here?"

Geoffrey made a great show of examining the bag, then he plucked out a thick red marker and held it up to his monocle. "An extraordinary ticket!" he announced. "Have fun."

He tucked the marker into the stand beside the papaya and gave Jenny a particularly melodramatic bow.

Micah thought Geoffrey was being absurd, but the longer

the ticket taker stood with his nose almost brushing the grass, the more Jenny smiled. By the time they left the ticket stand she was practically skipping.

"What was that all about?" Micah asked.

"It was just nice of Geoffrey to do that."

"He stole one of your markers."

"I wanted to do the ticket thing," Jenny admitted. "It's a big part of the Circus Mirandus experience, isn't it? I thought it would be silly to ask, but Geoffrey must have guessed anyway."

"Do you think his magic is something embarrassing?" Micah asked. "And that's why he won't tell us?"

"Maybe he makes umbrella hats," said Jenny, touching the bill of her ball cap.

Micah shook his head. "No. The Inventor makes these. Do you want to meet her? The souvenir tent's close."

The next few hours blurred past, no matter how much Micah and Jenny wished for time to slow down.

The Inventor added herself to the Artificer category of the chart before giving the two of them a special tour of her tent. Jenny spent more time admiring the workshop—a room full of beakers, burners, clockwork, and clever gadgetry—than the souvenirs that filled the tent.

The toys, games, and mementos the Inventor created for the souvenir shop were magical, but only a little bit so. The tops spun for longer than they should have. The balls bounced higher. The golden bells tinkled with a slightly different sound every time you shook them.

After browsing for a few minutes, Jenny chose a pen that would always write in the perfect color of ink to suit her mood, and she took it up to the counter.

Everyone who came to the circus could choose one souvenir, and they were always free. But the Inventor liked to check them one last time before they left her tent. She examined Jenny's pen through her jeweler's loupe, then she wrapped it neatly in silver paper and sealed it with a drop of orange wax.

"Thank you for coming to Circus Mirandus," she said formally, holding the package out to Jenny. "Carry it with you."

It sounded like she was talking about something more important than a pen.

Jenny tucked the parcel into her tote bag.

When they left it was drizzling, and the umbrellas blossomed out of their ball caps automatically. The Inventor's umbrellas were better than normal ones because they would fold and shift of their own accord to keep themselves from getting in the way in tight or crowded spaces. And no matter how hard the wind blew they would never fly off.

Micah and Jenny explored the midway, talking to every magician they could, then they headed to the mist maze. They wandered foggy corridors that twisted in endless spirals, and they might have been at it all day if Micah hadn't reminded Jenny there were other things to see.

He showed her how to get into the tent that held the nocturnal garden, even though it was officially closed to the public, and they sat on a big flat rock in the middle of one of the luminescent pools, eating a bag of chocolate sweets called brigadeiros that Dulcie had given them earlier.

After that, they caught the tail end of Firesleight's show, and by the time they left, it was raining in earnest. When Firesleight poked her head out of the tent flap to insist that Jenny come back for the full performance sometime, the raindrops sizzled in her hair and turned to steam.

"Do you think we could say hello to the Lightbender next?" Jenny asked Micah.

They headed for the black-and-gold tent. There was no line out the door, even though a show was just about to start. Bowler, who was wearing a waterproof poncho the size of a tablecloth, was letting everyone in early so they didn't have to stand out in the rain and mud.

The Lightbender spotted Micah and Jenny in the audience, and he included a couple of new experiences in the performance just for them. Jenny loved the tour of late-nineteenth-century Paris, complete with dinner at the newly built Eiffel Tower.

When the show was over, the two of them waited while the crowd filed out, several kids stopping to talk to the Lightbender on the way. As usual, the illusionist was sitting in his ugly, comfy armchair while he spoke to them.

Jenny leaned over and whispered in Micah's ear, "He didn't have that chair last time I was here."

"Yes, he did," Micah whispered back. "He just doesn't let most people see it."

He explained that the kids talking to the Lightbender probably saw him doing something terribly impressive—like floating in midair.

"That's just *cheating*," said Jenny.

The last member of the audience to leave was a small boy who asked the Lightbender to sign the back of his T-shirt. After he was gone, the illusionist said, "It is good to see you again, Jenny."

"You too," she chirped. "Thank you for the show. Paris was my favorite. Will you help with my chart?"

She grabbed the roll of wrapping paper, which was looking a little the worse for wear after being hauled all over the circus, and headed to the stage.

Micah watched the Lightbender's face carefully while Jenny explained how the chart worked. He didn't think his guardian would disapprove of the project, but what if he did? What if he thought it was rude of them to question all these magicians just to get ideas about Micah's own magic? Maybe it was the sort of thing Micah was supposed to be figuring out by himself.

But the Lightbender leaned forward in his chair to see the wrapping paper better and said, "How ambitious! Let us see what I can add to your endeavor."

Soon enough, the chart was spread across the stage. Micah was tasked with standing on one end to keep the paper from rolling back up while the armchair held down the other side. The Lightbender got down on his hands and knees beside Jenny and started making notes with a green marker.

Bowler came inside to watch.

"It's Strong*folk*," he said, shaking water off his poncho. He pointed at the category where his own name was listed alongside the other Strongmen at the circus.

"Yes," the Lightbender agreed, making a note. "You have not met the Strongwomen because they only visit us from time to time. They are a part of their own Sisterhood with its own goals."

"They are?" Jenny said, eyes bright.

"What kind of goals?" Micah asked.

"They are peacemakers," said the Lightbender. "They travel to some of the most dangerous places in the world to help bring an end to violence. When necessary, they are formidable warriors."

"Very good at arm wrestling," Bowler added. "We have competitions."

"What kind of names do the Strongwomen have?" Micah asked. He leaned over to see what the Lightbender was writing. Rather than choosing more traditional magicians' names for themselves, Bowler and the other Strongmen had all named themselves after the hats they wore. "Do they like hats, too?"

The Lightbender blinked. "No. The members of the Sisterhood customarily choose plant names for themselves. As for the hats . . . the Strongmen are going through a phase."

"My hat's not a phase!" Bowler protested.

The Lightbender examined the chart for a minute more. His name was the only one listed under the Mind Manipulation section, but it was that way for a lot of the categories. And quite a few people hadn't been able to fit themselves on the chart at all, so Jenny had been forced to add a new box labeled "Other Talents."

"Classifying magicians is a tricky thing to do," the Lightbender said, passing the marker back to Jenny. "Magic is a reflection of the people who wield it. It mirrors our characters. Or it represents something we hoped for or needed when we first discovered our power. It can be as individual, and as uncategorizable, as human beings themselves."

Jenny frowned thoughtfully. "What does Micah's magic say about him, then? I guess that's the question we need to ask."

"Indeed," said the Lightbender. He gave Micah a serious look. "But answering *that* question is the work of a lifetime. It's not something that can be accomplished in a single day."

With only an hour left before Jenny had to go back to Peal, the two of them headed for the menagerie, their shoes slipping in the mud.

Jenny was frowning.

"Are you upset you have to go home?!" Micah had to shout to be heard over the sound of the rain. "You know I'll invite you again!"

Jenny shook her head. "It's not that! I just thought the chart would help you more!"

Lightning crackled across the sky, and they picked up speed, sprinting the rest of the way to the scarlet tent. They dashed through the entrance into the welcoming brightness and warmth. The skylights had been shut against the rain, and the animals were all in good spirits.

Big Jean trumpeted happily when she saw Jenny, and she stomped over to them, waving a piece of sidewalk chalk in her trunk.

"Oh, Jean!" said Jenny, patting the elephant's leg. "I'm so sorry. I don't have time for the chalkboard right now. We've got to see Terpsichore, and I need to find Mr. Head. I've got a card for him."

The world's most intelligent elephant flapped her ears and knelt in the sawdust.

"Is she offering to take us to Mr. Head?" Jenny asked Micah.

"Probably," said Micah. "But she might also be planning to kidnap you and teach you geometry."

It had happened to him more than once.

They climbed aboard, and Big Jean tromped toward the manager's office. When she reached the hidden seam, Jean stuck her head right through it, as if she was sure she was welcome.

"Jean, we've talked about knocking," Mr. Head said. He came to the door before the elephant could force her way inside. "Hello, Jenny Mendoza."

"Hello, Mr. Head," said Jenny, once Jean had let them both down. "I made something for you."

She was busy rummaging through her tote bag, so she didn't see the look of surprise that crossed the manager's face. She pulled out a folded card made of heavy paper and checked it all over for bends and tears before handing it to Mr. Head.

"That's our dog, Watson, when we first got him from the animal shelter," she said, pointing at the photograph she had glued on the front. In it, her mom was grinning and holding a gangly German shepherd puppy. "And the one inside is him now. He goes to work at my mom's shop every day."

The front of the card said THANK YOU in bubble letters. Micah couldn't see what the inside said, but Mr. Head stared at it for a long time.

"You are very welcome, Jenny," he said finally. "And Watson is a beautiful creature. I'm glad to know he has a loving family."

An annoyed grunt came from across the room, and Micah saw Bibi's red velvet cushion shift. A moment later, the tiger appeared. She stood between the manager and Jenny, her posture unusually stiff, her blue eyes intent on Mr. Head.

"Really, Bibi." He sighed. "I didn't say the dog was *more* beautiful than you."

✧　　✧　　✧

They went next door to visit Terpsichore, who was so delighted to have a new guest that Micah was afraid she was going to expect Jenny to come every day.

Jenny cooed at the foal and brushed her while Micah sat comfortably propped against his backpack, studying the chart. He wanted Jenny to know that her hard work hadn't gone to waste, so he was trying to find some category he could possibly fit himself in. Finally, his eyes settled on the first one.

Artificers. People who made magical objects.

The Inventor's name was there. It would be great if Micah's knots could do even half the things her magical creations could. Maybe he could make umbrella bracelets.

Or exploding knots, he thought, remembering the gold ribbon he'd destroyed.

Suddenly, Micah could imagine a thousand things he wished his knots could do. If he were an Artificer, he could make shielding knots or levitating knots or knots that would work like tracking devices.

That last would even be useful. He could tie a tracking device knot around everything he owned, and then, when something got misplaced on moving days or stolen by one of the mousebirds, he could hunt it down.

"Maybe I'm an Artificer, Jenny."

He even liked the feel of the word in his mouth. *Artificer* sounded special. Talented. Definitely the kind of magician who belonged at Circus Mirandus.

"Do you think so?" Jenny asked. "Your bracelets would

qualify as magical objects. And if you could just make—"

"Different kinds," Micah said eagerly. "I know."

He was glad now that he'd put together his magician's kit. He had everything he needed right here. He unzipped the backpack and dug through it, pulling out a spool of black thread.

"Are you going to try something right *now*?" Jenny asked. She had brushed Terpsichore into a happy stupor and started braiding her tail.

Micah examined the thread. It wouldn't be a good idea to tie anything explosive in the menagerie, and he thought if you were trying to make a shielding knot you should probably use something more substantial than thread.

"A tracking device," he decided.

Thread was perfect for that. The knots would be nearly invisible, and they would be so small he could tie them to anything.

"How will it work?" Jenny asked.

Micah wasn't sure, but he was so excited by the new idea that he couldn't resist trying.

He started tying. *Don't get lost,* he told the piece of thread. He imagined he was attaching it to his own brain. He thought it would be like having a sixth sense, so that wherever the thread was, he would be able to find it.

Right away, the knot felt peculiar. The tingle in Micah's fingers told him he was doing magic, but something was different than usual.

He finished, bit off the piece of thread, and closed his

eyes. The tiny knot still didn't seem quite right, but he tossed it as hard as he could away from him and then waited, trying to picture where it must have fallen. He crawled around on his hands and knees, trying to get a sense of the knot's direction.

"Micah, what are you—?"

"*Shhhhh . . .*"

But he shouldn't have shushed Jenny. Because he didn't have anything like a sixth sense for the knot's location, and when he finally gave up and guessed, he looked down to see a patch of empty grass.

"Maybe a different technique?" Jenny suggested. She was working on Terp's mane now.

"No, I felt something," said Micah, frustrated. "I'm going to try again."

He went back to his backpack, picked up the spool of thread, and started over.

Micah tried a more complicated knot now. He would take his time, get it right. He worked slowly, pulling the thread tight *here*, twisting it around and around *there*.

After a while, the soft music that always filled the paddock helped him focus.

He stared at the thread, tracking its progress through the endless loops of the knot with his eyes, and suddenly, he saw . . . something else. Like a firefly, flickering in the periphery of his vision, desperate for his attention.

Micah turned his head to look, and it disappeared.

Jenny was petting Terpsichore, and the foal was soaking

up the affection, tossing her head to show off her freshly braided mane.

"Did you see . . . ?" Micah started to ask. But, of course, Jenny hadn't seen anything. She'd been focused on Terp.

He shook his head and went back to the knot.

It was done. This new design was exactly what he had imagined, but it had that same not-quite-right feeling to it. Micah knew it wasn't going to work any better than the last one had.

I'm missing something, he thought. *Something just out of reach.*

And there it was again. That glimmer. Micah didn't turn to look at it this time. He didn't want to scare it away.

What are you? His fingers searched the knot for an answer.

KRACKA-BOOM!

Jenny cried out in surprise.

Terpsichore whistled.

Micah dropped the knot and slapped his hands over his ears.

The sound shattered the air, and lights flashed overhead. Micah was vaguely aware of Terp scrambling to hide behind a pile of hay in the corner.

"Thunder!" Jenny said. She laughed nervously.

Yes, Micah realized. Thunder. That was what it had been. But the magical paddock did such a good job of muffling the sound of the weather that he hadn't ever heard thunder in here before.

He looked up and saw water smashing into the transparent roof. It didn't even look like rain. It looked like a giant was standing over the menagerie tent, emptying an ocean over the top.

"It's just the storm, Terp!" said Jenny. She hurried toward the unicorn, who was shivering in the hay. "It's okay. It'll be over soon. We're safe in—"

KRACKA-KRACKA-BOOM!

Micah felt the sound like a hammer against his bones.

Jenny yelled shrilly. "That struck us! Micah, I think lightning just struck the menagerie!"

Micah was still staring at the paddock's ceiling, which was no longer transparent but glowing with a light so bright it hurt. *It's the magic of the tent protecting us,* he thought. *That's what the light is.*

But that wasn't all there was.

Micah could see a different brightness. A tangled rope of light, burning and *wrong*.

He slammed his eyelids closed, but though the light of the tent dimmed, that wrongness was still there, high above him, twisting through the air like some terrible diseased vine.

A hand was on Micah's shoulder, shaking him. He opened his eyes, and the rope of light was gone.

"Are you okay?!" Jenny said.

"I . . ." Micah didn't know.

Jenny grabbed his face in both hands. "Micah? Are you going to faint?"

The rain was still pounding into the tent. Micah waited for something else to happen—some flash, crackle, or explosion. But it was just rain.

"Come on," Jenny said, grabbing his hands and pulling. "We should make sure everybody's safe."

"Did you see that?" Micah asked, climbing to his feet. "Did you see the light?"

"We got struck by lightning!" said Jenny. "The whole tent glowed for a second!"

"Not that," said Micah, shaking his head. "Did you see the rope?"

She pulled him toward the paddock's door seam. "What rope?"

"It was . . . there was a rope of light. I could see it with my eyes closed, and . . ."

But before he could figure out how to explain, Jenny opened the seam into chaos. Kids were running around and screaming, or they were crying and hunkering down in the habitats with the animals.

The huge center pole of the tent was blazing with white light, making Fish's aquarium shine like a bulb.

"It must work like a lightning rod!" Jenny exclaimed. "Micah, look!"

But Micah couldn't muster any excitement or curiosity over the tent pole. He felt dizzy and sick to his stomach. "Jenny, I think—"

"We need to calm people down," she said, her eyes

zipping back and forth to take in the frightened crowd.
"Let's—"

The tent fell silent. The kids who'd been running around
stilled. The ones who'd been climbing over gates and stalls
and startled animals stopped. Everywhere, children were
brushing sawdust off their clothes and helping one another
up off the ground. One girl even let out a merry laugh
when she saw that one of her flip-flops had gone missing in
the confusion.

Micah looked up and saw the Lightbender. The illusionist stood in the menagerie's doorway with Bowler at his
side. He was dripping wet, water streaming off his coat
onto the ground. And he was staring right at Micah.

Are you both well? his voice said in Micah's ear. *I've left
you out of this particular illusion. Do you need anything?*

Micah felt like he needed to throw up, but he didn't
think that was what the illusionist meant.

"We're good!" he shouted.

Stay in the menagerie for now, said the Lightbender. *It's
a safe place to weather the storm.*

He left, but he didn't drop whatever illusions were keeping the kids in the tent calm. Over the next few minutes,
Micah and Jenny stood with Big Jean and watched, wide-
eyed, as magicians came and went, making sure all was
well.

Rosebud was the first, striding into the tent with a bag
full of healing potions slung over her shoulder. There

wasn't much work for her, but she stopped to help a boy with a bloody elbow. A couple of the Strongmen appeared next. They set about righting overturned barrels and calming nervous animals.

Last came the Inventor. She'd brought something that looked like a spyglass with her, and she peered through it at the glowing tent pole, which was slowly going dark. Next, she took a tiny hammer and walked around Fish's aquarium, *tap-tapping* on the glass.

When she'd finished, she nodded at Mr. Head, who had just come from checking one of the private habitats. Then, she hooked the hammer back onto her belt, apparently satisfied all was well.

"What do you think these kids are seeing?" Jenny asked, watching a girl twirl in circles while a curious wallaby hopped around her.

"Something fun," said Micah.

"I like your guardian," said Jenny. "But he's a little terrifying."

Micah knew what she meant. It was always impressive to see the Lightbender's illusions during his shows, but watching him turn the mood of the tent around in seconds, without even lifting his hand, was more sobering.

"Jenny, when the lightning struck, did you see the *other* light? Like a vine or a rope, but really bright?"

Jenny turned to him, brow furrowing. "No?" she said. "Were you looking at the ceiling?"

"Yes," said Micah. "I mean, I was looking at the ceiling,

but when I closed my eyes, I could still see it. It looked . . . not right."

"Maybe it was an afterimage?" said Jenny.

"A what?"

"You know," she said. "It's like when someone uses a camera flash too close to your face, and you shut your eyelids, but you still see lights popping."

"I guess . . ."

It made sense. The lightning strike and the protective glow of the tent had been much brighter than any camera flash.

"Are you sure you're okay?" Jenny asked.

Micah nodded.

"Don't worry," she said. "I bet this kind of thing has happened before. Lightning's more likely to strike tall objects. And the menagerie tent's so big."

"Right," said Micah. He hadn't been worried about the tent. After all, he'd seen Firesleight cover hers in flames, and the fabric had never even scorched. But that ugly rope of light . . .

An afterimage, he told himself. *That's all it was.*

11

MAGICIANS WHO MATTER

The storm raged for over an hour, and long before the end of it, Jenny turned into an anxious mess.

"My parents," she moaned, wilting onto a folding chair in front of Big Jean's chalkboard. "They're going to wonder where I am. They're going to call the Greebers. Then they're going to call the FBI."

"Maybe they'll just think you're having fun at Florence's house," Micah said, sitting down in the chair next to hers. "You'll only be a little late."

"I left a note on my bed just in case I didn't make it back in time," said Jenny. "I didn't think they would ever actually read it!"

"But that's a good thing. They'll know you're safe."

"It said, 'Don't worry. I've gone to visit Micah. He lives at a magic circus. I'll explain when I get home.'" She pulled her feet up into the chair and pressed her face to her knees. "Why did I write that?"

"Well, it's the truth," said Micah.

"They'll think I've lost my mind."

"I'll come home with you and explain. I'll tell them I begged you to come, and it's all my fault."

She stared at him. "You can't do that! That will just make them mad at you, too!"

Big Jean turned away from her chalkboard at the shrill note of alarm in Jenny's voice. The elephant had been drawing a map of California, but she put down her chalk and reached out with her trunk to pat Jenny on the head.

"Oh, Jean," said Jenny. "Thank you. I know they love me, but what if I can't make them believe me? And what if I *can*, but they never want me to come back here?"

"Then I'll come see you in Peal," said Micah firmly. "And we'll both talk to them until they understand."

They watched the skylights, and when the battering rain became more of an ordinary flood, Jenny insisted they go wait by the door.

The fabric of the menagerie's entrance was drawn shut, and a pair of Strongmen stood there. They weren't letting people leave just yet. Not even people whose parents might or might not be on the phone with the FBI.

"It will be fine," Micah said for the seventh time.

Jenny sighed heavily. "You should keep this." She held the wrapping paper out to him.

"But you've worked so hard—"

"My parents might confiscate it. And, anyway, the chart was always about helping you figure out your magic."

"It helped." Micah took it from her. "At least I've got some new things to try now."

"You can keep adding more to it," Jenny said. "We didn't talk to everyone. And there are historical magicians to think about. Maybe if you keep asking, you'll find out that someone knew a knot magician in the past."

Micah was sure if anyone at the circus knew about knot magicians, they would have thought to tell him already. But since they were talking about adding people to the chart, he said, "You left the Zoo Mages category blank."

"We haven't met any Zoo Mages." But Jenny was shifting from foot to foot. She knew who Micah meant.

He glanced at the Strongmen by the entrance. They were just out of earshot if he talked quietly. "Victoria belongs in that category," he said. "She can . . . or she *could* mind control birds."

She could also fly, which meant she probably belonged in more than one category. But that was so terribly unfair that Micah didn't want to bring it up.

Jenny cut her eyes sideways at him. "I must have forgotten about her."

Micah crossed his arms. "Jenny, you even included the

magician who made the tents, and that guy's not alive any-more." Apparently, the Tentmaker had fallen in love with someone and moved away long ago. "Maybe Victoria's not either, but that's not why you left her out. Everyone else does it, too. Nobody ever talks about her in front of me."

Jenny bit her lip. "I thought it would hurt your feelings."

"I know," said Micah. "I would hate it if people were always bringing her up. But when she's never mentioned *at all*, it's obvious that everyone's still thinking about her. About what she did."

"Nobody blames *you* for it," Jenny said.

Micah knew that, or he did in his head at least. But it didn't change the worry he had sometimes, that he had to make up for Victoria Starling's crimes against the circus.

"You should tell the Lightbender how you feel," she said. "Or someone. Just so they know you don't want them to tiptoe around the subject."

"Maybe," Micah said. It would be an awkward conver-sation, but at least it would keep people from tripping over his grandmother's name when they spoke to him.

Jenny hesitated. "Earlier today, I wanted to bring some-thing up about Victoria, but I didn't know if it was a good suggestion or a bad one, so I didn't."

"What was it?"

"The storage tents," said Jenny. "There are so many of them. I bet her old things are in there somewhere. If you wanted, I'm sure they would let you look through them."

Micah stared at her. He couldn't imagine a single reason why he would want to look through the Bird Woman's stuff, if anyone at the circus had even bothered to keep it.

"It was a suggestion. That's all," said Jenny. "I would be curious if it were me. I would want closure."

Micah shook his head.

"Okay," said Jenny. Then she added, "I still don't think Victoria belongs on my chart."

"But—"

"My chart's for magicians who *matter*." She had a fierce look in her eyes. "And the Bird Woman doesn't. Not to me."

Somehow, Jenny always knew just what to say.

"Thanks," said Micah.

"Thank you." She looked toward the Strongmen. One of them was drawing a circle on the patch of fabric that would open the menagerie's entrance. "This was a really good day."

The fabric drew open. Outside, it still was raining heavily, but no lightning streaked across the sky, and the wind had died down.

"Maybe your parents won't be mad," Micah said.

"No, they will. They definitely will." Jenny reached for his hand. "It was worth it though."

She pulled him outside, and together they ran through the storm, heading for Porter's warehouse.

✧   ✧   ✧

Dear Micah,

I'm writing this with my new pen, and I think it's chosen gray ink because this is bad news.

I'm grounded. I can't even walk across the street unless my mom or dad is with me. Middle school starts next week, and I just hope they don't insist on escorting me to the bus stop.

I'm not sure they even believe I was with you at the circus. I showed them my pen and my friendship bracelet and explained about everything, but they look at me so strangely any time I mention magic.

I asked Chintzy to talk to them, so maybe that will do the trick. But would you please explain to her what a veterinarian is? I had to give her a whole jar of peanut butter because she thinks my dad is some kind of mad scientist who experiments on parrots.

I won't be coming back to the circus anytime soon, but we can still send letters. Please write as often as you can!

Your friend,
Jenny

PS—It was still worth it.

Dear Jenny,

I'm sorry about your parents. I'm writing them an apology note and sending it with Chintzy in case that helps.

She says your dad wants to pluck her tail feathers and put them under a microscope. But don't worry, she's flattered. Apparently, he told her she was unique.

We're all sick of the rain. I guess the lightning strike made everyone nervous, because they had a special staff meeting about it. (I wasn't invited.) And Mr. Head decided to move the circus south ahead of schedule. The last of the tickets will expire today.

We're going to be staying near a place called Santa Rosa dos Dourados.

Rosebud says we'll start classes after the move. I think I'm pretty lucky that she's agreed to be my teacher. She likes to travel a lot, and she says we can go on field trips to see Rio de Janeiro and São Paulo. She says you can come with us when you're not grounded anymore.

I'm still trying to make my tracking device work. Chintzy's been hiding different versions all over the circus for me. I'm going to call it the locator knot when it's finished, but so far I can't locate it at all.

Your friend,
Micah

FEATHERS

It was funny how time moved once you settled into a routine.

It felt to Micah like his first few months at Circus Mirandus had lasted forever. He'd met so many new people and learned so many new things that every day had been an adventure. At the same time, the absence of Grandpa Ephraim in his life had pricked him like a thorn over and over again, so that he feared he would never be able to go a whole hour without feeling at least a little of that hurt.

But the thorn stung him less frequently as time passed. And with Rosebud's insistence on schooling came a daily schedule for him to grow used to—up early for breakfast in the dining tent, lessons with Rosebud all morning, lunch with Terpsichore and Fish, math and geography with Big Jean. Then free time, supper, bed.

His new life was wildly different from the one he'd had in Peal, but something about the rhythm of it was similar, and Micah found the days zipping past him like the dotted lines on a highway.

The circus had left the strange weather behind in the Amazon, and it seemed to Micah that all the adults breathed a collective sigh of relief, though he himself hadn't realized there was anything to be truly worried about in the first place.

They spent September and most of October in a cornfield outside Santa Rosa dos Dourados. Then it was on to Colombia, where they stayed in a national park through most of December.

The new year found them in Argentina, northeast of a city called Azul, in the middle of a cow pasture that stretched to the horizon. After a couple of days, the cows started wandering right through the circus's meadow like they owned the place.

"Why don't we ever stop *in* town?" Micah asked Rosebud one day during a field trip. They had spent the morning in Buenos Aires, touring an art museum, and now they were walking down the sidewalk along a busy street. "Wouldn't it be nice if the circus was right beside a movie theater? Or a public pool!"

It was summer in the Southern Hemisphere, and Micah would have loved to go swimming. Fish would no doubt share his aquarium, but the Idea had grown again, and Micah figured he needed most of the room for himself.

"We travel to more heavily populated areas on occasion," said Rosebud, grabbing the back of his T-shirt before he could step in front of a passing bicycle. "We came to Peal for you, after all. But the Lightbender has more trouble hiding the circus in metropolises. He and Porter usually compromise by choosing places that are near enough to cities for easy Doors and far enough away for easy illusions."

"That makes sense."

"If you want a pool, duckling, you should talk to Bowler when we get back," she said. "The Strongmen have one. It's probably in one of the storage tents."

Later that afternoon, Micah did exactly that.

"The pool!" Bowler shouted. "Now that's an idea!"

He'd been standing out in the sun all day, and his forehead was wet with sweat. "I know where it is, too. Packed it away myself!"

He headed straight for the Staff Only section, apparently willing to leave the Lightbender unguarded if it meant he got to cool down. Micah trotted after him, imagining beach towels and swim trunks.

But when they reached the storage tent—a dull gray one that looked oddly misshapen and woebegone for Circus Mirandus—Bowler's cheerful demeanor turned suddenly awkward.

"Err . . . you'd better just stay out here," he said, when

Micah tried to follow him inside. "This tent's a bit disorganized. Don't want you stumbling over things in the mess."

"Bowler, I know how to watch my own feet," Micah said with a grin.

"No, no," said Bowler. He patted Micah on the back. "Be a good lad and keep watch over the door."

This behavior was sufficiently odd to make Micah suspicious. And while he stood outside, listening to Bowler rummage through the tent, Jenny's words from months before came back to him.

If any of the storage tents at Circus Mirandus *did* hold his grandmother's belongings, it would surely be this run-down one.

Part of Micah wanted to run right inside and tell Bowler not to be ridiculous. Micah wasn't going to fall apart if he saw Victoria's old suitcases.

But before he could work himself up to it, Bowler was back, balancing a huge crate over his head with both hands. "Better get some help," he said cheerfully. "We'll need extra hands to set up the high dive."

It turned out that the circus had not only an above-ground pool but also a tall diving platform. Both were part of an old routine, and that evening, after the Strongmen finished setting the high dive up behind the menagerie, they were overcome with nostalgia. They started a belly-flop contest so enthusiastic it rendered the pool unusable for swimmers who didn't have superhuman strength.

A crowd of spectators began to gather, and Micah knew

from experience that a competition among the Strongmen was likely to last for hours.

He abandoned his beach towel and headed back to the storage tent.

Micah wasn't sure he wanted to find Victoria's things, but he was sure that he was going to do it. It was like trying not to watch a horror movie playing in another room. You knew looking would give you nightmares, but you still had to peek from time to time.

Best to get it over with, he decided. Whatever was left of Victoria's stuff would be moldy and evil, but at least after he'd seen it, he wouldn't have to wonder about it anymore.

Inside, the storage tent was dark, and the air smelled stale. Most of Circus Mirandus's tents would turn on the lights whenever someone entered, but this one must have been broken. Or there was some trick to it Micah didn't know.

He trailed his hands along the fabric near the tent flap, drawing patterns with his fingers. And when that didn't work, he said, "Can I have some light?" out loud.

The tent itself didn't respond, but a faint glow came from something on the ground near the far wall. It wasn't much, but after Micah gave his eyes a minute to adjust, the silvery glimmer was enough. He could just make out the shadowy shapes of the crates and boxes that filled the tent.

Most of the storage tents were orderly, with everything neatly stacked and organized. But this one was as messy as Bowler had said it was. Micah picked his way through a maze of jumbled crates and tumbled barrels to get to the source of the light.

When he finally reached it, he froze.

He had expected to find a magical lamp, like the ones in his bedroom. He'd thought he would have to carry it around the tent for hours, peering into boxes, searching for something as wicked and unpleasant as he imagined Victoria to be.

But here, before him, were the Bird Woman's things. And they were beautiful.

The soft light came from a tent, carefully rolled and tied with ropes. Grandpa Ephraim had always described the Bird Woman's tent as silver, but that didn't do it justice. Even wrapped tightly and tucked away in this dim place, the fabric glittered like fallen stars.

The starlight tent would be huge when it was unfurled. Not quite as big as the menagerie, but close.

It would have to be, Micah realized. Victoria's performance had been a flight show. Something like that would require a lot of space.

The Bird Woman had soared through the air alongside her flock. It must have been wondrous, to see a person flying as easily as the birds themselves did.

She sang, too, Micah remembered suddenly. *She sang to the birds.*

Victoria had mesmerized the birds with her voice. She had called them to her. Charmed them. Taken care of them.

And then, when the Lightbender had refused to leave the circus with her to seek fame and fortune elsewhere, she had betrayed them.

She'd sent the birds crashing into one another, into the audience, into the ground itself. In the end, the Lightbender had used his own magic to put a stop to the carnage. He'd convinced the Bird Woman she could no longer fly.

Micah reached out to touch the tent fabric, but his hands stopped short.

What did the tent look like inside? Had Bowler and the other Strongmen had to clean it before they packed it away? Was it still full of feathers?

Was it stained with blood?

He drew back and turned instead to the two crates lying beside the rolled tent. Someone had written **Victoria Starling** on the top in black paint. Micah wondered if they had used the Bird Woman's real name because they thought she didn't deserve her magician's name anymore.

He lifted the top off the first crate. White feathers greeted him, ghostly in the silver light of the tent.

He took a deep breath and dug his hand in, exploring the crate. It was all fabric and feathers. Victoria's costumes. She would have looked angelic.

Micah opened the second crate and found a jumble of lovely things—pearl-colored shoes, an engraved silver mirror, bejeweled headbands, delicate makeup brushes. He set them aside one by one until he reached the bottom, where he found three heavy, leather-bound books.

Micah assumed they must be journals because the covers had no writing on them. He opened the first. It was written in a language he thought might be French, and he flipped through it curiously, trying to decipher some of the words.

Then he turned a page, and a drawing of a dragon, snarling as if it despised the very ink it was made of, glared back at him.

Micah stared at it.

It was a good drawing. Even in the faint light, he could make out the strong musculature of the dragon's two legs. He could see the bulbous joints that connected the spiny, bat-like wings to the scaled hide. The fangs curved inward, so that once the jaws locked, the beast's prey would have no hope of escape.

And there was something about those slit-pupiled eyes . . .

Micah could see why dragons were the only creatures unicorns had ever feared.

What was Victoria doing with a book about them? It made sense for Firesleight to be interested in dragons. She was a fire magician. But—

Firesleight, thought Micah. *I should have realized.*

When he'd questioned her about dragons, she had mentioned loaning her books to someone who'd never returned them. And then she'd changed the subject so quickly. Of course it was Victoria who'd taken them.

Apparently, she was a thief on top of everything else.

Micah set the book aside carefully. At least he could return it to Firesleight and put things right.

He reached for the next book. It seemed older than the first, and it didn't have much writing in it. Instead, it was full of hand-drawn maps covered in symbols Micah didn't recognize.

He held the pages as close to the rolled-up tent as he could, trying to catch the light. On one, he found what looked like a list. It was written in single column, with the symbols he'd seen on the maps arranged in order.

The list continued onto the next page. And the one after that. Until, in the margins of the book's final page, in fancy lettering, someone other than the original author had translated the last few items into English:

To Burn Is a Delight

I Eat the Horned Ones

The Sky Belongs to Me

Admire My Fire

The Mighty Conflagration

Micah remembered what Firesleight had said about dragons and draklings having a written language they used to scratch their names into the mud of their burrows. The names she'd mentioned were almost funny, and he'd thought at the time that it would be hard to take a creature who called itself "I Like to Burn Stuff" very seriously.

But these few names that someone—presumably Victoria—had chosen to translate seemed fancier than that.

The older ones had more dignified names, thought Micah. *That's what she said. That the ones who were real terrors in their day were smarter.*

Judging by this list, Victoria hadn't been interested in all dragons. Only the most dangerous ones.

Micah swallowed hard.

It doesn't matter what she was interested in years ago, he told himself. *The draklings are all in hibernation now. They're asleep because they're too weak to hunt other magical creatures. Firesleight said so.*

He picked up the third book, hoping Victoria had written something in it about how she'd gotten bored studying dragons and decided to take up a more wholesome hobby. Like stamp collecting.

But as soon as he opened the book, a torn sheet of floral stationery fell out. A single line was written on it, in that same ornate script:

They will wake as the Moment approaches.

13

SPECULATION

Micah stared at the piece of stationery.

He only knew of one moment important enough to deserve a capital M—Fish's. And it was definitely approaching. Micah had been using his knots to feed Fish bits of news and circus gossip every day, and he'd witnessed two of the Idea's peculiar growth spurts just last month.

What that Moment had to do with the draklings waking up was a mystery, but it seemed unlikely Victoria had been interested in the subject for *friendly* reasons.

Micah had to tell someone.

He grabbed the stack of books and headed for the door. Behind him, the sparkling silver tent was still glowing. He glanced back at it before he exited. It really was beautiful.

"Lights off."

Outside, the sky was cloudless and purpling toward night, and Micah couldn't help staring up as he headed for the Lightbender's tent.

Don't be ridiculous, he told himself. Of course the Bird Woman wasn't going to make an appearance just because he'd looked through boxes filled with her old costumes. But he'd shoved the thought of her to the back of his mind over the past few months, and now it loomed over him again, darker and more shameful than ever before.

Which was why he ended up standing frozen outside the Lightbender's room.

Micah clutched the books under one arm, and with the other, he reached for the bellpull that would let the Lightbender know he had a visitor. But when his fingers closed around the satiny cord, he found he didn't want to tug it.

He stared at the bracelets that covered his own arm from wrist to elbow.

Micah had never managed to turn his knots into the kind of fabulous magical objects he'd imagined, but he *had* nearly finished his memory bracelet project. He had tied bracelets for every show at the circus and for every magician except the Lightbender, who was still giving him trouble.

Gray twine, blue shoelaces, orange yarn, green floss, strips of leather, silk ribbons, fabric scraps—Micah's bracelets were an ever-present whisper at the back of his mind. They made him feel like he was taking part of the circus with him wherever he went, and they were a reminder of how good the place was.

The magicians here worked so hard to inspire kids, to make the world a little bit more magical. Firesleight had once told Micah that every time she performed, she hoped at least one person in the audience would change their minds about who they were and who they could be.

"You try to do something extraordinary," she'd said, "so that someone watching will begin to believe they can do extraordinary things themselves."

How was Micah ever going to belong here when his own grandmother had tried to ruin all that? The books seemed to grow heavier as that question filled his mind. He let go of the bellpull.

He was halfway across the Lightbender's stage, heading for the flap, when another question stopped him in his tracks: *How am I going to belong here if I don't do what's right?*

He took a couple of deep breaths, then spun on his heel and marched back to the bellpull. He yanked it hard before his nerves could get the better of him, and when his guardian appeared, he held out the books.

"Victoria was interested in dragons," he said without preamble.

The Lightbender blinked at him. "Beg pardon?"

"She took Firesleight's dragon books and never gave them back," said Micah. "And she wrote in them. She made a list of names. She talks about a Moment, and how when it gets closer the draklings will start to wake up, and I just . . . I thought I ought to tell you right away."

The Lightbender was silent, staring down at the books. When he finally took them from Micah, he opened one up and flipped through it, his fingers pausing every now and then to trace sentences.

At first, he didn't seem particularly concerned, and Micah began to relax. *See?* he thought. *It's all right. Old news. Nothing important.*

But then the Lightbender opened the next book, and his expression turned grim. He sat down on the edge of the stage, leafing through pages so quickly it seemed impossible he could actually be reading them.

After a few minutes of what felt like extraordinary patience, Micah burst out, "What do they *say?*"

The Lightbender frowned down at the page. "The author of this text was interested in how hibernating draklings might be affected by ambient magic."

"What's that?"

"Ambient magic?" said the Lightbender. "It's atmospheric magic. Or it might be more accurate to call it *potential* magic. It is around all of us, all the time, just waiting to become real."

He closed the book.

"An Idea like Fish is, essentially, unrealized potential. According to this book, the scent of an approaching Moment could make the draklings restless. Dragons hunted by sniffing out the magic of the creatures they preyed upon, you see."

"But they can't possibly smell Fish from wherever they're sleeping!"

The Lightbender rubbed the bridge of his nose and sighed. "I'm sorry. This is an abstract concept, and I'm not explaining it well."

He flicked his hand, and suddenly Micah was holding a large glass sphere. It was filled with tiny, flurrying specks of silver that made Micah think of a freshly shaken snow globe.

"Imagine this sphere is the world," said the Lightbender. "The particles inside it are potential magic. It exists every-where equally, as you can see."

"All right," said Micah.

"As the Moment approaches, the world fills with more potential magic." He snapped his fingers, and suddenly there were twice as many silver specks in the globe. "The specks just exist. For now. But if you were a drakling, with a nose finely attuned to magic . . ."

"The whole world would suddenly smell like dinner?" Micah guessed.

"Exactly," said the Lightbender. "And perhaps the smell would be strong enough to wake you from your slumber."

A tiny, snakelike creature appeared in the bottom of the globe. It was covered in slimy gray mud, and it was sniff-ing at the silver sparks hopefully.

"Okay," said Micah slowly. "But why would Victoria care about them waking up?"

"I am uncertain," the Lightbender said.

"But do you have a theory?" Micah pressed. He let go of the glass sphere, and it fell toward the stage, disappearing an instant before it hit the shiny black wood.

The illusionist said, "A sleeping drakling is of no use to anyone. A wakeful one little more so. They are too small and weak to hunt for themselves . . . but they can still eat."

It took Micah a second to catch on, but when he did, his stomach roiled. "You mean she would feed the draklings."

"It's only speculation," the Lightbender said, in a voice he probably thought was soothing.

Micah did not feel soothed. "You mean she would feed them magical creatures so that they turned back into dragons!"

"That *might* have been her plan. Decades ago. A full-grown dragon is a force unlike any other. Any reasonable person would never dream of attempting . . . but Victoria always did have an inflated opinion of her own abilities."

He saw the look of horror on Micah's face. "Please don't worry overly much," he said. "We know nothing for sure except that Victoria was once interested in the possibility."

"But that's *not* all we know," Micah said frantically. "We know that dragons liked to eat unicorns." One of the names on Victoria's list was I Eat the Horned Ones. "I thought maybe Terp's herd left her because they were scared of something, but I gave up looking because I couldn't figure it out. What if they were scared of this all along?"

If the herd knew that the draklings were awake, they would have tried to make sure their most vulnerable member was safe.

"The coincidence of the foal's arrival at the circus is unsettling," the Lightbender agreed. "But we do not know anything for—"

"I never should have stopped trying to figure out why Terp was here," said Micah. "We could have known months ago. If Victoria *is* out there, she could have an army of dragons right now."

"She certainly could not," said the Lightbender in a steady voice. "Even if our worst fears are true, I doubt she could manage to fledge more than one of them." He grimaced. "But one dragon is more than any magician can handle."

An emergency staff meeting was taking place in Mr. Head's office, and Micah was not invited.

"Why would they invite you?" Chintzy squawked at him.

The parrot was flapping around the stands collecting bric-a-brac the last audience had left behind. Micah sat slumped in the Lightbender's chair.

"I'm the one who found the books!" said Micah. "I want to know what we're going to do."

"Well, *I'm* the one who should've been invited," the parrot said. "I have expertise."

"On dragons?"

"On birds!" Chintzy said indignantly. "If they're talking about the Bird Woman, they should ask a bird for advice."

"Do you know a lot about her?"

"No," Chintzy admitted. She eyeballed a half-eaten caramel someone had dropped on the floor. "I was only a chick when she left. But I know she's evil!"

Micah hunched his shoulders. "Yeah. Everyone knows that."

Chintzy stretched her neck out to grab the caramel.

"Chintzy, don't. It's got germs, and it's pure sugar."

"Mind your business," said the parrot.

"Dulcie made it," Micah warned her. "You'll be coughing up snowflakes like last time."

Chintzy paused. "I can't deliver messages when I'm coughing! It's not professional."

"True," said Micah.

Chintzy clicked her beak and waddled toward a convenient piece of popcorn instead. "The sacrifices I make for humans!"

Eventually, the parrot grew tired of foraging and headed for her perch, but Micah stayed up, waiting on the Lightbender. He thought for sure his guardian would return soon, but the hours ticked by. When he went outside to examine the sign that was always posted by the entrance to the tent, he saw that the Lightbender's midnight showtime had disappeared.

And so had the two o'clock show for tomorrow.

How long, Micah wondered, *is an emergency staff meeting supposed to last?*

He wandered the circus for the next hour, making note of who was absent. It was mostly the oldest magicians who were gone, though Firesleight was missing, too. Everyone else was carrying on as usual.

I guess that's what I should do, too, Micah thought.

But he didn't.

Instead, he went to the menagerie. He tied knots for Fish, explaining what was going on, and as usual, Fish gulped them right down. He bumped the side of the aquarium with his nose when he'd finished, and Micah pressed his forehead to the glass.

"Don't worry," he said. "It's not your fault that you're making the whole world smell like magic. It's just how you are."

Next, he checked in on Terpsichore. He was proud that she was almost as big as a horse now, and glad that she was still every bit as much of a goofball as she'd always been. He stroked her powerful neck while she whuffled at his hair.

He didn't explain what he'd found out. For one thing, he didn't know how well the unicorn would understand, and for another, if Victoria *was* out there feeding magical creatures to some horrible drakling, he didn't want to give Terp nightmares.

Or make her wonder what had happened to her mother and her old herd.

Micah woke up the next day in the Lightbender's armchair. His stomach groaned with hunger, he had a crick in his neck from sleeping with his head at a funny angle, and his hair was stuck to the side of his face with what he hoped was sweat but thought might be drool.

Apparently, his guardian had come back to the tent and not seen fit to wake him up. Instead, the Lightbender had covered him with a cozy blanket and taped a note to the stage letting him know he'd been excused from morning lessons with Rosebud.

Which was a good thing, since he'd slept until well past noon.

Micah wanted information right away, but neither the Lightbender nor Chintzy were in the magician's room. And when Micah stepped outside, Bowler wasn't on guard duty.

He headed toward the dining tent. He'd missed two meals, and surely someone would be there who could explain what was going on.

The day was bright, and the circus was as festive as always. Micah looked around as he walked, expecting to see some evidence of a response to last night's revelations.

It wasn't that he wanted the whole circus to be in an uproar. He didn't even think they should be, necessarily. Not over news that Victoria *might* have had some mysterious plan involving dragons three-quarters of a century ago. But he felt odd walking past so many happy kids and smiling magicians.

When he reached the dining tent, he found it nearly empty. The lunch dishes had all been picked over, and the remainder had been relegated to a single table.

Someone Micah didn't recognize was standing over the

leftovers, digging into a dish of moussaka with a fork. The woman was short and round, with hair the color of a tangerine, and she had so much dirt on the back of her T-shirt and jeans that it looked like she'd been dragged along the ground for miles.

Micah, assuming she was one of the circus's shapeshifting magicians practicing for a new act, walked up and grabbed a plate. "Do you know what's going on?" he asked, scraping the last few grains out of a bowl of steamed rice. "And what happened to your clothes?"

The woman tilted her head to the side. "I lost a fight," she said. She had a strong Southern drawl. "Are you supposed to be here?"

"I didn't eat last night." Micah wondered why the shapeshifters had decided to put accents and fight scenes in their show. "And I missed breakfast. Are you going to eat all of that?"

He pointed at the moussaka. The woman stared at him for a moment before shrugging and scooping some eggplant and lamb onto his plate.

"Thanks."

The double doors to the kitchen swung open and a trio of women strode into the dining tent. They were beaming and talking excitedly with one another, their arms full of layer cakes, cobbler, and rice pudding.

"You found the dessert!" the orange-haired woman cried jubilantly. "Thuja, is that a flan?"

Micah stared at them all, counting. Circus Mirandus

had two shapeshifters. And here there were four women with unfamiliar faces.

The one called Thuja was tall and dark-skinned, and she wore armor made out of gold and silver leaves. Beside her stood a pale woman whose black cat-eye glasses and sharp business suit wouldn't have been out of place in a law office. And the final member of the group was a dimpled, gray-haired lady who wore a leather vest that revealed arms almost as heavily muscled as Bowler's.

They carried the desserts and half the leftovers to the corner table where Micah and Rosebud often had lessons in the morning. He followed them and was surprised to see the familiar mismatched chairs surrounded by assorted weaponry.

For Thuja, a longbow and a quiver full of heavy arrows, their wood a faint green as if it were still alive. A spiked club and a polished briefcase for the woman in the cat-eye glasses. And for the gray-haired woman, a sword that was longer than Micah was tall.

The double doors swung open again, and Yuri backed out of the kitchen holding a tray full of pastries. He was followed by Geoffrey, who was peeling a boiled egg.

"I found some more?" Yuri said, gesturing with the pastry tray. "Or I can pack these for your journey?"

"Thank you, Yuri," said Thuja.

"I swear the food gets better every time we visit," said the orange-haired woman. "By the way, are y'all letting the children into the Staff Only section now?"

She gestured to Micah, who was standing a few feet away with his plate, trying to figure out what was going on.

Yuri blinked. "No?"

"This is Micah," said Geoffrey. The ticket taker clapped Micah on the back with a hand covered in eggshell fragments. "Mentioned him to you in the meeting, didn't we, Pennyroyal?"

Micah assumed Pennyroyal was the one with the Southern accent and orange hair. He waved at her. "Hi."

"You're the Lightbender's kid!" she exclaimed.

Micah had never been called the Lightbender's kid before. He didn't know how to feel about it. "Yes . . . that's me."

They had all stopped eating to look at him. Micah had the feeling they were sizing him up.

"We call him String Boy," said Geoffrey in a jovial voice.

"No, we don't!" Micah protested, shooting the ticket taker a glare. String Boy was definitely the worst magician's name he'd ever heard.

Geoffrey grinned at him.

"Well, don't just stand there with your lunch," said Pennyroyal. "Pull up a chair!"

Micah soon found his plate piled high with food (most of it dessert) and his head stuffed full of new information. These women were members of the Sisterhood the Lightbender had told Micah and Jenny about over the summer, and they'd been called in to "patch up that little Victoria problem once and for all."

"It's always been a sore spot," Geoffrey explained. "Not

knowin' if she's alive or dead. Wonderin' if she's out there plottin' some kind of revenge. You usually hear things about a magician with powers as flashy as hers. But she dropped right off the face of the earth after she left the circus. Makes you curious why she's so keen on hidin'.'"

Victoria *hadn't* dropped right off the face of the earth after she left the circus. She'd been married to Grandpa Ephraim for a few years before she'd disappeared once and for all. But Micah didn't see any reason to remind everyone of that.

Instead, he asked how you were supposed to track down someone who'd been missing for such a long time.

"That book of maps," said Pennyroyal. "Good work finding it. It's got the locations of all the drakling burrows marked. They ought to be awake by now, thanks to that overgrown tuna in the menagerie. So, if Victoria's still interested in messing around with dragons, she'll have to visit one of the burrows eventually."

They told Micah the search would take a while, since the burrows were in far-flung locations without convenient Doors. And Firesleight would be traveling with them. Her knowledge of dragons would be useful, and apparently, she was old friends with the Sisterhood, who had raised her before she joined Circus Mirandus.

"Young magicians are prone to mishaps," said Geoffrey, who must have seen the surprised look on Micah's face. "And Strongfolk heal fast."

Micah had never thought of Firesleight as a kid magician

before, but of course she must have been. And he supposed
fiery mishaps would be much worse than the occasional
burst ribbon or snapped bracelet.

"What if you don't find any sign of her at the burrows?"
he asked, looking around the table. "Will you just give up?"

"We do not give up," said Thuja, her voice matter-of-
fact. "Ever."

"But when you do find her . . . if she's still alive I mean,
then what happens next?"

"Nothing," said Pennyroyal, running her finger over
the rim of a glass. "Or something. Depends on her."

Thuja nodded. "If she is living her life and harming no
one, then we have no quarrel with her. We will leave her in
peace. If she is harming others, whether human beings or
magical beasts, then we will stop her from doing so."

Micah glanced at the quiver full of strange arrows behind her chair. He decided it was best not to ask how, exactly, the Sisterhood would stop someone like Victoria
from doing wrong.

"What if she's got a dragon?" he said. "A fully fledged
one?"

"Then we will need more magicians to handle her,"
Thuja said calmly. "Here we have a circus full of allies, do
we not?"

The Strongwoman's certainty lessened Micah's fears.
Even if the worst happened, the Sisterhood and the circus could handle Victoria and a dragon. They would have
numbers on their side.

"That's right," he said, nodding at Thuja. "We're allies. We can help one another."

Geoffrey leaned back in his chair and raised an eyebrow at him. "If it's all the same to you, I'd rather *not* fight a dragon. Nasty beasts. *Terrible* breath. Let's just hope this is a lot of worryin' over nothin'."

14

LOST AND FOUND

Micah spent every moment of free time he had over the next few days hovering around Porter's tent, waiting to hear news from the Sisterhood and Firesleight.

"I *promise*," said Porter, when Micah showed up for the fifth evening in a row with a hopeful expression on his face, "if they find Victoria, or a dragon, or even an oddly shaped rock that bears a passing resemblance to either of those creatures, someone will tell you."

"You want me to stop visiting?" Micah said.

"Oh, for—you can keep visiting. But I want you to lower your expectations. They have to travel to northern Canada, Greenland, and a couple different deserted islands just to check the drakling burrows on that list you found. We're not expecting major news from them right this minute. We're not even expecting major news this *week*."

"I need to hear the minor news, too."

Porter sighed. "Come on, then."

Micah followed him to a freestanding wooden wall at the back of the tent. It was covered in mail slots. The newest addition was made of steel, and it didn't say "Mail" or "Post" or "*Lettres*." Instead, it had stylized flames etched on it.

Porter stuck his hand through the mail slot, and Micah heard Firesleight's voice shriek, "Porter! Shout a warning or something!"

Micah peered through the slot and saw feet. A moment later, Firesleight picked up the matching slot on her end. She smiled at him. "Here for the news again?"

Firesleight was in a tent, but not the magical kind. This one was small and made of neon-yellow fabric, and it was full of Strongwomen in coats and gloves.

"I rode my first snowmobile," said Firesleight. "And we should reach a drakling burrow tomorrow."

"Is that all?" said Micah.

"Well, I'm very gifted at riding snowmobiles," said Firesleight. "A natural, you might say."

"She fell off," said Pennyroyal.

"Twice," said Thuja.

"Don't listen to them," said Firesleight. "They're just jealous because I can keep myself warm without a parka."

"It's sweltering here," Micah said, sticking his face even

closer to the slot to feel the cold air on the other side. "And nobody can drag the Strongmen away from the pool."

A week later, Micah stepped out of the Lightbender's tent and found the ground covered with a thin layer of frost. Surprised, he scuffed his sneaker against the grass, watching the frost dissolve into a wet trail.

For a moment, he wondered if the Inventor had come up with some new way to cool everything off. He'd asked her once if she could air-condition the whole circus, and she hadn't said *no*. Only that it was impractical.

But he figured she hadn't had time to do something like that with everything else they had going on. The nights had been colder lately anyway, and the sun had just risen.

Micah inhaled, and the air pricked his lungs. His breath clouded in front of his face. Even his ankles were freezing.

He had grabbed a random pair of jeans this morning, and when he looked down, he saw bare skin peeking out below the hems. And now that he was paying attention to his clothes, he realized his T-shirt had collected a few holes in it, thanks to a certain unicorn.

He went back to his room to change into something warmer, but as he dug through his chest of drawers, a surprising theme emerged. The pants were all at least an inch too short. The long-sleeved sweaters left his wrists uncovered.

Micah hadn't given a single thought to his wardrobe since moving to the circus, and now that he finally was, he saw that the only things he owned that fit properly were his sneakers. Rosebud had bought him a new pair in December, after the two of them had spent the day visiting friends of hers in Bogotá.

Micah went to the Lightbender's door seam and tugged on the bellpull.

"Come in," the illusionist called.

Micah stepped inside. His guardian was fiddling with the silver coffee service by Chintzy's perch. The parrot wasn't there at the moment.

"Hello," said the Lightbender, pouring cream into his cup. "You're up early today."

"I've outgrown all my clothes," Micah reported. "And it's cold."

The Lightbender turned around. He looked Micah up and down, the expression on his face distinctly puzzled. "So you have," he said. "Come with me."

He left his cup steaming on the table and led Micah from the tent, pausing as soon as they stepped outside to stare at the frost and scuff it with his boot, just as Micah had.

"Is it weird that it's so cold?" Micah said.

"It seems unusual," said the Lightbender. "But brighter minds than mine will be trying to figure it out by now. The Inventor has a number of weather instruments in her tent."

They headed to the Staff Only section, then turned toward Porter's warehouse.

Micah wondered if they might actually leave the circus together and go to a store. He left often enough himself, with Rosebud and others. But the Lightbender always stayed at the circus to keep up the protective illusions.

Once, on a particularly slow day, Micah had worked up the nerve to ask his guardian if he might consider leaving, just for an hour, to get pizza. Instead, the Lightbender had taken Micah to the dining tent and shown him the chalkboard in the back of the pantry where anyone could write down special requests for the kitchen magicians. They'd added pizza to the board, and sure enough, sausage pizza had been one of the dinner items a few days later.

Micah still wasn't sure if the illusionist had missed the point of the invitation, or if he had just been saying *no* in the nicest way he could.

They passed by the entrance to Porter's warehouse, and the Lightbender nodded toward the storage tent next door. "In here."

Micah had glanced in this storage tent before, but it had looked so similar to all the others he hadn't bothered going in. Apparently, he had missed something.

"Have you ever been to the Lost and Found?" the Lightbender asked.

He clapped his hands rapidly three times, and the walls of the tent began to glow. Crates filled the tent, stacked into roughly cubic blocks. Every block was neatly wrapped in ropes as thick as Micah's arm.

"To keep them all together when the tent is packed up on moving days," the Lightbender explained, gesturing to the ropes as they strode through the tent. "We do not access these often, and you know how terribly things get jumbled."

Each of the crates had some kind of code painted on the side. Micah tried for a second to decipher them, but quickly gave up. "What do they say?"

The Lightbender stopped and pointed at a nearby crate. "Geoffrey dated these, and he is a stubborn creature. It annoys him that the Latin language is no longer in vogue. This says 'November 2443.'"

"It's a box from the future?"

"It's from 1943. Geoffrey starts his calendar on the day he met Mirandus—Mr. Head—in 500 BC. The group consisted of the manager and four others back then. Geoffrey and Rosebud are the only founding magicians left."

"That is a *really* complicated way to keep track of time," said Micah.

"I think he means for it to be amusing," said the Lightbender. "His attempts at comedy are often inconvenient. Do you mind getting the ropes?"

Micah reached for the thick ropes wrapping the pile of crates. He tapped his hand against them. *Come loose.*

The big knots the Strongmen had tied slipped apart in an instant, and the ropes fell to the dirt at Micah's feet.

The Lightbender twitched as if startled, even though he'd just asked Micah to do it. He eyed the ropes. "You are more adept at that than you were a few months ago."

"They're ordinary knots instead of magical ones," Micah said with a shrug. He'd been practicing so much and

failing at everything; even the locator knot had turned out
to be a complete waste of time. But he *had* gotten even better at the everyday sort of knots. He liked to tie his shoes
in the morning by flicking the ends of the laces.

The Lightbender picked up a couple of the smaller crates
and gave them a sharp shake. The first one rattled, and the
second clanged. But the third one he selected didn't make
any sound at all. He pried it open to reveal an assortment
of neatly folded clothes.

"For a time, in the 1940s and '50s, the souvenir tent held
versions of the performers' costumes. We discontinued the
practice when we realized how many children were leaving
their everyday clothes behind in hopes that they would be
allowed to wear circus uniforms to school."

"That would be a lot of fun, though."

"I don't disagree," said the Lightbender, "but I imagine
the children's parents and teachers did."

The clothes weren't strange looking, as Micah had worried they would be. And they didn't smell like they'd been
stuck in a dusty crate for decades, which was the important thing.

"Take whatever you like," the Lightbender said. "Tradi-
tionally, we wait a century before removing anything from
the Lost and Found, but I have never heard of anyone going to the enormous trouble of finding us just to reclaim an
old pair of mittens."

The illusionist sat on top of another crate with his el-
bows propped on his knees, watching Micah pick through

the clothes. Sweater vests must have been in fashion . . . or maybe not, considering how many had been left behind. Micah took a dark blue one that looked like it would fit. He found a couple of striped shirts with long sleeves and two pairs of pants that wouldn't leave his ankles bare.

At the bottom of the box was a red scarf that looked homemade. Some of the fringe had worn off on the ends, but Micah decided if someone had cared enough to knit it by hand, it would be wrong to leave it forgotten in a storage tent.

He wrapped it around his neck and looked up at the Lightbender. The magician held a gray peacoat out toward him.

"It's too big," said Micah.

"It is cold out," said the Lightbender. "And you will grow into it."

Micah took it and added it to the pile of things he was keeping.

When he began folding everything else back up, the Lightbender knelt down to help. He was not a good folder, and Micah wondered if his guardian just illusioned everyone into thinking his clothes weren't wrinkled.

"Micah," he said suddenly, not looking up from the dress shirt he was arranging, "have I missed your birthday?"

Micah dropped a stocking hat into the crate. "Oh. No. I didn't tell anybody when it was."

The Lightbender looked dismayed. "I'm sorry."

"It's no big deal," said Micah. "I'm the one who didn't mention it."

"But I could have known if . . . You see, I left legal matters concerning you up to those better suited to the task. I have no legitimate identity in the outside world. Most of us do not bother." He shook his head. "Porter has adopted you from your great-aunt, as far as the authorities are concerned. I assume he has papers of some kind. A certificate of birth. I should have asked him for it."

Micah stared at the Lightbender. It had never occurred to him to wonder what the government might do about him going missing. What if the police had thought that Aunt Gertrudis murdered him and buried his body in the desert?

She was bad, but not *that* bad.

"I do understand that such things are important," the Lightbender was saying. "I would not want you to think I did not—"

"June third," Micah interrupted. He'd been at the circus a month then. "But it's okay. Nobody here celebrates birthdays."

"Nobody else is eleven years old."

Micah didn't know what to do. The Lightbender seemed to feel guilty, but he shouldn't have. "I wasn't in the mood for a party anyway."

At that point, it would only have made him miss his grandfather even more.

The Lightbender said nothing while they finished packing up the crates. They put them back into their proper places, and Micah secured them with the ropes while the Lightbender watched.

It was harder this time, but only because the heavy ropes were awkward to lift into position around the crates. Micah was going to have to have a talk with the Strongmen about their choice of materials.

He finally finished and shook his hair off his sweaty face. It fell right back over his eyes.

"Your hair is getting long," the Lightbender said.

"I want a ponytail," Micah explained, hopping off the crates and collecting his new clothes. "Like Yuri."

"Yuri will be flattered, I'm sure."

"My hair doesn't tangle," Micah pointed out as they headed for the tent flap. "So, it won't be any trouble."

The Lightbender stopped walking. He reached out and put a hand on Micah's shoulder, shifting his head from side to side as if he were listening for something. "Wait here."

He strode to the Lost and Found's entrance.

Something wasn't right, Micah realized. Sounds from outside were dampened in many of the circus's tents, and this one was no exception. But now that he was on alert, he could hear a rushing noise.

Then the Lightbender opened the tent flap, and the sound became a ferocious howl. Snow blasted through the door. The whole tent shuddered, fabric snapping in the wind, the air suddenly icy. The Lightbender fought with the flap and barely managed to close it against the driving snow.

The roar was muffled in an instant.

"We seem to be caught in a blizzard," he said, brushing snow off his leather coat.

Micah's cheeks stung with cold. "But this is summer."

"Yes," said the Lightbender.

"Are blizzards something they have here in the summer?"

The Lightbender looked up at the roof of the tent, his eyes narrowing as if he could see through it to the storm raging outside. "No," he said. "No, they are not."

15

BLIZZARD

Micah and the Lightbender stood at the closed tent flap, trying to decide what to do.

The Lightbender was in favor of braving the storm in order to reach Porter's warehouse right next door. It was one of the most stable tents at the circus, since it would have been disastrous if thousands of doors were damaged during a rough move. The illusionist was worried that if the blizzard worsened, the Lost and Found wouldn't be safe.

Micah thought this was a fine plan, but he also thought they should search through the Lost and Found for weapons first. It seemed obvious to him that malevolent forces were at work, and they ought to be ready for anything.

"Is it a magician controlling the weather?" Micah asked.

"I do not know," said the Lightbender, heading for the

pile of clothes Micah had left behind. "Come here, please."

He held out the peacoat.

When Micah put it on, his fingers barely stuck out the cuffs. "*Are* there magicians who can control weather?"

"Not with any degree of reliability."

"But it's obviously magic. Isn't it?"

The Lightbender had started buttoning Micah into the coat, even though he could have done it fine by himself. "Yes," he said, frowning. "We hoped the lightning strike a few months ago was bad luck. Tents have been struck before, and we only moved the circus out of an abundance of caution. An unseasonable blizzard is another matter."

He finished buttoning the coat and reached for the red scarf. "I will tell you who I *think* may be responsible for this storm, but I would appreciate it if you did not cling so doggedly to guilt and worry as you have been doing these past few days."

"I don't cling!" Micah protested.

"Is that why you lurk around Porter's at all hours, waiting for news?" The Lightbender wrapped the scarf around Micah's ears and tucked the ends into the neck of the coat. "No one here cares that you are related to Victoria Starling."

Micah looked away.

"I do not care. Rosebud does not care. Porter does not care. Firesleight, Dulcie, Mistsinger, the Inventor, Geoffrey—"

"Are you going to name everyone at the circus?"

The Lightbender waited until Micah met his eyes. "Do I need to?" he said calmly.

Micah blinked. The Lightbender would really do it, he thought, even if it took all day. "No," he said hesitantly. "Only Mr. Head didn't want me to be here at first—"

"If the manager did not want you to be here," said the Lightbender, "then you would not. Mirandus is quite proud of the work you have done with Terpsichore, and he does not count your unfortunate relation to the Bird Woman against you."

The back of Micah's throat was burning in that odd way he associated with oncoming tears, but he didn't think he was about to cry. It felt like a swarm of confused emotions trying to escape all at once.

His guardian, apparently deciding that a single scarf was insufficient to keep him from freezing to death, had found a second one. He started wrapping it over the first.

"As for the storm," the Lightbender said, "it is much too great and complicated a force for a *magician* to control, but I have heard of animals that can manipulate the weather."

"Like birds?" Micah's voice was muffled by layers of wool.

"Several magical species of bird possess that power, yes."

"But if people can't, how—"

"Sometimes instinct outshines intellect. Chintzy, for example, has an extraordinary homing instinct. She can find her way back to the circus even if we move while she is away on a delivery."

"So, you think it could be Victoria," said Micah. "Using a weather bird."

"It is possible."

"She could be out there right now. Watching us."

"I am only making a guess," the Lightbender cautioned him. "But yes. If we assume it is her, then she must be staying close enough to maintain control over the bird. When I knew her, she had to be within earshot to direct most of her flock, but she has no doubt improved her range over the years."

"Can't you use your illusions to stop her?" Micah asked.

"I could if I had a clear idea of where she was," said the Lightbender. "But the kind of magic I would use to stop Victoria is not something I will send out into the world haphazardly."

Just then, the tent flap whipped open and a gust of wind swept through the Lost and Found. Snowflakes needled the tip of Micah's nose, which was the only part of him except for his eyeballs the Lightbender hadn't managed to completely smother in fabric.

Something that looked like the abominable snowman lumbered into the tent, and for a wild moment, Micah thought the Lightbender had been wrong about them not needing weapons.

"There you are!" shouted the snowman, shaking itself

all over. Snow spattered the ground, and Bowler appeared. He was wearing a furry coat, his hat was missing, and he had a wriggling, snowy bundle tucked under his arm. "Let's get you two out of here!"

They rode out the blizzard in Porter's tent, along with the wriggling bundle, which turned out to be an alarmed reading goat that had wandered away from the menagerie.

"Little fellow stumbled right into me," Bowler explained, giving the goat a friendly squeeze. "Must have gone out for a walk and gotten caught in the storm."

Micah was struggling to get out from under his coat and scarves. "What about all the other animals?" he asked when he was finally free. "What about the kids who are visiting today?"

"We got everyone into the tents," said Bowler. "We'll be fine."

"I've closed all the local Doors I was holding in the meadow," Porter added. "We won't have to worry about new arrivals until I open them again."

He led them to the back of the warehouse, to the freestanding wall where the mail slots were. "Do you think we should call Firesleight?" he said. "Or wait until we know for certain what's going on?"

"Best wait," said Bowler. "No point in worrying her until we know what move the manager wants to make."

"I agree," said the Lightbender.

"*Baaaaaa*," said the goat.

"Bowler, put that poor animal down," said Porter. "He needs some time to himself, I'm sure."

Behind the mail slot wall, the brown fabric wall of the tent itself stood taut, and set into that fabric was an ornately carved wooden door.

Porter reached for the knob. "Come in," he said. "Leave your shoes outside."

Micah toed off his damp sneakers and stepped through, blinking at the sight that greeted him.

Porter had a house in his tent. Micah had assumed the magician had private rooms just like everyone else did, but he hadn't pictured anything like this. The door opened into a comfortable living area, with a sofa, a coffee table, and two cushioned rocking chairs.

Micah took a seat on the sofa beside Bowler.

For the most part, the adults talked in circles, passing *what ifs* back and forth. No one was certain of anything, and Bowler, at least, was still hopeful that the blizzard would be revealed to be some freak natural disaster.

Micah didn't learn anything new until the Lightbender mentioned dragons.

"I *do* hope she thought better of it as she aged, and that we have sent Firesleight chasing after figments. I don't see what she could possibly hope to accomplish by fledging one."

Porter rocked back in his chair. "She probably thinks she'll be able to control it like it's a canary."

"That is absurd."

"You know how arrogant she is," said Porter. "Some of

the ancient dragons had feathered crests. I'm sure one of those books must have mentioned that they're distantly related to modern-day birds. That would be enough for her to start imagining what it would be like to have one under her thumb. No doubt she chewed on the idea for years, until it didn't seem *absurd* to her at all."

"Can't she control a dragon, though?" Micah asked hesitantly. "If they *are* related to birds, I mean?"

"They're related to birds in the same sense that the *Tyrannosaurus rex* is related to birds," said Porter. "I'm no scientist to explain how it all works, but I am absolutely sure that Victoria Starling cannot command a dragon. At best—or at worst, I should say—she'll have taken one of the draklings and bribed it into being civil by giving it everything it wants. Dragons are smart enough not to bite the hand that feeds them, but they can't be *tamed*. They're monsters, not miniature poodles."

The Lightbender was rubbing his temples. "The grandiosity of a dragon would have appealed to her on every level."

Porter nodded. "And if she means to attack the circus, instead of just annoying us with inclement weather, she'll need more firepower than she's got now."

Micah pressed himself back into the sofa cushions, trying not to imagine what a dragon attack on the circus would be like.

"You think she's out for revenge," said Bowler, his voice grim.

Porter snorted. "What else? Our illusionist knocked her out of the sky. Mirandus banished her." He smiled fondly before adding, "Bibi almost ate her."

If only, Micah thought. The tiger took her guard duties seriously.

The conversation grew repetitive again. It was all Victoria and dragons and endless *maybes*, and when the storm suddenly ended, three hours after it had begun, Micah was relieved. He hoped Victoria really had been out there in the blizzard, and that she'd accidentally frozen herself solid so that he would never have to think about her again.

When they opened the tent flaps, they found snow piled so high it came up over Porter's head.

"Delightful," he said drily.

"Well, at least nobody got hurt," said Bowler. "If it *is* Victoria trying to get revenge, then she's doing a bad job of it. She's made a lot of ruckus but hasn't done a bit of harm."

He put on his furry coat and started scooping out a path for them, his big hands as good as shovels.

"I doubt she wants to engage us too closely," said the Lightbender.

A sound came from somewhere deep in the warehouse, the echoing *baaaaaa* of a goat that had gotten lost wandering among all the doors.

"I guess I'll have to go find him," Porter groaned. "No doubt he's chewing on my inventory."

But instead of leaving, he turned to look thoughtfully

into the shadows. Micah followed the direction of his gaze and saw a large set of double gates.

"A good thought," the Lightbender said.

"I know how you feel about major cities," Porter said.

"I can manage."

Porter sighed. "So can I. I'll talk to Mirandus as soon as Bowler plows a path to his tent."

16

MOVE

Bowler was wrong about one thing. The blizzard *had* done harm, and more than a bit of it.

Two of the circus's animals were missing—the golden fleeced llama and a giant wombat. Both had apparently been outside the menagerie when the storm struck, and unlike the lucky reading goat, they hadn't bumped into a helpful Strongman in the snow.

Mr. Head was furious, and Bibi was worse. By that afternoon, most of the snow had melted in the heat of the day, and the tiger stalked the perimeter of the meadow, fully visible, looking like she wanted to rip someone limb from limb.

After the visiting children were sent back home through Porter's Doors, the magicians searched the circus for the missing creatures. Nobody found any sign of them.

"Stealing magical animals must have been the whole point of it," Micah said in a subdued voice. He and Geoffrey were working together, combing every inch of the nocturnal garden, but neither of them had much hope of finding anything. "This proves it's her. Doesn't it? She really *has* been planning her revenge against the circus all along. She just had to wait for the Moment to wake up the draklings."

"Seems like it." Geoffrey reached out to rustle the limbs of a flowering bush, as if he hoped a frightened llama might burst out of it. "Must've used the storm to cover an approach and a retreat. Didn't want to tangle with any of us yet, so she got us all out of the way. A lot of work for a little gain, if you ask me, but I guess it's not easy, tryin' to feed up a dragon."

The only thing they knew for sure was that the Bird Woman was no longer nearby. The Inventor had set up a magical telescope in the meadow, and magicians had been taking turns on watch all afternoon. They saw no sign of Victoria at all, not even a single sparrow.

"What are we going to do?" said Micah.

"You'll see," said Geoffrey. "Go to bed early tonight. Get some sleep if you can."

"Why?"

The ticket taker didn't answer.

Micah thought it was ridiculous advice. Who would be able to sleep under these circumstances? But it turned out that being caught in a blizzard in the morning and joining search parties in the afternoon was exhausting. When he finally closed his eyes that night, he was asleep at once.

It seemed like only seconds later he woke to find the Lightbender standing over him.

"What time is it?" Micah murmured, his brain still fuzzy.

"An hour before dawn," said the Lightbender. "We are moving the circus."

That's not right. Micah knew the travel schedule as well as everyone at Circus Mirandus did. It wasn't time for a move.

He rolled out of his hammock. Before his bare feet even hit the rug, the Lightbender was holding his magician's backpack out to him. It was already bulging, no doubt stuffed with everything in the room that was too delicate to be subjected to the Strongmen's version of packing up.

"When did you start sleeping in a hammock?" the Lightbender asked.

"I made it myself." Micah had tied it using different colored ropes and cords, making sure all the knots that held it together were full of comfortable, sleepy memories. He yawned. "Do you want one?"

"I do not," said the Lightbender. "But thank you. We need to hurry. We are making a much quicker leap than usual."

"We're running away?"

"It does us no good to stay here. We will travel somewhere unexpected. It is a wide world, and our pursuer cannot harm us if she cannot find us."

He left while Micah changed out of his pajamas.

When Micah exited his room a few minutes later, the Lightbender was gone, but he spotted Chintzy on the floor by the stage. The parrot was trying to drag her huge perch—stand, food dish, bell, and all—to the tent's entrance.

"Chintzy, you nut!" Micah exclaimed, running over to collect her. "You'll get packed up in the tent if you don't hurry. Forget the perch. Bowler can get it."

He grabbed Chintzy's scaly feet, and she flapped her wings, batting him in the face. "Not him!" she squawked. "Last time, he dented my bell!"

"Oh, please."

"It's a musical instrument!"

Micah rolled his eyes, unclipped the little silver bell, and hurried out of the tent with Chintzy clinging to his arm, muttering mutinously about people who didn't appreciate true artistry.

Outside, the confusion was palpable. Micah wondered if the manager hadn't told anyone they were leaving until the last minute, so that word couldn't reach the wrong ears. The magicians certainly weren't as prepared as they were on a normal moving day.

A few of the performers were still wearing their costumes. And others were in their nightclothes. People darted here and there, shouting questions to one another.

The Strongmen, however, were moving through the

circus like they'd been choreographed. One or two of them would approach a tent, fabric would buckle, pegs would fly, and a minute later they would be bundling it up and hauling it toward the edge of the meadow, where Micah assumed Porter must be setting up the Door.

They always used huge ones on moving days. Few entryways could accommodate circus tents, even neatly packaged ones, and though Big Jean was a sport about trying to fit herself wherever they wanted her to go, there was only so much bending and squeezing an elephant could do. Usually, the Strongmen were sent ahead in advance to set up the moving-day doors, but sometimes, they used gates or arches that were already in place.

Micah watched wide-eyed as tents fell and fell. A few of them were supported by center poles as big as sequoias, and they hit the ground with echoing booms he could feel in his chest.

"There you are!"

Micah turned to see Bowler striding toward him and Chintzy. All the circus's outdoor lights were blazing bright so that the Strongmen could see to do their work, and in the harsh white glow, Bowler's face and chest shone with sweat. "Emergency procedures," he said. "Beg your pardon."

Micah leaped out of the way, and Bowler grabbed two huge handfuls of the Lightbender's tent. He pulled, and Micah winced at the sound of twanging ropes and straining fabric.

Bowler wasn't playing around. He'd have the tent down in a minute, but everything inside was going to be flattened and battered.

"My perch!" Chintzy cried. "I can't watch!"

She launched herself off Micah's arm and flapped toward the meadow.

"Is there anything I can do to help?"

"Menagerie's the only holdup," Bowler grunted, his muscles straining.

Micah nodded and raced toward the menagerie, his heavy backpack jouncing against his shoulders as he ran.

Mr. Head's tent was almost always the last one standing, even on normal moving days. The animals disapproved of the whole procedure—having to leave their comfortable habitats, going through a Door to a strange new place. They weren't going to like this unexpected departure at all.

Micah reached the entrance to the menagerie, only to skid to a stop when he heard the sudden, stomach-churning sound of a tiger roaring. Bibi always helped keep the other animals in line on moving day, but Micah had hardly ever known her to roar. A second later, the two-headed camel scrambled out of the tent, both heads looking sorry for themselves.

Micah took a deep breath and headed in.

It was mayhem. Bibi was trying to round up the pangolins, who were rolling in twelve different directions like a bag of dropped marbles. And Mr. Head was gently prying a pair of bush babies off the wallaby, who was hiccuping with distress.

The mousebirds were zipping around in a complete frenzy, making everything worse by trying to steal tail hairs and tufts of fur from any animal that looked distracted. Two particularly bold ones came at Micah—one swooping down from above and the other scurrying along the ground. He dodged out of the way and smacked into the Inventor, who'd just strode into the tent.

Micah would have fallen flat on his face if the magician hadn't caught him and set him back upright.

"Sorry!" he said.

"Don't worry," the Inventor replied, a little breathless. She tucked a strand of hair behind her ear. "They are pests, aren't they? Always trying to take my creations."

As if to prove her point, a mousebird dove toward one of the pouches on her tool belt. She waved it away.

"Do you need help with Fish?" Micah asked.

"I can handle the Idea," she said. "It is always agreeable, and the tank is easily managed."

The Inventor waited for a pangolin to roll by, then she hurried on, her long skirt sweeping the sawdust. When she reached the aquarium, she began tapping certain places on the tank's metal plaque. In a moment, Micah knew, the tank would shrink down to the size of a lunch box, Fish included, and when it was finished, the Inventor would hook it to her belt.

Bibi roared, and Micah jumped. He was pretty sure the tiger wasn't giving *him* instructions, but he hurried toward Terpsichore's paddock anyway.

The unicorn was chewing on a pink plastic flip-flop. Terp had found the shoe somewhere not long after the lightning strike, and the manager had decided she could keep it. It was an odd choice of toy to begin with, and she had stopped playing with it months ago. But Micah guessed she must be feeling a little nervous right now.

"Hey, Terp!" he said in his most upbeat voice. "Let's get you ready to go!"

She chimed a hello and tossed the slimy flip-flop to him.

Micah caught the shoe out of the air. He considered it for a moment, then jammed it under one of his backpack straps in case he needed to bribe her later. "We'll play when we're through the Door, okay?"

The unicorn nuzzled his forehead. She never pretended to jab Micah with her horn anymore. It had grown wickedly sharp as she got larger, and now that she was nearing her adult weight, her blue-green coat was beginning to pale. She already had a few sparkling white hairs in her tail.

But she was still a total ham. She loved going on outings around the circus, and whenever kids cheered for her, she would start waggling her rump like a puppy.

"I'm going to put your halter on," said Micah. "You can show those animals out there how they *ought* to be acting."

Terpsichore had always had a rope halter and a lead for trips out of the paddock, but over the last couple of months, she had started breaking free whenever the Strongmen used it. No ordinary rope could hold her anymore, so Micah had devised something a little more suited to the unicorn's tastes and strength. He had let Terp pick the materials herself, and though the unicorn preferred delicate silk ribbons, Micah had knotted them together until he'd fashioned something even the Strongmen couldn't break.

Terpsichore let him put the halter on her and attach the lead. By the time Mr. Head appeared, the work was all done.

"Thank you, Micah," the manager said, stroking Terpsichore's nose. "It's a relief to see at least one of our creatures behaving this morning."

Terp nudged his hand.

"Where are we going, sir?" Micah asked.

"Far away," said Mr. Head. "Farther than Porter usually tries, and over an ocean, which is extremely difficult for him. We will all need to move more quickly than normal when he opens the Door."

Micah nodded his understanding.

"Take our friend here with you, and ask Bowler for help with her," said the manager. "Geoffrey informs me that if we leave in the next seven minutes, we will beat our previous speed record."

When Micah exited the menagerie, almost everything was ready. The tents were down and packed, and the magicians stood in loose marching lines in the meadow, waiting for

Porter to open the Door. It was a set of heavy double gates this time, and Micah realized after a moment's study that they were the same gates Porter and the Lightbender had been eyeing in his tent when the blizzard ended.

Porter stood before them, his face set in a serious, focused expression Micah recognized from past moving days.

Micah still didn't know where they were going, but he knew they would be there quickly. People and animals would leave first, then the Strongmen would chuck the supplies through the Door as soon as everyone was on the other side and out of the way. They would follow the supplies out, then Mr. Head and Bibi would come. Finally, Porter himself would step through, closing the Door behind him.

It was something like a fast parade, but with nobody there to see it.

The only thing that made this moving day different was the timing and the fact that a few magicians had binoculars and spyglasses pressed to their eyes, keeping watch on the dark skies.

Micah took a place in the back of the group, so that if Terpsichore decided to be contrary, they would hold up fewer people. The Inventor was just ahead of them, Fish's miniaturized tank sloshing on her belt. She collapsed her spyglass and smiled over her shoulder at Micah.

"Nothing to be seen," she said. "Not for miles."

Micah nodded, relieved.

He spied Bowler a few yards away, sitting on top of a

pile of bundled tents with two other Strongmen. When Micah waved, Bowler came over to stand with him.

"Hello, Terp," he said, patting the unicorn gently on the flank. He took the silky lead rope from Micah and wrapped it several times around his thick wrist.

Terpsichore was too busy sniffing at the flip-flop tucked under Micah's backpack strap to pay the Strongman any attention. "We'll play catch with it later," Micah reminded her. "If you're good."

Terp *toot-toot*ed hopefully and licked his hair.

"Looks like it's time to go," Bowler said.

Micah couldn't see the gates anymore because Big Jean was a few rows up, blocking his view. But he knew Porter must have been successful, because a few people applauded, and someone cheered. A moment later, they were all making their way toward the Door, much faster than they usually did. Some of the magicians were actually jogging.

"Get ready," said Bowler.

"We're ready, aren't we, Terp?" said Micah.

The unicorn didn't answer. She'd just gotten her teeth around the pink flip-flop and tugged it free of the strap.

"Hey!"

Bowler laughed.

Terp waved the shoe proudly over Micah's head. He jumped up, and to his surprise, he managed to grab it. The unicorn had gone still.

"Terp?" said Micah. "What's the—"

Terpsichore screamed.

17

LIGHT

A piece of the sky was falling.

At least, that was the last wild thought Micah had before Bowler picked him up and threw him out of harm's way. Something he could barely distinguish from the gray light of predawn plummeted toward Terpsichore. It was huge and silent as a whisper, and the unicorn screamed. Then, Micah was flying backward.

Too fast. Everything was happening too fast for him to keep up.

Big arms wrapped around his chest, caught him out of the air like he was a football, swung him around and down safely onto the damp grass. *One of the Strongmen,* thought Micah. Deep voices were shouting instructions in languages

Micah couldn't understand, and when he looked up, he saw clouds forming.

They roiled overhead, the color of a bruise, and the wind was picking up speed. Micah tried to get up, but someone pushed him back down and told him to stay there.

He curled into a ball. He crossed his arms over his head and held still because that was what they had always told him to do during emergency drills at school.

He took a breath. Another.

Think, Micah. Think.

Shouts. A rumble of thunder. Bibi roaring. And Terpsichore . . . what was wrong with Terpsichore?

She was Micah's responsibility. He forced himself onto his feet.

He stood amid the rolled tents and packed luggage. The magicians who hadn't made it through the Door yet were scattered everywhere. The Inventor and Yuri crouched several yards away, protected by a familiar shield of blue light. Others huddled among the baggage, calling to one another and pointing toward a terrible scene unfolding in the distance.

Terpsichore looked more like a nightmare than the friendly unicorn Micah knew.

Blood poured down her flanks, and her mane tossed in the wind as she bucked and reared and stomped. The Strongmen had formed a circle to hem her in, and other magicians were running to help, but she just kept stomping the ground.

No, Micah realized. *Not the ground.*

Terpsichore was stomping *someone* on the ground. Someone who struggled to his feet only to lose them again as the unicorn broke through the circle of Strongmen, sweeping them aside so easily they might as well have been paper dolls.

Bowler, thought Micah. *That's Bowler.*

With his arm wrapped in Terpsichore's lead rope, Bowler couldn't get away.

Or maybe he was trying to hold the unicorn, to wait for help . . . but Terpsichore needed to run. Something had hurt her, had made her afraid. Her screams were unlike anything Micah had ever heard—high enough to shatter glass and strong enough to pierce the storm that was building out of nowhere.

The rising wind stung Micah's eyes, but he couldn't look away.

Something terrible was going to happen. Micah could feel it coming. He remembered the Lightbender, saying unicorns could crush boulders into sand. He remembered tying the knots for Terpsichore's halter and lead, perfect and tighter than tight.

Stronger than strong.

Terp wouldn't be able to break free.

Bowler had to let go of the lead rope. He had to keep his feet for long enough to unwrap his arm.

"Let go!" screamed Micah, stumbling toward them, pushing through the wind. "Bowler, you have to let her go!"

But even as he shouted, it was too late.

Bowler pulled back on the rope with all his strength, his boots digging furrows in the earth, and Terp rounded on him. The unicorn reared and swung her powerful neck, snapping the lead tight, dragging the Strongman off balance and onto the ground once more.

Terp's front hooves came down again and again. Harder and harder. And Bowler was trying to get up. Trying to free his arm at last. But one of Terp's hooves connected with his forehead. A sound split the air, like the crack of a baseball bat, and Bowler stopped moving.

Micah's heart stopped beating.

But Terpsichore didn't even pause. She kept stomping, trying to break free of the Strongman she thought held her captive, trying to crush him into sand.

Micah ran.

He had to do something. He had to get to the rope. If he could just touch it . . . all he needed was to brush a finger against it. He could do it.

But someone grabbed his shoulders from behind.

"Micah!" said a voice with a strong Russian accent.

Yuri. The chef's voice was firm, and his hands held Micah like vises.

"I have to help Bowler!" Micah cried, struggling against the grip. "It's my fault! *I* tied it."

Bibi had joined the fray, her teeth long as knives. And there were magicians, so many of them, and nothing was working. The Strongmen were piling onto the unicorn, grabbing for the lead rope. But Terpsichore threw them off again and again.

"I can do it," Micah sobbed, stretching his arms out toward Terpsichore. Toward Bowler. Micah had never seen one of the Strongmen so still. "I just have to touch it. She just wants to get away."

Lightning crackled overhead, and in the sudden brightness, Terpsichore's hooves glistened, dark and shiny and wet. Why were they wet?

Micah cried out again, reaching and reaching and feeling . . . something new. Just in front of him.

The rope that locked the unicorn into battle with the unconscious Strongman was so far away, but Micah could sense it. Like a word on the tip of your tongue, like a dream you half forgot upon waking, it was faint. But it was there.

A tiny vibration so small Micah had never known to look for it before.

He tried to grab it, but his hands clutched at the air, and there was nothing to hold on to.

He stretched himself, all of himself, pulling so hard against Yuri's grasp that the magician's fingers would leave bruises. He flung his heart into the battle and his brain and whatever else there was inside of him, and he didn't care anymore about what he might be able to do with his magic one day.

As long as he could untie this knot right now.

"Come loose!" Even Micah's voice seemed to be reaching for Terpsichore's rope, sinking invisible claws into the ribbons, tearing at the halter knots. Pulling and tugging, ordering them to *snap*.

"Come loose NOW!" he screamed at the knots.

And they did.

And so did everything else.

For Micah, the real world went dim.

He was vaguely aware of the magicians around him, but they were only startled shadows, running here and there, so much less interesting than the shining new universe he'd found underneath the old one.

It was a golden place made of webs and strands of light.

Some of the strands wound around and around one another to form points of light no bigger than pinpricks. These tiny sparks were knots, Micah saw. Just ordinary knots. Tied into ropes or scarves or shoelaces.

These twinkles here were the knots that held the crates together in the Lost and Found. And those glimmers over there were the knots the Strongmen had used to secure the circus's luggage.

How interesting, Micah thought. *How nice to see you all like this.*

But even as he thought it, the small lights were winking out.

They faded one by one, the minuscule strands that formed them falling away from one another and going dark, as if they were candles someone had snuffed.

Did I do that?

Micah thought he might have.

But it was all right. There were so many other things to see in this place.

Strands of light as thick as rivers. Webs of it that stretched to the horizon. A knot was just a sort of *connection*, Micah realized. The smallest and least important kind.

Here, in this universe, were so many others.

The rivers of light were the connections between people, ties made not of string but of friendship. Of love. They burned strong and bright, and Micah thought it wouldn't be right to touch them. They were so perfect on their own.

But what's that? Up there? That's not right.

Overhead was a hideous snarl of knots that writhed like a pit of snakes. Just looking at them made Micah feel sick to his stomach.

I've seen something like this before.

All those months ago in Terp's paddock. A twisting, tortured vine of light.

As if the memory had called it into being, Micah saw it suddenly. That same light, less a knot and more a hideously stretched and tangled rope. It was on the edge of the writhing mass, and Micah reached up for it, intending to straighten out the mess.

But as soon as he brushed against the rope of light, it splintered and went dark.

Ow. He drew back, shrinking from the pain.

The snarl was smaller now. It writhed a little less. But it had *hurt* him.

Micah stumbled away from it, aching and unnerved. He passed gleaming rivers and glittering streams, careful not to touch, until he came across a huge tapestry of light, so magnificent he had to stop and admire it.

What are you? he thought, staring at it.

It certainly didn't writhe in that awful, nauseating way. In fact, it was beautiful. Not as grand as the rivers, not as bright as the streams, but fascinating in its own way. A big, powerful lacework of knots that connected . . . what?

Micah traced the pattern of light with his eyes, trying to figure it out. It was a funny thing, a golden connection that somehow joined *here* to *there*. It was like someone had used a tremendous net to bridge two places that didn't belong side by side.

Oh, that's very good! Micah thought admiringly. *I could never tie something like that.*

Too curious to resist, he reached for it, wanting to understand how it worked. But as soon as he made contact, the light began to dim.

That's not what I meant to do.

Micah was sorry, but the big connection was fading fast and he had no idea how to fix it. It dissolved into darkness.

And Micah felt utterly drained. The lights around him began to dim.

He'd been in this new world too long. And in the real world, something was going wrong. The shadowy magicians were upset. Someone was shouting.

At me? Micah wondered.

There was a thought trying to break through his confusion. He'd been worried about someone, only a moment ago. But though he wanted to help, Micah didn't think he had anything left to give.

Suddenly, he didn't even know where he was.

Both universes had gone dark.

Or maybe he was just too tired to open his eyes.

18

STRING BOY

Micah wasn't sure he was awake. He could hear voices, close and whispering, and he could feel that he was sitting—on the ground, he thought—with his back propped against something warm and sturdy.

But he couldn't tell his eyelids to open. Couldn't even make himself want to. His whole body was heavy, as if someone had tucked him in and piled far too many blankets on top of him. Even breathing was hard.

His ears still worked, though, and after a long while, he realized he could understand the people around him. Their voices were familiar. Friendly. And there were a lot them.

"You will have to try eventually, Yuri. It isn't good to fear your magic so much." It was a gentle voice. *The Inventor?*

"I did not think I should try during an emergency? On

a young boy?" And that was Yuri, of course. The cook had stopped Micah from running to save Bowler.

The next voice that spoke was definitely Geoffrey's. "You could've tried givin' him a little knock on the head. Just enough to scatter his brains before he collapsed an intercontinental Door."

Micah wondered whose brains the ticket taker wanted to scatter.

"I do not hit people?" Yuri's tone was surly.

"I'm not sayin' hit him *hard*." Geoffrey sounded almost merry. "Just a little wallop to distract the boy."

"Oh, that's terrific advice," someone said. "*Wallop* Micah. I'm sure the Lightbender would take that well."

Wait, thought Micah. *I'm Micah. That's* me they're talk-*ing about.*

He struggled to open his eyes.

"You'll see one day, Dulcie," said Geoffrey, a little more seriously. "Here we all are, thinkin' we've got a cute little knot-tier on our hands, and . . ." He trailed off.

"And?" the Inventor said.

"And he's awake," Geoffrey said.

It was unfair that Geoffrey knew that, when Micah was still trying to figure out how his eyelids worked. When he finally persuaded them to open a minute later, he saw more than a dozen magicians staring at him.

Most of the kitchen staff were there, sitting on top of crates. And beside Yuri, wagging its tail, was an oversized bloodhound that had to be one of the circus's shapeshifters.

It turned out that the sturdy prop behind Micah's back was Big Jean, and he thought he spotted a few more menagerie animals hiding among the luggage, which was strewn everywhere.

But the Lightbender and the Strongmen and the manager and everyone else—where were they?

The magicians present had gathered in a big, loose circle around a glowing copper sphere that hovered above the grass. The sphere crackled like a fireplace full of burning logs, and it gave off heat.

Only a knife juggler named Ten Hands was outside the group. He was circling the perimeter like a guard on duty, flipping his silver knives through the air so quickly that Micah couldn't begin to count them.

A thick, white fog obscured most of the world beyond them, and just as Micah wondered about it, Geoffrey spoke. "Mistsinger's keepin' us all covered, since you've gone and stranded our illusionist halfway around the world."

Geoffrey had somehow gotten hold of a lounge chair. The ticket taker sat with his arms behind his head and his boots kicked off, watching Micah closely.

Micah blinked at him. He had no idea what Geoffrey was talking about, but he had much more pressing questions. "Where's Bowler?"

Everyone was quiet.

"He's with Rosebud," the Inventor said finally. She held something soft and dark gray in one hand, and she was using her jeweler's loupe to examine it. "In her wagon. We're fortunate she was still on this side when the Door closed."

Micah tried to feel good about that. Bowler would be fine. Rosebud could heal anything.

Almost anything.

"And the manager is with Porter by the gates," said Geoffrey. "Givin' him a little bit of a magical boost. He'll be comin' around shortly, and I suggest you think up a good apology fast."

"Why?" said Micah. What had happened to Porter?

Geoffrey snorted.

"And where's Terpsichore?"

"Running?" said Yuri. "I think the Strongmen and the others cannot catch her?"

"They can't," said Geoffrey. "But they're keepin' pace with her and keepin' an eye on the sky. They'll protect her till she tires herself out. Shouldn't be long now. She's slowin' down."

"How do you know that?" Micah asked.

Geoffrey couldn't possibly see what was going on through all this mist. Instead of answering, the ticket taker put his hands behind his head and leaned even farther back in his lounge chair like he was thinking about taking a nap.

Micah didn't know what to make of that, but it didn't matter. He'd delayed long enough. This mess was his fault, and he had to tell them so.

"I'm so sorry," he said to the gathered magicians. "I don't know what happened. I was supposed to be taking care of Terp, and she was in a good mood. And then . . . then . . ."

Images came back to him—something falling out of the sky. Lightning. Bowler on the ground, sharp hooves coming down.

Several people answered him at once.

"You couldn't have known—"

"Bowler wrapped his arm in the lead. It was just a mistake."

"*None* of us were expecting—"

"But I tied the rope so that it wouldn't come undone," Micah tried to explain. "Bowler couldn't break free, and Terp was panicking, and I don't know why, but—"

"It's not your fault." It was Geoffrey who'd spoken. The ticket taker crossed one bare foot over the other and peered at Micah through his monocle. "It's not the unicorn's fault either. She's young, and even a full-grown adult might have spooked under the circumstances."

"What circumstances?" Micah put his hands on the grass and pushed, trying to sit up a little straighter. His muscles were aching and wobbly. "What scared her?"

"A dire hawk," said the Inventor, looking up from the gray thing she'd been inspecting. "The biggest I've ever seen. It dropped down on top of us."

A what? thought Micah.

Geoffrey grunted. "A dire hawk's a bird. Almost as large as Big Jean and strong enough to pick her up if it had a mind to."

"I thought I saw something . . ." said Micah. "It looked like a piece of the sky was falling?"

"Their feathers have a unique camouflaging property," the Inventor said. "They aren't quite invisible, but they blend in well. It's nearly impossible to spot them from a distance, and it's hard to keep them in your sights even when they're close. That's why we didn't see it sooner."

Micah took a breath. "So, it's definitely her then."

Of course it was. But he realized now that some tiny part of him had still hoped something else was causing all this trouble. He looked again at the soft, gray thing the Inventor was examining. It had feathers.

Geoffrey was still staring right at Micah. "It's a storm petrel," he said. "A seabird."

Storm petrel. That would explain the weather. And the little gray bird wasn't moving. It hadn't moved at all since Micah had woken up.

"It's fine that it's Victoria," Geoffrey said. "At least she's an enemy we know. It was clever of her to build up a flock of magical beasties to do her dirty work. But she's cocky, and prone to makin' mistakes when she's angry. And you can bet she's angry right now, considerin' the trouble you've caused her."

"I didn't do anything," Micah said.

Geoffrey chuckled. "Tell that to Porter."

Yuri stood up and walked across the circle to join Micah. He crouched down beside him. "Everything came untied?" he said curiously. "And the storm stopped at the same time?"

Micah frowned. He hadn't done anything at all to the storm. He'd only been trying to free Bowler from Terpsichore's lead.

"That wasn't me."

Yuri looked at the bird in the Inventor's lap. "It fell?" he said. "Right on top of the two of us?"

"Is it dead?" Micah asked.

The Inventor nodded. "Yes. Poor thing," she said, cradling the limp bird in her hands. "The Bird Woman must have been using it horribly, to create such huge storms. Few petrels have that power to begin with, and they never call it on land."

"You broke Victoria's hold on the petrel," Geoffrey said to Micah, "while you were busy untyin' everything else."

"No, I didn't," said Micah.

But he remembered now. He'd touched that rope of light. He'd been trying to fix it, but it had splintered and . . . died.

Horror grew in him, hollowing everything else out to make room for itself. That knot—that terrible wrongness he'd felt—had it been Victoria's connection to the bird? If it was, that meant the petrel's death was Micah's doing.

He couldn't have killed such a small, innocent—

"*You* didn't kill it," Geoffrey said, his voice sudden as a slap. "She did. The poor creature was being tortured, and you freed it."

Micah felt tears stinging at the corners of his eyes. "But—"

"The petrel was too hurt to continue, Micah," the Inventor said comfortingly. "It just gave up."

Micah swallowed. None of this made sense. "I can't do magic like that."

Geoffrey rolled his eyes so hard his monocle fell off. A couple of people laughed.

"You have not looked around?" Yuri asked.

Frowning, Micah did so. Everything was in such a shambles, and he couldn't see how it had happened. The Strongmen had roped everything together, but now the tents were in heaps instead of neat bundles and rolls. Barrels and crates that had been lashed together lay scattered on their sides.

Suspicion growing in him, Micah looked down at his sneakers. The laces were dangling, knots undone.

He reached for his wrist, and discovered, with a punch-to-the-stomach feeling, that his bootlace was gone.

Micah had spent months working on Grandpa Ephraim's knot, making it stronger and stronger. And he'd made *sure* the bootlace wouldn't come off without his permission. Not ever.

If he'd untied something like that without even realizing it . . .

What else did I do? he thought frantically, trying to remember.

Come loose, he'd said. Screamed.

And the world had gone strange—covered with all of those golden strands of light.

Knots, Micah had thought, but they weren't just that. They were connections. *Beautiful* connections between people. And those horrible ones . . . between Victoria and the petrel and all the other birds she'd enslaved to do her bidding?

"There was another thing, too," Micah said, thinking out loud. "This big pile of knots that looked different."

It had been a connection, but not between people. Between places.

And Micah had accidentally broken it.

"Um," he said, fresh shock numbing him. "Why are we all still in Argentina?"

The other half of the circus had already gone through the Door when Victoria attacked. And now they weren't here.

Scatter his brains, Geoffrey had been saying when Micah first awoke, *before he collapsed an intercontinental Door.*

"Oh, no," said Micah. He looked around the circle. "I didn't . . . I wouldn't have done something that *bad.*"

"Don't worry?" said Yuri, reaching into his apron pocket and offering Micah a slightly battered pack of crackers. "We won't let Porter kill you?"

Micah's fellow magicians seemed to think he needed cheering up. Unfortunately, every cheerful thing they pointed out was more than a little alarming.

"You probably knocked Victoria unconscious just like Porter. That's why she's not giving us any more trouble."

"Maybe she fell out of the sky. Ha!"

"Everyone's shoes came untied. It was funny. Geoffrey landed flat on his face."

"I'm takin' protective measures from now on," said the ticket taker, wiggling his bare toes at the group.

"And the Gardener won't be wearing lace-up breeches anymore, that's for sure."

"He needed a wardrobe update anyway."

"Plus, *we're* on the side with the tents. If it takes days for Porter to set up the Door again, we'll have somewhere comfy to sleep. The others will be stuck outside."

"Is it warm wherever they are?" Micah asked.

"Nope," said Geoffrey, who was one of the few people who knew where the circus had been headed. "But a little while out in the freezin' weather will be good for their constitutions."

Micah knew they were trying to make him feel better, and though he was grateful for that, he still found himself wondering if he could persuade Big Jean to roll over and squish him. At least if he was smooshed into the turf, he wouldn't have to imagine the Lightbender and everyone else shivering out in the cold with nothing but the clothes on their backs.

And what must they be thinking right now?

"Hey, Micah, maybe you need a magician's name!" someone suggested. *"Doorcrusher."*

"The UnPorter!"

"He could be Knot Boy?"

"That will confuse people, Yuri."

"String Boy is the obvious choice."

The idea of choosing a magician's name would have been exhilarating a few hours ago, but now . . . String Boy was so horrible Micah thought he probably deserved it.

"How did you do it?" Dulcie asked suddenly.

The candy maker was digging through her pockets, looking for something to feed Micah. Apparently, Rosebud had told them he needed to eat when he woke up, but he wasn't hungry. He'd already had the crackers Yuri had found and a plum, and he'd had to choke those down.

"I mean, you're a kid who makes bracelets," said Dulcie, reaching into the bib of her overalls and smiling when she pulled out a square of fudge. "And they're clever bracelets! Don't get me wrong. But what does that have to do with Porter's Doors?"

Micah looked down at his hands. It didn't make perfect sense, even to him. And he didn't think he could describe the golden world to them well. It already felt like a dream he'd had a long time ago.

"I think my magic isn't just knots. It's more like tying and untying all kinds of things? Does that make sense?"

He could tell by most of their faces that it didn't.

"It's like . . . there was a connection between the gates Porter set up here and the ones on the other side? And I broke it. Accidentally."

There was a moment of silence. The crackling of the copper fireplace sphere in the middle of their circle seemed unnaturally loud.

"Oh." Dulcie's voice had taken on a weird, high-pitched note. "Okeydokey then."

"I didn't *mean* to." Micah had to make sure they understood that. "I was kind of untying everything all at once because I was so scared for Bowler. And the Door was really pretty. I didn't know what it was. I just wanted to touch it."

He felt his face heating. It sounded foolish now. You couldn't go around poking magical things you didn't understand. Micah knew that.

He opened his mouth to say he was sorry again, but footsteps were approaching through the mist. A moment later, the manager appeared across the circle from him, the thick white fog curling away to let him pass.

Mr. Head's eyes pierced him like darts.

Micah's breath caught.

"Well done, Micah Tuttle," the manager said softly. "Rosebud tells me that Bowler will be fine, thanks to you. Though we would appreciate it, in the future, if you refrained from experiments that interfere with the work of other magicians."

"It's just *rude*," said an exhausted voice.

Porter appeared behind the manager, and everyone let out happy cries of welcome.

The magician looked ghastly. He was slumping where he

stood, and he had circles under his eyes as dark as bruises. He pointed at Micah.

"I'm forgiving you," he said. "But only because you said my Door was pretty. And because I like to imagine that wherever she is, Victoria feels even worse than I do."

"I am really, really sorry, Porter," said Micah.

"Don't do it again."

"I won't. I swear."

Micah's head felt a little lighter on top of his shoulders. Bowler was going to be all right. And Mr. Head didn't seem mad. He'd almost sounded proud.

"We will collect Terpsichore and be on our way," said the manager. "Those of you who know our destination, do not speak of it. I doubt the Bird Woman is in any fit state to be listening in, but we shouldn't risk it. We do not want to reveal our plans."

He looked at Porter. "Be ready."

Porter nodded, but as soon as Mr. Head disappeared into the mists again, he collapsed onto the ground. "I'm just going to lie here. *Don't* wake me when it's time to go."

"That might be a problem," said Geoffrey.

"Make Micah open the Door," said Porter, draping an arm over his eyes.

"I don't think I could do that," said Micah, remembering how complicated and impossible the Door had looked in that golden realm. "I think you have to create the connection before I can do anything to it."

Porter groaned and rolled over until he was facedown in the grass.

Micah didn't remember falling asleep, but when next he opened his eyes, he was curled up on a cushion on the floor of Rosebud's wagon.

The bundles of dried herbs hanging from the ceiling quivered and swung as the wagon rolled along. Bottles and jars rattled against one another on the shelves, and someone snored loudly on the bed. Micah pulled himself up for long enough to determine that it was Bowler.

Even in the dim wagon, the Strongman looked bad. A pair of lumps on his forehead made his skull look misshapen, and he had dried blood under his nose.

But he was snoring, and snoring people were never dead.

And that's good enough, Micah decided, collapsing back onto the cushion. *Even if everything else is messed up, that's good enough for now.*

19

CONSEQUENCES

Micah's bedroom looked like it had been put through a blender.

He wasn't sure how he'd gotten from Rosebud's wagon to the Lightbender's tent, or who had tucked him into his old bed, or how long ago that had been. He only knew that he hurt, from head to toe, like he'd tried to carry Big Jean on his back.

He thought he would have felt much better if he'd been sleeping in his soft hammock instead of with his nose smashed into the mattress. But as soon as he set his feet on the floor he realized that would have been impossible. His hammock was gone. The remains littered the rug, a mess of cords, not a single one of them tied to another.

And that wasn't the worst of it.

Micah shook his head, trying to make sense of the chaos around him—a scramble of wrinkled laundry and broken knickknacks. Half the clothes on the floor weren't his, and almost none of the books were. Bits of thread and twine were strewn everywhere, and he felt a twinge of frustration when he realized all his bracelets had been unmade.

The only thing in the room that didn't look like it had been caught in a bomb blast was his backpack. Someone had set it on the foot of the bed.

Micah reached for it. Maybe *something* was left. But when he dug inside, he found Chintzy's silver bell tangled up in loops of embroidery floss and ribbon. Those bracelets were gone as well.

It was all the work Micah had done as a magician—months of experimenting and fiddling with threads no thicker than strands of hair. And he realized, with a flash of panic, that if that had all come apart, then the rope ladder he'd taken from his old tree house must have been untied as well.

He leaped up and began searching the cluttered room for it, hoping that it had somehow escaped his magic, but when he found it under the tumbled chest of drawers, it was a heap of rope and scattered rungs.

The knots he'd tied with Grandpa Ephraim were gone.

That was me, thought Micah. *I did it without even being near them.*

He tried to be impressed with himself. It was a bigger burst of magic than he'd ever imagined he might be capable of.

But holding the limp ropes, he just felt wounded and surprised. Like he'd cut himself on something he'd never known was dangerous.

Mr. Head was proud of you, he reminded himself. *He said Bowler was all right thanks to you. And obviously the circus got where it was going, because here you are in your room. Porter must be okay, and the Door must have worked, and you've got bigger things to think about than a few silly ropes.*

Micah continued in this vein for a while, trying to convince himself that the rope ladder wasn't a tremendous loss. But those knots, the last his grandfather had ever tied, were gone.

You can tie it back. You can tie it just like he taught you, and it will still mean something.

That was the best he could come up with.

He coiled the two ropes and cleared a space on the rug for them, shoving the other detritus aside. Then he stacked the wooden rungs in the middle of the coil. It was the tidiest patch of floor in the whole room.

Micah dressed and left the tent. He wondered how long he'd been asleep. It could have been hours or days for all he knew, and the world outside didn't give him much of a clue.

It was cold, and the sky was a dreary gray, the sun completely hidden by clouds.

The circus looked half assembled. Many of the tents were up, but not all of them, and no one was busy putting together the missing ones. This was unusual, since the Strongmen usually worked straight through after a move, getting everything ready for the crowds in a few short hours.

But there were no crowds now. And the call of the pipes and drums was absent.

It felt wrong to Micah. Circus Mirandus was always so busy. He'd gotten used to ignoring the constant chatter and excitement, and without it, he felt unmoored.

It was even worse without Bowler watching over the tent. Micah wondered if he was in the Strongmen's dormitory, or if he was still in Rosebud's wagon.

Maybe he needed visitors.

Just as Micah was setting off in the direction of the dormitory, the Lightbender rounded the side of the tent holding a covered tray.

He stopped when he spotted Micah. "You've woken."

"You're all right," Micah said at the same time.

"I am quite all right," the illusionist said. "Though I nearly had the life frightened out of me when the Door collapsed. I haven't seen Porter lose control of one that badly since he was in his twenties."

He looked Micah up and down. "Are *you* all right?"

Micah nodded. "I think so. I didn't mean to do it. The Door . . ."

"I know. Are you hungry?" the Lightbender asked, shooing him back into the tent.

"Extremely hungry."

"Good. The kitchen is supposed to be serving sand-wiches while we sort things out, but apparently, Yuri cooks in times of stress. He's given me enough food for a small nation."

To Micah's surprise, the Lightbender settled in the stands in the main section of the tent, placing the tray on the bench beside him. He removed the lid to reveal an assortment of food—egg casserole and a vegetable stir-fry and a miniature pie that turned out to be full of chopped meat when it was cut in half.

Micah took the egg dish. "What meal is this, anyway?"

"An early supper, I think."

They ate in silence for a few minutes, and Micah real-ized that the Lightbender was tired. He was staring off into space as he chewed, and he wasn't bothering with the illusions he usually used to make himself look more magi-ciany. His coat hung limply from his shoulders, and he had bags under his eyes.

Micah swallowed a bite of his eggs. "Are you sure you're all right?"

The Lightbender blinked. "I am well. Only thinking about a great many things at once."

"I'm sorry about splitting up the circus."

The Lightbender waved his hand. "It was not badly done. The response was a bit extreme, but so were the circumstances."

"Mr. Head said Bowler's going to be okay?"

The Lightbender smiled. "Yes. You should hear him

complaining about his arm, though. You would think he was the first person in history to ever have broken a bone."

"He's awake!" Micah exclaimed. Something inside of him loosened at the news. "That's great! How's his head?"

"Hard. He had a concussion, but the Strongfolk are sturdy sorts."

"And someone found Terpsichore?"

"She has been tucked away in her paddock since you arrived, with a round-the-clock guard. I am sure she feels quite important."

"That's good," said Micah. "It wasn't her fault. She was scared of the giant hawk."

"Yes. We must talk about that. Among other things." The Lightbender brushed his hands together, scattering crumbs of piecrust on the ground, and cleared his throat.

"First, I should tell you that we are in a park in St. Albans, just outside of London. It is an unusual choice for us in many ways. The area is relatively populous, and we were not scheduled to tour England this year. Victoria has lost us once already, judging by the long period we had without any ill weather. And we are fairly sure that this move will keep her off our backs, perhaps for months."

"But she saw us going through the Door," Micah said quietly.

"She did not know where it led," said the Lightbender. "We never made this stop while she was part of the circus, and we are certain she did not follow us through. We think it likely, given your own actions, that she was not even conscious when the Door reopened. In which case, any birds she had in thrall will likely have scattered, and she will have to spend time recapturing them."

That was good news. Much better than Micah had thought. "She had a lot of them."

The Lightbender had been reaching for the other half of his meat pie, but at Micah's words he paused. "Oh?"

Micah set his plate down beside him. While they were talking, he'd eaten everything on it without tasting it.

"I saw this place." He stared at his knees, trying to remember it all. "It was like it was painted over the real world. These knots made of light were right there where I could reach them. And Victoria's flock was there, too. I could see it—like awful tangled ropes. I think it was her power, tying the birds to her."

The Lightbender said, "Your magic is different than you thought."

Micah nodded. He tried to explain his theory, that what he was really doing when he tied his knot bracelets was creating a kind of connection, not only between different pieces of string, but also between the string and his own thoughts and memories. "And I can do more, I guess. In that golden world, I might be able to tie all sorts of connections. Or untie them."

While Micah spoke, the Lightbender had been staring up at the ceiling of the tent, at the patch in the fabric where Micah had once fallen through the roof. "It suits you," he murmured.

"What does?"

"Your magic." The illusionist's expression turned serious. "Micah, I hope you will forgive me for telling you what I am sure is obvious. But you must be more careful now than you have been."

"Because I could accidentally close more of Porter's Doors," Micah said. "I know."

"No. Well, *yes*. Porter would appreciate it if you didn't do that again, but . . ." The Lightbender sighed. "Your power is lovely and unique. I do not think you realize how much so, yet. And it is also more complicated than any of us had imagined."

Micah thought he knew what the Lightbender meant. "There were so *many* connections," he said. "I couldn't even recognize most of them. I'll have to be careful what I touch."

He hadn't meant to shut the Door, after all. He'd just been bumping around cluelessly.

"It may be many years before you see the world in quite that way again," the Lightbender said. "You were extremely afraid for Bowler, and you reached much farther with your magic than you ever have before. I myself see the world through an overlay, much like the one you describe, though for me it is more a tapestry of minds I might affect at will. It took me decades to access that tapestry with any degree of certainty, and it has been the work of centuries for it to become a natural habit."

"You see threads of light, too?" Micah asked excitedly. "But all the time?"

He wondered what he looked like to the Lightbender.

"*That* is a subject for another day," the magician said. "I wish for you to understand that the scope of your magic is greater than we had realized. And the consequences of its use will be as well. It is easy enough for, say, Firesleight, to decide whether or not she should burn something to ash. That is not the sort of thing one does to one's friends, after all."

Micah laughed.

The Lightbender smiled, too, but his voice remained solemn. "My own power is not so straightforward. I must use my illusions carefully, and old as I am, I don't always know what is right."

"Your illusions are always meant to be nice, though," said Micah.

"When you are altering the thoughts of others, even good intentions can end in disaster," the Lightbender said, frowning down at his hands. "You had nightmares when you first came to stay with us. Do you remember?"

Micah had had such terrible dreams about Grandpa Ephraim dying. It was why he'd spent so much time tying knots with Fish.

"I was tempted to take them all away from you," said the Lightbender. "Replacing bad dreams with good ones is a simple thing for me to do. But Rosebud and Geoffrey

advised against it. Dreams can be your mind's way of working through something difficult. So, I helped just enough
to ensure you slept peacefully for a few hours each night."

"Oh," Micah said. He'd never even known. "Thank
you."

"You are welcome. Of course. But do you understand
what I'm telling you?"

"That you had to be careful. Because maybe what you
wanted to do to help me could have hurt me instead."

The Lightbender nodded. "You must be similarly cau-
tious. This idea that you manipulate the *connections*
between things—I believe you are correct. But I suspect
you do not yet understand the implications of that."

"I just woke up," Micah pointed out. "I haven't had time
to figure out everything."

He planned to sit down and have a long think about it
all after he checked in on Bowler and Terpsichore.

The Lightbender looked pained. "I am talking about an
understanding you might come to over the course of years,
not a few short—" He shook his head. "Let us agree that if
you feel even the *slightest* uncertainty about trying something new with your magic, you will ask someone more
experienced for advice. None of us will hold you back
from experimenting with your power; we will only help
you ensure that what you are attempting is reasonable."

Micah had never thought of his magic as dangerous
before. How could it be?

But then he remembered the storm petrel. That was

definitely a bigger consequence than he'd been expecting.

"I'll be *so* careful," he promised. "I'll stick to tying things into string for a while anyway. My bracelet collection is gone, and I need a new hammock. And maybe I can finally make the locator knot work. I think I've had the wrong idea all this time."

"Locator knot?"

"The tracking device I was trying to make."

The illusionist looked relieved. "That sounds like an excellent plan," he said. "And a safe enough first step."

Micah said, "Do you think I might be able to do something to help? If Victoria attacks again?"

"You helped quite enough as it was," said the Lightbender. "And I hope we have seen the last of her for a while. We've had word from the Sisterhood, who will be pursuing her now that we know her general location. She will not have an easy time of it with them on her trail."

"That dire hawk was trying to catch Terpsichore, wasn't it?" said Micah. "Victoria wants to feed Terp to her dragon."

The Lightbender sighed and rubbed his forehead. "That is the best theory we have," he agreed. "We've had word from Firesleight while you slept, and one of the draklings is indeed missing from his burrow. The Mighty Conflagration. Every sign points to Victoria having taken him away early last year. She could easily have fed him from her flock, but she no doubt hesitates to sacrifice too many of her own birds. She will need as many as possible if she means to mount an assault on the circus."

"So, she's going after our magical creatures instead," Micah said, anger tightening his voice.

The Lightbender nodded. "And a single unicorn has more magic than half the animals in the menagerie combined. Only Bibi compares. A meal like that might be enough to fledge Conflagration, and with a *true* dragon at her disposal Victoria could attack us directly, rather than taking these ineffective jabs."

Micah clenched his hands into fists. "We can't let that happen."

"Terpsichore is safe for now," the Lightbender said. "As are we all."

The two of them finished off the tray of food in silence. By the time they were done, Micah felt stuffed.

The Lightbender draped an arm over his stomach. "Yuri's cooking is as good as usual," he said. "And that reminds me . . ."

He stuck his hand into an inner pocket of his coat. When he pulled it out, his long fingers were wrapped around an old leather bootlace.

Micah gasped and reached for it. "Is this real?"

"I would not use my illusions for something like this," the Lightbender said, handing it to him. "Yuri picked it up for you."

The bootlace was soft with age, and it felt so familiar in Micah's hands. "I thought I had lost it. I was afraid I had."

"You did not. But there were other unintended consequences of your magic that you now must face." He clapped his hands together and stood.

"What consequences?" Micah said, confused.

"We will visit Bowler." The Lightbender's voice brightened. "He may well decide that he owes you his life! I hope you have resigned yourself to having a Strongman follow you around for centuries on end."

Micah stared at the Lightbender. "He *wouldn't*."

The Lightbender hummed. "Surely I can convince him that you are much more vulnerable than I. And so much more deserving of a bodyguard."

20
STANDING TALL

For the next several days, Circus Mirandus stood empty. Micah walked the same paths he'd always taken, but they felt foreign. Tent flaps were shut, the midway stalls had never been set up, and the music was quiet. He tried to tell himself it was peaceful not to have so many strangers around all day, every day. He even tried to pretend that the whole circus was on vacation together.

But it didn't feel like a vacation when, in every dark corner and out-of-the-way place, magicians could be found whispering together in worried voices.

Micah tried to eavesdrop on these conversations, but it was usually impossible. The adults at Circus Mirandus all spoke multiple languages, and when they thought Micah wasn't around, conversations tended to switch to Mandarin or French or Hindi—whatever a particular magician enjoyed or needed to practice. And when they finally realized he was present, the talk turned much more pleasant and casual.

"Is there a potion that can make people learn languages faster?" Micah asked Rosebud one morning during lessons.

They were sitting at their usual table in the dining tent, heads bent over a first aid manual. The circus's healer thought all knowledge was useful, so their classes focused on whatever Micah was curious about.

Rosebud slipped a bookmark between the manual's pages and closed it. "There are potions that help with memorization," she said. "But they won't do you any good right now, duckling. They're too dangerous for a growing brain. Do you want to spend more time practicing your Spanish?"

When Micah asked her for a long list of vocabulary words, she smiled knowingly.

He took the words back to his room and spent all night trying to tie a knot that would remind him of them whenever he wanted, but despite the new insight he had into his magic, the attempt was a failure. To tie information into a knot, he apparently had to know it well first, which meant he was going to have to study anyway.

"Don't know why you're botherin' with all the eavesdroppin'," Geoffrey said the next day when he found Micah skulking behind a set of cabinets in the kitchen. "Nobody's sayin' stuff you don't already know."

Micah didn't quite believe him.

"Don't believe me?" said Geoffrey, prying the top off a can of sardines. "Ask away. I'll tell you whatever you like."

Micah wasn't about to pass up an opportunity like that. "Have the Sisterhood found Victoria? Or Conflagration? How are they tracking her if she can fly?"

"No. No. And they're havin' some trouble," said Geoffrey. He licked sardine juice off his fingers. "The drakling's a tunneler, so that should make trackin' it easier, but she's got it fed up so well that it's tunnelin' deep and movin' fast."

Micah wondered if he could get away with a few more questions.

"Sure," said Geoffrey.

Micah was so startled to have his thought answered that his next set of questions fell right out of his head to be replaced by a much more pressing one.

"*Geoffrey,*" he said, aghast, "can you *read minds*?"

"Oho!" said Geoffrey. He slurped down a sardine. "Guess we won't have to wait until you're a hundred after all."

Micah's hands went automatically to the top of his head.

"Don't be silly. I don't have to look through your skull to see what's on your mind. And I won't pry as long as you think quietly."

Micah's thoughts were so loud right now that Geoffrey would probably be able to hear them from Mars.

"I think I'll just leave," he said, trying not to meet Geoffrey's eyes in case that would make the mind reading easier. "I need to check on the Lightbender."

"He's at Porter's," Geoffrey offered.

Of course he would know.

Micah headed to the warehouse and found his guardian sprawled across Porter's sofa, a cold cup of coffee on the floor beside him.

"He came by for a visit and didn't get three words out before he fell asleep," said Porter, shaking his head.

Even though he didn't have to perform with the circus closed, the Lightbender was doing more than usual with his illusions to keep them hidden. Micah was glad his guardian was getting at least a little rest.

"Let's leave him to it. I know how he feels," said Porter. He had slept for two full days after reopening the Door to England. "I've got something to show you in the warehouse."

Micah followed him out to the wall of mail slots.

"See anything new?" Porter said, gesturing at the wall.

Micah found it right away. It was a custom mail slot, like the one Firesleight had been using, but instead of etching flames into the metal flap, Porter had engraved this one with a square knot design.

"Since Chintzy's temporarily grounded, I thought you might need a new way to send letters to your friend," said Porter. "I put the matching slot in a box addressed to Jenny's house and dropped it through a cat flap in her neighborhood this morning. I figure she'll get it soon enough that way."

"That's perfect!" Micah said excitedly. A mail slot was even better than letters. He and Jenny would be able to talk face-to-face. "Porter, thank you."

"Just try not to blow it up," said Porter. "Or disconnect it. Or whatever it is you do. Even if it *does* look pretty."

To everybody's delight, Firesleight appeared in the dining tent the next day during breakfast.

She stepped through the entrance with a travel bag slung over her shoulder, and before she could say a word, the tent was in an uproar. Magicians cried out in welcome and ran to greet her.

Firesleight looked a little the worse for wear, her brown eyes weary and her clothes rumpled, but she brightened as she was surrounded by her friends. "I missed you all so much," she said. "It's good to be home."

Micah raced toward her, too, wanting to reassure himself that she was fine. And as soon as Firesleight spotted him, she slipped around all the people who were clapping her on the back.

"Micah Tuttle!" She wrapped her arms around him in a strong bear hug. "Look at you! I swear you've gotten bigger in the past few weeks! And is that a ponytail?"

Micah felt himself blush. He'd tried the ponytail for the first time this morning, and it was so short he couldn't decide if it looked interesting or just ridiculous.

"Are you okay?" he asked Firesleight. "Did you find Victoria?"

Firesleight let him go and shook her head. "I'm safe and sound," she said. "And we didn't find Victoria, but we did find this."

She dropped her bag on the floor and pulled a scale the size of a serving platter out of it. It was oval, with sharp edges, and the charcoal gray color of it was overlaid with iridescence like an oil slick.

"We found it in a fresh tunnel in Northern Mexico. So, we know the drakling hasn't fledged, and it's not heading toward us right now. Victoria must have lost our trail." She smiled. "I figured I would come home and share the good news. The Sisterhood will keep searching, and they'll call if they need a hand."

"What happens now?" said Micah.

"Well, since trouble isn't headed our way, we can reopen. We'll have to be extra careful, but—"

Whatever else she was going to say was lost in the general cheer that went up from the magicians. Apparently, Micah wasn't the only one who'd grown tired of an empty circus.

Two weeks passed, and Circus Mirandus held its breath, though the crowds never noticed.

The music played day and night, strong and true. The Doors opened again in the meadow, and children ventured through from St. Albans and beyond, never quite understanding how they had arrived. The shows went on, and if anything, they were more spectacular than ever.

The Strongmen played a stacking game in the afternoons, building a tower of logs so high it seemed to brush the clouds, while Ten Hands roamed the midway, juggling polished coins instead of his usual knives. The coins fell around him, flashing like raindrops in the sunlight, never once touching the ground. All the performers were at their best, and sometimes, Micah found himself joining the audiences and gasping with every bit as much astonishment as the guests did.

When he asked Mr. Head why everyone was putting forth so much extra effort when they were already stretched thin by the circus's new security measures, the manager said, "Because when evil asks us to bow before it, it is our job to stand taller."

Micah thought Circus Mirandus was standing very tall indeed.

The magicians had a thousand extra tasks to perform each day now.

There were patrols in the meadow and frequent emergency meetings in the manager's office, and whatever the Lightbender was doing with his illusions was taxing him. His shows were canceled, but still, he walked along like someone half in a dream. He answered questions ten minutes after people asked them, and he sometimes forgot his leather coat, which made him look so unlike himself that Micah always ran back to the tent for it, even if the Lightbender claimed he wasn't cold.

Micah had also gotten into the habit of fetching the

magician at mealtimes, just in case it didn't occur to him that he might be hungry. They ate quietly together, Micah busying himself with knot-tying when he was finished eating so that he wouldn't bother the illusionist with too much conversation.

He was working on resupplying himself with bracelets—replacing the old and making up new ones. It was different, now that he knew the point of his magic was connecting things. It was easier to decide what he wanted to do and exhilarating to understand that it wasn't the physical knot he tied that mattered so much as the one that existed somewhere in that realm of golden threads.

Micah hadn't managed to find that world—the overlay—again. He couldn't see it the way he had when he'd been afraid Bowler was dead. But now that he knew it was there, it was like a whisper on the edge of his thoughts, nudging him in the right direction.

He'd replaced all the memory bracelets on his left arm in record time. Memories were a special kind of connection, he'd decided, one that joined *then* and *now* together. Once he understood that, his knots grew stronger, the memories turning clearer.

"If you become any more skilled at that type of knot," the Lightbender said during a rare moment of alertness, "you will be halfway to an illusionist yourself."

It was lunchtime, and though Micah had managed to steer his guardian to their regular table, the Lightbender had barely eaten a bite.

"You can't go *into* the memories, though," Micah explained, nudging a plate full of tacos toward him. "Part of you always knows that they're not happening right now."

"Ah," said the Lightbender, blinking down at the food like he was surprised to find it on the table. "So, my job is secure after all."

Micah was starting to realize that he wouldn't want his guardian's job.

When the Lightbender finally started putting food in his mouth, Micah went back to work. He reached under the table for his backpack and pulled out the gray thread he was using for the new locator knot.

He was pretty sure he understood why it had never worked before. You couldn't use *one* knot to create a tracking device. He would need to use two. He would have to connect them somehow, so that one always knew where the other one was even when they were apart.

Micah had explained all this to the Lightbender. He'd been fairly sure the illusionist wasn't listening at the time, but when Micah pulled out the spool of thread, he said, "Have you had any luck with it?"

"Not yet," said Micah. "But I'm close."

A couple of days ago, he'd managed to get two knots to vibrate whenever they were separated from each other, and that was definitely progress.

"I think maybe I should try to make them identical. Because that's how Porter does it."

Porter had once said that it was much harder to create

a connection between doors if they didn't match perfectly. It stood to reason that connections between knots might work the same way.

The Lightbender was silent for a couple of minutes. Micah assumed he'd drifted off again, but then he said, "Yes. That makes sense. Porter's doors are tools he uses to make his magic easier to visualize and control. Your knots seem to be a similar kind of tool."

Micah nodded.

"When you finish your tracking device," the illusionist said, "I have another project in mind for you."

"What kind of project?"

"I would not dream of interrupting your current endeavor—"

"I want to be interrupted!" Micah protested. "What do you need me to tie?"

He'd been hoping, now that he'd started to figure things out with his magic, that he would find more opportunities to help out around the circus. But he kept drawing a blank when he tried to think of things that would make a real difference.

"I would like to have some way of knowing if you need help when you are away from the circus."

With Victoria thousands of miles away, Micah's field trips with Rosebud could resume. But he didn't want to add to the Lightbender's worries. "I won't leave the circus if it bothers you."

"It would bother me more if you were a prisoner

here when you didn't have to be," said the Lightbender. "However, it would ease my mind to know you had a way of contacting me if need arose."

Micah frowned. He didn't have any clue how to make a knot like that. But the Lightbender had made a special request, and Micah wasn't going to say he couldn't do it.

"I'll think of something," he promised. "Just give me a while."

21

THE LOCATOR KNOT

Two days later, Micah walked into the Lightbender's room. "I've done it!" he announced.

The illusionist was sitting on the clothes chest at the foot of his bed staring off into space. He turned and blinked blearily at Micah.

"You really need to sleep."

The Lightbender sighed. "You're not the first to tell me so."

He even sounded different.

"Why do you have an accent?" Micah asked. "Wait. Do you *always* have an accent?"

"Everyone does. It is merely a matter of the listener's perspective."

Micah supposed that was true, but though the Lightbender had always spoken formally, he'd always sounded familiar, too. Like he might have grown up in the house next door. Which was weird now that Micah thought about it. The Lightbender had been born in Scandinavia a long, long time ago. And he'd lived all over the world since then. He shouldn't have sounded just like someone from Micah's hometown.

"You use your illusions to change how people hear you!" Sometimes, Micah wondered if he knew anything real about his guardian at all.

"It is an unconscious habit," the Lightbender said, a hint of apology in his voice. "A little like smiling to make someone you have just met feel comfortable."

"It's fine," Micah said quickly. "I was only surprised."

"What did you wish to show me?"

Micah held up a pair of knot bracelets. He had made them out of thin black cords, and they were identical. "Give me your arm."

The Lightbender held out a hand, and Micah tied one of the bracelets around his wrist.

"Can you feel anything?" he asked, shoving the bracelets on his own arm apart to make room for one more.

The Lightbender touched the knot curiously. "I'm afraid not."

"That's okay. It'll still work." Micah *could* feel something. It was like an invisible string, thin as the thread of a spider's web, connected the two black bracelets.

"You wanted a way of knowing if I ever got into trouble," he said. "Watch this."

He hooked his index finger under the bracelet on his own wrist and gave it a tug.

Come loose. He felt a small *snap* in the back of his mind, and the bracelet came undone.

At the same moment, the matching bracelet unknotted itself and fell off the Lightbender's wrist onto the rug. The illusionist's eyes widened. He bent to pick it up.

I did it. Success was a warm rush in Micah's veins. *I really did it.*

"I think it's going to work over long distances, too!" he said. "I'll send one to Jenny to test it out. But this is what you wanted, right? We'll both wear one of these emergency bracelets, and if I'm ever in trouble, I'll break mine, and you'll know right away."

The Lightbender was still staring at the black cord in the palm of his hand. In a soft voice, he said, "How extraordinary."

Micah ended up making four different pairs of emergency bracelets. The Lightbender asked that he give one to Rosebud and another to Porter, just to be safe.

The final one was for long-distance testing purposes. When he'd finished it, Micah went to Porter's tent and passed it through the new mail slot to Jenny in Peal.

"Micah, this is so cool!"

Jenny was standing in the kitchen with her own mail slot propped against a cereal box. She was so close to the slot that most of the time Micah could only see her eyes and her nose, but he could hear the hum of the refrigerator running. And whenever she backed up a little, he caught a glimpse out the window. It wasn't dark yet in Peal, though it was nighttime in England.

Jenny slipped the coral shoelace he'd used for the test bracelet over her wrist and held her arm up to the slot so that Micah could see it.

"Try it out," he said. "It's supposed to work both ways, and I need to know how it handles distance."

"But I don't want to untie it," said Jenny. "Then I won't have it anymore."

It hadn't occurred to Micah that Jenny might want to keep the shoelace. "I'll give you another one when we talk next week," he promised. "I can't tie these as fast as the memory bracelets."

Jenny took a few steps back, and Micah saw she was wearing her new science club T-shirt. She'd been elected secretary, even though most of the other members were in seventh and eighth grade. Micah was so happy for her that he almost wished he still went to regular middle school, just so he could join her club.

Almost.

"All right," she said, prying at the knot with her bitten fingernails. "Here it goes."

She tugged the knot loose. All the way across the world,

the matching shoelace on Micah's wrist fell off as well.

"It works!" he shouted. "Eureka!"

Jenny laughed. *"Eureka?"*

"What?" said Micah. "Isn't that what scientists say when they discover something fantastic?"

"Sure," said Jenny, still giggling. "I've just never heard anyone say it in real life."

The success of the emergency bracelets spurred Micah on, and he spent the entire weekend sitting on top of his barrel in the menagerie, working on the locator knot while Fish watched curiously over his shoulder.

Fish was in a particularly good mood lately, and he had grown again.

Late Sunday night, Geoffrey came into the menagerie, stared hard at Fish for almost ten minutes, then announced that the Moment would happen sometime this year.

"This year?" Micah said, placing his palm against the glass. *So soon.* "How do you know?"

Geoffrey tapped his forehead.

"Oh." Micah guessed that a mind reader must be able to understand an Idea better than almost anyone else.

"Are you still feedin' it knots?" Geoffrey asked.

Micah nodded.

"It's an interestin' notion." Geoffrey eyed Micah. "Givin' the Fish an education. You might want to remind it it's supposed to wait for its Someone, though. It's startin' to get restless, and we don't want it to release its magic too soon."

"Fish wouldn't do that," Micah said. "He knows how important he is."

"It's happened before," Geoffrey said, "and it'll happen again. They get impatient, sometimes, Ideas do. They start to worry their Someone is never goin' to be ready for them."

Micah stared at Fish. "What if he *does* release his magic too soon? If it happens here at the circus, I mean?"

"That would be a bit of a waste," said the ticket taker. "Circus Mirandus has plenty of magic and inspiration flyin' around already. In some ways, we're in the same business as the Fish."

When Geoffrey finally left, Micah turned to the aquarium.

"It's not that I don't want you to find your chosen person," he said. "It's just that I don't want you to leave. Who else am I going to talk to while I work?"

Fish thumped the tank with his tail.

Micah sighed and turned back around, dangling his feet off the side of the barrel, trying to put his mind back on the locator. He had cut two pieces of gray thread off a spool, and he had measured them four times to be certain they were *exactly* the same length. He tried to reach for the overlay as he tied, to see the knot as it existed in the golden world.

But all he could see were his fingers working slowly with the threads.

He tied a simple knot into one piece of thread, precisely in the middle, and then he picked up the other and did the same thing. *You're twins,* he told the knots. *You're supposed to be together. You never want to be separated.*

He added a new twist to the knot, and a new thought to go with it. *You always know where your twin is.*

As he finished adding the twist to the second piece of thread, something happened. A brilliant spark leaped back and forth between the threads. Micah saw it for a split second, then it was gone.

But he could still sense it. It was almost like holding two strong magnets together and feeling them pull toward each other.

"Fish," he said, staring down at the threads. "Fish, I think I got it right."

Fish thumped the tank again, but Micah was already off his barrel. "Chintzy!" he cried, hurrying out of the menagerie. "Chintzy, I need you!"

He found the parrot in the Lightbender's tent. She was perched on the back of the illusionist's armchair while he sat below her, asleep and surrounded by the empty stands.

The Lightbender had been resting a little more often over the past couple of weeks at Rosebud's insistence. He took short naps in the oddest of places, somehow never letting his illusions drop all the way. Micah wondered what it was like to be so used to doing magic that you could literally manage it in your sleep.

He was always careful not to disturb his guardian during a nap, but it seemed Chintzy had different ideas. She leaned over the drowsing magician, intent on preening his hair.

"Chintzy, he's tired," Micah said. "Anyway, I need you."

He held up one of the locator knots.

"I'm helping *him*," Chintzy said, yanking at a strand of blond hair with her beak. "*He* doesn't like mail slots better than me."

"I don't either!" Micah said. "You're much nicer than a mail slot. And you can still talk to Jenny through mine any time you want. But right now, I need your hiding skills."

"*Hmmph*," said the parrot. "Last time you accused me of cheating!"

Micah had sent Chintzy out into the circus to hide almost two dozen previous versions of the locator knot. He'd been suspicious of her when he hadn't managed to find one even by accident.

"I'm sorry about that. Please will you help?" He showed her the knotted thread again. "Nobody hides knots as well as you do. You're the *best*."

Chintzy paused, watching the thread closely. Then she gave the Lightbender's hair a final tug and fluttered over to Micah's shoulder.

"Give it to me!" she squawked. "I'm a professional!"

She snapped up the gray thread and flew through the tent flap. When she returned ten minutes later, she looked smug. "You'll never find it!"

We'll see about that, Micah thought.

While Chintzy went back to preening the illusionist, Micah wrapped his own locator thread around his ring finger a few times and set off in search of its twin.

The tug of the thread was so gentle it felt almost like a butterfly had landed on Micah's hand, but it was definitely real. He focused on the pull and turned left.

It's happening! he thought, walking quickly. *I did it!*

Then the tug changed directions.

That can't be right. It's not supposed to move.

As Micah kept following the feeling, his enthusiasm dimmed. He'd been so sure this time.

When he ended up on the midway, right in the middle of the crowd, the tugging stopped abruptly. He looked around. He didn't see any likely hiding places, so he knelt down to inspect the ground, waving his hand over the grass.

The knot had to be here somewhere. Had Chintzy *buried* it?

No, she'd hidden it too quickly for that.

The tug came again, to Micah's right. He jumped up to chase it, running right into a group of kids who were stocking up on snacks at one of the booths.

Micah spun with his hand stuck straight out, trying to zero in on the feeling, but it had disappeared again. Frustrated, he turned around too quickly and bumped into another boy.

"Sorry!"

The boy was a couple of years older than him, with spiky hair and acne. He shrugged. "No problem, mate." He gestured at Micah with the bag of popcorn in his hand. "Do you want to come with us? We're all going to watch those big blokes stack trees."

"Yes, come," said a girl in a fancy school uniform. She was blowing on a mug of chai. "I saw them yesterday. You'll like it a lot."

"Aren't *you* the one who hangs around with that giant fish all the time?" a younger boy asked, squinting at Micah through his glasses. "Tying knots and talking to yourself?"

"That's me." Micah shoved up the sleeve of his coat so they could see the bracelets that covered his arm.

"Whoa. Those are great!" said the girl. "Do you sell them at school or something?"

"No, they're all mine."

"Bit of a weird hobby," the boy with the glasses muttered.

Micah rarely told the visiting kids he was a magician. Some of them were put out that he was allowed to live at the circus all the time, and others wanted him to prove he could do magic. It was easier to pretend he was just a normal guy whose passion was decorating himself with random pieces of string.

"I'd like a bracelet like that," the girl said, stepping close and pointing at one of the more elaborate ones. "They didn't have much jewelry in the souvenir tent. I've got to leave in a couple of hours, and I checked, but—"

"Have any of you seen a parrot around here?" Micah interrupted.

The tugging sensation was completely gone. The other thread had to be right here. He scanned the grass again, but he didn't see it anywhere. Surely Chintzy hadn't stuck it in a bag of popcorn? "She's big and red and—"

"Really bossy?" the girl asked, taking a sip from her mug and smiling. "I met her on the way here. I thought she was a boy parrot, though. I called her sir."

Micah was surprised the girl still had all her fingers. "Did she give you anything?"

"Just some thread. Bit strange, really. But my gran has a parrot, and they don't always make sense."

"That's mine!" Micah exclaimed.

He was going to pluck Chintzy. She was supposed to *hide* the knots, not give them to people who were leaving the circus forever. No wonder he'd never found one of the other locators, even accidentally.

"I mean . . . the parrot took it from me. She wasn't supposed to give it away."

The girl shoved her hand into the pocket of her school jacket. "Trade you for a bracelet?" she said, holding out the thread.

Micah blinked. "Okay."

"I want one, too!" a younger girl who'd just walked up announced.

"And me," said the boy in the glasses.

"You just called him *weird*," said the spiky-haired guy.

"So? He's giving out prizes."

Micah didn't want to give them the bracelets on his arm; they were each special to him in some way. But he'd left his backpack in the Lightbender's tent.

He dug through the pockets of his peacoat and searched his jeans. He'd become something of a magpie, he realized as he pulled stray scraps of fabric and frayed ribbons from every single pocket. He had more than enough material to make half a dozen bracelets for the girl and her friends.

They were in a rush to watch the Strongmen, so Micah didn't bother tying magical knots for them. He just tried for ones that looked interesting.

"Thanks," said the girl as Micah wrapped a braid of yellow and pink floss around her wrist. "You're pretty good. You should definitely sell these to the kids at school."

When he was done, she gave him the locator knot, and the group set off, arguing about whose new bracelet was the best.

Micah stared down at the gray thread, feeling a thrill of excitement. It didn't look like much, but he'd done it. He could track anything now, just by tying a piece of thread to it.

He wondered if distance would be a problem with these, but for some reason, he didn't think so. He almost thought the knots would tug *harder* if they were farther away from each other. After all, they wanted to be together.

"What are you smiling about?" Dulcie asked. She was

walking down the midway, a stack of empty trays balanced neatly on top of her head. As usual, the candy maker's overalls were covered in powdered sugar and edible glitter.

"I can do magic," said Micah.

Dulcie laughed. "Are you just now figuring that out?"

22

TAIL TWITCHES

Micah was so pleased with the locator knot's success that he sailed into the Lightbender's tent, waving his twin pieces of thread over his head.

"Chintzy, you big cheater! Look what I found!"

The parrot wasn't there.

The Lightbender, his hair sticking up in every direction, was still snoozing in his armchair, and the seam to Micah's bedroom was open. He could hear the sound of flapping and splashing from all the way out here.

"Aha!" he said, stalking into his bathroom.

Chintzy was in his sink, and the whole room was spattered with water. Micah held up the locator knot accusingly.

Chintzy ignored him in favor of dunking her head under the water.

"Go away," she said, when she came up for air. "My tail is twitching."

"Is it twitching with *guilt*?" Micah said, wiggling the thread at her. "You've been giving my knots away!"

"No!" she squawked. "It twitches when someone needs me to pick up a letter. I'm washing off first, because *I'm* a professional."

It was clear from her tone that she thought Micah himself was behaving in a highly unprofessional manner.

"I just talked to Jenny a couple of days ago," he said.

"Ha!" said Chintzy. "It's not a letter from her. This is major stuff. My tail twitches for *important* messages."

"Really?" Micah said doubtfully.

"The last time it twitched this hard, your grandfather was writing to the Lightbender!" Chintzy stretched her beak out toward Micah's toothbrush.

Micah snatched it away and tucked it into the pocket of his coat. Of course he knew that Chintzy had magic of her own, but since nobody ever sent the Lightbender mail, it was easy to forget she could sense when someone really needed her services as a messenger.

"Chintzy," he said, "I'm not doubting your tail twitches—"

"You'd better not!" She climbed out of the sink and started shaking herself dry.

Micah held up a hand to fend off flying water droplets. "You *know* if whoever is writing to the Lightbender is anywhere near Victoria, you can't go. Right?"

"It's not a letter for the Lightbender," said Chintzy. "It's for you!"

"But you said it wasn't Jenny."

She was polishing her beak on her damp chest feathers. "I don't know who the message is from. I just know where it is. And it's not in Peal."

Micah racked his brain, trying to think of who else might be writing to him. "Where is it?"

"Arizona." Chintzy looked up at him. "Is that near Victoria?"

"*Yes.* And it's . . ." Micah froze.

"Are you okay?" Chintzy squawked. "You look like you ate bad seeds."

"Arizona's where Aunt Gertrudis lives."

Micah stood outside Porter's door, knocking so furiously that Chintzy was having trouble clinging to his shoulder.

"All right, all right!" Porter called. "I'm coming."

He opened the door. "Why are you . . . What's wrong?"

Chintzy squawked, "I need to fetch a message!"

At the same time, Micah said, "Someone needs to check on my great-aunt."

"Gertrudis?"

"Chintzy says someone's trying to send me a letter from Arizona, and she's the only person I know there. And she doesn't even *like* me, so it's got to be—"

"Urgent." Porter rocked back on his heels. "Right. We'll take care of it."

The magician closed his eyes for a few seconds. "I'm shouting at Geoffrey," he explained to Micah. "In case he doesn't already know what's going on. He'll put together an away team."

"Can I do something?"

"Stand there. Don't panic. I've got to get a door."

"You could just send me through a cat flap!" Chintzy squawked. "I'm tired of being stuck in England!"

But Porter was already disappearing around a tower of doors.

Chintzy flapped off, muttering about people who didn't appreciate her tail twitches.

Micah was left on his own, wringing his hands and trying to come up with reasons for Aunt Gertrudis to be contacting him that weren't completely horrible.

He couldn't stop thinking about the fact that the Bird Woman had helped raise Aunt Gertrudis. She'd practically been her mother.

Micah should have warned Aunt Gertrudis that Victoria was still alive. She wouldn't want to hear it, but he should have tried.

You're getting ahead of yourself. She hasn't seen Aunt Gertrudis since she was a little girl. Why would she decide to bother her now?

A few minutes later, the Lightbender strode into the warehouse with Bowler, Firesleight, and Geoffrey on his heels.

"Why ever didn't you wake me?" the illusionist asked

Micah. His freshly preened hair was all sticking straight up.

"You look so awful lately. I thought you needed the nap."

"You do look awful," Bowler offered helpfully.

The Strongman had completely recovered from the incident with Terpsichore. And to Micah's relief, he'd refused to quit being the Lightbender's bodyguard, though patrols of the meadow were taking up a lot of his time.

"Terrible," Firesleight agreed, reaching up to mash the Lightbender's hair flat.

"I think he looks the same as always," said Geoffrey. "And I think Porter's ready for us."

Sure enough, Porter had just finished setting up the sliding glass door that would lead to Aunt Gertrudis's retirement community. They all gathered around it, and Micah waited, electric with nerves, to see what was on the other side. He half expected Victoria herself to step through, storm clouds and sharp-beaked monsters in her wake. But when Porter pressed his hand to the door, the glass shimmered, and someone's back patio appeared.

The most exciting things in sight were a pair of potted succulents and a dusty charcoal grill.

Geoffrey poked his head out the Door first. He was silent for a moment, apparently listening to the surrounding minds, but finally he nodded. "No Victoria nearby," he said. "Let's go."

He stepped through, Bowler and Firesleight following him.

"I'll reopen it in an hour," said Porter. "Be back then."

Micah's last glimpse before the Door slid shut was of Geoffrey in his tailcoat, pointing down the street, with Firesleight in her new black costume and a bare-chested Bowler flanking him.

"They are *not* going to blend into a retirement community," he said.

The Lightbender smiled faintly. "Ah, well. We magicians do like to make an entrance."

Waiting for the strange trio to return was excruciating, despite Porter and the Lightbender doing their best to take Micah's mind off things. And when the Door finally opened again, the Lightbender had to grab the back of Micah's coat to remind him he wasn't supposed to fling himself through it.

". . . can't fathom it!" Bowler was saying as the patio appeared through the glass. "How can anyone not like such a good lad? She's completely—"

"Are you all okay?!" Micah cried. He was glad Bowler thought he was a good lad, but he was more interested in making sure none of them had been attacked by dire hawks or his great-aunt.

"We're fine," said Firesleight, but her face was troubled. When she stepped into the warehouse, Micah saw she was holding an envelope. It had his name on the front.

Chintzy had been right.

Porter shut the Door, and Micah held out his hand for the letter.

"You probably don't need to read it," said Firesleight,

her fingers clenched around the envelope, wrinkling the ivory paper. "I mean, we questioned your great-aunt. She's totally fine. Just had a little visit from Victoria. Geoffrey's sure we know everything she does."

"Right," said Bowler. "Everything's fine in Arizona right now. Nothing to worry about."

Micah stared at them. "It's *my* letter," he said. "Why wouldn't I read it?"

When she finally gave it to him, he knew why.

THIS MESSAGE IS INTENDED FOR:
Micah Tuttle
Ward of the Lightbender
Circus Mirandus
PLEASE DO NOT REPLY

Micah,

I hope this letter finds you in good health.

I consider it my duty to inform you that your grandmother, Victoria, visited my home this past Thursday. She wished to speak to you, and she was under the impression that I had gained custody of you following Ephraim's death.

I informed her that you are now in the care of people more suited to your nature, that we do not keep in touch, and that I do not know where such people might be found.

She flew away.

I do not recommend you seek her out, and should she find her way to you, I advise you not to associate with her.

She is a noxious individual, and she should not be allowed around children.

This is all I know. I have no further interest in the matter, and I do not believe she will ever come back here. There is no need for you, or anyone else, to contact me.

Gertrudis Tuttle

The adults kept telling Micah to calm down, but he couldn't.

It was *him*. Victoria had attacked the circus because of him.

He was taking in great big gulps of air, and there was a ringing in his ears like he'd been hit on the head. "It's all my fault!" he said, a little hysterically. "She's doing all of this because of me!"

Firesleight sighed. "I knew I should have burned that letter."

"He's spinnin' himself into a tizzy," Geoffrey said, leaning back against the sliding glass door.

The Lightbender grabbed Micah's shoulders. "Micah, calm down! For heaven's sake. The attacks on the circus had nothing to do with you."

"They must have!" said Micah. "The letter! It says she's looking for me!"

"You're being ridiculous," Porter said, exasperated. "If you just think about what you're saying—"

"Porter, you have to send me away! So that everyone will be safe. You can send me to Antarctica!"

"The penguins don't want you there," said Porter.

The Lightbender leaned down until he and Micah were almost nose to nose. "It's extraordinarily *obvious* that the attacks were unrelated to your presence here."

"How—"

Geoffrey rolled his eyes. "Did you even *read* that letter?"

"I read it!" Micah said wildly. "Victoria went to Arizona because she wanted *me*! She wants to find . . . oh . . ."

"Exactly," said Geoffrey.

Micah felt his face heat. He *was* being ridiculous. "She thought I was in Arizona. She didn't even know I lived here, so the attacks can't have anything to do with me."

"That is correct," said the Lightbender, letting go of Micah's shoulders. "Unfortunately, her visit to your aunt brings up another question."

The mood in the room darkened as all the adults exchanged worried glances.

Micah knew what they were thinking. He was thinking it, too.

"If it's not my fault she attacked the circus," he said, "then what does she want me for now?"

23

MEETING

Micah shut himself in his room for the rest of the afternoon, hoping the tent fabric would prevent any mind reading. He was tangled up inside—confused and angry and scared all at once.

"I'm fine," he said, when the Lightbender came to check on him. "I just need to be alone. I'm fine."

Probably, he thought, *it's obvious you're not fine if you say it twice in a row.*

"All right," the Lightbender said quietly. "We can talk later."

As soon as the illusionist left, Micah sat on the floor, reading and rereading the letter from Aunt Gertrudis. Although, she hadn't called herself *Aunt* Gertrudis. Maybe she didn't want Micah to either.

He willed the letter to give him answers, and when it didn't, he wadded it up and threw it as hard as he could across the room.

It bounced off his chest of drawers and landed in the corner, on top of the coiled ropes that had once been his tree house ladder. Micah hadn't been able to fix it yet. It wasn't that he couldn't tie the knots; it was that the knots didn't mean anything to him when he did. The ladder, and the knots in it, had been a gift from his grandfather. Micah wanted *those* knots back. Not ones he'd tied himself.

He crawled over to the rope ladder. *Maybe today,* he thought. *Maybe today I can fix this one thing, and it will be like he's here with me.*

But it wasn't like that, and Micah ended up lying on his back with the ropes clutched to his chest, staring up at the ceiling. A few minutes later, twinkling stars appeared on the fabric. They swirled into shapes—frogs, people, trees.

The Lightbender was trying to make him feel better.

Micah watched the constellations shift, and he imagined his great-aunt, her hair pulled back in a painfully tight bun like always, opening her front door to find Victoria standing there.

Micah felt sorry for Aunt Gertrudis. Her letter hadn't been warm, but it showed she cared at least enough to warn him.

She flew away, Micah thought. That was what the letter had said.

What must it have felt like to look up and see the

Bird Woman flying, when all those years ago she had let Gertrudis fall?

Half an hour passed, and the swirling lights on the ceiling winked out. A moment later, sparkling letters appeared in their place.

MEETING IN THE MANAGER'S OFFICE

Micah frowned. Was the Lightbender only letting him know another meeting had been called? Or was Micah actually being *invited*?

He waited a minute, but the letters didn't fade.

I am being invited, he realized. He scrambled out of his room, almost running into his guardian, who'd been standing in front of the seam.

"I thought that would get your attention," the Lightbender said mildly. "Did you want to come to—"

"Yes!" said Micah. "I'm ready! Is the meeting about me?"

"Somewhat. I thought you wouldn't want to be left out."

Rosebud and Porter were standing by the aquarium when Micah and the Lightbender entered the menagerie.

Fish bashed his tail into the glass when he spotted Micah, and Rosebud gave the Idea a curious look. "It's grown again."

The adults all took their shoes off at the door before entering the manager's office, which made Micah feel guilty for all the times he hadn't done it himself. He left his sneakers by the Lightbender's boots before he stepped through the seam.

Inside the office, Mr. Head, the Inventor, Geoffrey, and Bowler sat waiting.

Micah decided it was best not to ask what seat he ought to take in case it was an amateur move for an important-meeting attendee. He headed toward a chair across the circle from the manager, looking around to see what the others were doing in case there was some special etiquette he ought to follow.

If so, the magicians weren't giving it away. Rosebud sat tall and straight, her hands folded in her lap. Bowler had plopped himself down onto the sofa beside the Inventor. Geoffrey and the Lightbender slouched in chairs by the manager, and Porter went to stand with his back to the fireplace.

"What have you learned?" Mr. Head asked, once everyone had settled.

"Not as much as we wanted to," Bowler said.

"Victoria knows Micah exists, and she assumed he would be with his great-aunt," Geoffrey said, nodding at Micah.

She's been checking in on the family over the years, Micah realized. If she hadn't been, she wouldn't even have known he'd been born. The notion of Victoria lurking near his house while he grew up, watching him and his grandfather from above, made him feel like insects were crawling over him.

"Gertrudis was shaken up to see someone she thought was long dead," Geoffrey added. "I'll give her credit for comin' to her senses after the fact and sendin' that letter. But it was done half out of guilt. She gave away more information than she should've, and she realized it after the Bird Woman flew off."

He glanced at the Lightbender, and the illusionist turned to Micah. "It seems Victoria had a lot of questions about your magic."

"She has some sense of its magnitude?" the manager said sharply.

Micah leaned forward in his seat. He wanted Mr. Head to explain what he meant by *magnitude*, but Geoffrey spoke up instead.

"Seems like Victoria didn't know what kind of magic Micah had inherited at all."

"Well, Aunt Gertrudis couldn't have told her anything about that," said Micah. "I couldn't talk about magic around her without starting a fight. She's spent her whole life trying to pretend like it doesn't exist."

"What an unfortunate point of view," Mr. Head murmured.

Bowler nodded in agreement. "All your great-aunt knew for sure was that you tied knots," he said to Micah. "She told Victoria that, and Victoria didn't like it at all. Kept asking Gertrudis questions about birds and how they behaved around you."

"Ah, of course," said the Inventor. "Victoria wants an ally."

Everyone turned to her. She had a thoughtful look on her face. "Perhaps I should say *an assistant* instead of an ally. Victoria was never one to share power, but I imagine she is regretting that now."

"What do you mean?" the Lightbender asked.

"Surely you've read the Sisterhood's latest reports?" she said. "So far, they've spotted three different dire hawks, golden swans, phoenixes, plague ravens. Not to mention the less dangerous species. She's collected hundreds of magical birds. It must have taken her years."

Micah sat back in his seat. He'd known Victoria had a large flock, but he hadn't known it was *that* large.

"Perhaps she can direct a flock that size *and* track us down *and* deal with The Mighty Conflagration at the same time. But it cannot be simple for her. The dire hawks alone would have given her trouble in the old days. They're intelligent, and they are too willful to be easily controlled."

The Lightbender frowned. "She hoped Micah had inherited her own magic, you mean. So that she could persuade him to help her."

Micah was fiercely glad that he couldn't fly or mind control innocent birds. "Well, I wouldn't help her," he said. "Not ever. She's just been wasting a lot of time."

"Of course you wouldn't," Rosebud said. "But Victoria never did have any respect for children. No doubt she thought you would be more easily bribed, or bossed around, than an adult."

The Lightbender was rubbing his temples. "I suppose this

is welcome news in a way. If Victoria is seeking help from a grandson she has never troubled herself to meet, it must mean she hasn't been able to find allies in other quarters."

"Not surpisin'," Geoffrey grunted. "Nobody with sense is goin' to pick a fight against Circus Mirandus just because Victoria wants a little revenge. The other unpleasant sorts are smart enough to stay out of our way."

"What unpleasant sorts?" Micah asked.

"Magicians are only people, duckling," said Rosebud, rubbing a hand over her scalp, smudging the delicate painted violets. "Good and bad and everything in between."

"We try to keep an eye on the bad ones," said Porter. "They make fewer messes when they feel like they're being watched."

Bowler laughed. "It's Porter's hobby! He pops Doors open near troublemakers, scares them half to death, then slams the Doors in their faces before they can retaliate."

"It's not exactly a hobby," Porter mused. "More like a calling."

"I'm *not* one of the bad ones, though," said Micah. He was still offended that Victoria, who didn't even know him, had imagined he might be on board with an evil plot. "Even if I had never met any of you before, I wouldn't want to hurt you."

"You're assuming she would have given you a choice," Porter said. "She might have harmed Gertrudis or Jenny. Or threatened to feed you to the drakling."

"I'd like to feed *her* to the drakling," Bowler muttered.

"I'd advise against it," said the Inventor. "I'm not certain, but I imagine consuming a powerful magician would be almost the same to the drakling as eating a unicorn."

"So why hasn't it attacked Victoria?" the Lightbender asked.

"Firesleight believes this one is unusually smart," said the Inventor. "And, of course, she can fly, and it cannot. Yet."

"You can tell it's smart by the name," said Micah. "Can't you? The Mighty Conflagration is a lot more impressive than most drakling names."

The Inventor gave him an approving smile.

Porter rolled his eyes. "Of course Victoria had to pick the dragon with delusions of grandeur to match her own."

"Maybe . . ." Micah said hesitantly, "if it's really smart, could we talk to it? And explain to it that we're good people and it should leave us alone?"

Everyone stared at him.

"No," said Mr. Head finally. "Though I appreciate the nobility of that thought, Micah Tuttle, I'm afraid dragons are as close to irredeemably wicked as a species can be. Once grown, they take great pleasure in violence. And they eat endlessly, gorging themselves until all other magical life in an area is extinguished. A dragon would consume every soul at this circus if it had its way."

Geoffrey nodded. "And then it would go lookin' for dessert."

24

EAVESDROPPERS

A few evenings later, Micah sat across from the Light-bender at suppertime, picking at a plate of chicken curry. The food was as delicious as always, but Micah couldn't seem to work up an appetite.

"Why do people like Victoria get to be magicians?" he asked, setting down his fork. "Why someone like her and not someone like Jenny?"

Micah didn't expect the Lightbender to reply. The illusionist had that distant, exhausted look on his face again. But he blinked a few times and said, "Do you remember the answer you gave me? When I first asked you what you thought magic was?"

Micah did. It had been the afternoon Grandpa Ephraim died. Micah and the Lightbender had been riding to the circus on Big Jean's broad back, and he hadn't known yet that he would soon be living there.

"I said it must be what's inside of people like you. I said I thought magic must be the part of you that was too big to keep to yourself."

"A fine description," the Lightbender said. "And insightful. But there is greatness within everyone, whether they are good or bad, young or old. And there are almost as many ways for that greatness to emerge as there are people. Sometimes the greatness shows itself as magic. But people also reach out and touch the world with their creativity, their intelligence, their patience, their sense of humor."

Micah thought about that. "Jenny's really smart," he said. "Is that like her magic?"

"If we are defining magic as something one puts into the world, then certainly," said the Lightbender. "And I would add that Jenny Mendoza's kindness and empathy are remarkable, especially for one so young. She has placed herself in difficult situations, many times, to be a good friend to you."

Micah knew that. Jenny hadn't believed in magic at all to start with, but she had been willing to help Micah find Circus Mirandus anyway. And she'd taken some pretty big risks to do it.

The Lightbender met Micah's eyes, suddenly serious. "I hope you will never fall into the trap of believing your ability to tie knots is the most important part of you. It is a common failing among magicians. Your talent is a tool you can use, but it is not the only tool you possess. Do you see?"

Micah nodded.

"Good," said the Lightbender. "I myself once made the mistake of thinking . . ."

The illusionist fell abruptly silent.

"What is it?" said Micah.

The Lightbender stood, tilting his head as if he were listening to something. All over the dining tent, other magicians were doing the same thing.

"Is something wrong?"

"I have to go," said the Lightbender, distracted.

An emergency meeting must have been called, Micah realized. He wondered if Mr. Head had some way of contacting everyone that Micah didn't know about. His guardian could use his illusions to spread the manager's messages over the circus, but how did the manager get in touch with the Lightbender in the first place?

"Can I come, too?" Micah had been invited once before, after all.

But the Lightbender was already striding away. As he neared the exit, Rosebud grabbed him by the sleeve of his coat. She leaned down to whisper something in his ear, and the Lightbender nodded shortly. For a split second, he looked back over his shoulder at Micah.

The expression on his face was unreadable. He turned and left with Rosebud.

The magicians who'd stayed behind in the dining tent

were muttering to one another now, looking worried. They must have heard the silent announcement, too. A few of them glanced in Micah's direction before quickly looking away again, and Micah's throat tightened.

Something *was* wrong, he realized.

And it was something to do with him.

For a moment, Micah sat frozen, trying to imagine what could be so wrong that the Lightbender would leave without explaining anything. The illusionist had been trying to be forthcoming with information ever since their talk in the Lost and Found. He was the one who'd made sure Micah was invited to the last meeting, and he had promised to keep Micah filled in.

Which meant that whatever this was, it was worse than Victoria hunting down Aunt Gertrudis. Worse than dragons.

Micah couldn't stand not knowing. He left his food on the table and headed for the menagerie.

Terpsichore was delighted to have company until she realized all Micah wanted to do was press his ear to the wall of her paddock. It was hard to tell, with magical spaces, but he was fairly sure the manager's office was on the other side of this wall.

But he couldn't hear anything except for the paddock's classical music and Terp's annoyed foot stomping and fluting.

"Shhh," said Micah. "You know I'll play with you later. I'm trying to concentrate."

The fabric was soft against his face. It didn't seem like it should be able to block out sound so thoroughly. He got down on his hands and knees and ran his fingers along the edge of the fabric, where it met the ground. It was tight— much too tight for him to lift up.

"Warn me if someone's about to come in, okay?" Micah said to the unicorn. "You'll be my lookout."

Terpsichore stared at him.

"Well, don't step on me at least."

Micah planted his fingers into the grass right at the edge of the fabric and started to dig. It wasn't easy. The ground was hard, and his fingernails felt like they were trying to come off. But after a couple of minutes, he'd dug a hole the size of his fist under the tent wall.

Terp thought this was some sort of new game. She pranced off to the center of the paddock and started gouging her horn into the grass with enthusiasm.

Micah shook his head and lay down on his stomach. He scooted as close as he could to the wall of the tent and pressed his ear to the new gap he'd made between fabric and ground. At first, he thought it hadn't worked. Then, beneath the sound of the music, he heard voices.

They sounded odd and farther away than they should have, like they were echoing from across a canyon instead of the next room over. But maybe that was the magic of the tent itself interfering.

Micah closed his eyes and concentrated. He could pick out the Lightbender's voice. And Rosebud's. They were speaking urgently in a language he didn't know.

He listened anyway, hoping someone would slip into English. Or say his name. But the first word he recognized didn't come for several long minutes.

" . . . Victoria . . ." someone said.

Then someone else—Micah thought it might have been Geoffrey—said another familiar name.

"Peal."

Micah's breath caught. *What about Peal?* Was Jenny all right? He wanted to leap up and burst into the meeting to demand answers. He wanted—

"It's my turn!" a voice squawked right in Micah's ear.

He shrieked and scrambled to his feet, heart racing, but it was only Chintzy. The big red parrot stood in the grass beside him, and before Micah could ask what on earth she was doing in Terp's paddock, she waddled forward and stuffed her whole head under the tent wall.

"Chintzy!" Micah protested, dropping back onto the ground. "I'm trying to listen."

"Hush," she said. "They're probably talking about me."

"No, they're not," Micah hissed, reaching to pull her out of the way.

She screeched ferociously. "Not my tail!"

"Dig your own hole!"

"You don't even speak Latin!" Chintzy squawked.

Micah froze with his arms stretched out to grab her. "Do you?"

"I'm not some second-rate chicken!" she said. "I'm a professional."

"Chintzy, that's great!"

"I know."

"Can you translate?" he asked eagerly.

"Don't touch my tail feathers."

"I'm so sorry," said Micah. "That was wrong of me."

He did his best to cram his head in beside Chintzy, but she was too big. "Mmm . . ." she was saying. "Of course she did! That rotten egg!"

"What is it?" Micah whispered. "What are they talking about?"

"Victoria's on a bird-killing rampage," she reported. "She crashed a flock of pigeons into the windows."

"*What* windows?"

"Pigeons are rude, you know. Almost as bad as ducks."

"Chintzy, I swear . . ."

"The windows in Peal," said Chintzy. "Victoria's mind controlling all the birds in Peal!"

"Is Jenny all right?" Micah breathed. "Are her parents?"

"Don't worry," said Chintzy. "Victoria can't make people crash into windows. Oh . . . oh, dear."

It took all of Micah's self-control not to scream at the parrot. He managed to pry the conversation out of her bit by bit, and every new scrap of information made him feel more nauseated.

The events in Peal had made international news. No

magical birds had been spotted, at least none that the news channels were reporting, but every normal bird for miles around had been involved in the chaos. They'd smashed themselves into shop windows all over town. A flock of crows had attacked children on the playground at Micah's old elementary school, and there had been accidents on the freeway when panicked birds crashed into windshields.

"This can't be happening," Micah breathed. "It can't."

Victoria would never have even *thought* about Peal if not for him.

What if Jenny was hurt? What if her dad had been driving when the attacks happened? What if her mom's shop was destroyed?

Jenny had asked to keep the emergency bracelet, and Micah had told her *no*. He'd told her he'd make her another one. Why hadn't he done it right away?

"Is anyone . . . Are people . . ." Micah didn't want to say the word *dead*. What if that made it real?

The parrot had fallen silent.

"Chintzy?"

She didn't answer. Micah realized her feathers were quivering. "Chintzy, please," he whispered. "I have to know."

"She's bad," Chintzy said quietly.

"Have they mentioned Jenny's family?"

"Porter can't reach them through the mail slot. They're not at home yet. He's going to keep trying."

That made sense, Micah told himself. Because of the time difference. It was still the middle of the day in Peal.

Jenny's mom was probably at work. Her dad would be at work or school. And Jenny would be in class, wouldn't she?

She couldn't have been outside like the elementary school students, because they didn't let you have recess in middle school. She was fine. They were all fine.

"They're safe," he said. "They're safe. They're safe."

If he repeated it over and over again, it would start to sound true.

Chintzy pulled her head out from under the wall. "I want to go back to my perch."

"Is the meeting over?"

Chintzy's feathers puffed. "I don't want to translate anymore."

"But—"

"I want my perch."

"Okay," said Micah. "That's okay. I'll keep listening, and I'll tell you if I learn anything."

Chintzy waddled toward the door. Micah sat up and watched her go. She was a large bird, but she looked so small suddenly. So easy to hurt.

And even though Micah knew it didn't make sense, even though he knew Victoria was busy terrorizing an entirely different continent, he suddenly thought it would be his fault if anything happened to Chintzy on her way back to the Lightbender's tent.

He jumped to his feet. "Wait!" he called. "Chintzy, wait. I'll come with you."

As he left, Terpsichore tootled proudly and gestured to the enormous hole she'd dug in the middle of the paddock. Micah tried to give her a smile. He patted the unicorn's neck good-bye and scooped Chintzy up.

She didn't even make a joke about how she could fly faster without his plain old human legs slowing her down. Micah held her close to his chest and she buried her beak in his shirt.

"Jenny's nice," she said as Micah left the menagerie. "She made me a plate with my name on it."

It's going to be okay, Micah tried to say. *Jenny will have treats waiting for you on that plate the next time you see her.*

But his throat had closed up, and he couldn't find enough breath to get the words out.

25

FIGHTING THE DARKNESS

W hen the Lightbender returned to the tent, he didn't
seem surprised to find Micah waiting for him in
the stands. He came to sit beside him, looking as tired as
he ever had.

"You are aware of the attack on Peal."

It wasn't a question. Geoffrey must have told him Micah
knew.

Micah was stuffed so full of worry and hurt there was
no room left to feel ashamed of himself for spying. He set
aside the new pair of emergency bracelets he'd been trying to tie. "Is Jenny . . . did someone get in touch with her
family?"

"Just a few minutes ago," said the Lightbender. "They

are all well. The Sisterhood detected a flock of birds building near Peal right before the attack. One large enough to show up on Doppler radar. They called Jenny's family to warn them."

Micah let out the breath he'd been holding.

"Victoria never targeted Jenny specifically," the Lightbender added. "The windows of her mother's shop were broken, but so were many others in the area."

"What about . . ."

He didn't know where to start. What about Florence Greeber and her family? What about the kids at the elementary school? What about all of them, every single person in Peal? Were they okay?

"Micah, I know how you must feel about this. Victoria—"

"She's a *monster*," Micah interrupted. His own voice sounded strange to him, quiet and sharp as a knife in the dark. His hands curled into fists without his permission. "I wish she was gone. Why can't she just be gone?"

"Micah—"

"It's not *fair*." He grabbed his bootlace and squeezed it hard. "It's not. Everyone else is gone. Grandpa Ephraim and my parents and all sorts of wonderful people. But *she's still here*."

He shouldn't be saying these things, part of him warned. The Lightbender was the kind of person who caught spiders in coffee cups so that he wouldn't have to squish them. He would never understand.

But a truth had built up inside of Micah until it was so big he couldn't hold it back anymore. "I want her to be dead."

Micah felt more ugly and hateful than he ever had in his life. And feelings like that didn't belong in a place like Circus Mirandus. He knew it down to the soles of his shoes. He rubbed at his eyes with the sleeve of his shirt and clenched his jaw, waiting for his guardian to recoil from him.

The Lightbender placed a hand on his shoulder. "You seem to expect me to react with horror," he said in a measured voice. "I assure you, I am not so easily horrified."

"I shouldn't want her to be dead," Micah said. "It's not right."

The Lightbender sighed. "It's not. But I can hardly hold the sentiment against you when I feel much the same way."

Micah blinked at him.

The Lightbender squeezed his shoulder, then allowed his hand to drop. "You underestimate my anger, Micah, or perhaps you overestimate my compassion. I thank you for that, but you are not the only person to imagine how much simpler our lives would be, how much safer the *world* would be, without Victoria Starling in it."

Micah swallowed hard. "Is anyone else in Peal hurt?"

"A great many people had minor injuries. A few are wounded more severely. No one has died."

Yet. The word hung unspoken in the air.

"Why would she do it?" Micah asked. "Does she *want* us to know where she is?"

"I am afraid that is exactly what she wants." A grim look crossed the Lightbender's face, and the whole room seemed to dim.

"We thought Victoria would continue to search for us. We thought it might take her years. But apparently, she hasn't the patience for that course of action. She seems to hope that by attacking innocents, she might flush us out of hiding." His mouth twisted with distaste. "No doubt she chose Peal in a fit of spite when she found out we had taken you in. She is sending a message."

"You mean she wants us to come to her, instead of the other way around."

"Yes. It would be convenient for her if we abandoned reason and raced to Peal."

"Aren't we going to?" *Of course we will,* Micah thought. Someone had to keep Victoria from attacking again.

"No," the Lightbender said.

"They need us!" Micah protested. "They're not magicians. How are they going to protect themselves?"

"We will send a handful of magicians to help, and the Sisterhood will bring all their resources to bear, in addition to the few Strongwomen you have already met."

"But—"

"I know how you feel," the Lightbender said, meeting his eyes. "I do. But Peal will be well protected by morning. And if Victoria is foolish enough to stay, she will be found."

Micah shook his head. It wasn't enough. He wanted to

check on Jenny and her family in person. He wanted to be there to help his former classmates and neighbors however he could.

"The Sisterhood is far more accustomed to dealing with trouble of this nature than we are," the Lightbender said. "And it is best to let them do it. Many of the magicians here at Circus Mirandus *can* fight, however—"

"Then why won't we?!"

"Micah," said the Lightbender, "there is *always* a violent battle taking place somewhere in the world. If we devoted ourselves to engaging in each one, we would be a society of warriors, and there would be no circus at all."

Micah tried to understand, but it was a hard thing to wrap his mind around—the idea that a battle might be taking place in his old hometown and every capable magician wouldn't rush to defend the people who lived there.

The Lightbender seemed to know what he was thinking.

"Some fight the darkness head-on," he said. "Others try to create so much light that it cannot take hold in the first place. We need both sorts of people in this world."

"Why can't we get rid of the darkness forever so that things like this don't happen anywhere?"

"We are trying," said the Lightbender. "So many of us have tried for so long. I have to believe one day we will be victorious."

26

A GREAT MANY SEAGULLS

Micah spent most of the next day in Terpsichore's paddock.

He had caught a glimpse of the overlay there once before, during the lightning strike, and he hoped the peaceful music and the presence of the unicorn would bring him luck again. He tied knot after knot, reaching out with his mind.

If I could just find that golden place, he thought, *I could fix all of this. I could stop her.*

He would snap that writhing mass of connections he'd seen, and Victoria's birds would be free.

The Lightbender had said it might be decades before he could do something like that. He'd said Micah would have to practice and learn more about himself and his power.

But surely, if you really needed to do something and you tried your best, you would find a way.

Only Micah *did* need to find the overlay. And he *was* trying his best. And hours later, all he'd gotten for his trouble was sore fingers and hundreds of useless knots.

Decades of practice, he thought dismally, rubbing his aching hands into the cool grass. *I don't have that long.*

He packed away his supplies and went to see Fish.

A couple of curious girls were admiring the aquarium, but they left when they saw Micah's gloomy expression.

He stepped up to the glass. When Fish swam around to see him, Micah met one of his big, silvery eyes and whispered, "Listen, I know the chances are one in a few billion, but if I *am* your Someone, I could really use some help right now. Things are pretty dark, and I think you're a kind of light. So if you can do anything . . ."

The minutes trickled by as Micah stared deep into Fish's eye, trying with all his might to open his mind up, making room for some spectacular new idea that would put a stop to the Bird Woman once and for all.

"Well," he said, when the silent staring match finally became too much, "I guess you know best. But just in case."

He reached into his pocket and pulled out a piece of gray thread. "This is the locator knot." He held it up to the tank. "See?"

Fish twitched a fin.

"The matching one is on my finger." Micah tapped his

ring finger against the glass. "I made them so that they would pull toward each other. And if I give you one, then we can always find each other. So, when the time's right—if it's ever right—you'll know where I am."

Before he could chicken out, Micah climbed on top of his barrel and tossed the tiny knot over the rim of the tank.

Fish swished his tail and caught it the instant it hit the water.

Micah, heart fluttering, waited to see if there was any reaction. Fish circled the tank at top speed and stopped again right in front of him, but that was what he always did lately when Micah gave him a knot.

Fish didn't transform, and there was no huge outpouring of magic. No flash of inspiration came.

And later that night, Micah heard the news—Victoria hadn't been caught in Peal. She had flown on, and in another town, more innocent people had looked up to see the sky darken, the sun hidden behind thousands of beating wings.

Victoria attacked another town two days later, and then another, four days after that. And rather than racing to meet her, Circus Mirandus kept up its usual work, just as the Lightbender had said it would.

To the children who arrived in droves, Micah guessed it must seem that everything was as beautiful and fun as always. But he saw a different side of the circus.

Porter had taken on the job of helping a select few

magicians and members of the Sisterhood travel from battle to battle, and his warehouse had turned into a command center.

When the flocks were big enough, the Sisterhood tracked them using radar. Those were the good fights, because the magicians could anticipate which town would be hit and arrive in advance. They would go through Doors and be on hand to meet the waves of birds, and they would fight or subdue them as necessary.

But smaller attacks came, too—ones they couldn't do anything about until after the fact. And on those days, everyone felt like failures.

Victoria was traveling impossibly fast, in so many scattered directions that they could never completely anticipate her next move.

Most days, the Strongfolk and the others met in the warehouse to discuss tactics. Micah went every chance he got, and as long as he stayed out of the way, nobody seemed to mind him listening in on their plans. At first, it was encouraging to watch them all set out—brave and ready for anything—but as the days turned into weeks, Micah began to fear that Victoria was too clever to be captured at all.

Half the battle party was always dedicated to tracking down the Bird Woman, but she never allowed herself to be seen on the battlefield.

"She's a coward!" Pennyroyal shouted, stomping into the warehouse after a particularly frustrating day, her orange hair covered in feathers and bird droppings. "Or a genius! I'm not sure which. We're running ourselves ragged dealing with swarms of pigeons while she keeps herself and the dangerous creatures out of the fight."

Micah didn't tell Pennyroyal, but he was glad Victoria hadn't risked her magical flock in any of the fights so far. He already spent his long hours in the warehouse trying not to stare at the space Rosebud had set aside for medical emergencies; he hated to think of the magicians dealing with even more danger.

Just yesterday, Thuja had come through the Door with a bleeding Ten Hands slung across her shoulders. The juggler was an expert with his knives, and he had refused to be left out of the fighting.

"It was a gigantic dire hawk that did this to me," Ten Hands told Micah, pointing to the long scratches on his cheeks. "The size of a rich person's house."

"Oh, was it now?" said Rosebud, rubbing the juggler's arms with a minty-smelling potion. "You were fearless, I'm sure."

"Did it pick you up?" Micah asked.

He had been trying to learn everything he could about Victoria's most dangerous birds, and Porter had told him that dire hawks killed their prey by dropping it from great heights. He leaned in closer to examine Ten Hands, assuming there must be broken bones.

"No. It was the kind of dire hawk that likes to scratch people," said the juggler. "Very terrifying."

"It was seagulls," said Thuja from her seat on top of a

stack of doors. She was checking the fletching on one of her strange green arrows, and Micah was relieved to see that the tip of it wasn't dirty with blood. The magicians were doing their best to fend off the birds without hurting them. "And a goose."

"*Thuja,*" Ten Hands protested.

Thuja grinned at him. "A great *many* seagulls," she said placatingly. "And a *fearsome* goose."

She stuck the arrow she'd been checking back in her quiver.

Micah had asked the Strongwoman last week why her arrows were so big, and she'd given him a long look. "Sometimes the enemies of peace are big," she'd said. "And when they will not be swayed by kind words and good reason, they might be swayed by something sharper."

Micah was a little alarmed by the archer, but he was glad, at least, that she was on their side.

He wished with every bit of himself that he could join the fight in a more active way, but the Lightbender thought he was spending too much time at Porter's as it was.

"Even were you as strong as Bowler, we would not send you into battle," the illusionist said. "Because you are eleven, and there are many other ways for you to be helpful."

He suggested that Micah start going with other magicians on supply runs into St. Albans and London. "There is absolutely no reason for you to confine yourself to the circus when Victoria remains an ocean away. I know how you enjoy field trips."

But Micah couldn't let himself *enjoy* touring England, knowing that any day now, someone might go through one of Porter's Doors and never come back.

Instead, he came up with the idea of making unbreakable nets. His sleeping hammock was only a kind of net, after all, and the magicians needed some way of capturing and containing Victoria's birds. So, he set out to tie nets that even the Strongfolk couldn't destroy.

Unfortunately, he was a little too good at the job.

The knots that made up the nets were simple, and they came together quickly. Once he laid out the ropes on the floor of the warehouse and started tying, his magic did more than half the work for him. The strands twisted around one another obligingly, like they had minds of their own. And since the nets were unbreakable, they didn't suffer from wear and tear.

It wasn't long before Pennyroyal, a little less polite than some of the others, said, "Honey, you've got to stop. The nets are fabulous, but we've already got more than we need."

Even as she said it, the Strongwoman was hauling nets full of shrieking crows and honking geese. All the birds they caught had to be released somewhere far away from civilization so that they could recover from whatever Victoria had done to them.

Micah kept sneaking behind stacks of doors to make more nets anyway, just in case Pennyroyal was wrong. And when he wasn't busy with that, he was trying to reach the overlay.

He'd even gotten Jenny involved. They'd talked several times since the attack on Peal, and when Micah ran out of ideas for methods to try, she came up with some new ones.

Closing his eyes, holding them open until he couldn't stand it anymore, wearing tinted glasses, sleeping with his backpack full of knot bracelets on top of his face, drinking six mugs of coffee, dangling upside down from one of Porter's door frames so that the blood would rush to his brain—none of it worked.

The last time they'd spoken, Jenny had crammed a book on meditation through the mail slot, in case that might help.

"Thanks, Jenny," he said. "How are things in Peal?"

"Almost back to normal," she said. "People aren't even talking about it much anymore."

"Really?" Micah said, his mood brightening. The attack on Peal had been the biggest one. If his old hometown could recover, then maybe other places could, too.

"Really," Jenny confirmed. "And did I tell you I got a call from the Sisterhood the other day? Just out of the blue."

"What about?" Micah knew Jenny had met Pennyroyal, Thuja, and some of the others when they went to help Peal, but he didn't know why anyone would be calling her now.

"Apparently they fund educational programs for kids all over the world. The programs don't have anything to do with magic, but they sound amazing. The Sisterhood even sponsors a summer camp. It's not too far from here. They called to say if I wanted a scholarship, I was a shoo-in."

"Jenny, that's great! Do you think your parents—?"

"I don't know," Jenny sighed. "They were so mad about my trip to the circus last summer, but I *think* they're over it now. And they appreciated how the Strongwomen helped us out."

"I hoped they would let you come back here this summer," Micah admitted.

"I guess we'll see," Jenny said. "What about you guys? Any luck figuring out Victoria's master plan yet?"

Micah shook his head. Nobody at Circus Mirandus could understand why Victoria kept up her attacks when they obviously weren't luring the circus out of hiding. One theory was that she was just too hateful and too stubborn to give up. Another was that she had some scheme to find one of Porter's Doors and breach the circus that way.

"I don't see how that would work," Porter said when it was brought up. "It would be a suicide mission on her part."

It did sound far-fetched. The Strongfolk were always the first through a Door, so even if Victoria knew where one was she'd end up facing down Thuja's bow or Bowler's fists.

And Porter had assured Micah that he could close Doors quickly.

"It's hard to hold them *open*," he said. "They want to be closed, and I pity whatever, or whoever, is stuck in one when it does."

"What would happen?"

"I'm not sure," Porter had replied, gazing at the painted metal door they were using to reach the latest town under attack. "I've never hated anyone enough to try it."

27

LONDON

As the end of March approached, the situation improved. The attacks became less frequent, and the flock Victoria called to each town grew smaller. In at least one case, she even lost control of her birds. A few minutes into the attack, they turned on one another instead of the people in the city below, then flew off, scattering in different directions.

Despite these encouraging developments, Micah felt like Victoria was a stone laid across his shoulders, the weight of her growing heavier and heavier as the days passed. Nobody had come close to catching her. No one had even seen her.

And though things were better, it only meant he had to wait for three days, or five, before hearing the same bad news all over again. Children were swarmed by ravens at a birthday party. Songbirds flung themselves into the path of floats at a parade.

Micah was afraid Victoria would never be caught, that she would exist in the background for the whole of his life, vanishing for days or weeks only to return as soon as he let down his guard.

He went to Porter's every day to stare at whatever Door the response team had disappeared through last. Unless the Lightbender caught him before he got there. The illusionist would give him comic books to read and chores to do and gentle reminders that the world was moving on without him while he wasted away in a dark warehouse.

"Why don't you make friends with some of the children here?" the Lightbender said. "Or offer to give them tours of the circus! You have a unique perspective to share."

This last suggestion was almost tempting.

Only months ago, Micah would have relished the chance to be a Circus Mirandus tour guide. And it wasn't as if he could do it any time he pleased. He would be a poor guide once the circus moved on to a country where he didn't speak the language. They'd only stayed so long in England because of Porter, who couldn't move the whole circus and send groups of fighting magicians across the Atlantic at the same time.

So, on one unseasonably frigid morning, Micah tried following his guardian's advice. He collected a gaggle of younger kids and spent a couple hours showing them around, giving them inside information about every tent, animal, and magician they encountered.

But he found he was awkward around them. They were so happy and wonderstruck, clapping their mittened hands at every new spark of magic they saw. And Micah was worried about so many things. It made him feel tired and somehow alien, and he worried he might say something to spoil their fun. He left them watching the shapeshifters and went again to the warehouse, hoping for news that would cheer him up.

He arrived to find Porter huddled in one of the rocking chairs that usually sat in his living room, while Yuri tried to force-feed him a piece of baklava. The chef had been supplying the away teams with food ever since the attack on Peal. He seemed to be feeling every bit as frazzled and helpless as Micah.

Yuri was always hovering around looking agonized, as if he expected dead bodies to fall through the Doors the second Porter opened them. When Porter inevitably got frustrated and pointed out that he was in the way, Yuri would apologize and leave, only to return half an hour later with a tray full of sushi or pot stickers or bread rolls stuffed with stewed lamb.

As Micah approached, the chef dropped the baklava back on a tray and reached for a brownie. Neither magician had spotted Micah yet, and he froze a few yards away when Porter suddenly snapped, *"Stop it!"*

Micah had never heard Porter speak so harshly. He was holding up his hand to fend off the brownie.

Yuri drooped. His ponytail hung limp and tangled down his back, and he was shaking as he set the tray of food on the small table beside Porter's chair.

"I'm sorry, Yuri," Porter sighed, rubbing his face with both hands. He hadn't been shaving regularly, and he had the beginnings of a beard. "I didn't mean to yell at you. Forgive me, my friend. But also, quit feeding me."

"I do not know what else to do?" Yuri's shoulders hunched.

Porter patted his arm. "I know," he said. "But I feel like I'm being fattened for slaughter. You don't have to cook or make excuses to stay here. Just take a seat and stop feeling guilty."

Yuri wrung his hands. "I should be helping the others with the battle?" he said softly. "My magic . . . I cannot manage it?"

Porter rocked back in his chair. "You can," he said. "You just need to practice. Hiding in the kitchen and talking in questions because you're afraid of your power is no way to spend your life."

"How am *I* supposed to practice?" Yuri said, a note of deep frustration in his voice.

"*Carefully,*" said Porter. "With a great deal of fore-thought and a willingness to make a few mistakes. It's not as though you're the first of us with a difficult and dangerous magic. You might talk to the Lightbender or Firesleight about the trouble they caused when they were starting out."

Micah really wanted to know what kind of mistakes a young Lightbender might have made, and he was more curious than ever about Yuri's talent. But what kind of friend would he be if he found out this way?

"Hi!" he said loudly, smiling and waving as if he'd just walked into the room.

Yuri jumped and spun around, gaping at Micah like he'd never seen him before.

Porter didn't seem surprised, though. "Hello, Micah," he said. "You can't be here."

"What?" Micah was startled. "But I'm always here."

"Exactly," said Porter. "Rosebud *and* your guardian *and* the manager have come by this morning to make sure you aren't moping around my warehouse. If you're not going to attend lessons, we'll have to find something else for you to do that doesn't involve sitting here like an unhappy lump for hours on end."

Mr. Head had come by? Himself? Micah didn't know whether he should be flattered or alarmed.

Porter looked between him and Yuri. "Honestly, you two are turning into hermits. It's been *months* since you left the circus, Micah. And it's perfectly safe here in England, so you don't have any excuse. And Yuri! You haven't been anywhere in . . ." Porter trailed off, frowning. "*Have* you been anywhere lately?"

"Yes?" said Yuri, sounding worried. "I went to Moscow to see my mother?"

Porter stared at him. "That was four years ago."

Micah found himself staring, too.

Of course, being younger than all the other adult magicians at the circus, Yuri must still have family and friends in the outside world. Micah couldn't imagine going four *years* without seeing Jenny. And though he didn't remember his own mother well, he was sure if she were still alive, he would want to visit her all the time.

Porter stood up and pointed at the two of them. "Travel is good for the soul," he said. "And it's good for getting you two out in the fresh air. Have you ever been to London? It's a great city. And here we find ourselves practically on top of it!"

"I do not want to go to London?" said Yuri.

"I need to stay here in case something happens with the battle," said Micah.

"I'm glad you're both so enthusiastic," said Porter. He headed over to a bright purple door that was propped against a nearby stack. "You're going to have so much fun! I'm jealous of you, really, getting to take a day off to explore."

He grabbed the purple door and maneuvered it toward one of the few empty frames he had left. It was at the end of the warehouse, near the entrance, and neither Micah nor Yuri followed him.

"Is he going to *make* us leave?" Micah asked the chef.

Yuri didn't answer. He was just standing there wild-eyed, as if he'd been told the purple door led straight into the heart of a nuclear reactor instead of a neighboring city.

Porter let the door hit the floor with a thud that echoed through the warehouse. "It's either London for the afternoon or Tahiti until all this wretchedness is over," he called. "I would choose Tahiti. But then, *I'm* sensible."

Micah didn't think Porter would actually send him to the South Pacific while everyone else dealt with Victoria, but he wasn't one hundred percent sure. The magician had been under a lot of pressure lately.

"I've always wanted to see London," he said.

"That's the spirit!" Porter beckoned him toward the door. "Yuri?"

Yuri didn't move.

"Suit yourself." Porter shrugged. "But Micah's going to London right now. This very minute. With or without adult supervision."

Yuri looked alarmed. "The Lightbender will not like it if he goes alone?"

"Not at all," Porter said cheerfully. "But you're the one who's going to have to explain it to him."

The Door opened into a shop that sold fancy crystal and ceramic figurines. When it slammed shut behind Micah and Yuri, hundreds of delicate ornaments tinkled against one another on their shelves.

A pointy-nosed shopkeeper, who had been nestling a

porcelain chicken into its proper place, rounded on the two of them. "What was that about?" he asked, glaring.

"Sorry," said Micah. "The wind caught the door."

"That's a pretty chicken?" said Yuri. "This is a nice store?"

Micah heard the polite note in Yuri's voice and understood he was offering a compliment. But judging by the confused expression on the shopkeeper's face, that wasn't obvious if you weren't used to the way Yuri talked.

Micah grabbed the chef's arm. "We were looking for a different shop," he said, opening the purple door and pulling Yuri out onto a city sidewalk. "We got lost."

He shut the door behind them—carefully—and looked around.

They were on a bustling street, lined with cars and delivery vans, and as it always did when he first stepped outside the circus, the change in atmosphere surprised him. The smells he'd become so accustomed to were gone—no chocolate or smoke or sweet hay. And no musical undercurrent filled the air. Instead, he heard the sounds of traffic and people talking on their phones and a bell chiming as a woman exited the florist's shop next door.

The day was chilly, and the sky was gray, but at least Micah had put on his peacoat this morning before he gave the kids their tour. Yuri was in short sleeves, and he wore a flour-dusted apron over his jeans.

Micah pointed at the apron. "Shouldn't you take that off?"

Yuri looked down at himself and groaned. "I wasn't prepared for traveling?"

Neither was Micah. This became apparent when they decided to make the best of their situation by exploring the shops, only to realize money was going to be a problem. All they had was a five-dollar bill Micah had stuck in his coat pocket at some point. It was the same as having no money at all, since London shopkeepers understandably didn't want to be paid in American dollars.

Porter had said he'd pick them up at sunset, which was at least seven hours away by Yuri's reckoning, and they had nothing to do.

"We could find a museum to hang out in?" Micah suggested after they tired of window-shopping.

They set out looking for a museum, in no particular hurry and with no particular direction. Micah didn't feel like asking someone for help, and Yuri definitely wasn't going to. The chef hadn't spoken to anyone since the porcelain chicken incident. When groups of people passed by the two of them, he pressed his lips together as if he thought words might burst free without his permission.

"Are you okay?" Micah said finally.

"I don't want to make mistakes?"

Micah hesitated before asking, "Is your magic really that dangerous?"

Yuri nodded.

Micah felt bad for him. He could sense all his bracelets against his arm right now, and it was a good feeling.

The memories were warm and vibrant, and the emergency bracelets were comforting. The locator knot on his ring finger gave a light but steady tug toward the northwest—reaching for Fish in his aquarium at the heart of the circus.

"It's not always terrible?" Yuri said, an earnest expression on his face. "But it's hard to catch? The magic gets away from me, and it will not stop?"

Micah was baffled. "What? Is it like a pet or something?"

Yuri shook his head. "My words sound true to people? And I can't make them sound untrue after I have said them?"

Micah still didn't get it. Wouldn't it be a positive thing, for people to believe whatever you said?

They turned the corner onto a short, one-way street. It was quieter here, with only a few parked cars and no people around except for a woman who had just stepped out of a hotel.

Micah had more questions, but he knew Yuri wouldn't answer with someone standing close enough to hear them. The woman was thumbing her cell phone, staring at the screen, and she barely glanced up as the two of them passed.

Micah would decide, later, that he'd made a mistake. If he'd only kept walking, if he hadn't looked in her direction . . .

It took him three steps to realize who he had just seen, and when he did, he stopped breathing. His legs locked him in place. Though his mind was suddenly running at full speed, screaming for him to *do something*, *say something, warn Yuri*, his body wouldn't cooperate.

Yuri stopped beside him. "What's wrong?"

Micah stared back over his shoulder.

The woman appeared to be middle-aged, and she was stylishly dressed. She had pulled her blond hair back in a tidy bun. Her oversized gray scarf was arranged in elegant swoops over the front of a dark blue dress.

The scarf matched her eyes. Micah knew this because she was looking right at him.

For a long moment, she didn't seem to know him. Then, her mouth opened in surprise. Her phone tumbled from her grasp and smacked onto the pavement. She slapped one hand over her scarf, almost as if she were clutching at her heart, but when she dropped her arm a split second later, she held a small green bird that glimmered in her palm like a jewel.

She whistled a single, high note, and the bird shot toward Micah and Yuri, moving so fast that it blurred.

Micah jerked back, but the bird hadn't been aimed at him. The tiny creature plunged its sharp beak into the side of Yuri's neck, and Micah realized with shock that it was a hummingbird. It zipped up and away, leaving a bead of bright red blood against Yuri's skin.

The magician didn't seem to understand what had happened. He raised his hand toward his neck. And then he went still. His eyes were half shut, as if he'd been in the middle of a blink, and his mouth was wide, forming the shape of some question.

"Hello, Micah darling!" said Victoria. Her shoes hit the ground with sharp little taps as she approached.

Micah wanted to run. He wanted to hit her. He wanted to shout for the Lightbender and Grandpa Ephraim and every good person he'd ever known.

But Yuri? What about Yuri? Micah couldn't leave him.

Victoria smiled, and some ridiculous part of Micah's brain informed him that it was a nice smile. It didn't look fake.

She stretched up and pressed her hand to the center of Yuri's forehead. She gave a push, and the magician toppled over, not a single joint bending on the way down. He hit the pavement hard and lay there.

Micah wasn't even sure he was breathing.

"They say it's better to be lucky than good." Victoria sounded so calm. Like attacking people in the middle of the street was no more startling than saying good morning. "Of course, it's best to be both."

She nudged Yuri with the tip of her shoe and smiled sunnily at his still body.

Then she looped her arm through Micah's, as though they were dear friends. He tried to pull away, and her grip tightened just enough to show she didn't mean to let him.

"What did you do to him?" Micah's voice shook. He was surprised he'd managed to say anything at all. He felt like there was nothing in his lungs but dust.

"Oh, he'll be fine," she said. "He's only paralyzed temporarily thanks to my pretty friend here."

She looked up at the green hummingbird, which was flitting around them. It stopped suddenly and flew back into her scarf to hide.

"Come along, darling." She gave Micah's arm another squeeze. "We need to catch up on the last . . . eleven years? I was just on my way to lunch."

Micah stared at her. "I'm not going anywhere with you!"

He would fling himself onto the sidewalk first. He would scream for help.

Her face darkened. "Don't be such a child."

"Get *away* from—"

"Careful." Her fingers dug into his arm, and she pulled him toward her. They were so close he could see the faint lines in the makeup around her eyes. "Have you ever seen a dire hawk slaughter its prey?"

They drop them, thought Micah. He couldn't say it out loud.

"They always choose *exactly* the right height," she murmured. "Just far enough to kill without making a mess."

Micah didn't hear the bird. He didn't even realize it had arrived until it landed beside them, so quiet it might have been a ghost. The hawk was huge—bigger than the cars parked along the narrow street. But its feathers blended in with the sidewalk and the buildings so perfectly that it was more of a shadow than anything else.

Only its bright yellow eyes stood out. There was a rage in them that pierced Micah like a blade.

He gasped and reached for Yuri, already knowing there

was nothing he could do against a beast that size, but Victoria dragged him back as the hawk wrapped the paralyzed magician in talons as long as Micah's arm. It took off with a single beat of its wings, lifting Yuri up and over the buildings.

"Don't hurt him," Micah said. "Please don't hurt him."

Victoria had her back to the dire hawk. Apparently, she didn't need to see the bird's progress to control it. Instead, she was studying Micah.

When the Bird Woman had appeared in Micah's nightmares, he had always imagined her to be a hateful, angry version of the person he'd seen in his grandfather's old photographs. He had pictured a terrible, cackling monster dropping out of the sky with a cloud of cawing minions at her back.

But the look she was giving him now wasn't hatred. It was more like he was a stray cat she'd found, and she was deciding if she wanted to take him home.

"I didn't recognize your friend," she said, her voice pleasant once again. "He must be new at the circus. What kind of magic does he do?"

She asked the question so casually.

But Micah knew.

If he said the wrong thing, Yuri was dead.

"He works in the kitchens." He tried to sound normal, tried not to blink. "We came to pick up groceries."

Victoria narrowed her eyes at him.

"Well, everyone loves a kitchen magician," she said

after a moment. "Do they still make those sugar whistles on Fridays? Those were always my favorites."

Micah wouldn't let himself breathe a sigh of relief.

"Come on then." She gave his arm a sharp yank. "We have *so many* things to talk about."

They set out, and Micah craned his neck, searching the sky for the dire hawk. They had turned the corner onto a busier street by the time he managed to spot it. The bird had landed on the flat roof of a building less than a block away.

Micah swallowed. The building was only a few stories tall, but if it decided to drop Yuri . . .

A few stories would be, as Victoria had said, just far enough.

28

LUNCH DATE

Micah couldn't use his emergency bracelets.

He wanted to. Badly. If ever there had been an emergency, this was it, and Micah knew the Lightbender would expect him to do as they had agreed.

But they had never counted on a situation quite like this.

Micah had no way to explain to his guardian that, while he was in trouble, Yuri was in *much worse* trouble and would have to be rescued first. If help arrived for Micah and not for Yuri, Victoria could order the dire hawk to drop him.

And that was assuming Victoria didn't get suspicious when he untied the bracelets in the first place. She still had a tight grip on his arm. She was sure to notice, and when she did, she might decide to kill *both* of them before rescue could come.

So. Something else.

He could run, but Victoria could fly.

Micah looked up at the sky. The gray clouds blanketing the city might hide hundreds of her birds. The magical flock, Micah was guessing, since it hadn't been spotted at any of the North American attacks. And even if it was only the other two dire hawks up there, how much damage could they do in a place like this?

This was London. *Millions* of people lived here. With their magical camouflage, the dire hawks might pluck pedestrians right off the street without anyone noticing.

A round-cheeked woman pushing a baby stroller down the sidewalk smiled at Micah and Victoria as they passed, and Micah forced the corners of his mouth up. He didn't want any innocent bystanders to suspect that he needed help. What if the woman realized he was in trouble and tried to intervene? What if Victoria hurt her and her baby?

Micah didn't doubt she would do it.

"Almost there!" Victoria said in a chipper voice. "I think you'll love this place. You eat French, don't you?"

Micah had never met an evil mastermind before, but he was pretty sure they weren't supposed to behave the way his grandmother did.

Wasn't she supposed to say something like, "Join me, or die?"

Shouldn't she threaten to break his arms if he didn't tell her where the circus was?

At first, Micah had even suspected she might take him

into a quiet alleyway and order some razor-beaked bird of prey to rip out his throat.

But no. Victoria Starling was strolling along, talking about pointless things—her broken cell phone, an expensive purse she liked in a shop window, her mansion in Nova Scotia, powerful friends she'd made over the years.

And she seemed to think the two of them were going to sit down and have lunch together.

It's a cruel joke, Micah thought. *She's going to feed me to her dragon. Or question me about the circus.*

But now she was explaining to Micah that he must be on his best behavior. It was a fancy place they were going to, and of course he hadn't been included on her original reservation. She didn't want him to embarrass her.

"No one likes an ill-mannered child in a fine restaurant," she concluded.

Micah thought she was lying right up until the moment she dragged him toward the door of a restaurant with a French name written on the sign in fancy script.

Micah stared at her as she reached for the door. "What is *wrong* with you?" he demanded. "Yuri is—"

"Who?"

"The kitchen magician. My friend."

"What about him?" Victoria said, impatient. "The dire hawk will sit on him like he's a good little egg, and you and I will have a pleasant luncheon."

"I'm not hungry."

Victoria shrugged one shoulder. "Suit yourself, but I

always eat a nice meal before a battle, and I won't have any time for you later. So."

She pulled him inside.

Micah was surprised that the atmosphere in the restaurant didn't shift when he and Victoria walked in. He was so on edge himself that he thought others must surely feel it, too.

But nobody looked up from their menus. None of the conversations stopped.

It was a small and elegant place where well-dressed people sat around tables draped with bright white cloth. They were talking in soft voices, laughing now and then.

Danger had stalked into the room, and everyone was still exclaiming over their entrees.

I didn't think it would feel like this.

Micah had imagined meeting Victoria. He had imagined fighting her with his magic and his fists. He had thought he would be furious and scared and determined. And he was, but . . .

He looked around at this room full of everyday people. He stared into the faces of these adults who wouldn't be able to help him at all when Victoria finally finished playing her strange game and turned violent. And he felt so utterly, wrenchingly *alone.*

It's up to you now. Keep them all safe. Think of something.

"May I take your coat?" said a polite voice. It was the woman who greeted customers.

Micah shook his head. "I'm fine." He forced another smile. "Thanks."

He had stuffed a roll of twine and a few pieces of string in his coat pockets that morning, and now they were the closest things he had to weapons.

They were seated, and Micah tried to behave normally while their waiter fussed with the glasses and napkins. As soon as he left them to study their menus, Micah said, "I'm not going to tell you where the circus is."

Victoria didn't even look at him. "I've known it was near London for a couple of weeks now. Smart of them— moving it here. It's so difficult for the Man Who Bends Light when they settle in cities. I didn't expect it."

Micah went cold. *Maybe she's bluffing. Maybe it's a test, and she doesn't really know.*

"They're not anywhere near here," he said. "They're hundreds of miles away."

Victoria set her menu on top of her plate.

"You're determined," she said. "And not the worst liar I've ever met. Useful qualities, though wasted in this case. I know exactly where the circus is thanks to the mousebirds. Odd little things. I've never been able to control them, but I can sense them when I'm near enough."

She took a sip of water and smiled at him over the rim of the glass. "I can be there in five minutes by air, when I'm ready."

The waiter returned, and Victoria ordered three courses off the menu. Micah had never looked at his own copy, and the tiny print swam across the page when he tried.

Five minutes by air. Even if he did get word to them somehow, five minutes wasn't enough time to evacuate all the children. *A plan. You need a plan.*

When the waiter turned to Micah, he thought of asking if it might be possible for the cook to poison Victoria's food. Instead, he pointed randomly at a few things. The man raised his eyebrows and whisked the menu away.

"To business, Micah darling," said Victoria as soon as he was gone. "I have a proposition for you! I thought we'd lost the opportunity when I found out you'd gone to the circus, but here we find ourselves by happy chance. Tell me—your magic? Is it the same as Ephraim's?"

"All I can do is tie knots," said Micah.

Victoria nodded. "Good old Gertie said as much when I visited her, but I wanted to be sure. You see, I was rather hoping my grandson might have taken after me."

"I didn't."

The Inventor was right, he thought. *She wanted someone to help her control her birds.*

"Well, no matter," said Victoria, tapping her fingernail absentmindedly against her glass. "You're family after all. Have you put much thought into your future? I suppose you must have considered joining the circus on a permanent basis. Immortality is quite the job perk, I admit, but what good is it, if you're a slave to a ridiculous purpose for the whole of your life?"

"The circus isn't ridiculous," Micah said.

Victoria smirked. "You think not? What would you call it then? Geoffrey could blackmail every businessman in the world. Rosebud's potions could make her a billionaire. The Man Who Bends Light could topple governments. And what do they do instead?"

Micah knew how powerful the magicians of Circus Mirandus were, but he'd never thought about it like this. In terms of governments and money and—

"They fritter their endless days away, putting on pretty shows for children."

"They're putting *magic* into the world. They give people—"

Hope, he was going to say. He'd seen it himself. He'd felt it. Something about visiting Circus Mirandus made you believe that no matter how bad things were in the outside world, there was still a chance for them to turn out all right.

But Victoria didn't let him finish.

"It's practically a crime! The way they waste themselves—slaving away for the sake of *inspiring* and *nurturing* and *listening* to a parade of human children who will grow up to become every bit as insignificant as the countless generations that came before them."

Human children, thought Micah, as if Victoria imagined there was some other kind.

"Do you know how rare magicians are? How precious our power is?" She pointed at him. Her fingernails were painted a pale shade of peach.

Micah's heart beat fast. Victoria was clearly working

herself up now, and he didn't want her to *do* anything. Not here with all these people sitting so close.

"Do you know how many people can command more than a *million* birds from the other side of the world?" She let her hand fall onto the table hard. The glasses rattled.

Micah jumped in his seat.

Victoria blinked, and then laughed lightly, as if nothing she'd just said was that important.

Micah was thinking frantically. She couldn't possibly control birds from so far away, could she? Nowhere would be safe.

"A million."

When Victoria's smile widened, he realized he'd said the number aloud.

"Impressive, isn't it? And all for the sake of a little distraction. I learned how to do it from the Man Who Bends Light."

"The Lightbender wouldn't teach you anything." Micah said it quietly, but with absolute conviction. "He wouldn't help you."

Victoria's eyes narrowed into slits, and he thought for a moment that contradicting her might be an unforgivable mistake. But after a pause, she went on as if nothing had happened.

"No. He certainly didn't *mean* to help me. He has no ambition beyond performing tricks for snotty brats. And when I tried to show him how unimportant his precious circus is, how small it is in the grand scheme, he tortured me for it."

Micah thought torture was an extreme description. Victoria had been soaring around her tent, slaughtering birds for sport and crashing them into an audience full of little kids. All the Lightbender had done was illusion her into thinking she'd forgotten how to fly.

But when Victoria spoke next, there was a vicious undercurrent in her voice.

"He told me I was falling from the sky." Her eyes burned with the memory. "I, who have *never* fallen. And he poured so much magic into the illusion that I couldn't look away from it. Not for years. He stamped his lie deep in my mind so that every time I tried to fly the terror overcame me. He made me think I was nothing. He made me think I was *human*."

Micah held himself very still in his seat. It was ludicrous for Victoria to keep saying the word *human* like it was a dirty species that didn't have anything to do with her. But he knew if he argued right now, she would hurt him for it.

"I thought I would never be myself again. I left the circus and met Ephraim. Played at being a mother to Gertrudis. Gave birth to your father. But inside of me . . . oh, can you imagine the despair, Micah? Of knowing that you had such power and it had been taken from you? It was a kind of death."

It would be terrible to lose his magic, but Micah didn't think it would be anything at all like dying.

"I learned from it," Victoria said, drawing in a deep breath. "I learned how a strong enough command can warp a mind so that it remains obedient *long* after it has left the magician's influence. And I practiced once I regained my powers, so that I could do it, too."

She sighed. "No more sweet songs for the Bird Woman, but so much more impact. Of course, the trick won't work on most of the magical species. They have to be handled directly. But ordinary flocks can be so easily overwhelmed. They'll continue following my instructions even though they haven't seen me in weeks. Oh! Appetizers!"

Their waiter had appeared with plates.

So that's how she did it, Micah thought, staring down at the food that had been placed in front of him. Apparently, he'd ordered a salad, though the leaves and nuts and tiny drops of vinegar had been arranged until they looked more like abstract art than lunch. A poached egg was nestled in the middle of it all, oozing yolk.

"Aren't you going to eat?" Victoria said. A bowl of pale soup steamed in front of her.

Micah made himself take a bite. He felt like he was trying to swallow paper.

She tucked into her soup, and he tried to use the few minutes of quiet to work out an escape plan. He stuffed salad and egg into his mouth without paying attention, chewing mechanically, and he thought, *It's important to do things in the right order.*

First, sever Victoria's connection to the dire hawk. Hope it doesn't eat Yuri out of spite. Second, use the emergency bracelets. Last, run as fast as you can toward the Door.

The bracelets were easy. And Micah thought he knew his way back to the china shop he and Yuri had arrived in.

Porter would have the Door open the instant he called for help.

But breaking Victoria's connection to the dire hawk was going to be a problem.

"Conflagration's a brute," Victoria admitted, digging a spoon into a dish of ice cream. "But he's *my* brute. Do you have any idea how much a dragon can eat? Feeding him has been a full-time job."

Micah was letting his own dessert melt in his bowl. He had been trying to distract Victoria with questions the whole meal, hoping she would go off on such a long monologue that he would have time to find the overlay he'd seen when he collapsed Porter's Door. If he could just touch the connection that tied Victoria to the dire hawk, he could free the bird. But he couldn't focus his mind.

He'd learned more than he ever cared to know about his grandmother over the past hour or so, and he hadn't caught even a glimmer of light at the corner of his vision. He was beginning to think he was taking the wrong tactic altogether.

He crossed his eyes, hoping that might help, and Victoria said, "What are you doing?"

Time. He just needed time. *Ask another question. Ask a whole bunch of them.*

"So, is that why you attacked the circus when we were

going through the Door in Argentina?" he said, trying to match the overly friendly tone Victoria was so fond of using. "You wanted a unicorn to feed to Conflagration? So that he would be able to fly and help you get revenge on all of us? Or do you only want to kill the Lightbender?"

Micah figured he knew the answer to these questions. And he couldn't believe the Bird Woman seriously thought he might join her "little team," which apparently consisted of Victoria herself and the dragon. She believed that Conflagration would be more controllable when he grew his wings, but for now, she seemed to think of him as a large and badly behaved dog.

Victoria pursed her lips. "I hope you weren't frightened by the attack. It wasn't intended to hurt anyone at the circus, you know. And I had no idea you were even there."

Micah didn't answer. He was staring deeply into his bowl of ice cream, trying to see anything at all but melted dairy.

She sighed. "No wonder you don't want to join me. You seem to think my goals are so common."

Connections, thought Micah. *Knots. Rivers and streams of light. Come on, please?*

"Well, there's no harm in letting you see the big picture now, I suppose. Conflagration's already in position. Micah, darling, I'm not out for *revenge*. And I hope you don't imagine me to be some cinema villain bent on world domination. Revenge is for backward thinkers, and conquest is for people with wounded egos and too much free time. What I want is much simpler."

Her spoon clinked against the side of her bowl.

"What I want," she said, her voice fervent, "is something new. A fresh start. A big, bright, and shining chance to make my mark on things again. Oh, darling, you don't know how hard it is, to reach old age and find yourself facing down obscurity. I should have *been* somebody—a name on every human tongue, a song in every mortal heart. And I would have been . . . but I have had to spend all my life in hiding for fear that the circus would come after me. No more. Soon, so very soon, I will be more powerful than ever before, and I will have something that not even the manager, not even the Man Who Bends Light, can take away from me."

So passionate was this speech, so filled with longing, that Micah couldn't help but stare at her. "What are you even talking about?"

Victoria's lips curved up at the edges. "You're so young," she murmured. "Micah, I'm talking about starting over. About reinventing myself. About putting my name in lights for all the world to admire. All I need is a big enough idea."

And, finally, Micah understood what Victoria wanted. What she'd wanted all this time. "Fish," he said. "You want Fish."

That lightning strike last summer—it had been aimed at

the center of the menagerie for a reason. If Fish's tank had been damaged, the Inventor might have taken it away for repair. Fish would have been vulnerable.

And when that hadn't worked, Victoria had used the blizzard. She'd known it would prompt the circus to move. The dire hawk hadn't been going after Terpsichore that day after all. It had been trying for the aquarium on the Inventor's tool belt.

Victoria didn't *want* to fight the circus. She'd wanted to snatch Fish without doing battle at all.

Then, Micah realized something else. Victoria might not want to fight, but she was willing to. She was prepared for it. The dragon and the huge magical flock were her backup plan in case everything else failed.

"I told you," said Victoria, dabbing her mouth with her napkin, "you have entirely the wrong impression of me. I'm not some frightful boogeywoman. I'm a visionary. The Idea will choose some random nobody if left to its own devices. It belongs in the hands of a magician. When its time comes, if I am the only one nearby, it will have no other choice to make."

The locator knot on Micah's finger was still tugging toward the northwest. *Not Fish,* he thought. *Not that.*

Fish had waited his whole life for his Someone. He had done everything he was supposed to do. He was here because he was meant to make the world a better place.

And Victoria wanted to steal his power for herself. She wanted all of that inspiration and magic to be hers, so that she could have one last shot at glory, and she didn't care what it cost everyone else.

"That's why you'll have to wait a while to join up with me," she was saying now, motioning for the waiter to bring the bill. "I hope you understand. I can't have anyone else around confusing the Idea or taking a portion of its power. I'll contact you again after the Moment has passed. Just stay out of my way today. This will all be over in a few hours, and as long as you don't interfere, I'll consider us allies."

She said the last part as if Micah had already sworn an oath of fealty to her. He opened his mouth to tell her exactly what he thought of being her ally, but then the rest of what she'd said registered.

"What do you mean *a few hours*?"

Victoria reached into some hidden fold of her enormous scarf and threw a handful of money on the table.

"Well, I can't hold off any longer," she said in a reasonable voice. "Not now that you and your kitchen friend have seen me. Better to get a move on anyway. I've only been dawdling these past few days out of nerves."

"You're going to attack Circus Mirandus *now*?" he said. "Like, right now, this minute?"

Victoria winked at him and stood up. "Five-minute flight. Sorry, but I'm going to have to leave you here."

Out of time. Forget the plan.

Micah stood up, too. "My magic isn't quite the same as Grandpa Ephraim's."

Victoria tilted her head. "What do you mean?"

He leaned across the table as if he were going to whisper in her ear. Victoria leaned in as well.

"You should've wondered," said Micah. "You should've cared enough to wonder what happened to your storm petrel."

Victoria's eyes widened, but Micah's fingers were already wrapped around her scarf.

Tighten up, he thought.

29

FIVE MINUTES BY AIR

Micah hadn't planned it, but he *had* meant it. The scarf tightened around Victoria's neck in an instant, and she staggered back from the table, her hands clutching at the layers of soft gray fabric. She pulled at it, trying to free herself, but the giant scarf tightened even more.

Victoria's pale face was turning red.

People in the restaurant shouted as they realized something was wrong. The waiter and the woman who'd offered to take Micah's coat ran toward the table. Someone was calling for an ambulance. Someone else was babbling about the Heimlich maneuver.

That won't help her, Micah thought.

He realized he still had his arm stretched out toward his grandmother, and as she fell to her knees, scrabbling at the scarf so frantically that her painted nails left bloody scratches on her cheeks, he lowered it.

I should save her. Numbness seeped into him as he realized what he'd done. *I don't want to see someone else die.*

But then he thought of Terpsichore with scratches from a dire hawk's talons on her flanks. He thought of Bowler, bruised and broken on the ground. He thought, *darling* and *humans* and *five-minute flight.*

And he took a step back. Away from Victoria.

He reached under the sleeve of his coat and hooked a finger through his emergency bracelets—all of them—and pulled hard. He felt the *snap.*

The waiter was kneeling over Victoria, yanking on the scarf. Her face was turning purple. *So fast.* It hadn't even been a minute.

Her eyes met Micah's. She looked afraid.

I could . . .

What? He couldn't let her go. He couldn't stand here and watch her die. Where was the Lightbender? Where was someone who would tell him the right thing to do?

Victoria's movements were slowing. She was still fighting the scarf, but weakly now.

And then Micah saw it—a flutter against her cheek. There was a little ball of desperate movement, a live thing trapped inside the scarf's folds.

The hummingbird, Micah thought. *I'm killing it, too.*

It was too much.

I don't want this. I don't.

He felt something loosen in his mind and knew it was the scarf. But he didn't stay to see what happened next. He ran, shoving past people, bumping into a table. He knocked over a glass and heard it shatter, and then he was out the door, on the sidewalk, his shoes slapping against the pavement.

Micah was running as fast as he could, and he wasn't sure what scared him more. Victoria? Or himself?

Micah expected the clouds to break open. He expected to be lifted off his feet and hauled into the air by huge grasping talons. Or the hummingbird—surely the hummingbird would come after him, and a quick jab from its beak would send him crashing to the ground.

But Micah ran and ran, his feet carrying him toward the place he'd last seen the dire hawk, and though people called out in confusion or annoyance as he dashed by them, nobody tried to stop him.

And above him was nothing but lifeless sky.

"Micah!"

He whirled at the sound of his name, his momentum making him stumble, and he raised his fists, ready to hit and kick and scream if he had to. But then he saw who had shouted.

"Yuri!"

The magician was clinging to a lamppost. His T-shirt was soaked in blood, and his face was frighteningly white. Micah had run right past him.

He hurried back, panicked. "Yuri, what—?"

"The bird put me down. And then it flew away." Yuri leaned toward Micah. His eyes seemed to be having trouble focusing. "I don't know why."

"I strangled Victoria with her scarf," Micah said quickly. He scanned Yuri's bloody chest and abdomen, trying to find the wound. It had to be bad if the magician wasn't remembering to talk in questions. "Where are you hurt?"

"*Strangled!*"

"Yuri, where?!"

"Shoulder," Yuri grunted. "One of its claws."

Micah saw it then. The dire hawk's talon had torn a hole in Yuri's shirt and left a deep puncture in his shoulder. Blood was flowing freely from the injury.

"We have to get to the Door," said Micah. "Right now. Victoria's going to attack the circus."

Yuri swayed.

"Yuri?" Micah said frantically. "Do you understand me?"

"Yes."

"Okay, come on." He reached for the arm on Yuri's uninjured side and threw it over his shoulder. "We have to hurry."

Yuri staggered, and Micah barely managed to catch his weight.

"Sorry," said Yuri. "I'm sorry."

They made it a few painful steps before a woman in a business suit saw them and gasped, "Oh my g—"

"Everything's fine!" Micah panted, half dragging Yuri forward. "Just get out of our way."

"Victoria is attacking?" Yuri whispered to Micah as the woman hurried toward them. "You are sure about this?"

"*Yes,*" said Micah, adjusting Yuri's arm over his shoulders. "In minutes."

He didn't know if he'd bought them time with the scarf, but even if he had, it couldn't have been much.

Yuri closed his eyes. He was taking fast, shallow breaths. "Okay," he said, "I'll try it."

The woman had reached them. "Sir, you need to sit down!"

Yuri pulled his arm free. He swayed but managed to stay on his feet.

Micah stared at him. "What are you doing?"

"Take these," said Yuri, reaching into his pocket and pulling out a pair of pink earplugs.

Micah didn't understand, but there wasn't time to argue. He grabbed the earplugs and stuffed them into his ears.

Yuri said something to the woman.

The earplugs didn't block every bit of sound, but they muffled it enough so that Micah couldn't make out the magician's words. The woman, who'd been reaching into her bag, stiffened. She blinked at Yuri a few times, then she nodded and turned, running for the door of a nearby office building.

Micah started to take out the earplugs, but Yuri shook his head. "Keep them," he mouthed. And he mimed covering his ears.

"The Door," said Micah. He pointed. "I think it's that way."

Yuri nodded and stumbled off in that direction. Micah went with him, chafing at the slow pace but unwilling to run ahead when Yuri looked on the verge of passing out.

He didn't understand why he had to keep his earplugs in, since Yuri wasn't talking to anyone. Then he noticed something strange.

No one else was trying to stop them, though Yuri was a gory sight, shuffling alongside Micah. And besides that, the sidewalk was clearing. Everywhere Micah looked, people were ducking into shops and restaurants, and nobody was stepping back outside.

He watched, shocked, as a taxicab stopped right in the middle of the street he and Yuri were waiting to cross. The driver and his passengers all jumped out, ignoring the angry honk from the car behind them. The passengers—a man and a woman—hurried toward a café, and the driver shouted something at the car behind him before doing the same.

What did he say? Micah wondered.

It hadn't been intelligible through the earplugs, but the people in the other car had obviously understood. The engine cut off, and they all climbed out, following the taxi driver inside.

People believe whatever Yuri says, Micah thought. So maybe he had told that first woman she needed to get in a building and stay safe, in case Victoria's birds attacked the city. But what about everybody else? Yuri hadn't spoken to them at all.

Then Micah remembered the other thing the magician had said: *The magic gets away, and it will not stop.*

It had to be like a rumor, he realized as the street emptied around them and even the more distant sounds of traffic in other parts of the city began to grow fainter and fainter. Yuri had told one person to stay inside, and she had told somebody else, and on and on. . . . The magic was spreading like a juicy piece of gossip, only faster because every single person who heard it thought it was true.

"Yuri, what did you *do*?"

He hoped Yuri had said exactly the right thing. What if this didn't wear off, and everyone thought they had to stay indoors forever? He covered his ears with his hands, just to be extra safe, but excitement flashed inside him alongside a new thought: *Maybe Victoria's caught in it, too!*

Maybe the Bird Woman hadn't flown away from the restaurant in time, and the magic had spread fast enough. Maybe she was stuck there, convinced she was supposed to stay indoors.

"Yuri!" he said. "Do you think it got Victoria, too?"

Yuri looked over at him, mouth open, eyes glassy. And then he crumpled, his knees giving way. Micah made a grab for his shirt, hoping to slow his fall.

He missed, but Yuri didn't hit the ground. Instead, the chef's body floated weirdly in midair, curving over some invisible obstacle so that his head and arms dangled, while his feet dragged limply along the concrete.

Micah jumped back, alarmed, and then he realized. "Bibi!"

The tiger appeared, looking pleased with herself. Yuri was slumped across her back, and her fur was turning red under his bloody shirt.

"Bibi, I'm so glad to see you!" Micah cried. "Victoria was here, and . . . and . . . who else came with you?"

He looked around, and a moment later he saw Firesleight rounding the corner. She had ripped half the skirt off her long black dress so that she could run faster, and the ferocious expression on her face was only slightly diminished by the fact that she had her hands pressed to her ears.

She sped toward Micah and Yuri, not seeming at all surprised to see them or the state they were in. "It's Victoria!" said Micah as she skidded to a stop. "She's here!"

"We know!" Firesleight shouted loud enough for him to hear through the earplugs.

Her eyes skimmed over Yuri, and she plunged one hand into the front of her dress, pulling out two small vials of silvery liquid. She ripped the cork out of one with her teeth and bent over the unconscious cook, prying open his mouth while Bibi watched.

Since Firesleight had dropped her hands, Micah decided it must be safe enough to take the plugs out of his ears.

"Victoria wants Fish," he said in a rush. "She said she's got the dragon in position. She was going to head to the circus right away, so I strangled her with her scarf, but then I couldn't, and I don't know if Yuri's magic got her in time."

Firesleight didn't seem to be paying attention. She spun away from Yuri and grabbed Micah by the arms, her eyes darting over him. "You're not hurt, right?!" she yelled in his face.

Micah blinked. "I'm okay. I can hear you."

"Sorry," said Firesleight, letting him go. "And good. Geoffrey said you were fine, but I worried. Take this." She thrust the other vial of silvery stuff at him. "If you get seriously hurt, or you think you're about to, drink it."

Micah took it and shoved it into his pocket. "What does it—?"

"From Rosebud. No time to explain," she said. "Bibi's got Yuri. You come with me."

Firesleight set a breakneck pace, and Micah was gasping a couple of minutes later when they met Geoffrey. The ticket taker was in the middle of a street full of abandoned vehicles. He made a peculiar sight in his tailcoat and boots. He stood right in front of a stopped bus with his eyes closed and his head tilted as if he were listening for something.

"Did they get her?" Firesleight asked when they reached him. She didn't even sound breathless.

Geoffrey kept his eyes shut. "She's in the air."

Firesleight swore.

"Save it for later," said Geoffrey. "She's just flown out of my range. We need to get to the Door."

Five minutes by air, thought Micah, ice creeping into his burning lungs.

"It's not all bad news," Geoffrey said. "Yuri's outdone himself. That suggestion of his will hit the edge of the city soon and keep going. We won't have to worry about gawkers getting in the way."

He opened his eyes. "Sleight, you have to head back. Your talent will be needed before the day's through. We'll follow you."

Firesleight covered her ears and darted away, leaving Micah to stare up at Geoffrey.

The city was so quiet now. Micah knew people must be hiding in the surrounding buildings, but he couldn't see anybody. Not a single face peered through the windows. It felt like it was just the two of them, alone in the middle of what had been a bustling metropolis moments before.

"Interesting choice," said Geoffrey.

"What do you mean?" asked Micah. *Not using the bracelets until the last minute? Trying to kill Victoria? Letting her go?*

"I mean you're doin' just fine," said Geoffrey, dropping into the casual, lilting voice Micah was accustomed to. He slapped Micah on the back. "Come on, String Boy. They'll be needin' us back at the circus."

30
THE MIGHTY CONFLAGRATION

The moment Micah stepped through the Door, his feet shot out from under him. His chin smacked into the floor, his teeth cracking together painfully, and a second later, a heavy weight toppled onto him, cursing in Latin.

Did we trip? Micah thought.

Geoffrey rolled off him, and Micah scrambled upright only to fall again, onto his hands and knees this time. Somewhere nearby, Porter was shouting, and Geoffrey was shouting back. Micah couldn't understand either of them, but he suddenly knew why he couldn't stay on his feet. The ground was shaking.

Victoria couldn't cause an earthquake, could she?

"What's going on?" he said, clinging to the floor.

Nobody answered. He heard the purple door to the china shop slam shut behind him.

"What's going on!?"

Big hands grabbed him under the arms and lifted him into the air. Micah yelped, but it was only Bowler, hat askew.

"The dragon!" said the Strongman. "It's been hiding underground." He took off running for Porter's living quarters, clutching Micah to his chest.

Over Bowler's shoulder, Micah saw doors and gates sliding from their stacks, smashing into the floor.

Porter must have called everyone back to the circus to deal with the emergency, Micah realized. Strongwomen raced around, snatching falling doors out of the air with their bare hands and flinging them away before they could hit other magicians. Micah saw Pennyroyal, her tangerine hair wild around her face, leap over Geoffrey to intercept a barn door just before it landed on the ticket taker's head.

Bowler reached the entrance to Porter's house and tossed Micah through the door. He landed on the sofa.

"Stay here until it's over!" Bowler shouted. And then he was gone.

Micah clung to the sofa cushions while mugs and cups tumbled from the cupboards in Porter's kitchen, the sound of them shattering against the floor a minor echo of the crashing noises in the warehouse.

The shaking went on for almost a minute. Then, all at once, it stopped. Micah heard a few more crashes before everything went silent.

He took several steadying breaths and got to his feet. His chin throbbed, and he tasted blood in his mouth. His lip was busted. For a couple of minutes, he waited, expecting someone to come through Porter's front door and explain what was going on.

When that didn't happen, he crept out into the warehouse himself, crouching low in case the shaking started back up and he needed to grab a convenient patch of floor.

The warehouse was in ruins. The cavernous space, once filled with towering stacks of doors, now looked like a box of spilt dominos. Only a single stack was standing. The others lay in heaps.

Metal gates had twisted on impact, and heavy wooden doors had split and splintered. The air was full of dust that glittered in the faint sunshine coming through the skylights.

"Hello?" Micah called.

Nobody answered. He couldn't hear anything but the sound of his own blood rushing in his ears.

Micah realized that when Bowler had said, "Stay here until it's over," he had probably meant the whole battle, not just the dragon-induced earthquake. But he started picking his way toward the tent's entrance. He clambered over the wreckage, wincing as he thought of how many centuries of Porter's hard work might be ruined.

He hadn't gone far when he heard a faint and frightened voice whimpering, "Help. Help. I need help."

"Who's there?" Micah took a step toward the voice, careful not to trip over the brass knob of the door he was standing on top of.

"Micah?" said the voice. It echoed oddly.

"Yes." Micah peered around. "It's Micah. Where are you?"

"COME GET ME!" the voice squawked. "IT'S ME! COME GET ME! I'LL NEVER USE YOUR TOOTH-BRUSH AGAIN!"

"Chintzy!" cried Micah. "I can't see you!"

"A WHOLE MOUNTAIN OF DOORS FELL ON ME! I'M STUCK!"

Micah was so horrified by Chintzy's panicked screeches that he ran around in circles, falling all over himself and bruising his shins against a portcullis. After a minute of frantic searching, he almost stepped on the very parrot he was trying to rescue.

Chintzy was not buried under a mountain of doors. She'd only been pinned under the lid of an old top-loading washing machine.

"Thank goodness!" said Micah, reaching down to grab her. "What are you doing in here?!"

Chintzy was breathing hard. Her chest feathers were aquiver. "The Lightbender told me to get to Porter! Where is he!? I need to get away!"

"I don't know," said Micah. "I guess he's evacuating people?"

"He's supposed to be evacuating me!" Chintzy shrilled. "Victoria will get me!"

"No she won't," said Micah, gripping the parrot's feet tightly and bringing her closer to his chest. "I won't let her. Where's the Lightbender?"

"He's using illusions on the dragon so everyone can get away!" Chintzy shouted. "He's no good at animals! He'll mess up! We'll die!"

"That's not a helpful attitude!" Micah shouted right back. "He won't mess up, and we won't die!"

They stared at each other.

Chintzy puffed her feathers out stubbornly, and Micah shook his head.

He looked around, trying to figure out what to do. He couldn't take Chintzy outside the tent. She would be a danger to herself and others if Victoria's magic took hold of her.

His eyes landed on the washing machine lid. The edge of one of his own nets was peeking out from underneath it.

"I have a plan," said Micah. "You're not going to like it."

That was an understatement. Chintzy yelled at Micah the whole way back to Porter's house, and when he stuck her in Porter's claw-foot bathtub and started securing the net over the top and sides, her volume increased. "You're trapping me in a cage!"

"It's not a cage," said Micah, yanking the corner of the net tight around one of the tub's feet, telling it not to come undone no matter *what* happened. "It's a bunker. A birdie bunker. Super safe. Even if the whole tent collapses you'll be fine."

"It's not a birdie bunker! It's a tub!"

Micah didn't have time to argue with her. He shrugged his peacoat off, took the ball of twine and the potion Firesleight had given him out of the pockets, and threw the coat over the tub. He hoped it would help keep any small pieces of debris from falling through the holes in the net.

"Stay here," he said.

"Do I have a choice!?" Chintzy squawked as Micah hurried out the door.

Micah's second trip through the warehouse was hastier than the first had been.

He could feel the tug of the locator knot against his ring finger. It might have been his imagination, but the pull felt more urgent, somehow, than it had ever been before. Fish was on the other end of that tug. Victoria would be heading for him.

And somewhere outside this tent, the Lightbender and the others were fighting a dragon.

Micah clambered up a hill of tumbled doors as quickly as he dared, then slid down the other side on a battered metal hatch.

It was still so quiet in the warehouse that Micah's footsteps echoed as he ran the last few yards to the tent flap. He reached for it, steeling himself for whatever lay beyond, but before his hands touched the fabric, a roar unlike anything he had ever imagined shook the tent.

The sound broke the air. It pummeled Micah's bones. His ears throbbed in time with his split lip, and he threw his shaking hands up to cover them.

The Mighty Conflagration, he thought.

It was at that moment that Micah realized he'd been wrong about something. After meeting Victoria, he had been so sure that she herself was the biggest threat to Circus Mirandus. But she was only a magician, only *human*, no matter what she told herself.

Whatever had made that sound was something more.

That's not an animal, he thought, still clutching his head. *It's a force of nature.*

The roaring cut off abruptly, and after a few seconds, Micah stepped cautiously out of the warehouse. He stared around, shocked. Everything looked exactly as it should have.

Afternoon sunlight pierced the clouds, shining down on the tents. They gleamed, bright as always, and over the multicolored rooftops Micah spied the huge, scarlet menagerie.

The knot tied around his finger was tugging toward it, and the pull was definitely harder than it was supposed to be. Micah was close to Fish now. The tug should've been faint, more of a suggestion than anything else.

He looked down at the knot. "You'd better not be malfunctioning. Not today."

He set out, trying to be smart and sneaky about it. He

didn't want to get himself in trouble when his emergency bracelets were all gone and the whole circus was engaged in a battle.

But where *was* the battle? Where was the source of that enormous roar?

Micah passed the dining tent, storage tents, the greenhouses. He didn't see a soul. It was eerie, and he had to resist the urge to rip open every single flap he passed. He wanted to shout, to demand that someone appear and explain to him what was going on.

Suddenly, the ground *thumped* underneath his feet. He froze, ready to get down in case it was another dragonquake, but it was only a thump.

He took a few steps, and the *thump* came again.

It was a feeling he recognized from moving days, he realized, like the largest of the tent poles falling. Something heavy was hitting the ground in another part of the circus.

Okay, he thought. *No need to panic yet. You don't even know what it is.*

A shadow fell over Micah. He ducked automatically, and whatever it was passed by. But another shadow came, and then another. Huge dark blots, silent and winged. They skated over the grass, heading toward the menagerie.

Micah looked up. The dire hawks, nearly invisible, were cutting through the air, only their shadows giving them away. And soaring just above the lead bird, her hair catching the sunlight, was Victoria.

She did not, Micah noticed, have on her scarf.

He opened his mouth to shout a warning to whoever might hear it. But as Victoria approached the menagerie, that bone-shaking roar came again.

And this time, Micah saw where it was coming from.

The Mighty Conflagration rose up among the rooftops, his iridescent scales gleaming. His head was the size of a dump truck, and as he opened his maw, Micah drew in a breath at the rows of fangs lining his jaws, every one as long as Micah's arm and turned inward.

Conflagration didn't have wings yet, but Micah couldn't see why he would ever need them. His serpentine body, his roar, that snout full of teeth—it was already too much to fathom.

For almost half a minute, the dragon shook his head furiously, like he was trying to clear it. Then he bellowed with rage and struck at the menagerie tent, biting at the roof like a snake.

In an instant, the volume of the day was turned up to full blast.

Magicians shouted. Animals cried out in panic. Tent fabric creaked. Ropes snapped.

The Lightbender, Micah realized. He'd been doing what Chintzy had said—calming the dragon so people and animals could make their escape. He must have been using so much power that the illusion had bled out, creating that strange false quiet.

But that was over now. The Lightbender hadn't been

able to hold the dragon forever, just as he hadn't been able to trick Terpsichore into eating her dinner when she was a foal.

The game was up. The battle was starting in earnest.

Micah ran for the scarlet tent, trying not to imagine what must be going on inside.

The rest of Victoria's flock came before Micah reached the menagerie—a storm of rainbow-colored birds descending all at once.

Micah saw a small green parrot drop an egg that sizzled and hissed when it hit tent fabric, eating through like acid, and he spied a giant eagle dragging what he was afraid was one of the pangolins into the air. But most of the birds began to circle over the menagerie, swirling in tighter and tighter rings.

Micah kept looking up as he ran, but he couldn't spot Victoria. She'd left two of her dire hawks behind. They were diving toward the ground again and again—fighting magicians, Micah assumed.

But Victoria must have flown off with the third hawk. No doubt she was trying to stay out of sight and out of range. The drakling, so close to the menagerie, was such a threat that nobody could afford to hunt down the Bird Woman yet.

Micah dashed around a tent, approaching the menagerie from behind. He could see his fellow magicians now, fleeing and fighting and trying to round up frightened animals. But in the chaos he couldn't make sense of who was doing what. He had no idea how to help.

He dove under Rosebud's wagon and paused for a few seconds with his forehead pressed to the ground, trying to catch his breath. Then, he crawled forward on his belly to get a better look at what was happening.

No, he thought. *No way.*

Conflagration was so massive Micah could barely believe he was real. The drakling had burst out of the ground on the midway. Half the booths and stalls and a couple of neighboring tents had disappeared into the pit he'd left behind in the soil. It looked like he had slithered straight to the menagerie, but the Strongfolk had intercepted him before he made it inside.

They were still holding him off. Five of the Strongmen and Pennyroyal had grabbed the drakling by his massive tail, and they stuck to him like burrs no matter how he thrashed. Other members of the Sisterhood were dealing with his head.

They had thrown nets over Conflagration's crest—a comb of flattened spines that started on top of his head and ran halfway down his powerful neck. They almost looked like feathers, but hard and razor sharp.

Not sharp enough to cut through my nets, Micah thought with satisfaction.

The Strongwomen were using the netting to scale the drakling's spine. As Micah watched, one of them made a powerful leap for one enormous green eye, swinging with her sword. But even though she landed a blow on the eyelid that would have felled a tree, the sword barely left a scratch in Conflagration's scales.

The real damage was coming from Thuja.

The Strongwoman stood a couple dozen yards away from the drakling, nocking arrow after arrow into her bow. She fired them methodically, her face so calm she might have been shooting at a wooden target. Sometimes, she took a shot at Conflagration's head to distract him, but most of the greenish arrows buried themselves with sickening thwacks in the beast's side. They all hit a small spot over what Micah assumed must be the heart.

Thuja's plan seemed to be to punch through the wall of thick dragonflesh one arrow at a time.

The rest of the fight was harder to understand.

Micah looked everywhere for the Lightbender, but he couldn't see him. He spied Rosebud, though. She was helping a magician who'd been hit by one of the acid eggs.

And there was Firesleight. She crouched behind Thuja, her face intent, her eyes fixed on the arrows digging into Conflagration's hide. If she was trying to set the drakling on fire, it wasn't working at all.

Almost everybody else raced around the menagerie tent, dodging the drakling's crushing coils as they went. They were trying to protect the circus's animals from dive-bombing birds and the enraged Conflagration, but it wasn't an easy task. The frightened creatures had scattered in every direction.

Micah gasped when Big Jean stomped out of the tent, a dozen smaller animals clinging to her broad back. She was too large and too slow; there was no way she could escape without attracting the drakling's attention.

But the world's most intelligent elephant waited for one of Thuja's arrows to bite deep. As Conflagration rounded on the archer, Big Jean made a break for it. She ran right toward Rosebud's wagon and then past it, not pausing for a second.

A moment later, Terpsichore burst out of the menagerie.

Unlike the other animals, the young unicorn hadn't seen fit to use the entrance. She'd charged right at the patch of tent wall nearest the wagon. Her sharp horn ripped through the fabric, and the rest of her followed.

Run, thought Micah. *Run away. Go.*

But Terp snorted and turned back to the hole she'd made in the tent.

"No!" shouted Micah, scrambling out from under the wagon. "No, Terp! Go! You have to leave!"

He ran toward the menagerie, swatting at something feathery and shrieking that flew into his face. But before he reached the hole in the wall, Terpsichore emerged again. She had the tail end of the Lightbender's coat clamped in her mouth. The unconscious illusionist was dangling upside down, his head trailing on the ground, only one arm still caught in a leather sleeve.

Terp dragged him easily, apparently unaware that she was scraping the Lightbender's face along the rough ground. When she spotted Micah, she dropped the illusionist and started chiming, trumpeting, and tootling for all she was worth, like she was trying to explain that there was a dragon here and they really must get away from it.

"I know, I know!" shouted Micah, dodging sideways as she tried to grab on to him with her teeth. Apparently, Terp was in a rescuing mood, and she thought Micah would do just as well as the Lightbender.

Micah fell to his knees beside his guardian and reached for his neck. Rosebud had taught him how to check pulses as part of their first aid course, and he was so relieved to find the Lightbender's that tears sprang into his eyes.

He wasn't sure what had knocked the magician out. It might have been the dragon breaking free of the illusion, or it might have been Terpsichore herself. The unicorn was stamping her feet and whistling shrilly at Micah. He had a feeling she wasn't going to stick around for long even out of loyalty.

"I need you to help me," Micah said, fumbling for his ball of twine. "Please lie down."

He'd thought it would be difficult, calming Terp enough to get her to cooperate, but he managed it quickly. "Good girl," he said. "Thank you. Just hang on a second."

He grabbed the Lightbender's coat and heaved, dragging his limp body onto the unicorn's back.

Terp froze. Her ears twitched. She stared at Micah, a look of such utter offense in her eyes that he was sure she had forgotten about the battle altogether.

Unicorns did *not* do horseback rides.

"He's not really riding you," Micah said breathlessly. He strung twine around Terp's neck and then started securing the Lightbender in place, his hands shaking. He didn't even know what kind of knots he was tying; he was just trying to hurry. "He's totally unconscious. Think of him like a package."

Terpsichore looked like she was thinking about bucking the Lightbender right off.

In less than a minute, Micah was done. He broke the twine and stuck what little was left back into his pocket. He decided against making the knots holding the Lightbender unbreakable. After what had happened with Bowler, he couldn't risk it.

"Go," said Micah. "Please, go. Take him away from here."

Terp stood. She shifted her weight. She *was* going to buck the Lightbender off.

"It's a game!" Micah blurted.

Terpsichore loved games. She tootled at him questioningly.

"I'm giving the Lightbender to you," said Micah. "He's your new toy. And you have to keep him away from everyone else. Now go."

He swatted the unicorn's rump. She didn't even notice.

"Go!" Micah yelled, pointing in the direction Big Jean had run.

The raised voice brought Terp back to her senses. She tossed her head once, then trumpeted and took off, horn aimed down like a lance to threaten anyone in her path. As she galloped away, her tail streamed behind her and the Lightbender bounced against her back.

Before Micah could call out a good-bye, before he could tell the unicorn to stay safe and run fast, she was already out of sight. *She'll be halfway to London in a minute,* he thought. And he was so relieved he almost cheered.

But not all of the animals had Big Jean's good sense or Terpsichore's speed and determination. Too many of the creatures were confused. They snarled and roared and shrieked with fright, some of them fighting the very magicians who were trying to save them, others fleeing aimlessly through the melee.

Micah spotted the two-headed camel standing petrified not far from Rosebud's wagon, and he hurried over to give it directions. As soon as he approached, one of the heads butted him in the stomach, and he ended up on the ground, clinging to the spokes of a wooden wagon wheel while he waited for the world to stop spinning.

He'd gotten the camel moving, but it almost trampled the reading goat in its haste to leave. The goat, not a tower of courage in the first place, panicked and turned, running straight for the dragon, bleating in alarm.

Micah was sure the goat was a goner. It had no magical powers that could save it, only a passion for reading magazines and newspapers. But to Micah's surprise, one of the Strongmen flung himself off the drakling's tail and raced toward the goat, tackling it out of the way at the last second.

It seemed like a terrible risk to take. Then Micah realized—they were all afraid to let even a single animal, no matter how small, fall prey to the drakling's jaws.

They didn't want Conflagration to eat. He was so big that any magical meal—be it magician or goat—might give him the last bit of power he needed to grow his wings.

And then how would they stop him?

Suddenly, Conflagration dropped his head to the ground and rolled, over and over. None of the magicians expected the maneuver, and several of the Strongfolk were thrown off. Bowler skipped over the grass like a stone across the surface of a lake, sending up fountains of dirt with every strike until he landed a couple of yards from Micah.

But the rolling motion drove the arrows in the drakling's side deeper. He hissed as his own dark blood stained his scales.

He rose up again, his head soaring over the top of the tent, and Micah poked his own head around the side of the wagon to see better. He covered his ears, expecting another roar, but instead, Conflagration made a plaintive, whistling sort of hiss. It was almost *cute.*

Micah didn't understand what it meant, but then a bird with feathers the color of a sunset flew into the drakling's mouth and down his throat.

Conflagration made the noise again, more insistently this time, and *five* golden swans flew into his mouth in a glittering V.

"Why that rotten, foul . . ." Bowler muttered as he got back to his feet.

Micah knew how he felt. The drakling was tired of trying to catch the menagerie animals, so Victoria was feeding it her own birds. It was an *obvious* thing to do, but it was so revolting that Micah couldn't quite grasp it.

The drakling didn't even chew the offerings. He just let them fly down his gullet, and then he reached up to beg for more.

Wherever she was, Victoria gave in. The huge flock circling the menagerie began to funnel down, not to attack but to pour themselves into Conflagration's waiting mouth. One after another after another, the birds' lives winked out of existence so fast Micah couldn't count them.

This is it, he thought, dread taking root in him. *They can't stop it now.*

Micah watched, unable to look away, until suddenly something gave his ring finger a sharp yank. *Ow!* He blinked down at the locator knot. *What was that about?*

The knot pulled so hard that Micah's hand was jerked out from under him.

It's not supposed to do that.

Then, something happened inside Micah's head.

It was like hearing a voice, but not quite. Like having a dream, but not exactly. A certainty blossomed inside him, and he knew it as deeply and clearly as his own name.

Fish was scared.

And he wanted Micah to come save him.

THE
DIRE HAWK

Micah raced past Conflagration's coiling scales and whipping tail. He didn't look up to see if some awful bird was about to fall on him, and he didn't glance to the sides to find out if worried magicians were trying to stop him.

Speed, he figured, was as good a tactic as any under the circumstances. And anyway, if you ran hard enough, then you couldn't think about being afraid.

The locator knot wasn't tugging toward the menagerie. It had changed direction during the battle. Which meant someone had *taken* Fish, either to protect him or . . .

Micah pumped his arms. He forced his legs to go faster.

Tents and animals and magicians flashed past, and he didn't have the presence of mind to recognize any of them.

Where are you? he thought. *Fish, tell me.*

But he didn't get that jolt of certainty again. All he could do was follow the locator's pull.

He dashed past the ticket stand and into the meadow. To the left, half a football field away, Porter was chivying a clamorous group of animals and magicians through a Door.

Micah wanted to go to them, to see if the Lightbender and Terpsichore had made it out that way, but the locator knot was urging him toward the right. He followed, running flat out into what looked like nothing but empty meadow.

By the time he spotted the distortion in the air, it was too late to slow his pace. The dire hawk stood in the tall grass with its huge wings outstretched and angled—a wall of meadow-colored feathers. Micah barreled right into one of those wings and toppled backward, feeling like he'd smashed into a stack of bricks.

He tried to cry out, but he couldn't stop gasping. He lay in the grass, panting for air, and waited for the hawk to fall on him. There was no escaping now. Not when the bird was this close.

Micah shut his eyes. The last things he would hear were the bellowing of the dragon and the distant shouts and screams coming from the menagerie.

Let the Lightbender be all right, he thought. *Please let them all be all right.*

But nothing happened.

Why wasn't the dire hawk attacking? It couldn't possibly have missed someone running into it. Micah opened his eyes and looked cautiously up at the bird.

It was staring right at him over the top of its wing, pinning him with one wicked yellow eye. They gazed at each other for a long moment, then the hawk blinked.

It turned away as if it hadn't seen Micah at all.

Shocked, Micah sat up. *What's it doing?*

He took in the bird's posture, tracing its nearly invisible form with his eyes. The way the huge wings were spread . . . it was almost like the hawk was shielding something in front of it from view.

And the locator ring was pulling Micah in that direction.

Still breathing hard, but trying to do it more quietly, Micah crawled forward through the grass. The bird heard him. It must have. But it didn't move a muscle.

When he reached tail feathers, he got to his feet, staying in a crouch. He was too short to see over the tops of the dire hawk's wings. He slowly rose up onto his tiptoes, but the bird was still just a little too tall.

Micah started to shuffle sideways, intending to walk around the hawk, but it whipped its neck around and glared at him, this time with both eyes, as if to say *Don't you dare.*

Its hooked beak was bigger than Micah's head.

Micah held up his hands in a gesture he hoped the bird would find placating.

He was sure now that whatever was in front of the dire

hawk was important, that he needed to see it, and that the creature *wanted* him to do so. But how was he supposed to manage that when the hawk wouldn't let him go around it? And why wouldn't it just move its wings out of the way?

Because it couldn't?

No, Micah realized. *Because someone has given it an order.*

Maybe he'd been wrong to think of the dire hawk as an enemy. After all, it had set Yuri down when Micah distracted Victoria for a minute. It was so large compared to a human that it probably hadn't even realize how much damage its claws had done to the magician's shoulder.

Maybe, just maybe, it was doing everything it could to help defeat its mistress.

Well, there's only one way to see over it if I'm not allowed to go around.

Micah approached the dire hawk's back and reached for a handful of soft feathers. When the bird didn't move, he decided that was as good as an invitation.

With the way the hawk stood, straight and tall, the climb was awkward. But Micah managed it by jamming his foot against the base of the huge tail and clambering with his arms and legs up the bird's back. After a brief struggle, he got his hands around the place where one of the dire hawk's wings met its body.

Trying not to pant too loudly, Micah craned his neck and peeked over the feathered shoulder.

The Inventor lay on her side in the grass, covered by a familiar shield of blue light.

She was hurt. Micah couldn't see any wounds, but he could tell by the way her lips pressed against each other and the way she held her body so very still. Her eyes were shut tight, and only her hands were moving, twiddling knobs and buttons on her shielding device.

Some of the knobs were missing from the metal cylinder, one of the little glass bubbles on the end was broken, and as Micah watched, the blue light *flickered.*

Victoria Starling, kneeling on the ground just outside the shield, stretched out her hand.

The Inventor smashed her thumb into a button, and the protective light brightened.

Victoria chuckled quietly. "Go on then," she said, her voice hoarse. "You can't keep it up forever, and your friends are all distracted."

Her eyes were fixed on the Inventor's belt. Clipped to the side, as it usually was on moving days, was Fish's shrunken aquarium.

Inside his small tank, Fish was burning with such a brilliant white light that it looked like the Inventor was wearing a star on her belt.

No! thought Micah, horrified. *No, Fish. This isn't it. This isn't your Moment.*

But as he slid down the dire hawk's back, he remembered Geoffrey saying, "They get impatient sometimes, Ideas do."

And if Ideas could be too impatient to wait for their Moment, Micah was betting they could be too terrified as well. Fish must know somehow what Victoria planned to do with him. She was going to take him far away, so that his Moment wouldn't count for anything, and the only way Fish could stop her was to go out in a glorious blaze, a big flash of inspiration that would fall on everyone at Circus Mirandus.

Instead of just Victoria Starling.

Micah's feet hit the grass, and he clamped his eyes shut, thinking hard. He brought the locator knot to his lips and pressed them to it. *Not yet*, he thought. *Not yet. I'll save you. I promise.*

He had no clue whether or not Fish heard him.

But he knew what he had to do. What the dire hawk *wanted* him to do.

He just . . . didn't know how.

Micah tried to see the overlay.

He had done it before, when he was afraid. And he was afraid now—for the circus and for the Inventor and for himself and for Fish. He thought it ought to be enough.

But though he stretched his mind in every direction, he couldn't find any golden connections. And though he stared at the knot bracelets wrapped around his arm until his eyes burned and blurred, he couldn't see anything but string.

He couldn't speak aloud. Not so close to Victoria. But inside his soul, he begged and pleaded for something to *happen*.

None of it worked.

The dire hawk was hiding Micah from Victoria, but he knew he didn't have forever. The Inventor was hurt. She would pass out. Or she would . . .

And then it would all be over.

I did it once, he thought. *Why, oh why, can't I do it now?*

Victoria would kill him this time. Micah knew it.

But somehow, the thought of losing Fish this way was even more painful.

Grandpa Ephraim brought you to the circus in his boot, he thought. *And he told me so many stories about this place. And because I can't do it, that's all going to be for nothing.*

Micah felt like he was breaking in two.

His body started to shake, and he realized he was crying silently. He clutched at the bootlace on his wrist and fell against the dire hawk, pressing his face into the warm feathers.

I'm sorry, he whispered in his heart. *You didn't deserve this. None of the birds did.*

How many had died for Victoria? How many had flown into the dragon's maw? Was it still happening, even now?

The dire hawk's body trembled, and Micah remembered Chintzy, her chest feathers quivering as he carried her to Porter's bathtub. How could one helpless red parrot possibly have survived everything that had happened today?

He dug his hands deeper into the hawk's feathers, and he imagined he could sense the war raging within the bird, the way it fought against Victoria's bonds.

He admired its courage. Inside of himself, Micah felt

like some battle had already been lost. *I've got nothing left.*

His focus was shattered, and his heart ached. He was drained. Maybe he had enough energy to untie his own shoelaces, but as for freeing the dire hawk? He just couldn't do it.

I've got to give the dire hawk something. Even if it's small.

The bird was trying its best. Micah owed it every last bit of magic he could find. He sighed into the feathers, and thought, *Well, if I can still untie my shoes, then you can have that.*

He thought of how simple it was, to tap the laces of his shoes so that the knots fell apart.

He tightened his grip on the bird. *You're a big feathery sneaker now, dire hawk. And whatever ties you to Victoria is just a shoelace.*

So.

Come loose.

Somewhere, in a world Micah couldn't quite find, a rope of golden light splintered.

And in the back of his mind, he felt it. Just like when he'd untied the rope ladder from the tree house all those months ago.

The *snap.*

32

A FEW
SECONDS

The dire hawk lunged forward.

Micah fell on his hands and knees.

A high-pitched scream split the air, but it was cut off so quickly Micah wasn't quite sure he'd heard it. Something warm and wet spattered against the back of his shirt. He was so startled it took him a few seconds to get back on his feet, and by the time he did, it was over.

Victoria Starling was dead.

Micah stared, barely understanding, as the dire hawk launched itself off the ground, carrying what was left of Victoria into the sky.

Clutching its bloody prize in a single claw, the bird called out, and in its voice, Micah heard not victory.

But joy.

33

FAR

Micah knelt on the ground by the blue shield, trying to ignore the blood-splattered grass beside him. The dire hawk was still calling overhead, its voice piercing, and from somewhere farther away, Micah heard the other two hawks cry out in answer.

"Inventor," he said, reaching toward the shield, not sure if he should touch it. "Are you all right? It's Micah."

It took a minute, but the Inventor opened her eyes.

Micah breathed a sigh of relief. "Victoria," he said. "She's gone."

It felt like an ending, but he knew it wasn't. As the Inventor's shield dissolved, Conflagration roared. Even this far away, the sound made Micah's stomach clench.

But something about the roaring was different from before. There was less anger in it and more pain. Micah looked around quickly.

Conflagration had heaved himself on top of the distant menagerie tent. The drakling bellowed. His scales began to split. He shook himself all over, and from one of his sides, a single, damp wing unfurled like a sail.

Heart galloping, Micah turned back to the Inventor. He couldn't watch the dragon's metamorphosis. It would only distract him.

He plunged his hand into his pocket and found the vial of silver potion Firesleight had given him. He held it out to the Inventor. "It's from Rosebud," he said. "Firesleight said to take it if I was hurt. I'm okay, so you should have it."

She nodded and opened her hand. Micah placed the vial in it, and she closed her fingers around it.

At her belt, Fish was still shining bright enough to hurt Micah's eyes. And the locator on his finger was pulling so hard that it had begun to cut into his skin.

"What do I do?" Micah asked. "How do I help?"

"Take the Idea," she said, her voice weak but sure. "Run." She pulled in a shallow, shuddering breath and winced. "Run to Porter."

Micah was so grateful to have clear, easy instructions that he would have hugged the Inventor if he'd thought it wouldn't hurt her.

"But what about you?"

She gave him a tiny smile. "I'll be fine." She opened her hand to reveal the potion. "But you . . . you must hurry. The Idea can't be allowed to disperse. Not so near the dragon."

Micah had worried about so many things, but not that.

"But Conflagration's . . ."

A monster who feeds on magic, he thought. And the Lightbender had once said that an Idea was the purest sort of magic. If Fish's power fell over the circus, would it affect the dragon, too?

"What would happen?" Micah breathed.

"Not sure," said the Inventor, her voice thin. "Can't take the risk."

Micah reached for the clip that held Fish's aquarium to the tool belt and found the tiny hinge that released the tank. He grabbed the cool glass and felt the contents slosh, but he couldn't even see Fish. The light was too painfully bright.

He stood up to go, and the Inventor drew in a shuddering breath. "Micah," she said.

"Yes, ma'am?" He leaned over to hear her better.

"Far," she said. "Tell Porter . . . to send you far."

Micah was too tired to run anymore, but he stumbled forward as fast as he could, Fish's aquarium blazing in his hands.

He headed across the meadow toward Porter, forcing himself not to look back at the tents when he heard screams and crashes and those terrible roars. *Almost there,* he thought. *Just get to Porter.*

Then came the blast of heat.

It was so sudden and so powerful it felt like something had slapped him. Micah couldn't stand not knowing. He spun and saw The Mighty Conflagration soaring over the roof of the menagerie. Deep red flames danced in the air around him, dissipating as he swooped through them.

The dragon's scales were a vibrant shade of emerald now, and his immense wings—clawed at the tips—were an almost translucent lime. He threw his head back, and red fire shot up, fountaining toward the clouds. And *hanging* there.

The crimson flames burned and burned even though the dragon had stopped producing them. He flew around the fire fountain, roaring with a dark delight, and Micah realized with shock that the dragon didn't just breathe fire.

He could control it.

Conflagration hovered above his flames, and they grew, fanned by the wind from his wings. They spread, boiling over the menagerie, moving in a way that was more like liquid than any fire Micah had ever seen.

Then Conflagration tucked his wings in close to his body and dropped like a stone toward the roof of the tent.

The flames fell with him.

"No!" Micah yelled.

The flames splashed down against the fabric, and the dragon's full weight landed on the roof. The biggest tent at Circus Mirandus didn't catch fire. It vaporized. The entire menagerie disappeared in an eye-searing flash of red flame.

The wind and heat from the explosion reached Micah a moment later, blowing his hair back and forcing him to slam his eyelids shut. He held Fish's aquarium to his chest. The locator knot was jerking on his finger so hard that he thought it might break the bone.

Get to Porter.

He sprinted the last few yards, pushing past a pair of scratched and bruised acrobats who were trying to drag a panicked orangutan toward the safety of the Door without hurting it.

"Porter!" he shouted, waving one arm. "Porter, it's Fish!"

The magician had been staring up at the dragon, his face horrified. When he heard Micah, he whirled.

"Micah!" he exclaimed. "You need to get through the Door."

"Where does it go?" Micah asked, stopping in front of him.

Porter had a cut on the side of his face and dried blood on his neck. "Does it *matter*?"

Micah held up Fish's aquarium.

"Oh, wonderful," Porter grumbled, holding his hand up to block the blinding light.

"Where does the Door lead to?" Micah said urgently.

"Norwich."

"Is that far?" Micah asked. "The Inventor said Fish had to go far away. Because of the dragon."

Porter looked taken aback. "How far away?"

"I don't . . . I don't know."

Porter grimaced. "Micah, this is important. Did she mean it had to go a few miles away? Or does it need to leave the country?"

Micah was breathing hard. "I'm not sure," he said. "I'm sorry. I didn't ask. She was hurt, and she only said *far*."

"You're covered in blood," Porter said, his eyes widening. "Is—"

"It's not the Inventor's," Micah said quickly. "The dire hawk ate Victoria. Porter, what do we do?"

Porter turned to look at the tents. The dragon was back in the sky, searching for another target.

"I think we have to assume that far means far," he muttered. "But that's going to be a problem."

Porter's long-distance doors were all back in the warehouse, Micah realized, and half of them were in splinters.

Conflagration was exhaling fire into the air, building up another pool of that deadly red flame. *Please no,* thought Micah. *Not again.*

Which tent would it be? Who might be standing in the dragon's path?

But suddenly, Porter was smiling.

"Will you look at that?" he said. "She really can do it."

At first Micah didn't understand. Then he saw that the dragonfire was behaving differently this time. As Conflagration fanned it with his wings, it was dimming instead of building. The outermost whorls of flame were being snuffed out.

"Firesleight!" shouted Micah. "She's fighting back!"

"A magician who can control dragonfire," Porter said. "Now that's something I've never seen."

All at once, the flames were gone, and Conflagration shrieked with rage. He swooped low over the tents, looking for whoever had spoiled his fun, and Micah, so proud of

Firesleight that he wanted to clap, didn't realize the danger until Porter said, "It's looking at us."

"What?"

Conflagration had spotted the evacuating magicians in the meadow. Or, more likely, the brilliant magical light coming from Fish's aquarium had drawn his gaze.

Even as the dragon circled the tents, his head turned, eyes fixed curiously on Micah.

"Everyone through the Door!" Porter yelled, motioning the straggling magicians and animals through. "It's about to close!"

Then he turned to Micah and said, in a much calmer voice, "Step closer."

Micah, unable to tear his gaze away from the dragon, did.

"Listen to me," said Porter. "I've only done this a few times. It's important that you don't move."

"Okay?" said Micah, barely paying attention.

Conflagration was turning in the air. He was heading for them. It would just take a few beats of his wings.

"Hold on tight to Fish," Porter said.

Micah squeezed the aquarium in both hands.

He felt something on his chest and looked down. Porter had pressed his palms to the front of Micah's shirt.

"You can do this," the magician whispered.

Micah didn't think Porter was talking to him.

"Porter?"

"Far," said Porter. And he shoved Micah hard.

34

FISH

Micah stumbled back a step, and Circus Mirandus was gone.

The day was brisk, the sky cloudless, and as Micah turned to see where Porter had sent him, smooth pebbles crunched and rolled under his feet.

He stood on a small, abandoned beach. The sea was only a few steps away, the waves so slight that the cold, gray water looked almost like glass.

It was quiet. Micah's breath sounded loud next to the faint swish of the ocean and the clacks the pebbles made as they tumbled at the edge of the lapping water.

He knew exactly where he was.

"Fish," he said to the blazing light in his hands. "This is it. This is the beginning of our story."

Micah sat on the water's edge, staring at the horizon.

Somewhere over the ocean, a battle raged. Micah's friends—his family—were fighting a great evil, and he would have walked across the sea to them if he could.

But it felt right to be here on the beach where his grandfather had first heard Circus Mirandus's call, holding Fish's aquarium in his lap.

They both had decisions to make, and there was no better place to do it.

"We're safe now, Fish," said Micah. "Do you think, maybe, the two of us could have a talk?"

The light in the small round aquarium didn't flicker.

"That's okay. I'll go first."

Micah told the story again, about a tiny fish that had swum into a boy's boot. About how the boy had grown up, grown old, and passed magic on to his grandson, who had loved him more than anything.

"I've been thinking all this time, Fish, about how much I wanted you to stay at Circus Mirandus. I knew you had your own work to do, but it seemed like it would be perfect for the two of us to be there together. It would be almost like one last gift from Grandpa Ephraim, if I was your Someone, and you were my Fish."

Yes.

It wasn't quite a thought. Nor a word. It was more a feeling inside Micah, and he knew it had come from Fish.

He nodded. "If you decide you want me to help you, I'll do my best. Whatever kind of Idea you are, I'll try to make it happen."

Fish burned so bright suddenly that Micah had to cover the top of the tank with his hands so that he could still see. And Fish's feelings were clearer now.

Safe. Micah was a friend, and he would keep the Idea safe. And maybe it wouldn't be perfect, but it would still be good. They would still do great things together. Fish could feel it, like a tug deep in his belly.

Micah understood.

"I guess you didn't realize how scary the world could be," he said. "And now you know terrible things can happen. But, Fish, that's exactly why you have to do what you came here to do. You're important, and this isn't your Moment."

Micah looked down at his hands. The light was shining through his fingers.

"I would love to keep you," he said. "But I've got magic of my own I haven't even figured out. And I've got an idea of my own about who I want to be. I'm going to be a magician at Circus Mirandus, Fish. And that's right for me, but that doesn't mean it's right for you."

He reached for the locator knot tied around his finger. It was still pulling at him, tugging his hand toward Fish, who was swimming below. Micah dug his thumbnail under the gray thread, took a deep breath, and ordered it to come loose.

It snapped, and for the first time since Micah had picked it up, the light in the aquarium dimmed a little.

"There," said Micah. "I think that might have been confusing you."

He ran his fingers over the top of the aquarium, feeling for the tiny dimple in the glass that would open it. He found it and prodded it until the glass on top of the shrunken tank disappeared.

"Hi," said Micah, staring down into the water, where a goldfish-sized spark swam in frightened circles. "I think I need to show you something."

He reached for his left arm and tugged one of his bracelets over his wrist. "Here's a memory of Rosebud," he said. "The circus couldn't do without her. She's a healer, and she's saved so many people's lives with her potions."

He dropped the bracelet into the water. It shrank to a speck, and Fish, as always, swallowed it.

"This one's for Firesleight," said Micah, tugging off an orange-and-copper bracelet and dropping it into the tank, too. "Do you know she can control dragonflame? I bet nobody else has ever been able to do that in the whole history of the world. And if she'd gone off and done something different with her life because she was scared or because it seemed easier than mastering her fire magic, then everyone at the circus might be dead."

He went one by one, memory by memory, magician by magician. He kept on until his left arm was bare, and then he reached into his pocket and pulled out the last piece of twine.

"Hold on, Fish," he said. "This one's never worked well before."

After meeting his grandmother, Micah understood what he'd been getting wrong with the Lightbender's bracelet all this time. He tied the twine carefully, and the knots came together one by one. He included the illusionist's magic, his leather coat, the way he talked. He included memories of that day in the Lost and Found, when the Lightbender had been so upset about missing Micah's birthday. He included his own worry about the magician, his hope that Terpsichore had carried his guardian to safety.

And through it all, he wove in one final truth that made everything come together.

"This is the Lightbender, Fish," he said, holding the knotted twine over the water. "He could have done just about anything he wanted. Victoria thought he should have been rich and famous and powerful. But instead he catches spiders in coffee cups, and he puts on shows for little kids. And when someone asks him to adopt a boy he barely even knows, he says *yes*."

He let the twine fall into the aquarium, and he watched Fish gulp it down.

"If the Lightbender had done something else with his life, then neither one of us would be sitting on this beach right now," said Micah. "It's important to do the right thing. Even if it's hard."

Many of the things Micah had done today had been difficult. But at some point, he thought, you had to take your own stand against the darkness in the world, whatever it might cost you. Circus Mirandus did it one way. The Sisterhood another. And Micah could do his part, too, by telling Fish the truth.

"We've got a lot in common, Fish, and I'd love to be your Someone. But I'm not."

Micah knew Fish understood because his light was steadily dimming. A few minutes later, he was a little silver fish. Small enough, Micah figured, to swim into somebody's boot.

"Good for you," said Micah. "Now I guess we wait here until someone decides to come and get us."

No, said Fish.

It wasn't hard to understand him at all now. Micah was getting used to the language of Ideas.

It's time to find my Someone. They're ready for me, and we've got a lot of work to do.

Micah wasn't sure what would happen when Fish left the aquarium. If he turned huge right away, Micah didn't want him to be stranded in the shallows.

So he waded into the ocean, ignoring the achingly cold water that soaked his pants and his shirt. When he was up to his chest, he said, "You're sure, right?"

And he knew Fish was.

"I'm going to miss you," said Micah. "You've been the best listener in the world."

He lowered the tank into the water, and Fish swam out.

He circled Micah a few times, growing bigger and bigger, his silver scales flashing in the sun. And then, with one swish of his powerful tail, he headed out to sea.

Micah stared at the horizon, waiting and hoping, and a couple of minutes later, Fish leaped. He was as big as a whale, and the splash he made when he landed sent a wave of water right over the top of Micah's head.

35

THE MOST IMPORTANT PART

Micah walked up and down the beach, rubbing his arms and shivering, willing his wet clothes and hair to dry faster. He worried a little more with every step he took. Were his friends all right? The animals? The Lightbender?

There was a town, he knew, a short walk from here. And it occurred to him that the smart thing would be to head in that direction.

Maybe he could find a warm drink. Or a towel.

Maybe he could borrow someone's phone and call Jenny's house.

Peal wasn't nearby, but Micah was sure her parents could get here in a few hours. And he knew that they would do it, too, the second he told them what had happened.

It sounded like a good idea. But Micah decided not to go through with it.

This beach was where Porter had sent him, and it felt almost like Micah would be jinxing the circus if he left. And anyway, every inch he walked away from the ocean would be an inch farther from home.

Tonight, he decided. *If nobody comes for me, I'll find a phone and call Jenny.*

He looked up at the sun. He thought it was noon here, maybe a bit later. He still had hours to wait.

Micah's clothes dried. He shivered a little less.

Soon, he thought. *Someone will come.*

He sat down and played a game with himself, trying to figure out who would come and get him, and when they would arrive.

The Lightbender was out of the question, of course. Rosebud would have patched him up by now, but his illusions would be needed to hide either the circus or the magicians and animals Porter had evacuated.

Bowler would definitely volunteer for the job. He hadn't looked hurt when Micah had seen him during the fight.

He would come when Micah counted to a thousand. Porter would send him in that same strange way he'd sent Micah. He would push Bowler from England right to this beach in *nine hundred ninety-eight, nine hundred ninety-nine, nine hundred ninety-nine and a half . . .*

Well.

Bowler was probably busy. The Strongfolk would be

up to their shoulders in work for ages. The menagerie had burned, after all. There would be animals to manage and wreckage to deal with.

Rosebud couldn't come. The healer probably wouldn't sleep for days. She'd be tending to people and animals, saving all of them, each and every one.

And Firesleight—she'd be too exhausted from dealing with the dragon.

It would be Dulcie, Micah decided. The confectioner would show up with the pockets of her overalls stuffed full of experimental sweets, and Micah wouldn't complain when she forced him to try some. Not even if they made him cough up snowflakes.

She would appear when Micah counted to *three* thousand. He'd do it more slowly than before.

"Two thousand nine hundred ninety-nine and three-quarters," Micah said out loud over an hour later. "Three thousand."

He looked around. He was still alone on the beach.

Circus Mirandus can handle a dragon, he told himself. *Circus Mirandus can handle anything.*

The sun was sinking steadily at his back.

It was nearly evening when Micah finally heard feet crunching toward him.

He'd been lying with his face pressed to the uncomfortable pebbles for a long while, and when he stood up, his whole body was stiff and achy. But that didn't stop him from running toward the magician in the long leather coat.

"I knew it would be you!" Micah shouted, grabbing the Lightbender around the middle. "I knew you were all right!"

The Lightbender made a pained sound, and Micah let him go. "I'm so sorry," he said. "Did I hurt you when I strapped you to Terp?"

The Lightbender had two black eyes, and his nose was swollen. But he was smiling.

"Cracked ribs," he said. He leaned forward and hugged Micah back gingerly. "Although I think that happened when Terpsichore threw me off in the middle of a parking lot in Norwich, not when you tied me to her."

The Lightbender scanned Micah from head to toe, his eyes pausing on the split lip, the busted chin, the shirt dried stiff with salt from the sea and Victoria's blood.

"You are freezing," said the illusionist. He held up one arm, and Micah realized his peacoat was draped over it.

"I left this on top of Chintzy's bunker," Micah said, reaching for it. "Does this mean she's okay? And Porter's warehouse?"

"They would argue with that assessment," the Lightbender said. "But, yes, Chintzy is safe. And the warehouse still stands, though we had difficulty finding a door that would lead to this place in the mess. Most of the tents will be all right. Only the menagerie is unsalvageable."

"And everybody. Is everybody . . ."

The Lightbender's face was serious. "A few of the animals are missing, and we presume at least some of them must have been taken by birds. But we hope most are in hiding. As for the magicians, we will all be fine."

"Even the Inventor?" Micah said quickly. "And Yuri? And Firesleight?"

"All of us," he said. "And you? Are you all right, Micah?"

Micah knew the Lightbender wasn't asking about his physical injuries. He'd had plenty of time to think about what had happened to his grandmother and the role he had played.

"Victoria's dead," he said.

The Lightbender nodded.

"I untied her connection to one of the dire hawks. And it killed her."

"Porter said as much." The Lightbender spoke cautiously. "The hawks joined in to defeat the dragon. Most of the remaining magical birds did. They appeared to be in a . . . celebratory mood."

Micah sighed. "It was horrible," he said. "And I'm glad she's gone."

The Lightbender put a hand on his shoulder. "I am so sorry you had to play a part in it. But more than that, I am so very *proud* of you."

Micah smiled. "Can we go home now?"

The Lightbender grimaced. "I wish so," he said. "But I am afraid we're on our own for a couple of days."

"Days? Don't you need to get back to the circus?"

"Porter's feeling a little under the weather," said the Lightbender.

Micah said, "He sent me here without using a Door. I didn't even know he could do that."

The illusionist nodded. "A tremendous magic, and he was nearly insensible from the effort when I found him and dragged him to Rosebud."

Micah raised his eyebrows at his guardian. "Did you ask her to heal Porter just so you could come here?"

"Yes, I did," said the Lightbender. "He told me if I even *suggested* he bring us back tonight, he would send me to the South Pole."

"That sounds fair," said Micah.

"It does," the Lightbender agreed.

While they watched the sun sink into the waves, the Lightbender told Micah about the end of the battle. Once Firesleight had gained mastery over the dragon's flames, the fight had turned. The birds from Victoria's flock had distracted Conflagration, harrying him until he flew close enough to the ground for the Strongfolk to engage.

"They drove Thuja's arrows deeper into his sides, toward his heart, and Firesleight set them aflame."

Apparently, that was how dragons killed other dragons—by burning their hearts, which were the only parts of them that weren't completely fireproof.

Micah shuddered, feeling a little sorry for Conflagration, despite the fact that he would have gone on slaughtering everyone and everything at the circus.

Then it was his turn to talk.

When he told the Lightbender about giving Fish all his bracelets, the illusionist looked surprised. "That was kind of you," he said. "I know how hard you've worked on those."

"I kept my bootlace," said Micah, lifting his sleeve to show the Lightbender his wrist. "I can replace everything else. Do you think Fish will find his Someone soon?"

"Yes," said the Lightbender. "Geoffrey did think it would be sometime this year."

"But will we know when it happens?"

The Lightbender shook his head. "I do not think so," he said. "At least not right away. It can take an Idea many years to come to fruition, you know. Even after someone has conceived of it."

Micah knew that, but a part of him still hoped there would be some sign that Fish had succeeded.

"If you do not mind answering . . ." The illusionist trailed off.

"What?"

The Lightbender looked somewhat embarrassed. "I would be interested to know what made tying a bracelet to represent me so difficult."

"Oh," said Micah. "I was being silly. It should have been really obvious."

"I had wondered if it was the fact that I am an illusionist," said the Lightbender hesitantly. "I am aware that it is almost the same as being a professional liar, and many people find that upsetting—"

"No," said Micah. "That's not it. I just didn't realize something about you until today, when I met Victoria."

The Lightbender turned to Micah, both of his eyebrows lifted in alarm.

Micah said, "She was my grandmother. And she didn't care about me at all. She didn't hate me. She didn't like me. She just thought that I wasn't much of a threat and maybe I would be useful to have around one day. I didn't expect her to be so . . ."

"Indifferent," the Lightbender said softly.

Micah nodded. "I've been so ashamed of being related to her. But then, when she called me her *family*, it was like the word didn't mean anything to her at all. I realized she didn't even know what a family was."

Micah touched his bootlace and watched the curved edge of the sun disappear on the horizon.

"*I* know what a family is," he said. "I used to have a grandfather who loved me a lot. And now, I've got you."

The Lightbender smiled. "You do."

"You love me," Micah concluded. "That's what the bracelet was missing—the most important part."

36

MAIL SLOT

"**I** can't believe I wasn't there to help!" Jenny said through the mail slot several days later. "Micah, are you sure you're all right?"

"I'm great. The circus is still closed. It will be until we get the menagerie sorted out. But everyone's going to be okay."

Micah and the Lightbender had arrived home to find that the circus's animals were being housed in every tent with even a little bit of spare room. The dire hawks had flown off, but many of Victoria's birds had stayed, either because they were too injured to leave or because they didn't have anywhere else to go.

Afraid that she might be asked to share her perch with the newcomers, Chintzy had taken it upon herself to invite Big Jean and Terpsichore to stay in the Lightbender's tent instead.

Micah had walked into the tent on his first day back to find Big Jean drawing math problems on the Lightbender's

stage with a piece of sidewalk chalk. Terpsichore was
outside, rolling in the grass.

"You *do* realize we have one of the smallest tents, right?"
he said to the parrot. "And you invited the biggest animals
at the circus to live with us?"

"Exactly!" she said proudly. "No room for anyone else now."

"All right, Chintzy." Micah had been too pleased to see
her alive and well to be annoyed. "That makes sense."

Jenny pressed her face so close to the mail slot that
it looked as if she were trying to squeeze herself through it.
"How are they going to replace the menagerie?" she asked
worriedly.

"Victoria's old tent." Micah had suggested the idea to
the manager himself. Repurposing the glittering, silver
tent would be a way of erasing some of the damage
Victoria had done. "When the Inventor's fully recovered
she's going to start working on it. She thinks she can
expand it and make it even better than the old one."

"That sounds perfect," said Jenny. "It's going to look
impressive at the center of the circus. I wish I didn't have
to wait so long to see it."

"You still can't visit?" Micah asked, disappointed. He'd
hoped that with Victoria gone and summer approaching,
Jenny's parents would have decided it was fine for her to stay.

"Actually . . ." Jenny's voice was nervous. "My mom and
dad said I could visit once school let out. But you know
how I told you about the Sisterhood offering me a spot at
their summer camp?"

"I remember."

"Well, they've got a different theme every year, and this summer it's about protecting the environment. It's something I'm really interested in. The campers will get to talk about ecology and green energy, and there's going to be a river cleanup day and—"

"That sounds like a lot of fun," said Micah.

"You're not mad? I'll still be able to come *later* in the summer."

"Of course I'm not mad!"

"It's not an all-girls camp," Jenny said quickly. "I bet they would let you come, too."

Micah thought about it. The members of the Sisterhood who'd fought in the battle against the dragon and Victoria were all still here. They had decided to stay a while and help the circus get back on its feet. He could go right now and ask one of them about camp.

"No," he decided. "I want to stay here. We'll be reopening at the start of the summer."

"And the circus needs all its magicians," said Jenny.

"That's right," said Micah. "You're not mad either, are you?"

Jenny shook her head. "We'll both be doing what we're passionate about. We'll both have a great summer, and we'll see each other at the end of it. I'm sorry I'll miss your twelfth birthday, though."

"That's all right," said Micah, smiling. "The Lightbender's taking me out for pizza."

37

THE SHOELACE WIZARD

By early August, Circus Mirandus was more or less back to normal.

Micah and the Lightbender sat together at a small wooden breakfast table in the illusionist's room. The Lightbender had found the table in one of the storage tents, and he had presented it to Micah as a birthday present, complete with wrapping paper and a badly tied bow.

Going out for pizza wasn't something they could do on a regular basis, he'd explained apologetically, but eating meals together more often could certainly be managed.

Every morning since, Micah had fixed a to-go tray in the dining tent, knowing that by the time he returned, his guardian would have chosen their view for the day. The wide picture window beside their table wasn't real, nor were the scenes on the other side of it. But Micah didn't mind.

Today the window looked out on a quiet, brick-paved street. It had obviously rained not long ago, and the puddles reflected the bright yellow and blue awnings of the shops and cafés across the road. A man in old-fashioned clothing walked by, carrying a bundle of newspapers on one of his shoulders. Micah could make out the sound of his footsteps through the glass.

It was a pretty, peaceful view, and nobody was there to see it but the two of them.

Victoria had been wrong about a lot, including this. She'd said the magicians at the circus wasted their power on things that didn't matter. She'd missed the point, Micah thought.

Putting something beautiful and good into the world always mattered.

Big or little, impressive or simple, magic was supposed to be about giving something of yourself to other people. In the end, despite her power, Victoria's life hadn't counted for much, because all she'd ever done with it was *take*.

"Deep thoughts this morning?" asked the Lightbender, watching him over a tall stack of toast.

Micah shook his head. "I was just looking out the window."

The sound of wings beating the air made him jump, but it was only Chintzy, flapping in without bothering to call out a warning.

"Is that mail?" Micah asked, eyeing the thick shipping envelope clutched in Chintzy's claws.

A second later, the parrot dropped it on top of Micah's

waffles. Melted butter and raspberry sauce spattered his shirt.

"*Chintzy.*" Micah grabbed the envelope in one hand and a napkin in the other as the parrot landed right in the middle of the table.

"That girl!" she said, ruffling her feathers. "She wrote to you the whole time she was at camp, and she used *thick* paper."

Chintzy helped herself to the piece of toast the Lightbender had just spread with marmalade.

Micah felt himself grinning. Jenny should have just gotten home from camp last night, and he hadn't expected to hear from her so soon.

He tore open the envelope and found a pile of letters inside, each neatly sealed except for a single sheet of paper that had been tucked in on top of the rest. It was covered in Jenny's sloppy handwriting.

Micah pulled it out and started to read.

"She says hello. And that something exciting happened this summer, and she wants to tell me about in person. Do you think Porter would mind sending me to Peal?"

Porter had recovered slowly from the battle, even with Mr. Head and Rosebud helping him. The circus had stayed in place all summer on the manager's orders. When Porter had regained his strength, they would all be heading back to South America to finish their interrupted tour and search for Terpsichore's herd. Mr. Head said that with Conflagration gone, the unicorns might have come out of hiding.

"I think Porter would be delighted to send you any-where," said the Lightbender, reaching over Chintzy to grab the bowl of marmalade. "He claims he is tired of our coddling and more than ready to get back to work."

Chintzy, still munching on her stolen toast, turned her head sideways to eye the Lightbender's wrist as it passed over her. A new black-and-gold bracelet adorned it, the knots tied flat against one another until they almost resembled a fish's scales.

"When do *I* get a bracelet?" Chintzy asked plaintively, holding one of her feet out behind her as if she expected Micah to tie something to it on the spot.

"Oh," said Micah. He hadn't realized that Chintzy might wear jewelry. "Um . . . really soon. It's just taking a while because I want to be sure it's perfect for you."

The Lightbender smiled knowingly at him.

"Well, that makes sense," the parrot said, putting her foot back down. "I'm unique, after all."

After breakfast, Micah went to Porter's. He found the magician in his workshop, applying a welding torch to a damaged gate.

Only a small percentage of the doors in the warehouse had been broken so badly they wouldn't work, Porter had told Micah, but that still meant he would be repairing things for years to come.

He shoved up his welding helmet and put down the torch when Micah entered the workshop.

"Finally!" he exclaimed when Micah asked about visiting Peal. "Do you know how long it's been since someone asked me to send them out of the country? I was starting to worry I'd be forced to retire from lack of interest."

Porter offered to open the Door straightaway, but Micah shook his head. "There's something I have to do first."

He returned a couple of hours later, carrying the rope ladder. He'd repaired it, making sure each and every knot was exactly as he remembered it.

"So that's what kept you," said Porter. He already had the scuffed door to the Greebers' gardening shed set up in its frame.

"It came untied with everything else," Micah explained. "Back when I collapsed your Door and knocked you out."

"Such a fond memory," said Porter. "I love how people keep bringing it up."

Micah laughed.

Porter opened the Door with his usual flourish and waved Micah through.

It was morning in Peal, not long after sunrise. When Micah knocked on the front door of his old house, the woman who answered was wearing her bathrobe and slippers.

"I'm sorry to bother you," he said, gesturing with the bundled rope ladder. "I used to live here with my grandpa. We built the tree house in the backyard together."

He was nervous, explaining himself. He'd been afraid the woman might not be as nice as Jenny had said she was, or that she wouldn't appreciate a random twelve-year-old showing up on her doorstep.

But she seemed to understand what he was trying to do perfectly.

She took him into the house and led him to the storage closet under the staircase, though Micah had already known where it was. He borrowed a tall stepladder, and she helped him maneuver it out the door.

They positioned it under the oak tree, and she went back inside to tell her kids they had company.

Micah stood for a while at the base of the oak, looking up at the tree house nestled in its branches. Grandpa Ephraim had never meant for it to sit empty. And though Micah had lost the knots his grandfather had tied into the rope ladder, he would never lose the memories. Those were his to keep.

Micah climbed up and secured the ropes to the beam beneath the tree house, exactly where Grandpa Ephraim had once tied them. He checked the knots several times, even though he knew they were right.

"Tuttle knots," he whispered. "Tighter than tight."

By the time he was finished, two little kids were standing under the tree.

The girl's name was Josie, and the boy's was Daniel, and they were excited at the thought of being able to use the tree house.

"Mama says we can try the ladder if you show us how," Josie said.

Her little brother was still in his pajamas, and he was already reaching for the rope ladder, his face determined.

Micah glanced toward the house and saw their mother watching through the upstairs window.

"I hope you two are good climbers," he said, stepping over to hold the ladder still.

"I'm better than he is." Josie pointed at her brother. "But that's because I'm older."

Micah showed them how to go up and down the rope ladder, holding on tight and being careful not to lose their balance. They were great at it, and in no time, all three of them were sitting in the tree house together, waving at the kids' mom through the window.

"It's so high!" Daniel exclaimed. "I can see the whole city from up here."

That wasn't true at all. Mostly, they could see oak leaves and a few neighboring yards and hedges. But Micah didn't argue.

"Mama says you used to live here," said Josie, throwing her legs off the side of the tree house's platform so she could swing her feet. "Why'd you leave?"

"Be careful near the edge," Micah reminded her. "I did live here, but I have a new place to live now."

He didn't think he ought to tell them that his grandfather had died in their house.

"Does your new place have a *treeeee* house?" Daniel asked. He had gotten up and started walking around and around the platform, stomping on every board hard with his bare feet, as if he hoped he might find a trapdoor hidden somewhere.

Micah shook his head. "No tree houses," he said. "But it does have an invisible tiger and a unicorn and an elephant who can do math."

Daniel stopped stomping. Josie stopped swinging her legs. They exchanged a look that said they'd suddenly realized they were stuck in a tree with a very strange person.

"For real," Micah said. "I'm a magician."

"Prove it!" the little boy shouted enthusiastically. He waved his arms up and down. "Turn me into a dog!"

"I'm not that kind of magician. I can show you something else, though."

Micah thought for a minute, then said, "Can I see your shoe?" to Josie.

She turned and stuck out one of her pink sneakers. The laces had been carefully double-knotted.

"Watch this," said Micah.

The little girl stared hard at her shoe. Her brother leaned over her shoulder.

Micah tapped the laces, and they untied themselves, then he tapped them again and they spun themselves into a complicated knot that looked like a daisy.

"Wow!" shouted Daniel.

Josie's eyes were huge. "Do it again!"

Micah did it again. And again.

Daniel let out an excited squeal. "He's a shoe wizard!" he said, as if a shoe wizard was the most spectacular thing he could imagine.

"He's a shoe*lace* wizard," his sister corrected.

They made Micah tie the sneakers over and over until their mother called them back into the house.

"Will you come back and tie my shoes tomorrow?" Josie asked after all three had their feet on the ground.

"Not tomorrow," said Micah. "I live pretty far away."

"With your tiger!" Daniel said.

"Right," said Micah.

"Are there a lot of shoelace wizards?"

"I'm the only one," said Micah. "But there are plenty of other kinds of magician."

He carried the borrowed stepladder back inside and put it away in the closet. The children's mother was surprised to hear them shouting about invisible tigers, but she told Micah that if he wanted to come back and visit the tree house sometime, it would be all right.

Micah thanked her and left.

It felt like he'd finished something bigger than a rope ladder. And if the kids were more impressed by the "shoelace wizard" than the tree house, that was all right.

It wasn't even a bad name. Much better than String Boy.

Not quite perfect, Micah thought, mulling it over as he turned the corner onto Jenny's street. *But close.*

THE
MOMENT

The plastic bottle had once held an energy drink. Its label still said BLUEBERRY ZAPPER, but it had been a long time since the bottle was filled with anything so nice.

It had flown from the hand of a girl riding a bike. It had hit the sidewalk and rolled down a storm drain and stuck there, collecting muck, until a heavy rain washed it away. Down the sewer pipes it went, floating out of the city, until it fell into a river that flowed slowly on, taking a long and meandering route toward the sea.

The energy drink bottle never made it that far.

It drifted in the current for miles, tumbling over rocks and brushing up against the banks, until finally, it caught on the limb of a tree that had fallen into the river. And there it stayed, just under the water's surface, while the months passed by.

Hello, said a voice the bottle couldn't hear. *I am on a mission. You are supposed to help me.*

Something flashing and silver wriggled itself inside the bottle.

It's harder than it used to be, said Fish. *Making myself so small.*

"Wait a second, Pennyroyal! I think I see something right there."

Jenny Mendoza leaned over the side of the boat, her orange life vest making it more difficult than it should have been. "Something's caught on a limb under the water. Just . . ." She stretched as far as she could, then sat back. "Can you paddle that way? I can't quite reach it."

The tangerine-haired woman in her camp leader's uniform shook her head. "Sorry. Can't. My arms are tired."

"You poor thing," said Jenny, smiling. "You help slay a dragon, and then river cleanup does you in."

"It's a tragedy," Pennyroyal agreed. She dug her paddle in the water, easing the boat along. "And if you keep talking about dragons, the other campers are gonna start to wonder about you."

"I'll tell them I like fantasy books," Jenny said, reaching down into the water to scoop up the bottle. "Got it!"

Light flashed in Jenny Mendoza's head, bright as the sun, and she froze with her arm still under the water.

"Jenny?" said Pennyroyal. "What are you doing?"

When Jenny didn't answer, she frowned.

The Strongwoman stowed her paddle and stepped over the pile of garbage they'd already plucked from the water. She crouched low in the boat and reached for the bottle. She pulled it out, her eyes widening when she saw the little fish swimming around and around, delight apparent in every twitch of its fins.

"You," Pennyroyal breathed. Then she narrowed her eyes at it. "Aren't you supposed to disappear or something? After you've done your job?"

I had extra magic left, said Fish. *My friend fed it to me.*

Pennyroyal tilted her head, as if she were listening hard. She nodded slowly. "Okay. I think I understand. I'm guessing you don't want to go back into the river, then?"

I am done with my mission, said Fish. *Can I have my aquarium back?*

Pennyroyal dug through the litter in the boat and found a plastic cap that matched the energy drink bottle. She screwed it into place and sat back down, tucking Fish safely under the boat's seat.

Three minutes later, when Pennyroyal dragged the boat onto the bank of the river, Jenny toppled over and blinked.

"Holy smokes!" she said. "HOLY SMOKES! I just had the *best* idea."

THE END

ACKNOWLEDGMENTS

I began working on a sequel to *Circus Mirandus* in 2014. The first book wasn't even on shelves yet, but I knew I'd left so much of the world unwritten. I wanted readers to meet Micah on the other side of his grief. I wanted to introduce people to the magicians I'd been imagining for so long.

Nearly five years later, I've got a box full of manuscripts that weren't quite right. And I've got a heart full of gratitude for all the people who helped me find my way to *The Bootlace Magician*. Many thanks to:

Elena Giovinazzo, my agent, who believed in the circus from the very beginning.

Nancy Mercado, my editor, whose advice and encouragement made this a better book.

Lauri Hornik, Rosie Ahmed, Rosanne Lauer, Regina Castillo, Tabitha Dulla, Lily Malcom, Samira Iravani, Jason Henry, Vanessa DeJesus, and the rest of the team at Dial/Penguin. They work so hard to put great books in readers' hands.

Monica Roe, for her thorough and thoughtful critique.

Namrata Tripathi, who read my early attempts at a sequel and helped me figure out what this book should be.

Cindy Beasley, my mother, and Kate Beasley, my sister. They've read every version of this book many times, and it's infinitely better for their advice.

And finally, thanks to you, the reader. I was imagining you as I wrote. I was praying that this book would make your world a little brighter. Wherever you are, I hope the fish you need is headed your way.